Okay, she'd allow herself one more kiss.

Just one more kiss, and then she'd call a halt to this, tell him that he was being incredibly hasty and foolish and a whole host of other things as well, ending it by saying that one of them had to be sensible.

In a second, in just another second, she'd tell him all that and more.

More.

The single word shimmered in her head, a silent entreaty to the man who was knocking out all the carefully laid foundations of her world. Very effectively reducing her to a pile of palpitating rubble.

She had one last card to play.

"What about your sons?" Tracy asked as, tapping the last of her strength, she created yet another chasm between their lips.

"Let them get their own women," Micah told her, kissing her again.

Melting her again.

Dear Reader,

When I first came up with the idea of MATCH-MAKING MAMAS, it was going to be only a three-book series. But as you might have noticed, I have a great deal of trouble letting go.

This time around, our ladies, Maizie, Theresa and Cecilia, bring together two people who really need one another in more ways than one. Tracy Ryan is an extremely successful lawyer who is a dynamo in the courtroom but very lonely when she closes her door at night. Micah Muldare, a senior reliability engineer, had an extremely happy marriage that ended when his wife died of a brain aneurysm, leaving him with a mountain of medical bills and two very young sons. But a ring of hackers hijacking computers places his future—not to mention his freedom—in jeopardy just as his aunt turns her attention to his non-existent love life. Maizie brings Tracy and Micah together, and the lady lawyer stays to fix more than his legal problems. She fixes his heart, and he returns the favor.

I hope you enjoy this latest installment of one of my favorite series. As ever, I thank you for reading, and from the bottom of my heart I wish you someone to love who loves you back.

All the best,

Marie Ferrarella

ONCE UPON A MATCHMAKER

BY

MARIE FERRARELLA

First published in Great Britain 2012
by Mills & Boon, an imprint of Harlequin (UK) Limited,
Eton House, 18-24 Paradise Road, Richmond, Surrey TW9 1SR

ISBN: 978 0 263 89453 0
ebook ISBN: 978 1 408 97126 0

23-0812

Harlequin (UK) policy is to use papers that are natural, renewable and recyclable products and made from wood grown in sustainable forests. The logging and manufacturing processes conform to the legal environmental regulations of the country of origin.

Printed and bound in Spain
by Blackprint CPI, Barcelona

Marie Ferrarella, a *USA TODAY* bestselling and RITA® Award-winning author, has written more than two hundred books, some under the name Marie Nicole. Her romances are beloved by fans worldwide. Visit her website, www.marieferrarella.com.

To
Gail Chasan
who, mercifully, gets
my sense of humor

Prologue

"He's a good, decent man," Sheila Barrett said.

The "he" the tall, striking woman referred to was her nephew, the young man she'd taken into her home and raised when her sister and brother-in-law were killed in a car crash.

That had been nearly twenty years ago. Micah Muldare was more like a son than a nephew to her and, like a mother, she worried about him. In her opinion, she had good cause to be worried. He'd all but become an emotional hermit.

"But ever since his wife, Ella, died, he's become almost driven, throwing himself into his work. If I even try to mention socializing, he tells me he's too busy." She pressed her lips together, trying to suppress the wave of sadness welling up within her. "It's like he's always trying to outrun the pain."

Sheila didn't usually pour out her heart this way, even to a good friend like Maizie Sommers, but at this point, she needed help getting through to her nephew. If anything, the situation was getting worse, not better.

"What about his sons?" Maizie asked. "Didn't you tell me that he has two little boys? How is he with them?"

Sheila nodded, pausing for a moment to take another sip of the exotic-tasting tea she'd ordered. Maizie, a real estate agent, had suggested that they meet here in this little café to discuss what was bothering her. The problem, it seemed, was right up Maizie's alley.

In addition to having her own real estate company, Maizie, along with her two lifelong best friends, Theresa Manetti and Cecilia Parnell, dabbled in matchmaking. Initially undertaken just to match up their own single children, they'd come to enjoy such success that now they did it for their friends. Knowing about this sideline, Sheila had come to her, worried about Micah and looking for help.

"Gary and Greg," Sheila confirmed. "They're five and four, and he adores them. But the boys are seeing less and less of their father because he's immersing himself in his career. And it's not helping," she confided. "Any of them."

"Work is never a substitute for a good relationship," Maizie maintained.

Sheila couldn't agree more. "The boys need a mother and Micah needs someone to love who loves him back." She looked at her friend, feeling somewhat uneasy. "I don't usually meddle in his life—"

"And I'm sure he appreciates that, but sometimes those we love need a little push in the right direction. Nothing wrong with that," Maizie assured her.

"He'd be really upset if he knew I was even discussing his life like this—"

Maizie flashed the other woman an encouraging smile. "Don't worry. This'll all be discretely handled. Let me see what I can do," Maizie told her. "Mother's Day is coming up," she noted, thinking that could somehow be utilized in this case, then promised, "I'll get back to you before then."

The wheels in Maizie's head went into high gear as she began to consider possibilities. Operation Micah Muldare had begun the moment Sheila had sat down at her table.

Chapter One

So this was what all the secrecy, giggling and whispers had been about.

Micah Muldare sat on the sofa, looking at the gift his sons had quite literally surprised him with. A gift he wasn't expecting, commemorating a day that he'd never thought applied to him. He'd just unwrapped the gift and it was now sitting on the coffee table, a source of mystification, at least for him.

His boys, four-year-old Greg and five-year-old Gary, sat—or more accurately perched—on either side of him like energized bookends, unable to remain still for more than several seconds at a time. Blond, blue-eyed and small boned, his sons looked like little carbon copies of each other.

They looked like Ella.

Micah shut the thought away. It had been two years, but his heart still wasn't ready for that kind of comparison.

Maybe someday, just not yet.

"Do you like it, Daddy?" Gary, the more animated of the two, asked eagerly. The boy was fairly beaming as he put the question to him. His bright blue eyes took in every tiny movement.

Micah eyed at the mug on the coffee table. "I can honestly say I wasn't expecting anything like this," Micah told his son. "Actually, I wasn't expecting anything at all today."

It was Mother's Day. Granted he'd been doing double duty for the past two years, being both mother *and* father to his two sons, but he hadn't expected any sort of acknowledgment from the boys on Mother's Day. On Father's Day, yes, but definitely not on this holiday.

The mug had been wrapped in what seemed like an entire roll of wrapping paper. Gary had proclaimed proudly that he had done most of the wrapping.

"But I put the tape on," Greg was quick to tell him.

Micah praised their teamwork.

The mug had World's Greatest Mom written on it in pink-and-yellow ceramic flowers. Looking at it now, Micah could only grin and shake his head. Well, at least their hearts were in the right place.

"Um, I think you guys are a little confused about the concept," he confided.

Gary's face scrunched up in apparent confusion. "What's a con-cept?"

"It's an idea, a way of—"

Micah abruptly stopped himself. As a reliability engineer who worked in the top secret missile defense systems department of Donovan Defense, a large national company, he had a tendency to get rather involved in his explanations. Given his sons' tender ages, he decided that a brief and simple explanation was the best way to go.

So he tried again. "It's a way of understanding something. The point is, I'm very touched, guys, but you do understand that I'm not your mom, right? I'm your dad." He looked from Gary to Greg to see if they had any lingering questions or doubts.

"We know that," Gary told him as if he thought it was silly to ever confuse the two roles. "But sometimes you do mom things," he reminded his father.

"Yeah, like make cookies when I'm sick," Greg piped up.

Which was more often than he was happy about, Micah couldn't help thinking. Greg, smaller for his age than even Gary, was his little survivor. Born prematurely, his younger son had had a number of complicating conditions that had him in and out of hospitals until he was almost two years old.

Because of all the different medications he'd been forced to take, the little boy's immune system was somewhat compromised. As an unfortunate by-product of that, Greg was more prone to getting sick than his brother.

And every time he did get sick, Micah watched him carefully, afraid the boy would come down with another bout of pneumonia. The last time, a year and a half ago, Greg had almost died. The thought haunted him for months.

Clearing his throat, Micah squared his shoulders. His late mother, Diane, had taught him to accept all gifts gracefully.

"Well, then, thank you very much," he told his sons with a wide smile that was instantly mirrored by each of the boys.

"Aunt Sheila helped us," Gary told him, knowing that he couldn't accept all of the credit for the gift.

"Yeah, she drove us to the store," Greg chimed in. "But me and Gary picked it out. And we used our own money, too," he added as a postscript.

"'Gary and I,'" Micah automatically corrected Greg.

The little boy shook his head so hard, his straight blond hair appeared airborne for a moment, flying to and fro about his head.

"No, not you, Daddy, me," Greg insisted. "Me and Gary."

There was time enough to correct his grammar when he was a little older, Micah thought fondly.

Out loud he marveled, "Imagine that," for his sons' benefit. A touch of melancholy drifted over him. "You two are growing up way too fast," he told them. "Before you know it, you're going to be getting married and starting families of your own."

"Married?" Greg echoed, frowning as deeply as if his father had just told him that he was having liver for dinner for the next year.

"To a *girl?*" Gary asked incredulously, very obviously horrified by the mere suggestion that he be forced to marry a female. Everyone knew girls were icky—except for Aunt Sheila, of course, but she didn't count.

"That's more or less what I had in mind, yes," Micah told his sons, doing his very best not to laugh at their facial expressions.

Covering his face, Gary declared, "Yuck!" with a great deal of feeling.

"Yeah," Greg cried, mimicking his brother, "double yuck!"

Micah slipped an arm around each little boy's very slim shoulders and pulled them to him. He would miss this when the boys were older, miss these moments when his sons made him feel as if he was the center of their universe.

"Come back and tell me that in another, oh, ten, fifteen years," he teased.

"Okay," Gary promised very solemnly. "We will, Daddy."

"Yeah, we will!" Greg echoed, not to be outdone.

Micah's aunt, Sheila Barrett, stood in the living room doorway, observing the scene between her nephew and her grandnephews. Her mouth curved in a wide smile. While she lived not too far from Micah, it felt as if this was more her home than the place where she received her mail. She took care of the boys when her nephew was at work, which, unless one of his sons was sick, was most of the time.

"They picked that mug out themselves," she told Micah, in case he thought that this was her idea. "They absolutely refused to look at anything else after they saw that mug. They thought it was perfect for you."

"And of course you tried to talk them out of it," Micah said, tongue in cheek. His amusement was there, in his eyes.

Sheila shrugged nonchalantly. "The way I see it, Micah, little men in the making should be as free to exercise their shopping gene as their little female counterparts."

"Very democratic of you," Micah commented, the corners of his mouth curving. Aunt Sheila had always had a bit of an unorthodox streak. He learned to think outside the box because of her. He sincerely doubted that he would be where he was today if not for her. "Well, just for that, I'm taking all of you out for lunch."

"Aunt Sheila, too?" Greg asked, not wanting to exclude her.

"Aunt Sheila most especially," Micah told his younger son. There was deep affection in his voice. "After all, Aunt Sheila is the *real* mom around here," he emphasized pointedly.

Clearly confused, Greg turned to look at the woman who came by every morning to take him to preschool and his brother to kindergarten. Every afternoon she'd pick them both up and then stayed with them until their father came home. Some nights, Aunt Sheila stayed really, really late.

"Aunt Sheila has kids?" Greg asked his father, surprised.

Sheila smiled, answering for Micah. "I have your dad," told the boy.

They had a special bond, she and her sister's son. When the world came crashing in on him when his parents were killed in a car accident while on vacation, Micah had been twelve years old. Injured in the accident, too, he'd been all alone at that San Jose hospital. She'd lost no time driving up the coast to get to him. She'd stayed by his side until he was well enough to leave and then she took him home with her. There was no looking back. She'd raised him as her own.

Greg was staring at her, wide-eyed, his small face stamped with disbelief. "Dad was a kid?"

"Your dad was a kid," she assured him, biting her tongue so as not to laugh at the expression of wonder on the little boy's face. "And a pretty wild one at that."

"She's making that part up," Micah told his sons. "I was a perfect angel."

"When you were asleep, you looked just like one," Sheila agreed, then added, "Awake, not so much."

"Can you tell us stories about when Daddy was a kid?" Gary asked eagerly.

Sheila's smile was so wide, her eyes almost disappeared. "I sure can."

"But she won't," Micah interjected with a note of finality. "She's going to save those for when you're older."

Gary's forehead crinkled beneath his blond bangs. "Why?"

"I'll tell you *that* when you're older, too," Micah promised him. Changing the subject, he asked, "Now, who's hungry for pizza?"

The words were no sooner out of his mouth than a chorus of "We are!" rose up. It was hard to believe that two little boys could project so much volume when they wanted to.

Micah gazed at his aunt who'd made herself comfortable in the love seat opposite Micah and the boys. "I thought we'd go to that little Italian restaurant you like so much. Giuseppe's." The boys bounced up to their feet. His aunt rose to hers, as well. "Luckily for me, it's kid-friendly."

"As it happens," his aunt said, placing a hand on each boy's shoulder in order to usher them out the front door, "so am I."

"You know there's no one here to impress, right?" Kate Manetti Wainwright said to her friend, Tracy Ryan, as she stuck her head into the latter's office.

It was Sunday and the law firm was closed. Or should have been. The sound of typing must have drawn Kate to Tracy's small office, which meant an interruption.

Tracy looked up from the brief she was working on. "You're here," she pointed out.

"But I'm not supposed to be." *And neither was anyone else,* she added silently. "I just stopped by to grab the sweater I left here on Friday." She held up the powder-blue article of clothing as exhibit A. "And besides, I don't count."

"You do to me," Tracy told her, flashing a quick, fleeting smile at her friend. "And for your information, I'm not trying to impress anyone, I'm just trying to catch up on my workload."

Kate rolled her eyes. "You already work twice as

hard as anyone here," she pointed out. "How much catching up do you possibly have to do?"

Tracy's slender shoulders rose and fell in an absentminded shrug. "Enough," she said evasively, then, cocking her head, she leveled a piercing gaze at the woman who had been her friend all through law school. They'd been each other's support group through the bad times, and each other's cheering section through the good ones. "Don't you have somewhere to be?" she asked. After all, today was Mother's Day and, unlike her, Kate was lucky enough to still have one.

Kate feigned innocence. "As a matter of fact, I do—and you're coming with me," she declared as if she'd just thought of it.

Instead of automatically demurring, Tracy felt she needed to arm herself with information first so that she could come up with a good reason to say no. Kate didn't take "no" easily. "And just where is it that I'm supposed to be going, too?"

"Giuseppe's. Lilli and I are taking my mother out for Mother's Day," she said, referring to her brother Kullen's wife.

Tracy shook her head. "That's okay, I'll just stay here and finish this brief."

"I'm not taking no for an answer, Trace," she informed her friend.

"It's Mother's Day," Tracy said out loud, taking care not to lace her protest with emotion. "I'm sure your mother doesn't want you dragging a stray along on her afternoon out."

"Then you definitely don't know my mother—and

you're not a stray," she tagged on as an afterthought. "You're more like family." She smiled at her. "Like the sister my mother never got around to giving me," she told Tracy.

Tracy suppressed a sigh. Mother's Day was particularly difficult for her on two counts. The mother she adored was no longer part of her life. She hadn't been for close to three years now. Moreover, added to that was the numbing fact that her blink-and-you've-missed-it marriage that came and went four years ago had left her pregnant and hopeful. Tracy had always loved children and the idea of being a mother herself was thrilling. But the thrill became tragedy when her baby came into the world prematurely—and stillborn.

That, more than the painfully short marriage she'd endured, had left her with the feeling that she was one of those people who was meant to go through life alone. She faced that the same way she faced everything else she found overwhelming: she threw herself into her work. Buried herself in a hundred and one details. Anything so that she didn't have any time to think, to dwell on her own situation—or lack of one.

When the loneliness came at her full force, as it did sometimes, Tracy just worked a little harder until she was able to make herself numb again.

The important thing was not to feel. Since she was a normally caring person, she channeled her emotional connections into the cases she took on—and the people whose hand she figuratively held while she worked on their cases.

"I am not taking no for an answer," Kate repeated

with more feeling, adding, "And don't worry, this isn't some kind of a setup. Jackson is out of town on bank business this weekend, so it's just going to be us girls," she promised. "C'mon," Kate coaxed, "It'll be fun.

"That can wait," she insisted, nodding at the brief on Tracy's desk. "Unless it suddenly grows legs—and if it does, we'll have bigger problems than just your workload—it's not going anywhere," she concluded with finality. Her tone left no room for a rebuttal. Tracy was coming with her even if she had to find a way to carry the woman out of the office and to the restaurant.

For now, she made a show of tugging on Tracy's arm, gently but insistently nonetheless.

With a sigh, Tracy gave in. She supposed that being around pleasant people was preferable to being here by herself. Except for the very low hum of her computer, the office was bathed in silence. Silence allowed memories to pop up, painful memories that were liable to sneak up and ambush her at any time.

She knew the danger in that. Dwelling on either one of her losses for even a minute tended to devastate her. As long as she outran the memories or banked them down, she was all right. She could function. She desperately needed to function.

The alternative, sinking into a darkness where grief could eat away at her until there was nothing left, was not an option she was willing to accept. She'd been there once, and once was more than enough.

"Okay, I guess a girls' afternoon out does sound pretty good," Tracy agreed.

"Great!" Kate declared, already way ahead of her.

Coming around to Tracy's side of the desk, she nimbly pressed a combination of keys to save the document Tracy had been working on, and then shut down the computer. "Done," she informed Tracy, then hooked her arm through her friend's the moment Tracy got up from her chair.

"Knew you'd come around," Kate told her, doing little to hide the triumphant note in her voice. "Let's go. I don't want to keep my mother waiting. Oh, by the way, did I tell you that Nikki and Jewel were going to be there with their mothers, too?"

It was in the form of a question, but Tracy knew her friend was dispensing information slowly. Tracy could acknowledge Kate was a dynamo in the courtroom and the complete opposite in a private setting.

"I hope you don't mind," Kate added. "My mom and those women have been friends forever. I knew she'd enjoy things more if they were there, too."

What was that saying Mom used to say? In for a penny, in for a pound, Tracy recalled. Since it was Mother's Day, she'd follow the old adage.

With a nod of her head, Tracy allowed herself to be dragged along.

Tracy had met Theresa Manetti a couple of times, once at Kate's wedding, the other at Kullen's. The woman reminded her a little of her own mother. Consequently, she had taken an instant liking to the intelligent, savvy woman as well as the two women she'd introduced as her "best friends since third grade," Maizie Sommers and Cecilia Parnell.

She'd discovered that by combining the three women's characteristics, she came practically face-to-face with her own mother. She savored the experience for a moment, then refocused herself to enjoy the individual company of each of the women.

"See," Kate said as she, Lilli and Tracy all sat down at the extended table, "I told you it was going to be girls' afternoon out."

Theresa laughed shortly. "You're stretching the word, dear," she told her daughter. "I haven't been a girl since the last century."

"It's all in your attitude," Maizie told her. "Me, I'm never getting old."

Theresa suppressed a laugh and asked Cecilia, "What's the female counterpart to Peter Pan?"

"Happy," Tracy chimed in without hesitating.

Maizie smiled her approval. "I do like the way you think, Tracy." Picking up the menu, she began to scan it. "So, what looks good?" she asked the others.

"Offhand, I'd say he does," Theresa Manetti answered. She wasn't looking at the menu but at the occupant of a table three tables away.

Maizie looked up at the dark-haired man her friend was referring to. She pretended to look surprised. In reality, all three of them—she, Cecilia and Theresa—knew *exactly* where Micah Muldare would be sitting, thanks to prior arrangements with Sheila.

"You were saying about Peter Pan?" Maizie teased. And then she leaned forward, squinting just a little. "Oh, I think I know the woman he's with."

Now all the women at the table were looking in the

direction Theresa was. "A little old for him, isn't she?" Cecilia asked.

"That's his aunt, Sheila Barrett. I sold her a condo a few years ago," Maizie explained, slanting a glance toward Tracy.

"Then she's really a client, not a friend," Tracy guessed.

Maizie smiled as she looked at the newcomer. "She's both."

"Mother makes friends easily," Nikki confided.

Tracy looked at the table in question. "Cute little boys," she commented. Her smile was genuine. And wide.

Maizie nodded in approval. "Yes, they are. He's doing a wonderful job, raising them by himself, I hear. Of course, Sheila comes by to help out when she can, but there is no real substitute for a mother's love, is there?"

The question was directed toward Tracy, but it was her own daughter, as well as Theresa's and Cecilia's, who chorused in a singsong voice, "No, Mother, there really isn't."

Maizie only laughed softly. She had a really good feeling about this. There was a definite smile in Tracy's eyes when she looked at the children. That was very telling in her book.

Another match would soon be in the offing, she thought with satisfaction.

It would be only a matter of time.

Chapter Two

Maizie waited until she saw Sheila glancing over in the direction of their table, then she raised her hand high and waved at the other woman.

Seeing her, Sheila smiled and returned the wave. That in turn had Micah's sons twisting around in their chairs to see who was waving at their great-aunt—a title, when they first heard it, both boys took to mean that their aunt Sheila was really terrific. Delighted, Sheila never bothered to correct them.

Micah looked over to his oldest son. "Turn around in your seat, Gary."

"I *am* turned around," the boy told him, confused by the instruction.

It took a second before Micah realized the communication problem. At five, his son took everything literally, just like his brother. "Turn *back* around," he corrected.

"Oh, okay." Doing as he was told, Gary turned his face toward the others at his table. He focused his attention on his great-aunt.

"Do you know those ladies?" Gary asked her solemnly, doing his best to seem every bit as grown up as his father.

"What ladies?" Micah asked. This time, he turned around to see what had caught his son's attention. Nothing seemed out of the ordinary.

Twisting back around again, Gary said, "*Those* ladies." He pointed to the table where he had seen someone waving to his great-aunt.

"Don't point," Micah reminded his son patiently.

Total confusion descended on the small, angular face. "But if I don't point, Daddy, how are you gonna know which table has the ladies?" he wanted to know.

Sheila suppressed an amused smile. She glanced at her nephew. "He does have a point, Micah."

"I know," Micah said with a sigh, then tousled Gary's hair. "He's got the makings of a great lawyer. Too bad that won't be for another twenty years or so. I could use him now."

"Why?" She looked at her nephew a bit more closely. Beneath the smile, there was tension. More tension than usual. "Are you saying that you need a lawyer, Micah?"

"Probably," he admitted. He upbraided himself for his moment of weakness and flashed her a deliberately wide, easy grin. "Forget that," he told her. "This is your special day, Aunt Sheila. Let's not spoil it by talking about lawyers and necessary evils." Which was the way he viewed lawyers as a whole.

Given a choice, he would have avoided the whole lawyer route altogether, but he had a feeling that this was something where he wasn't going to be able to rely on just his wits to get him out. And knowing that he wasn't guilty of what he was being accused of didn't seem to matter, or help.

He looked at the other three occupants at the table. "I just want to have a nice meal with my three favorite people."

But Sheila didn't seem satisfied. Covering Micah's hand with her own, she looked intently into his eyes. "Well, I won't be able to have that 'nice meal' unless you promise to tell me what's wrong the moment we get home."

It was a compromise he could live with. Micah nodded. "Done."

"I'm going to hold you to that," she told him.

Though he would have wanted it otherwise, he knew that the woman was as good as her word. He wouldn't be able to put her off.

"I know that."

For now, Sheila relented. "All right, then." Sitting back in her seat, she opened the menu again out of habit. "Let's get this party started."

"You didn't answer my question, Aunt Sheila," Gary reminded her, shifting in his seat restlessly.

The boy had the tenacity of a pit bull. For a second, Sheila's eyes shifted to Micah.

"Definitely the makings of a lawyer," she said,

agreeing with her nephew's assessment of his older son. Leaning her head on her hand, she looked directly into Gary's sky-blue eyes and asked, "And what question is that?"

"Do you know those ladies?" Gary repeated with just a trace of exasperation. He slanted a look at his father. "The ones I can't point at," he added.

"I know some of them. The lady who waved sold me the condo I live in. Those two other older ladies are her oldest and dearest friends."

"Doesn't she have any young friends? Besides you," Gary asked. His smile was broad and earnest.

Micah's older son was seated to her left. Sheila leaned over and gave the boy a long, heartfelt hug. "Best present I ever got," she told him.

At any other time, Gary would have preened at the compliment. But right now, he was dealing with a more immediate problem. "You're squishing me, Aunt Sheila," the boy protested.

She released him immediately, making a show of raising her hands and removing them from his small body. "Sorry, I got carried away," she apologized. There was a glimmer of humor about her mouth that only Micah took note of.

Greg scrunched up his face. It was clear that he didn't understand the expression.

"No, you didn't," the younger boy told her. "You're right here. Nobody's carrying you away."

Greg looked around as if to make sure no one had sneaked up on them. As he scanned the room, he made eye contact again with one of the ladies at the other table. She was looking right at him.

Shy, he shifted back around and hid his face in his hands.

"What's the matter?" Micah asked his son. What had caused *this* reaction, Micah wondered.

"That lady, she's looking right at me." Greg giggled, saying the words into his hands.

It was Micah's turn to look at the women at the table in question. He assumed his sons were both looking at the same table. Scanning it quickly, he saw that there were eight women seated around the table. Seven appeared engaged in conversation and the eighth, a blonde—Greg had to be referring to her—was looking in their direction.

His eyes met hers unexpectedly and for a very long second, neither of them looked away.

She had a nice smile, he caught himself thinking. He saw her mouthing something and belatedly realized that she was saying, "Cute little boys." Not knowing what else to do—and ignoring her seemed rather rude—he mouthed, "Thank you."

Her smile curved even more, pulling him in a little further. For some reason, he was having a difficult time looking away. There was something almost hypnotic about the smile, yet incredibly soothing at the same time.

"How come you're not making any noise?" Greg asked, then explained the reason for his question. "Your mouth's moving."

"He's using his inside voice," Gary informed his

brother importantly. Then, raising his chin, he added, "I can hear him."

Even at four, Greg knew a lie when he heard it. "No, you can't," he insisted.

"Can, too," Gary shot back, ready to go to war against his worst enemy/best friend in the blink of an eye.

"Boys," Micah interjected sternly, "what did I tell you about arguing?"

"Don't," both boys chorused, their eyes downcast. Both appeared to be properly chastised, although Micah suspected that a little playacting was going into their performances.

Satisfied that they were going to behave for at least the next five minutes, Micah nodded and turned his attention back to the meal. Their waiter was approaching the table.

"All right, let's order the food while it's still Mother's Day," he urged his sons.

"Why didn't you tell me?" Sheila asked, looking dismayed, annoyed and worried all at the same time.

"But I just did," Micah pointed out, spreading his hands wide.

They had barely crossed the threshold to his house before his aunt had pounced and demanded to know what was going on. They'd stayed at the restaurant a good two hours and apparently she had enjoyed every minute of it. But now, she informed him in a no-nonsense voice, it was time to come clean.

"What's wrong and why do you feel you need a lawyer?" she'd asked—and he'd told her.

Told her everything.

Granted it was a summarized version, and he'd left out a few details because she was outside the realm of those who had a need to know, but he'd relayed the general gist of it.

She'd taken it all in quietly, making no comment while he talked. But he could tell that she was upset.

"Besides," he pointed out, "it's Sunday. There's not much I can do about this until tomorrow." Everything had blown up on him late Friday afternoon. He'd spent Saturday trying to come to terms with the unexpected, jarring turn his life had taken.

"Oh, yes, there is," Sheila informed him in no uncertain terms. She went directly to the kitchen and the phone on the wall.

To his knowledge, no good law firm did business on a Sunday. "Who are you going to call?" he asked sarcastically. "Lawyers R Us?"

Granted he wasn't an expert, but in his opinion, any attorney who was in his office or on call on a Sunday was either desperate, ridiculously expensive or not any good. None of which were qualities he was seeking in the person he needed to represent him. He needed someone good who charged a reasonable fee, one that he had a fighting chance of paying off before the turn of the next century.

Sheila stopped just short of dialing, looking at her nephew over her shoulder. "Remember that woman who waved at me in the restaurant?"

He remembered. Remembered, too, the tall, striking blonde he'd made eye contact with. It had been an odd feeling, a little like déjà vu, as if he'd been in exactly the very same spot before.

But of course he hadn't. He blamed it on his overwrought nerves.

Shaking off the feeling, he got back to his aunt's question. There seemed to be only one reason why she would refer to the other woman.

"She's a lawyer?" he guessed. But the moment he said it, he knew that didn't make any sense. "I thought you said she sold you the condo."

He didn't want to hurt his aunt's feelings, especially not on a day that celebrated mothers. He was ever mindful of the fact that she had taken him in when she didn't have to. No law would have made her open her home—not to mention her heart—to an orphaned relative. She'd done that out of the goodness of her heart and he loved her for it.

Still, this was his life—and quite possibly his freedom—they were talking about.

"Usually anyone who wears two hats doesn't wear either one well," he told her diplomatically.

The boys were sitting on the floor watching a cartoon video his father kept on hand just for occasions like this, when Gary looked up, his attention captured by the phrase his father had used.

He frowned thoughtfully. "She wasn't wearing any hats, Daddy. Don't you remember?"

"My mistake," Micah said.

It was easier saying that than getting involved in an

explanation that cited the sentence as an old expression. Since Friday, when his life had suddenly been upended, it was all he could do just to try to hold himself together and not think of the possible consequences if things went awry.

He couldn't even afford to let his mind go there. He had sons to provide for and an existing pile of medical bills—both for Ella and for Greg—that he still had to pay off. That meant keeping a clear head and being prepared at all times. Prepared to defend himself, prepared to answer charges—and somehow get to the bottom of all this to find out how he'd become implicated in these criminal allegations to begin with.

All he knew was that he was innocent. The tough part was getting everyone else to believe him. In the meantime, he had to hang on to his job while getting himself emotionally ready to face the kind of charges that could very well be leveled against him.

"Maizie's not a lawyer," Sheila told him. "But I need her to get in contact with one of the other women at the table—Theresa Manetti."

"She's the lawyer?" Micah asked.

Sheila sighed. It would have been simpler just to say that Maizie had arranged for a beautiful, unattached woman to be at their table just so that she could see him and he her—and that woman just happened to be a damn good lawyer. At that point, no matter how good she actually was, Micah would definitely *not* avail himself of her services. So she went the long way around, just to eventually get to where she needed to be.

"No, she runs a catering business." Then, seeing his

confused expression, she quickly added, "but her son and daughter are both lawyers."

"There are lots of different kinds of lawyers, Aunt Sheila," he pointed out tactfully. "What I'm going to need is a criminal defense lawyer—"

Gary, who was openly eavesdropping, appeared horrified. "Daddy?" he cried uncertainly. "Are they gonna put you in jail?" His eyes were suddenly huge, watery saucers as he contemplated his own words.

"No!" Greg cried, not waiting for his father to answer. The small boy jumped to his feet and immediately threw his small arms around the first part of his father he came in contact with: his elbow.

Micah sighed. He'd always tried to protect his sons, doing his best to keep them away from topics that he considered too adult, despite the fact that both boys seemed, at times, to possess old souls. He made sure that the parental block was in place on a host of programs and channels. Yet, the world obviously had a way of intruding and circumventing all his best efforts.

"Nobody's putting anyone in jail," Micah quickly assured both boys. "I just want to ask a lawyer some questions, that's all." Gently extricating his arm from Greg's surprisingly strong grip, he put that arm around the boy and his other one around Gary. "There's nothing to worry about."

Sheila could almost believe him—if she didn't know him as well as she did. The only time Micah lied was to spare someone else's feelings. In this case, he was trying to make all three of them believe that everything was all right.

Except that it wasn't, she thought.

She called Maizie's number. Counting off the number of rings, she heard the receiver being picked up on the fourth. Sheila began talking immediately. In short order, she told Maizie that what had begun innocently enough as an effort to get her nephew back to the dating scene had just taken on far more serious ramifications.

On the other end of the line, Maizie listened.

Several moments later when Sheila paused, Maizie jumped in. "I'll talk to Kate directly," she promised. She'd already made the decision to bypass Theresa for now. Her friend could be filled in on this newest development later. They no longer had the luxury of allowing things to progress naturally and gradually. Sheila's nephew needed legal aid *now,* which meant that he had more of a professional need for Tracy than a personal one.

She got right on it.

Kate was a little confused as to why Maizie was calling her, but she listened to the woman patiently and tried to answer her questions to Maizie's satisfaction.

"Yes," Kate told her mother's best friend. "Tracy is very good. She's extremely dedicated. I had to literally drag her away from work today."

Maizie put her own interpretation to the information. "Then what you're saying is that Tracy is booked up," she said, disappointed.

She was surprised to hear Kate laugh. "The thing about Tracy is that she always makes time for more cases. I'm beginning to think that she hardly ever sleeps. What I'm saying," she summarized, "is that

I'm sure she'll be more than willing to look into the case for your friend's nephew. And if she thinks she can win, she'll let your friend know. As far as I know, she's never lost a case," Kate said with a note of envy. "Let me give you her cell phone number." She rattled it off, then added, "But, knowing Tracy, I've got a feeling she's probably back at the office right now. I'll give you her number there just in case your friend has trouble getting through on the cell."

Maizie made a note of that number, as well, then turned around and called Sheila with both.

Sheila, in turn, spun around and handed the two numbers to Micah.

Despite the fact that she had a burning desire to handle this for him, to set up everything for him in order to minimize what he had to deal with, she knew that doing so sent the wrong message to Tracy. Although Micah had a softer, gentler side to him, he was definitely not one of those neutered males that a woman could easily lead around by the nose and lose respect for by the hour.

"Here," Sheila said, placing the two phone numbers in front of him.

It had been less than twenty minutes since he'd given his aunt a general summary of what he was dealing with. To spare her, he'd left out the more troubling details. She didn't have to know about that unless it was absolutely necessary.

This was fast, he thought. He looked from one phone number to the other.

"Which one belongs to the better lawyer?" he asked.

"They both belong to the same lawyer. That's her cell number—" Sheila pointed to the first piece of paper, then to the other "—and that's her office number. According to my friend, she's there now. In her office. Working."

That sounded like his kind of person, Micah thought. If he didn't have his sons, or if they'd been older and away at college, he would have buried himself in his work and not even bothered to come up for air unless he absolutely had to. It wasn't that work soothed him, it was just that it kept him so busy, he didn't have time to think.

To remember.

And regret.

"Okay," he said. Picking up the pieces of paper, he started to put them in his pocket.

"Now," Sheila insisted, drawing his hand back so that he was forced to place the phone numbers back on the counter in front of him. "Call her now." And then, in case he had any suspicions as to why she was being so adamant, she said, "The sooner you start to tackle this, the sooner it'll go away."

She was right, Micah thought. Taking out his cell phone, he began to tap out the phone number on his keypad. Charges of treason and espionage were not something to take lightly or ignore—no matter how much he desperately wanted to.

After five rings, the answering machine on the other end kicked in. He almost hung up but then decided against it. Dutifully, he gave his name, phone number and a "brief message." He was almost finished when he heard the line pick up.

"Hello? Mr. Muldare?" Tracy said, picking up on the name he'd given as he started leaving his message. "This is Tracy Ryan. How may I help you?"

The voice was soft, melodic, and drew a response that took Micah entirely by surprise. He felt an uncertain tremor at the core of his stomach, definitely *not* the kind of response that a person had to their potential lawyer.

Chapter Three

Several seconds went by as Tracy waited for the man on the other end to say something.

Had he hung up? Or was he just reconsidering his options? If it was the latter, she had a sneaking suspicion she knew why. Over the phone, she sounded younger than she actually was. Youth didn't exactly generate confidence in clients who found themselves in need of a criminal lawyer. That was why she always preferred to meet a client face-to-face for the first time.

While at five-six, slender and blond, Tracy knew that she would never be mistaken for a football lineman, at least she didn't look as if she was a senior in high school, which was the way she sounded on the phone according to Simon, her ex. In reality, she was twenty-nine—going on sixty.

Some days, she felt even older than that.

"Mr. Muldare?" she prodded after another minute had gone by. If he'd hung up, where was the dial tone? "Are you there?"

The sound of her voice had thrown him. He'd come very close to asking to speak to her mother before realizing that *this* was the lawyer his aunt's friend had referred him to.

"Micah," he told her. "Call me Micah." After all, if she was going to be his attorney, he had a feeling they were going to be spending more than a little time together.

"All right, *Micah,*" she said, deliberately emphasizing his name, "just how is it that I can help you?"

You can wave your wand and make this all go away. Wouldn't that be a neat trick? he couldn't help thinking sarcastically. Out loud he asked, "You're a criminal lawyer, right?"

"Right," she echoed, then waited for him to continue. Instead, she heard him sigh. "Is something wrong, Mr. Mul—Micah?"

She heard him laugh. It was more of a disparaging sound than a happy one.

"Chronologically or alphabetically?" Micah asked.

"Excuse me?"

"Well, I really don't know where to begin," Micah admitted somewhat helplessly.

"In my experience, the beginning is usually the best place." And then, because there was another, somewhat long pause on his end, Tracy decided a few questions might be in order. "Why don't we start with where you got my name and number." She gave him several choices. "Was it off the internet or did you—"

"My aunt got your name from one of her friends. I'm not sure of the exact relationship but I think it's safe to say that it was a friend of a friend." He stopped, realizing how ridiculous all this had to be sounding to her. "I'm afraid I've never done anything like this before—looked for a lawyer," he explained in case she didn't know what he was talking about—and why should she? Rattled by this unexpected turn his life had taken, he was barely making any coherent sense. It had all served to put him on the hairy edge. "And I usually don't ramble like this," Micah added.

Rather than make some sort of belittling noise or say something that conveyed the presence of an attitude, he heard the woman on the other end say, "I'm sure you don't. Finding themselves needing a criminal lawyer usually knocks the average person for a loop. Why don't you come into the office tomorrow and tell me why you feel you need my services?"

He'd have to see about arranging for some comp time at work. The way things were going there lately, though, making up time was the least of his problems. He was already facing restricted duty, and his security clearance had been suspended pending further notice.

"Sounds good. What time?" he asked the adolescent-sounding woman.

Tracy pulled over her desk calendar—the existence of which the administrative assistant she shared with two other lawyers at the firm always found incredibly amusing—and glanced at the appointments that were listed for tomorrow.

The page was full.

She suppressed a sigh, thinking. "How about after hours?" she finally suggested. "Ordinarily, I'd say lunchtime, but I'm going to be working through it tomorrow. If you can come in around five-thirty, I can see you then," she told him.

"Five-thirty," Micah repeated. It was doable and this way, he didn't have to make up any work time—as long as he got in early. His department had been on flextime for eighteen months now. "I'll be there."

He sounded as if he were ready to hang up, Tracy thought. She talked quickly to stop him. "Oh, Micah, just so I know what I'm up against, how serious is the alleged crime you've been accused of?"

Micah glanced over his shoulder to see if either one of his sons had quietly sneaked up behind him. For the most part, Gary and Greg were as quiet as train wrecks, but every so often—most likely through the use of magic—they managed to approach his space without making a sound, and almost always when he was saying something they weren't old enough to hear yet.

But when he looked, both boys were still on the floor in front of the TV. Gary was laughing and chattering to his brother. Greg wasn't answering. The younger boy appeared to have fallen asleep.

Taking a breath, Micah said, "The word *treason* should cover it."

"Oh." Tracy paused a second to get her bearings and

regroup. "You're being accused of treason? Seriously?" she asked, her voice echoing disbelief.

"That's it in a nutshell. Treason," Micah repeated. He half expected the woman with the teenager's voice to beg off, saying something along the lines that she'd just realized she had a prior commitment—like for the next eighteen years.

But instead, he heard her say, "Okay, then. I'll see you tomorrow at five-thirty."

Well, that was a surprise. The woman had taken it in stride. "Five-thirty," he repeated, feeling both numb and, for the first time in two days, somewhat hopeful. Numb because he still couldn't believe this was happening to him, and hopeful because at least he'd taken the first step toward resolving this nightmare.

God knew he'd never been an angel, nor had he presented himself as one, but anyone who knew him knew that he took pride in his work, pride in the fact that in some small way, he was helping to defend the country that he loved. He could no more do what he was being accused of—selling top secret information to this country's enemies—than he could suddenly grow a viable set of gills and live the rest of his life in the ocean.

And yet, the company he'd gone to work for straight out of college was saying he *was* guilty.

"Daddy," Gary called, breaking into his thoughts. The boy beckoned wildly for him to come over and join them. "Come see this. It's funny!" the little boy said, laughing.

"I could use 'funny' right about now," Micah told his son. Putting his cell phone away, he went to join the two little boys. He sat down on the sofa directly behind his sons and glanced in Greg's direction. His younger son was curled up on the floor and from the looks of it, had fallen asleep. "Looks like this put Greg to sleep," he commented to the other boy.

Gary waved a dismissive hand at his brother. "He's a baby," he taunted the sleeping boy. "He still needs naps." And then, suddenly becoming animated, Gary looked over his shoulder at his father. "Want me to wake him up for you?" he asked eagerly.

"No, that's all right," Micah assured his son. "Let him sleep. He probably needs it."

He heard Gary mumble "Big baby" under his breath. The next moment, the boy was scrambling up onto the sofa, taking advantage of the fact that with his brother asleep, he had his father all to himself. "Just us guys, huh, Daddy?" he asked, puffing up his chest.

Just then, Sheila came out of the kitchen. She'd placed all the food they'd brought home in doggie bags from the restaurant into the refrigerator.

"So how did it go?" she asked, sitting down on the other side of Micah. She nodded toward to phone in his pocket to make her point.

"Well enough, I guess." It was hard to glean anything from the few minutes he and the lawyer had talked. "I'm meeting her at her office tomorrow."

"Good," Sheila approved, nodding her head. "This'll be over with before you know it," she promised, then smiled warmly at him as she patted his hand. "Just you wait and see."

"Shhh," Gary said loudly. He put his finger to his

lips. "You hafta listen," he insisted, looking at his great-aunt. "You're missing all the good stuff."

"No, I'm not," Sheila told him, her eyes crinkling as she regarded the little boy fondly. "The 'good stuff' is right here."

"This is the good part," Gary alerted his father and his great-aunt just before he turned his eyes back to the screen and watched in rabid attention.

Yes, Micah thought, eyeing both his sons, *this* is *the good part.* No way would he allow some baseless, false accusations to destroy that for him.

Certainly not without one hell of a fight.

Tracy's last appointment wound up leaving early, for once sticking to the facts and cutting his rhetoric short. That allowed her a few minutes of breathing space before her last client of the day, Micah Muldare, arrived.

Treason. Well, that was certainly a new one. She'd never handled a treason case before, nor had any of the other lawyers at the firm. She very well could be in over her head.

But, she reasoned philosophically, the only way to learn was to learn, right? She tried to look at each new challenge that came her way as an opportunity for her to grow as a person.

Each new *professional* challenge, she amended.

She had absolutely no interest in expanding or growing on a personal level, no matter *what* Kate blatantly hinted at.

Been there, done that.

Her one incredibly brief foray into marriage had

been nothing short of an unmitigated disaster, the likes of which she had no desire to repeat or relive ever again. The only way to avoid it was not to come within a ten-mile radius of the institution of marriage.

That meant no dating, no mingling with any representative of the opposite sex in any form except professionally.

Speaking of which…

Tracy glanced at her watch. It was five minutes past five-thirty. Her last client of the day was now officially late.

So where was Mr. I'm Not Guilty of Treason, anyway?

Maybe she should have questioned him a little more thoroughly about who had referred him. Her time was too precious to waste, sitting here and waiting.

Another five minutes went by.

Okay, she'd been patient enough, Tracy decided. Time to go home to a hot bubble bath and a cold pizza, she told herself, thinking of what waited for her in her refrigerator.

She'd really enjoyed the food at Giuseppe's. So much so that she'd taken an order of pizza—classic flat, with extra cheese and three meat toppings—home with her. She'd had a couple of slices last night for dinner and planned to have two more tonight.

Never a big eater, Tracy figured that the pizza would probably last her about four, or maybe five days, depending on—

Her phone rang, breaking into her thoughts and demanding her attention. Since it was now a quarter to six, she debated ignoring it and letting the caller go straight to voicemail.

Maybe it was her errant client, calling to say that he was running late—or just running. Tracy chewed on her lower lip, weighing the odds.

There was only one way to find out.

Tracy finally picked up the receiver and said, "Hello, this is Tracy Ryan."

The voice on the other end of the line immediately launched into an apology. She'd discovered years ago that it was hard to remain annoyed when there was an apology rushing at you.

"I'm sorry, Ms. Ryan, this is Micah Muldare. I'm afraid I'm not going to be able to make our meeting tonight."

He sounded very sincere, she thought, giving him the benefit of the doubt.

"Nothing serious, I hope," Tracy said mechanically. Mentally, she was already drawing the hot water and pouring the bath salts into the tub.

"My younger son's running a fever and my usual babysitter just called to tell me she's stuck on the freeway," he explained. "I can't leave my sons home alone. They're much too young."

"Your sons," Tracy repeated. Suddenly an image clicked in her brain. The little boys from the restaurant.

No, it couldn't be. What were the odds?

"By any chance, did you have lunch yesterday at Giuseppe's with a striking dark-haired, older lady and two very cute, very blond little boys?" she asked him.

He probably thought she was crazy, Tracy told herself, but her instincts told her to ask anyway.

"They didn't tell me you're clairvoyant," Micah said dryly. The woman's question had caught him completely off guard. How had she known?

"I'm not." Although God knew that would have come in handy in her line of work. "I was there."

There were other women to choose from, but his thoughts immediately gravitated to the woman who had smiled at his sons. "That was you?" he asked without any preamble.

Tracy wasn't sure how, but she knew exactly what he was asking. They'd made eye contact over his sons' heads. It had been brief, but enough to have left her with a lasting impression.

"That was me," she confirmed. Now that she knew who he was, she relaxed just a notch. "I hope it's nothing serious with your little boy," she told him, this time with all sincerity.

"Greg has a tendency to run really high fevers," he told her. There was more to it than that, but he saw no point to going into detail. She didn't need to know that in order to properly represent him.

"I don't like taking chances," he added. "Otherwise, I'd bring both of them with me."

Tracy nodded to herself. She liked that. Liked the fact that Muldare put his sons first, ahead of what had sounded like it could easily escalate into a very serious problem for him.

After a nonexistent debate with herself that took all of half a second, she made up her mind.

"Listen, I was going to go home right after seeing you, so why don't you give me your address and I'll just swing by your place before I call it a night?" she proposed. "I have to admit, I am rather intrigued," she told him. "You're the first person who's ever come to me because he was being accused of treason."

He was glad that someone was intrigued. As far as he was concerned, he was just oppressed by the very weight of the whole ordeal.

He debated her offer for exactly fifteen seconds and decided that he had absolutely nothing to lose. But he didn't like the idea of putting the woman out. "You're sure you don't mind?" he asked her.

"Why should I mind?" she asked. "If I minded, I wouldn't have suggested stopping by in the first place."

Her bubble bath became a distant memory—but it was for a good cause. Picking up a pen and tearing off a two-day-old page from her desk calendar, she got ready to write.

"Okay, where do you live?"

Greg was coughing in the background. Distracted, Micah answered, "In Bedford."

"Bedford's gotten to be a big city," she quipped. "Mind narrowing that down a bit?"

"Sorry."

Right now, he felt as if everything was coming at him at once. The accusation, Greg's fever, his aunt getting stuck in traffic—he'd always hated the idea of traffic ever since his parents had been killed in that car accident. He knew it was unreasonable of him, but he couldn't harness his response, couldn't do away with it. Belatedly, he recited his street address.

Rather than make some inane comment—or say nothing at all—he heard the woman say "Huh" in what seemed like preoccupied wonderment.

"Something wrong?" he asked her uncertainly, although for the life of him, he couldn't begin to imagine the reason for a positive answer. It wasn't as if he lived in a haunted house or anything of that kind. Why had she made that noise?

Tracy stared at the address she'd just jotted down. It seemed rather incredible to her, but she actually lived in his development.

What were the odds of that happening?

But she didn't want to disclose that little tidbit to her prospective client because then she'd be leaving herself open to all sorts of things she might not be too happy about down the road. Besides, once out of the office and off the clock, she was a very private person who *valued* her privacy.

She wanted that to continue.

So all she said in response to his question was, "No, I'm just surprised—I'm fairly familiar with the area." Glancing at her watch, Tracy did a quick calculation. "I can be there within the half hour—if it's all right with you and—your wife?" she ended her statement with a question since she wasn't entirely familiar with his situation. He'd been at the restaurant with only his sons and his aunt, but that didn't mean he wasn't married. After all, Kate's husband hadn't been there with Kate yesterday at the restaurant. There were all sorts of reasons why this Micah could have been there without his wife.

Wife. The word still hurt after all this time. Rather than say he was no longer married, or that his wife had died, he told the attorney, "It's just me and the boys. And Aunt Sheila," he added.

"That would be the striking brunette who was at your table," Tracy surmised.

Micah laughed to himself. Hearing herself described that way would certainly be good for Aunt Sheila's ego, he thought.

"I'll be sure to tell her that when I see her. It's bound to brighten her day," he told the woman on the other end of the line.

Tracy caught herself listening to his soft chuckle. It was a nice sound. Hearing it seemed to generate a feeling of well-being within her.

You're just being punchy, Tracy. It's been a long day and you put in more than your share of hours. Maybe you should just go home.

But she couldn't just go home, not after telling Muldare that she was coming over. He'd think he was dealing with a dizzy blonde. As a natural blonde, she had fought against the image all of her life.

"I'll be there in less than half an hour," she repeated and then hung up.

Tired or not, her mouth curved in just a hint of a smile as she walked out the door.

Chapter Four

The residential development where Tracy lived was one of the oldest ones in Bedford. It was also one of the smaller developments.

Maizie Sommers, the real estate agent who had sold her the house she lived in, had happily given her all sorts of positive statistics about the area. According to the woman, Bedford Ranch had seven hundred and fifty homes within it. The agent had called that "cozy."

Oddly enough, though the word normally suggested fireplaces and warm comforters to her, Tracy decided that the word *did* seem to fit the community. She was also happy to learn that this particular development didn't come with myriad rules and regulations that covered everything from the number of hours that residents could keep their garage doors opened to when and *if* they could park their cars in the street or had to leave them strictly in their driveway.

But the thing that Tracy liked best about the relaxed atmosphere within the development was that she was free to paint the outside of her simple, two-story home any color she wanted without having to submit the request first in triplicate to some nebulous association for their approval.

Obviously, Muldare found this sort of freedom as appealing as she did. Otherwise, the newer, more rigidly structured developments would have certainly lured him away. They had the bigger, more modern houses.

Most likely equally appealing—at least to her prospective client—was the fact that there was an elementary school on the southern perimeter of the development. Los Naranjos was the name some clever pencil pusher had given it.

She wondered if his sons went there. It certainly made drop-offs and pickups easy for whoever looked after the boys while he was at work.

Maizie had gently touted that feature to her, as well, saying, "When you have kids, you'll find that this is an excellent school for them to attend. All the schools in Bedford are ranked in the top 5 percent scholastically," the woman had told her proudly.

Little had the woman known that for her there was never going to be a "when." Much as she adored her mother who had raised her by herself—she'd never known her father—Tracy truly believed that kids needed a full set of parents, not just one. After that humiliating experience with Simon, she was not about to get married ever again, which sort of closed the door for her when it came to having kids.

Tracy pulled up to the curb before his house. Muldare lived closer to her than she'd thought he would. Only one vehicle was in the driveway—his, she assumed—but she didn't feel as if she could take the spot beside it in case someone dropped by while she was still here.

After getting out of her vintage white sedan, Tracy came up the walk to the front door. Her ex-husband had been into status symbols, big time. The fact that they couldn't afford to buy things like super-expensive cars and a cabin cruiser made no difference to him. Debt was just an annoying detail that he left for her to handle while he drove around in a vehicle that could have easily been a down payment on a house in the more affluent part of the city. He'd accused her of being a stick-in-the-mud when she'd tried to show him the discrepancy between their salaries and the lifestyle he was living.

Tracy rang the doorbell and heard the beginning notes of Beethoven's Fifth symphony. A classical music lover? Or had that just come with the house and he hadn't gotten around to changing it?

She waited until the strains faded away, then pressed the doorbell again, a little longer this time. He had to be home, right? At least, that was what he'd said when he'd called to cancel their appointment. Maybe he was one of those people who didn't like to stand up for himself and this was his way of backing away from the problem.

If so, he'd probably seen an ad for her law firm and was intimidated by what representation would wind up costing in dollars and cents.

She hadn't told him that if she was going to take the case, it would be pro bono. But she also wanted to judge the merits of the case for herself before she committed to it. If she told him about pro bono up front, he'd be eager for her to take the case and if she didn't believe in his innocence, or didn't think there was at least a slim chance in hell of winning, she wouldn't take it on.

About to ring and listen to the Beethoven piece a third time, she was spared the encore when the front door suddenly opened. Her prospective client was on the other side.

"I was beginning to think that maybe I had the wrong address," she said by way of an ice breaker. "Hi, I'm Tracy Ryan," she said, extending her hand out to his.

Caught off guard—today was *not* going to go down as one of his better days—he said the first thing that popped into his head. "I'm Micah Muldare—but then, you already know that."

"Yes. I do." He was still holding her hand and, while that did generate a rather exceptionally warm feeling within her, she did need it back sooner than later.

She glanced at his hand, then raised her eyes to his, waiting.

Realizing that he'd spent too long staring at her, Muldare flashed her a quick, grateful smile that was gone almost before it arrived. At the same time, he released her hand.

It was easy to see that he was worried. About the case? Or about his son? Most likely, it was a little of both. The old adage about "when it rains, it pours" floated through her head.

Because Muldare continued standing where he was, blocking her way, she was forced to ask, "May I come in? Conducting initial interviews in doorways leaves a little something to be desired," she quipped, surprising herself at the dry comment.

"Oh, sorry." Belatedly, Micah stepped to the side, allowing her in. "I guess I just didn't realize you'd be this young—I mean, there's nothing wrong with being young, but—"

"I assure you that in this case youth isn't synonymous with lack of experience," she told him as she came inside.

There was a warmth here, she thought, looking around. A charm. Love had been in this house—in place of a cleaning lady, she thought as she side-stepped a stuffed animal on the floor. Given a choice, she would have picked love every time—if it had been hers to pick. The house she'd briefly shared with Simon had been so neat, it all but sparkled on its own. And she couldn't remember ever being in a colder place.

"How's your son?" she asked, passing both Micah and a very animated-looking little boy. He certainly didn't appear sick to her. But then, she'd heard somewhere that children had a way of bouncing back almost immediately.

Gary, who was shadowing his father step for step, took the question to mean him. "I'm okay," he told her, speaking up immediately. "But my little brother's not feeling so good. He's sick," he confided in what could have passed for a stage whisper.

"So your dad told me." She turned to look at Micah. "Have you called his pediatrician yet?" she asked. It seemed like the logical thing to do.

"I thought I'd give the fever another thirty minutes before I start sounding like a panicky father." Because she seemed to be interested and because she'd voiced the inquiry before diving into the reason for her drive-by visit, he found himself giving her a little more information. "This isn't exactly the first time I've sat beside his bed, holding his hand and making bargains with God."

Bargains with God? Now, *that* surprised her. Turning, she took a closer look at him. A hint of a boyish smile met her, but then it was gone, replaced by the expression of an extremely worried-looking man.

Her eyes slid over him, taking full measure of her potential client.

"Funny," she finally commented, "you just don't seem like the type to bargain with God."

Micah laughed shortly. "Believe me, once a kid or two enters the picture, you'd be surprised how quickly you wind up changing and start bending all sorts of rules and regulations you'd never even thought to question or challenge before."

"You probably don't want to admit that in exactly those words right off the bat when the other counsel questions you," Tracy advised.

Realizing what he'd just said, Micah nodded. He

wasn't accustomed to having to censor himself. "Yeah, right," he agreed.

Was that an embarrassed flush on his cheeks, or a reaction to the unseasonably warm weather they were having, she wondered. This was June, best known for June Gloom in Southern California, but rather than hiding behind clouds, the sun had been out every single morning, warming everything far beyond the customary cool, agreeable temperatures.

Rules and regulations. The term echoed in Micah's brain. He'd surprised himself, rebel that he'd once been, at how well he'd adapted to this secretive world he'd found himself in with its strict, strict rules. On the black programs that he'd been working for the past eighteen months—he was currently handling the bulk of seven different programs, complete with files that had pages where huge sections were blacked out with permanent laundry markers—every step of the process, every breath of the day was regulated to the extreme. And he had *really* surprised himself by doing his best to play the game and adhere to all the different stipulations because ultimately, he was working to defend not just his homeland but his sons, as well.

His sons were everything to him. If they hadn't been around, he was fairly certain that he wouldn't have been, either.

"You have any kids?" he asked her suddenly as he closed the door behind her.

There it was, she thought, that small, sharp prick, the one that sought her out each and every time someone asked if she had children. You'd think by now it would begin to fade. Instead, at times it felt stronger than ever.

I would have, but things just didn't work out. I guess I'm just not supposed to have any.

Out loud, Tracy said, "I'm not here to talk about me." She wanted that to be the end of it, to close herself off to that part of herself, the part that always, *always* bled when the topic came up. But she couldn't just block it out. There was this absolutely adorable pint-sized shadow next to her, following his father's every move, being oh so serious about it and succeeding in being oh so adorable, as well.

She grinned down at the little boy behind Muldare and thought back to the restaurant and her first impression of the duo. "But you seem to have struck the lottery with your two guys here. What's your name?" she asked Gary.

"Gary Muldare," he told her both proudly and promptly. "The sick one's Greg Muldare. He's just four," he added disparagingly.

"Four's not such a bad age," she pointed out tactfully.

"What's your name?" Gary asked. It was obvious that he hadn't heard her introduce herself to his father.

Micah loved both boys fiercely, but there were times they made him think of puppies, all big paws and charging clumsily into places that they had no business going.

"Gary—" Micah chided.

Gary's head bobbed up, a defensive protest already

on his protruding lips. "You said I could talk if someone talked to me. Well, she's talking to me."

Tracy did what she could to smother the laugh. "He's got a point, you know, Dad. From now on, you're going to have to watch how you word your instructions. Kids have a way of cutting straight to the chase."

Turning her attention back to the little man beside her client, she extended her hand to him just the way she had to his father. "Hi, I'm Theresa Ryan, but you can call me Tracy."

"Tracy," he repeated, as if testing the name out on his tongue to see if he liked the sound of it. His brow scrunched as he tried to make sense out of what he'd just been told. "Is 'Tracy' your name, too?"

"Tracy's my nickname," she explained. The look on his wide-open little face told her she'd made no headway in the explanation department. And why should she? she thought, suddenly realizing the problem. At his age, Gary probably didn't know what a nickname was. "So, yes, it's my name, too."

If Gary had ever been shy, he'd completely forgotten about those days. Taking her hand confidently in his, he said, "If you wanna see Greg, I can take you to him," he volunteered.

Micah gave his older son a look that was supposed to take the place of a reprimand. It didn't work. So he tried a verbal restraint. "Gary, Ms. Ryan didn't come here to visit—"

"But a visit to a bedridden family member wouldn't be entirely out of order," Tracy said, interrupting. She wanted to get on Gary's good side. It never hurt to have an ally, no matter how short, and something told her that having allies in this case might prove to be helpful. Children often said things that offered a different insight. “Where is your little brother?”

“Back in bed. In his room. Being sick.” The answers came out like rapid gunfire before Gary slowed down. “He’s sick a lot,” the boy told her dramatically, ending with a deep sigh.

Hollywood was missing one of its more talented actors, Tracy couldn’t help thinking, more amused than she’d been in a long while.

She looked over her shoulder toward the boy’s father as Gary pulled her along in his wake, obviously taking her to see his brother. “Maybe you should have some lab tests done on him,” she suggested.

Wasn’t that what you did for a child with a recurring illness? She herself didn’t know. She had been a healthy child, which was lucky for both her and her mother since there was no extra money to be had for luxuries like doctors.

“We already know what’s wrong in general,” Micah told her, wondering why she wanted to discuss Greg in the first place. “There were some residual problems due to his being born prematurely. He spent the first two years of his life in and out of hospitals. As a result, the doctors found that Greg’s immune system was compromised somewhat. It takes him twice as long to get over something than it does Gary.”

“That’s ’cause I’m healthier than he is,” Gary said to her, all but thumping his small chest.

“And because you are,” she told him, saying it as if

he should be very proud of himself, "you can help your dad take care of your little brother."

The large, glowing smile faded, to be replaced by a frown. Gary's expression indicated that he'd actually felt as if the rug had just been pulled out from under his feet.

"I guess," he said in a far more dispirited tone than he'd used just a minute ago.

"That means that you're a very important young man. Not just anyone gets to do this kind of thing," Tracy told the little boy solemnly.

Gary began to come around. "Or get a nickname?" he tagged on eagerly.

"Or get a nickname," she echoed.

"You're a natural at this," Micah observed, letting her walk into his sons' bedroom ahead of him. "You sure you don't have any kids?"

"Very sure." She policed herself to make sure that the yearning in her soul didn't manage to work its way into her voice. "My best friend, though, was the oldest in a houseful of kids. I got put on kid patrol every time I walked into the house." She smiled fondly, remembering the O'Sullivans who'd lived in the house next door to hers. They had been a noisy crew, especially on Sundays as they got ready for church. She was over at their house more than she was in her own. They helped fill the loneliness when her mother was out, working two jobs so that they could survive. "After a while, I had the feeling that if my mother ever put me up for adoption, Rosemary's parents would have grabbed me up in a heartbeat."

Her heart twisted a little in her chest as she found herself gazing down at the pale, sickly little boy lying in bed, his back propped up by several pillows. He looked so small and helpless.

"Hi, I'm Tracy," she said, putting out her hand to him as if this was a serious meeting.

Taking her hand, he blinked a couple of times, clearly mesmerized by this pretty lady with his dad and brother. "Are you my guardian angel?"

Stunned, it took Tracy a second to collect herself. "No." But even as she said it, she had to admit she rather liked the reference. "But I might just turn out to be your dad's guardian angel," she added, slanting a look in his direction.

"Daddy's too big for a guardian angel," Gary protested.

Tracy squatted down to be more on the same level as the two boys. "Ah, but there you're wrong. Nobody ever outgrows their need for a guardian angel. We're the ones—if we're doing our job right—who help you gain your goals, help make the cacti grow—" She said the latter because she'd seen a small cactus garden behind a proper miniature picket fence in the front yard.

"How about flowers?" Greg asked. "Do you help make them grow, too?"

"Absolutely. The next time you see a flower in the field, just think of me," she told both boys, concluding with a wink.

Her suggestion was met with far more eagerness than she'd thought was possible. "Okay, I will," Gary promised enthusiastically.

Tracy rose back up to her feet. Standing over Greg, she brushed her hand along the boy's forehead, subtly checking to see just how hot it was.

"Me, too?" Greg asked her hoarsely. "Can I think about you when I see flowers?"

"Absolutely," she told the boy. "I'd be honored." He did look pretty miserable, she thought. "Tell me, Greg, how long have you been feeling sick?"

"I didn't feel so good after having that pizza yesterday," he confessed.

She looked at Micah. "Anyone else have the pizza?"

"Try everybody," he told her. "Including my aunt Sheila."

So much for that theory. But there was no harm in asking. She glanced at Gary before looking at Micah again. "And you two are feeling okay?"

"Yes," Micah answered.

"Sure am," Gary crowed, then, seeing his brother's pale face, he became just a wee bit contrite. "Sorry, Greg."

Another little boy wouldn't have even noticed his brother's complexion, much less been sensitive enough to connect it to his own revelry at not being sick and think to apologize. Someone was doing a good job raising them. Was Muldare responsible, or was it that older lady who'd been at their table, that friend of Maizie? In either case, the boys were a credit to whoever had taken the time to raise them right.

"Did you eat anything else, Greg?" Tracy asked.

He thought a minute. "Just the orange pieces. They fell on the floor, but they didn't look dirty. Just sticky."

Sticky, as in something had gotten on the slices? Or from their natural juices? "Can you remember what floor they fell on, honey?" she pressed.

"The garage," he mumbled, his eyes downcast. "When I was getting out of the car. Nobody noticed," Greg confessed.

Tracy continued to follow the thin thread. "What's on your garage floor?" she asked Micah.

"As little as possible," he answered. He was forever moving things out of the boys' reach. And then he suddenly remembered. He'd been transplanting plants on Saturday. "I spilled some liquid fertilizer I was mixing, but I thought I mopped it all up."

"Maybe you missed a spot," she suggested.

The full impact of what had possibly happened hit him like a nine-pound hammer. "I've got to get him to the E.R." He looked at his other son. "Gary, we need to get Greg to the hospital."

"Ask for Dr. Nikki Connor," she told him suddenly. When he looked at her quizzically, she explained, "She's a top-notch pediatrician with a very gentle bedside manner. Sometimes you need that." Tracy paused a second, debating with herself. She knew what a hassle any outing with two children could be. Going anywhere with a sick child while the other one, full of energy, would be bouncing off the walls—literally—was trying for anyone. "I can stay with Gary," she finally volunteered. "Just until you get back."

Stunned, Micah stared at her. She'd gone out of her way to drop by his house in order to talk to him about the sudden turn his life had taken. So far, they hadn't talked about it at all. Instead, she'd charmed his sons and left no small impression on him. And now she was volunteering to occupy his son until his aunt came home. The woman probably cost a fortune, but she was well worth it.

"I can't ask you to do that."

"You didn't. I volunteered, remember? I hope you pay attention at work better than you do at home," she said solemnly.

It took him half a minute to realize she was kidding.

Chapter Five

Micah debated taking Tracy Ryan up on her offer. It would certainly make things easier if all he had to worry about and take care of was Greg. Gary could be a handful when he wanted to be.

Still, he didn't really know this woman. Yes, she'd come recommended by way of one of his aunt's friends, but he was rather protective of his sons and the bottom line was, attorney or not, he didn't know this woman.

He vacillated, weighing pros and cons the way he always did.

In the end, because he was fairly certain that his aunt would be arriving at his house within the half hour, he decided that it was all right to leave Gary with Tracy. The boy seemed to be very taken with her, which ultimately tipped the scales in her favor.

"Okay," he told her. "I'll be back as soon as I can and my aunt will be here before then."

Tracy nodded, placing a hand on Gary's shoulder. "I'll keep a candle burning in the window for her."

Gary looked up at her, excited. "You mean like a birthday candle?"

Tracy bit back a laugh. "Something like that."

Telling Gary to behave, Micah hurried off to the hospital with Greg, hoping he hadn't just made a huge mistake trusting this woman.

Maybe he was teetering on the edge of paranoia again. Because of the nature of his work, he had become so suspicious of everyone and everything.

It hadn't always been that way.

He'd never been one of those stupidly reckless adolescents, leaping before looking and thinking nothing through. He had always been naturally cautious, but moderately so.

All that had changed in the past two years. That was when his company had switched him into the black programs. These programs, the ones that were ranked far beyond top secret and required him to have fourteen different passwords, had turned him into someone who saw at least two sides to everything and usually the darker explanation.

Trust no one wasn't just a catch phrase for a cult classic TV series, it was an actual way of life for people involved in the black programs. A way of life that he wanted to abandon once he was cleared of the charges looming over him. He had no intentions of leaving in disgrace. He'd given Donovan Defense his all but he was *not* about to let them claim his soul and step all over it.

He wondered if Tracy Ryan was amenable to low weekly payments. If she was as good as she seemed, he'd probably be paying her installments until long after Greg graduated from college.

As he stopped at a light, Micah turned to look at the little boy in the backseat. Strapped securely in his car seat, Greg appeared miserable.

"Hang in there, buddy," he told his son, sounding as upbeat as he could. "We'll get you back to your old self in no time. I promise."

"Okay, Daddy," Greg responded with a weak little smile.

Just like Ella, Micah couldn't help thinking. Greg was always ready to cling to the positive. *Thank God,* he couldn't help adding.

The trip to the E.R. lasted longer than he'd anticipated. It wasn't until close to three hours later that he finally pulled up into his driveway again. He parked beside the black Ford Mustang, noting that his aunt was home and no longer stuck in traffic. Given the hour, she probably had Gary tucked away in bed.

It was only after he'd gotten out of his car and rounded the trunk to lift Greg out of the boy's car seat that he realized the white car was still parked at his curb.

Was she still here? Or had someone else with a white car taken the parking space? It wasn't unusual for people visiting one of his neighbors to park in the first space they found, and white was one of the more popular colors for a car. He hadn't noted the make and model of Tracy's car when he'd hurried to the hospital with Greg.

Why would the attorney still be here? It didn't make sense. The car had to belong to a neighbor's visitor, he reasoned.

Carrying Greg in his arms—his son was curled up into him the way he always did when he wasn't feeling well—Micah stopped at the front door. He was about to fish out his house key when the door opened.

"There's my boy," Sheila said, looking at Greg. "How is he?"

After entertaining notions of his four-year-old suffering from some sort of poisoning, he'd envisioned Greg getting his stomach pumped. The diagnosis had been an utter relief.

"Turns out that he has a touch of the stomach flu. According to the doctor, he should be fine in a couple of days or so. In the meantime, he gets to stay home and watch cartoons, don't you, buddy?" He ruffled the boy's hair.

He received a sleepy smile in response.

"Well, I'm going to take our boy up to his room and get him ready for bed," Sheila informed both father and son. Very gently, she extricated Greg out of his father's arms.

Micah was about to ask his aunt about the car parked at the curb, but as she stepped away, he found he didn't have to. Tracy Ryan had been standing behind his aunt, silently observing. The moment Sheila took the boy, she stepped forward.

"So, I'm guessing that Greg didn't ingest any of the fertilizer?" she asked.

"No, thank God." His voice all but vibrated with palpable relief. And then, because she had seriously aroused his curiosity—no easy feat these days—he had to ask, "What are you still doing here, if you don't mind my asking?" And then an answer occurred to him. "Did my aunt just get home *now?*"

"No," Tracy assured him, "your aunt got home a few minutes after you left." She saw the question in his eyes. "I thought I'd just stick around for a while to find out how Greg was—I didn't think you'd mind," she added.

"Of course I don't," Micah assured her quickly. "I was just surprised that you stayed after my aunt got home, that's all."

He would have thought she'd be eager to get home. Because she seemed genuinely nice, he felt he owed it to her to be completely honest. Even if it wasn't easy.

"Look, I have to tell you right up front that I'm not going to be able to pay you right away. Or after a little while, actually." He looked at her face, searching for a telltale sign that she'd suddenly changed her mind about being his attorney. So far, there didn't seem to be any indication that she was thinking any such thing. "If you're not averse to getting the money in installments—*lots* of installments," he emphasized, "then I'd be more than happy to have you represent me."

She waited until he was finished, sensing that he'd

gotten a full head of steam up and wouldn't appreciate being interrupted. But now it was her turn to talk. "Didn't your aunt tell you?"

All his aunt had said was that Tracy Ryan was a friend of one of her friend's daughters. He had a feeling that wasn't what the woman was referring to. "Tell me what?"

"This case is pro bono." When Micah said nothing, Tracy tactfully began to explain, "That means that there's no charge to—"

"I know what the term means," he told her, sounding a great deal more formal than he had a moment ago. "And if it's all the same to you, Ms. Ryan, I like to pay for what I get." He drew himself up a little straighter, as if wrapping his dignity around himself. "I'm not a charity case."

Ah, there it is. Pride, she thought. Replaying her words in her head, she decided that she could have stated her offer a little better.

"No one said you were, Micah. It's just that legal representation is rather pricy these days—especially legal representation from my firm. They have an excellent reputation," she told him matter-of-factly. "An excellent track record. And for that, they feel justified in charging an excellent fee." The smile on her lips was a self-deprecating one. "Actually, a prohibitive fee for the average citizen," she pointed out. "In order to give a little back to the community, so to speak, on occasion my firm agrees to do a few pro bono cases."

He held up his hand to stop her before she could go on. "I understand all that," he told Tracy. "But I'm not going to fill that requirement for your firm. I pay all my bills no matter how long it takes."

"Yes, I know you do." She saw him raise an eyebrow quizzically. "I always do my homework before I agree to undertake any case," she informed him. "I looked into your background."

His life, he had begun to believe, seemed to be a matter of record. Not an easy fact for a man who valued his privacy. But then, he reasoned, he'd given up all claim to privacy when he signed the papers agreeing to go into the black programs. He had given them permission to turn his life into an open book.

"Thorough," he acknowledged. "That's very admirable."

"Thank you. Now, you're probably too exhausted to talk about the case tonight, so why don't you come by my office tomorrow, say around lunchtime, and tell me your version of the story?"

Her choice of words, intentionally or not, had his back going up. "It's not a 'version,' it's the truth." Even as he said the words, Micah knew he was being testy, but then given the circumstances, he felt he had a right to be.

"I didn't say it wasn't," Tracy pointed out calmly. "But trust me, there are always different versions of the same story out there. It's my job to prove that the true version *is* the true one. And also yours," she concluded with a smile. "So, tomorrow at lunchtime?" she asked.

Somehow in the past five seconds, he'd gotten a second wind. Feeling a little more like himself, Micah made her a counter offer.

"If you're not in a hurry, I'd rather get this out in the open now." He saw her hesitate for a moment and guessed at why. She was probably hungry. "I can feed you," he offered. Realizing that hadn't exactly come out right, he tried again. "I know you haven't had dinner and there's lasagna in the refrigerator that I just have to heat up—unless you're a vegetarian," he said as the thought suddenly occurred to him.

"Nope, not a vegetarian," she assured him, and then she asked, "Your aunt made lasagna? What was the occasion?"

"No occasion," he told her. Beckoning for her to follow him, Micah led the way to his kitchen. "And actually, she didn't make it." He stopped by the refrigerator and opened it. "I did."

She stared at him. "You?"

"Why is that so surprising?" he asked.

Taking out a large, rectangular pan from the refrigerator, he placed it on the counter and removed the foil from the top. Micah cut two healthy-sized portions and placed them on a plate. He brought that over to the microwave and pressed the appropriate numbers on the keypad.

"Because to most of the men that I know—make that *all* the men I know," she amended, silently including her ex amid that number, "*cooking* means putting something frozen into the microwave and making it hot."

Well, that wasn't the case with him, Micah thought, amused. As he waited for the microwave to go off, he gave her a thumbnail sketch of his background.

"My mother liked to cook. I used to spend time

hanging around in the kitchen, watching her make these fantastic meals. When I cook, it makes me feel like she's still around."

She knew he was an orphan, that he'd lost both parents in a car accident when he was twelve. A lot of people would have closed up emotionally because of that—especially if their wife had died on top of that. But he obviously hadn't.

She liked the fact that he didn't seem embarrassed by the admission. Here was a man who was obviously secure in his identity. Had she not made up her mind to represent him already, this would have easily pushed her to making that decision.

The microwave bell went off. Opening the door, he gingerly removed the plate then divided the two pieces, placing each on a separate dish.

Tracy could feel her taste buds arousing in anticipation of the meal that accompanied the sumptuous aroma. Her stomach was already pinching her in protest for having been neglected. Lunch had been a highly unsatisfying protein bar.

"Well, if the aroma is any indication of your culinary abilities," Tracy told him, "you might have a whole new career opening up for you if you decide you want to leave the engineering world behind you."

It wasn't engineering he wanted to leave behind, but there would be very little arm twisting involved to get him to leave the black world. There was still a great deal of defense system work available that didn't involve taking his computer hard drive out every night and having it locked up in a vault until he retrieved it the following morning.

All in all, he'd had more than his fill of paranoia. A man could only live so long with that sort of specter hovering over his shoulder before it started infiltrating and affecting every aspect of his life.

He smiled at the compliment she'd given him. "Why don't you wait until you've tasted it before you have me wearing an apron full-time?"

Tracy inclined her head. "Fair enough."

Using her fork, she cut off a piece and slid it into her mouth, aware that he was watching her and waiting for a reaction. Her taste buds were greeted with a combination of hot, spicy and sweet as well as savory. She said nothing as she took a second bite, discovering it to be even more flavorful that the first. The entire experience was a revelation to her.

Ordinarily, most of the time she ate merely to sustain herself. The only simple requirement she had was that the food not be spoiled or foul tasting. Beyond that, she was fairly easy to please and definitely not demanding or discerning. This, however, felt like a carnival was going on in her mouth.

After her fourth forkful, she paused long enough to look at him in unabashed admiration. "And you actually made this?"

He already knew her reaction to the meal. He wondered if she was aware of the fact that she'd made a little noise of pleasure between the second and third forkful. A completely stray thought floated through his head, wondering if she did the same when she made love. Startled at the sexual thought, his first about another woman since he'd first met Ella, he shut it down. It was almost too much for him to handle.

Clearing his throat, he replied, "Yes."

She knew there were male chefs around. The cable channels were full of them. But she herself had never met an ordinary male who was any better at boiling water than she was. As far as she could ascertain, this meal was beyond perfect.

"Without help?" she pressed.

"Well, I didn't make my own ricotta cheese, if that's what you mean," he told her, amused rather than annoyed or insulted by her skepticism. "I bought it in a container at the supermarket. But I did make my own sauce and grate my own parmesan cheese."

"I'm not an expert," Tracy freely admitted—life, and her vocation, had taught her to be cautious in the way she worded her statements, "but this has got to be the best lasagna I've ever had." She began to eat with gusto, something she was quite unaccustomed to doing. "Forget about pro bono or monthly installments, just pay me in lasagna and we'll call it more than even." She paused for a second, not wanting to talk with her mouth full. "Do you make anything else?"

He had a fairly diverse list of meals he made, but for the most part, he tended to favor meals with an Italian flavor. Rather than launch into a long explanation, he answered her question simply.

"Yes."

The one thing she did have was a sweet tooth, hence the chocolate-covered protein bar for lunch rather than grabbing a sandwich from the vending machine. "Des-serts, too?" she asked.

He could tell by the way she asked that she'd just revealed her weakness. He nodded in response to her question, then told her, "There's some leftover tira-misu—that was what Aunt Sheila wanted as her cake for Mother's Day."

"Tiramisu?" she repeated. She could almost feel her mouth begin to water.

Tiramisu was one of the very few things she actu-ally went out of her way to order whenever she could. Done correctly, it was a sinfully delicious, light deli-cacy that felt as if the calories were floating just above her tongue whenever she had a slice.

This man could actually *make* that?

He picked up on the wistful note in her voice. "Would you like a slice when you're finished with that?" he asked, nodding at her plate.

"I wouldn't want to take any away from your aunt and the boys," she told him, but even as she said it, she hoped that he would offer her a piece despite her polite protest.

"No worries," he assured her. "I made a very large cake."

Feeding her was the least he could do, Micah thought, seeing as how she was apparently taking on his case. He wondered if she knew what she was get-ting into.

Micah continued to watch her, enjoying her simply enjoy her dinner. Most women her age picked at their food, determined to remain some absurdly small size.

It was obvious to him that his lawyer wasn't a slave to being a stick figure.

They were going to get along. He found the thought reassuring as well as oddly comforting. He couldn't really explain the latter reaction, but for now, he didn't even try.

Chapter Six

Tracy couldn't remember the last time she'd felt this full. Her usual habit was to eat only until the empty feeling in her stomach was no longer a problem, and then stop.

Tonight, she'd eaten well beyond that point.

Even now, filled to capacity and feeling somewhat drowsy, to boot, she could have *still* slipped in another few mouthfuls of the sinfully delicious dessert.

Putting her fork down, she gave her full attention to Micah. "I suggest you tell me what you want to tell me before I wind up curling up in front of your fireplace and purring like a contented kitten." When she saw the surprised expression in his eyes, Tracy realized that he might be misconstruing what she'd just said to him. "Between the lasagna and the tiramisu, I think I just ate enough to sustain me for an entire week. You know how old men usually fall asleep after eating too much turkey at Thanksgiving? Well, I'm very close to reaching that point."

He laughed. A dozen ways to describe her occurred to him. Not one involved likening her to an old man. "You're not an old man," he pointed out, "and you didn't just take in an inordinate amount of tryptophan."

Okay, now her brain was going to sleep. She looked at him, confused. "Excuse me?"

He grinned at her. This had been nice. He'd forgotten what it felt like just to have dinner with a woman his own age, never mind that it was at his kitchen counter and that he had made the meal. Some of his best memories of Ella involved this exact same scenario.

The thought startled him, and he immediately pulled back, his feelings jumbled and confused.

"Which part is giving you trouble?" he asked. "The old man part or the tryptophan part?"

She nodded when he mentioned tryptophan. "The second part. What is that?" she asked, referring to what she assumed was a strange ingredient.

"Tryptophan is what puts people to sleep," he told her simply. "It's a natural calming agent and turkey is absolutely loaded with it. Hence, people who eat a large portion of turkey tend to feel very sleepy."

"And here I thought it was just because they stuffed themselves," she quipped. Was it her imagination, or had he somehow gotten physically closer? Neither one of them had moved off the stools or drawn them in nearer. Maybe it was just getting warm in here, and her mind was playing tricks on her.

In either case, she didn't draw away from him but remained sitting exactly where she was, just possibly a little more erect.

"Well, that helps, too," Micah allowed. She was telling him she was sleepy. He could take a hint. "Maybe I should just take you up on coming over tomorrow at lunch."

She couldn't pay him back like this after he'd gone out of his way and made her dinner. Tracy took a deep breath, trying to wake herself up.

"No, no, you said you wanted to get this out on the table tonight and we're not going to postpone anything on my account." She had to pause to stifle a yawn. She really *was* tired. One glance at his face and she could see he was aware of it, too. "Okay, I tell you what, just give me the highlights and you can fill in between the lines tomorrow, how's that?"

"Sounds like a reasonable compromise," he answered. And, if he was being honest, he did feel rather tired himself. Or maybe *drained* was a better word for it. God knew he certainly felt drained. Worrying about his sick son had worn Micah out clear down to the bone.

Between that and agonizing about what would happen to the boys if he was found guilty of selling secrets to a foreign power, Micah felt as if he'd been turned inside out, and then used to mop up all the floors at John Wayne Airport.

"Because of the nature of the work—" He paused

for a moment, then interjected, "and you know I can't tell you what that is."

"I don't need to know specifics for this," she told him complacently. "Go on," she urged.

It was all such a jumble—and it had been ever since he'd been placed on restricted duty—that he wasn't all that sure just exactly where to begin. So he started with his daily routine—beginning with the end of it.

"Every night," he told her, "I need to take out my hard drive and have it locked up in the department's vault."

She stopped him. "Do you know the combination to the vault?"

"No." They'd asked him if he wanted to be part of a select few who had access to the ever changing combination and he'd turned them down. That responsibility was above his pay grade. "Only Justin Reed does at the moment—and they make a point of having him change it at the beginning of each month." His eyes narrowed. She had taken out a pen and was jotting things down on the napkin he'd given her. "Are you taking notes on a napkin?" he asked.

"It was handy," Tracy answered.

"I'll get you some paper," he offered. Turning his stool away from her, Micah was about to get up.

"No need," she told him. When he turned back to look at her, he saw that she'd opened up the napkin to show him how much writing space she actually had. "Go on."

Whatever works, he thought, shrugging. "Anyway, I pick up my hard drive every morning and put it back into the computer. The software and everything I work on is completely encrypted. As is the information on my laptop," he added.

She raised her eyes to his. "Your laptop?"

He nodded. "They issued me one so that I can work from home if I have to. For when Greg gets sick," he explained.

Professionally, she was far more interested in the fact that his company had issued him a laptop than why they'd issued it to him. But personally, she found the thought of his caring so much about his younger son endearing.

"Obviously you can't take the same precautions with your laptop, since if it's locked up at Donovan's, you defeat the initial reason for *having* the laptop in the first place," she reasoned. "Which computer is the reason for this investigation?"

He liked the way she shifted the blame onto the inanimate object and steered it away from him. But the laptop was his, *had* been his for the past eighteen months. As far as he knew, no one so much as touched the computer in all that time.

"The laptop," he told her.

She asked him the first thing that occurred to her. "Any chance that one of your boys—"

He cut her off before she could finish her question. "No. I treat it as if it were a firearm." Then he explained what he meant by that. "I lock it up when I come home unless I'm using it. And even then, when I'm finished I put it under lock and key in the back of my closet. Neither of the boys can reach it," he assured her.

Little boys could be very resourceful, but for now, she let what he believed to be true stand. "All right, go on."

"The company does random surprise tests on computers. They send in their man—nobody ever knows when they'll happen or who they'll target—and when he asks to see either your desktop computer or your laptop, you've got to immediately stand back and give him total access to your hardware."

Tracy could tell that he took this to be the ultimate show of distrust, even if he could probably see the reason for the random tests.

"No last-minute keying in of any codes or saving any material you might have been working on," Micah continued. "You have to instantly raise your hands away from the keyboard and give the guy room to run his test."

Tracy saw the need for this, but at the same time, it was incredibly invasive. It showed that there was no trust, no bond between management and the people who worked for them.

"Have you ever had one of these tests run on your hardware before?" she asked.

"No, but I've only been working on black programs for the last two years—I've had the laptop for eighteen months," he added, trying to give her as much information as he could.

"Black programs," she repeated.

"That's what they're called," he explained, answering her unspoken question. "Most likely because whenever there's any paperwork involved, whole sections are indelibly and permanently blacked out with a black marker."

Interesting though it was, she was getting sidetracked and got back to the pertinent questions. "All right, so this is the first time that this has happened?" she asked again.

His smile was just the slightest bit lopsided as he told her, "There is no second time if they find something to arouse their suspicions. This kind of thing is grounds for instant dismissal, not to mention being brought up on charges."

"But you haven't been dismissed yet, have you?" she asked. He'd told her that he was working today. If what he'd just told her was true, then he'd lied about working. Something wasn't adding up here.

"Due to all the layoffs that have been taking place in the last couple of years, the company's really shorthanded. I've been with Donovan Defense for more than ten years—I interned with them while I was still in college," he explained, in case the numbers didn't work for her. "Because of that, and the fact that I've worked for several different areas within the company, I've got a broad spectrum of knowledge that they need so they don't want to get rid of me altogether. But I have been placed on restricted duty," he assured her, none too happily. As far as he was concerned, he was now doing grunt work and he hated it. "They have me doing end-of-day reports and quantifying—well, never mind. It's actually even more dull than it sounds," he told her.

And he didn't do "dull" well, she thought. Who did? Tracy mused, knowing how she'd feel in his place. A person liked to be challenged, to strive to do their very best. Rote work didn't allow for that factor. It tended to put the person who was doing it to sleep.

"So exactly what was found when they did their impromptu raid on your laptop?" she asked.

He'd gone over this a hundred times in his mind, trying to figure out how it had happened—and when. He still had no answers.

"That the firewall had been breached and it looked as if someone outside the company got into my hard drive. These laptops are programmed so that only certain internal computers can communicate with them."

A closed circuit, she thought. "In other words—ideally—if I sent you an email from my office to your laptop, it would just bounce back," she asked, wanting to make sure they were on the same page with this.

Micah nodded. "Exactly."

She was fishing now, but she had to start somewhere. "Could you have done something to, say, tweak your laptop so that you could receive messages from me if you wanted to?"

She was asking him if he was a hacker, Micah thought. "That is entirely above my pay level," he told her whimsically. And then he became serious as he gave her a little more background about himself. He had a love/hate relationship with computers. "Computers for me are an acquired taste. When they're working properly, they can be extremely efficient, but when they're not..." He allowed his voice to trail off.

She picked up his meaning immediately. "It's like that old nursery rhyme about the little girl, that goes,

'When she was good, she was very, very good, but when she was bad, she was horrid.'"

Micah brightened. "Exactly. There're people who can make their computers tap-dance and sing. I feel victorious if I can just get mine to work properly." He realized that she was looking at him intently as he talked. So much so that he felt the attorney was practically looking right *into* him. "What?"

She was just trying to get a feel for him, for what he was thinking. She wanted to be able to read him easily. For that she would need his cooperation—and to build up some trust. The latter was a two-way street.

"You realize that anything you say to me is going to be kept strictly confidential." It was a given, but it didn't hurt to make sure that it was understood.

"I'm aware of that feature, yes."

"And that you *have* to be completely honest with me," she emphasized. As she spoke, her voice gained in passion. "If I find out that you're not, that you've been lying to me—for whatever reason," she stipulated, "I *will* drop you like a hot coal and remove myself as your attorney from your case so fast that your head will spin, possibly for days."

"That creates quite an image," he told her.

Micah understood why the woman had to say that, although he didn't particularly like the fact that she seemed to believe him capable of lying to her.

Still, she didn't really know him, right? Didn't know that he prided himself on being a man of integrity. Plenty of liars out there, both men and women. There was no stamp on his forehead, informing her that he was exempt from that.

He cut her some slack.

"I don't lie," he told her matter-of-factly.

She nodded. She intended to believe him—until given proof otherwise.

"Good to know." Tracy got back to asking her questions. "Did the person who discovered the breach tell you anything else? Like who he thought you were selling those secrets to?" It would be nice to have a name or a face to put on the nebulous "enemy." It made her fact checking easier.

"No, all I was told was that the contents of my laptop had been breached and that I was on restricted duty pending an investigation into the matter—starting immediately. That was on Friday," he told her. "In their world, I'm guilty until proven innocent."

And she could see how much that was really bothering him. His reputation meant something to him. So did being brought up on charges of treason. Not exactly a walk in the park, was it?

"I know that," she said.

This next part would sound hokey to her, but he didn't care. It was how he felt and she needed to know that, too.

"Okay, well, I also want you to know that I love my country and that I would never do anything to compromise it in any way or to make my sons ashamed to call me their father."

He said it with such feeling that she was moved just listening to him. He meant every word, she could see it in his eyes, hear it in his voice. He was a man of integrity.

She believed him.

That made things easier for her. She could passionately defend someone she believed in. That he sounded sincere was a huge plus, as well. If this wound up going to trial, his appearance—as long as the jury was made up of more women than men—could only help them. It was easier to convict an unattractive person than an attractive one—as long as the latter didn't smirk, and she doubted that Micah could, even on a dare.

Nodding absently at his remark, she looked down at the napkin she'd unfolded and had been making notes on. "Well, I seem to have run out of napkin space, so why don't we stop here for tonight." It wasn't really a question, more like a rhetorical suggestion.

Tracy rose to her feet and picked up the two plates that were on the counter in front of her. She turned toward the sink. "Tomorrow, I'll see what I can find out from Donovan for you," she told him.

"You don't have to do that." He went to take the plates from her and their fingers brushed against each other. "I mean bus your dishes," he explained, in case she thought he was referring to talking to someone at his company.

She picked up on the words he'd used. People were like jigsaw puzzles to her. She liked filling in the missing pieces. Most likely, he'd done some waiting on tables himself. Probably when he was in college, she guessed. To earn some extra money.

"I always clean up after myself," she protested.

Micah continued to hold on to the dishes from his end. "You looked after Gary for me. The way I see it, I'm the one who still owes you."

"You fed me dinner," she reminded him. "I consider myself paid in full—and then some." But because she had no intentions of playing tug-of-war with the plates, Tracy did retract her fingers, allowing her host/client to take possession of the dishes.

He brought them over to the sink, then put his own on top of them. For now, he ran some water over them to keep the food from sticking.

Shutting off the water, he turned toward her. "How about some tiramisu to go?" he suggested.

Normally she turned down offers of doggie bags at restaurants whenever the food server asked if she wanted to take any of her food home with her. But there was absolutely no way she would turn down this offer.

So, instead, she smiled at him and said, "You certainly do know how to tempt a girl."

The phrase—along with her smile—seemed to nudge loose something distant in the back of his brain, a half memory he couldn't quite get hold of and bring forward. But it did manage to rouse a tiny inkling of nostalgia, as if what Tracy had just said was something that Ella might have said to him once a long time ago.

It also, for just an instant, made him acutely aware that his attorney was an extremely attractive young woman, the kind that brought conversations to a screeching halt whenever she entered a room.

Added to that package—and a pair of possibly the longest, sexiest legs he'd seen in a long, long time—

was her utterly unassuming air. If anything, it made her doubly attractive.

He had a strong feeling that Tracy Ryan had no idea just how sensual, how beautiful, she actually was. The more genuinely beautiful women usually didn't.

The next moment, Micah realized that he seemed to have completely frozen in place and that she was waiting for him to make good on his offer.

Embarrassed, but able to hide the fact well—a trick he'd learned as a freshman in college—Micah reached into one of the overhead cabinets, took out a role of aluminum foil and then pulled out a length of foil slightly larger than he needed.

He used it to wrap up a generous slice of tiramisu for her to take, then held out the wrapped piece to Tracy.

She smiled as she took the cake from him. Holding it up, she told him, "Consider this a down payment on my services."

Micah laughed shortly. As far as he was concerned, he made better desserts. Maybe if she came back to dinner sometime, he'd show her. "You get me my life back, and I'll make you a cake every week for the rest of your life," he promised.

Tracy's smile, already wide, spread even further. It seemed to light up her entire face, making her appear radiant. She shifted the wrapped dessert to her left hand. "Deal," she declared, holding her right hand out to him.

When he realized that she was actually being serious, he was quick to put his hand in hers. "Deal," Micah echoed.

She probably thought he was kidding, Micah surmised. But he was willing to do anything to ensure that she had enough incentive to prove him innocent.

Because he really was.

Chapter Seven

Jewel Parnell Culhane was one of the private investigators that Tracy's firm utilized whenever they needed to do a background check on a client or gather details necessary for a case.

Tracy knew she would need more than a little help in cracking the technology involved in Donovan Defense's allegations against her client so she put in a call to Jewel early the following morning. Since the nature of the charges being levied against Micah involved treason, she decided it was best not to discuss anything about the case over the phone.

Though she hesitated for a moment, Jewel finally agreed to come to the office that morning.

"But it'll practically be a drive-by," Jewel warned. "I'm up to my ears in cases, interesting ones for a change," she told Tracy. The situation, they both knew, was in sharp contrast to the days when the bulk of her work revolved around tailing cheating spouses and capturing compromising photos for divorce proceedings.

"Don't worry, I promise I won't keep you long," Tracy told her.

"You might not even be able to keep me short," Jewel cracked. "I'm meeting my one and only for lunch." Tracy could almost hear the smile in Jewel's voice as she said, "He insisted. Between his work and mine, we're like two ships in the night, except that we're hardly even passing each other. We just seem to be sailing off in opposite directions."

"One of you needs to rework your schedule," Tracy suggested. "From the little bit I know of your husband, he's much too good a catch to throw back into the sea. He wouldn't be there five minutes before some other woman would get her hooks into him."

"Said the woman who never dates," Jewel commented, laughing softly. And then she immediately held up her hands, as if anticipating Tracy's next words, even though Tracy had no way of seeing her. "I know, I know, it's like the pot calling the kettle black—but I'm a reformed 'pot.' I'd give up this gig in a heartbeat if keeping it meant losing Christopher, not to mention losing Joel."

Joel was her husband's orphaned nephew and the reason the two of them had met in the first place. Christopher had hired Jewel to find Joel's absentee father when his sister had died suddenly. When Jewel finally located the man, Joel's father wanted nothing to do with his son. By then, Christopher had formed a bond with the boy and readily adopted him. As a bonus—to himself—he added Jewel to the mix as his wife.

Tracy had met Christopher and Joel at her firm's last Christmas party. Seeing them, she couldn't help thinking that they made a really nice family. That in turn had aroused such longing within her that it had taken her a while to lock down her emotions and tuck them away again. It did no good to long for something she wasn't destined to have.

"Understood," Tracy replied, then requested, "Just get here whenever you can."

"I'll see what I can do," Jewel promised just before she terminated the connection.

"Treason?" Jewel repeated incredulously some ninety minutes later in Tracy's office after the latter had given her a thumbnail sketch of the case. "And here I thought you lawyers led a pretty boring existence," she deadpanned.

"Boring's good," Tracy told her. "Boring I can win." She shifted in her chair, fidgeting slightly. "This case has me nervous."

"Well, that's a first," Jewel observed. And then she leveled a look at the other woman. "Wait, is it the case that has you nervous—or the guy?"

Both.

The response popped up, unbidden, in her head, surprising Tracy. Where had that come from? And why was Jewel asking her this?

To forestall any more probing, personal queries,

she ignored the question and said, "He has two little boys—ages four and five. I'm taking the case because I'd hate to have them grow up seeing their father only on visiting day."

Jewel nodded. Obviously Tracy and she responded to the same kind of stimuli. "I see your point. Anything else I should know about this case?"

She might as well tell her everything up front, Tracy thought. Jewel would find out sooner or later and it was better that the investigator was prepared instead of broadsided.

"Micah Muldare is up to his neck in debt. Specifically, medical bills—his late wife's and younger son's. He's too proud to declare bankruptcy and is paying them off as much as he can each month."

"You realize you just made a good case for the prosecution, don't you?" Jewel asked. "They'll claim he sold highly classified information to the highest bidder because of his situation."

"If he was the kind of person who'd sell out his country, he wouldn't be trying to pay off bills, he would have gone with the bankruptcy option. It's easier," Tracy pointed out.

"It's also humiliating," Jewel countered. "But for the record, as far as I'm concerned, he's innocent until proven guilty."

Tracy smiled. "Nice to know the justice system is still alive and well."

"So exactly what is it that you'd like me to do for this honest man?" Jewel asked.

The problem was so involved, Tracy wasn't sure

just how to go about asking. "For starters, answer a question for me."

"If I can," Jewel qualified.

"The official accusation against Micah is that his laptop was compromised. Someone breached his firewall and got into the information on his hard drive. He swears it has to be a hacker. I know his company takes extreme precautions to keep the information on the laptops impenetrable. They employ state-of-the-art techno security safeguards." She took a breath. "So my question is, could someone *have* hacked into his laptop, or is that not really a possibility?"

"Oh, it's *always* a possibility," Jewel assured her. "Like the old saying goes, 'the difficult we can do, the impossible takes a little longer.' If someone builds a better mouse, someone else is guaranteed to come up with a better mousetrap."

Tracy was trying to follow this reasoning. "So is that a yes?"

Jewel nodded. "That is most definitely a yes. And, the worst part of all this is that whoever actually hacked into your client's laptop is going to hide their trail really well. So if someone actually hacked into Donovan Defense's system—"

"*When* someone hacked into Donovan Defense's system," Tracy insisted.

Jewel inclined her head, correcting herself. "*When* they hacked into the system, if they're good enough to get in, they're good enough to make it close to impossible to track them down."

Tracy picked up on what seemed to be the all-important word in Jewel's statement. *"Close?"*

Jewel smiled and nodded, the picture of confidence. "Now, this is why your firm keeps me on retainer," she reminded Tracy. "I happen to know a computer tech who makes Harry Houdini look like a rank amateur."

"I'm sure that with computers, Houdini probably would have been," she commented. The man had been a world-renowned magician, not a wizard with technology. "If at all possible, I want your techno wizard to try to find out just who it was that got into Micah's system."

"And if he does manage to find the guy—or the ring—doing the hacking, do you also want to know why he, or they, hacked into Micah's hard drive?"

That was the one thing Tracy felt she didn't need to find out. She assumed she already knew why. "He—or they—hacked into his system because Micah has sensitive material on his laptop that no one outside of a select few at the company is supposed to be aware of or is allowed to see."

"There's that," Jewel allowed with a nod. "And then again," she said with a wide, knowing smile, "you might just be surprised."

"Okay, I'll bite. How so?" Tracy asked.

"For all you know, if his hard drive was hacked into by an outside party—"

"And we're assuming that's the case," Tracy reminded her firmly.

"His laptop might actually be just part of a wide network hijacked by the hacker."

Tracy stared at her. Just what was Jewel telling her? "Come again?"

"A network," she repeated, then began to explain. "It's called a botnet and it's not as uncommon as you might think. What it boils down to is that his laptop might just be one of many computers that are remotely accessed and controlled by hackers. The hackers use these infected computers to troll other computes for credit card numbers, bank account information and various other 'useful' things they can get their hands on and eventually deplete. It's very possible that initially, the hackers might not even know what they have in their hands here," she told Tracy.

Now, there was both a hopeful—and a chilling—possibility, Tracy thought. Hopeful because if they didn't know and weren't looking for it, the data on the hard drive pertaining to the ongoing missile work might be safe. Chilling because there were now skilled rings emptying people's life savings with a click of the right key. *People like that should be shot,* she thought. *No ifs, ands or buts.*

Looking at Jewel now, she asked, "And you think there's a chance that this is what happened?"

"Could very well be. But do us both a favor and don't get your hopes up until I can get the chance to talk to my techno guy and have him get started."

"There's just one problem," Tracy said, none too happy about the matter.

"Just one?" Jewel quipped. "Hardly seems worth the effort."

It might be just one problem, but it was a huge one in her eyes.

"I can't get my hands on my client's laptop. It's been confiscated by his company and he said it's scheduled to be scrubbed, whatever that actually means." She knew it couldn't mean what the word ordinarily suggested. No one submerged a laptop into water and expected to be able to use it ever again. Something else was going on with the machine.

Jewel sighed. "It means that all traces of any infecting virus will be erased, as well as any and all existing programs. The company's tech department will have to reinstall all the programs from scratch in order for the laptop to be of any use to your client."

That was what Tracy was afraid of. "Won't that get rid of all the evidence?"

Her question made Jewel grin. "You underestimate what a really *good* tech can accomplish. There's always a trace to follow. Footprints in cyberspace, so to speak."

Tracy shook her head in wonder. It seemed as though the impossible was possible these days. She couldn't begin to wrap her head around that. "I can't even retrieve files that were accidentally deleted."

"That's why you need people like me—who in turn need people like Neal—that's my techie," she explained. Glancing at her watch, Jewel quickly rose from her chair. "Looks like I'm out of time," she told Tracy. "If I leave right now, I've got just enough time to reach the restaurant—provided all the lights on the way there are green."

"Good luck with that," Tracy said.

Grabbing her things, Jewel promised, "I'll get back to you." As she hurried out, Jewel added, "This sounds like a really interesting case."

She supposed that was one word for it, Tracy thought as she watched her firm's primary investigator disappear. Another word for it was *challenging*. Very, very challenging.

Suppressing a sigh, Tracy got back to work.

She had other cases. Trials to prepare for. God knew she didn't lack for things to keep her extremely busy and occupied for marathon days on end. But the odd thing was, her mind kept reverting back to Micah's case.

Or, more specifically, to Micah.

Though she hated to admit it to herself—because it signified that she wasn't being objective—there was something almost sensually attractive about the man, some kind of chemistry between them. A chemistry that she would rather not acknowledge existed—except, perhaps, and it was a big "perhaps," in the deep recesses of her own mind.

She tried to tell herself that she was confused, that her reaction was due to the fact that he was a single father trying to raise two sons, which she found very admirable. He was like an underdog in this situation. She'd always had a weak spot for underdogs and people struggling against the unexpected blows of life.

Despite her excuses, deep down Tracy knew she was rationalizing and trying not to acknowledge that she found the man not just sympathetic but knee-weakeningly attractive.

Since when did she even think that way? Tracy upbraided herself. It had been years, *years,* since she even glanced at a man with something other than impartial interest—and then only if he was involved in a case of hers. That little zip that most women experienced and were acutely aware of, the suddenly igniting spark that made women do stupid things in an effort to meet the object of their attraction, had been M.I.A. in her life since she climbed out of the disaster known as her marriage. And she liked it that way.

It kept life simple, uncomplicated. As far as she was concerned, her cases were all the complexity she wanted. And yet, though she tried to squelch it, a little thrill snaked through her each time she thought of Micah Muldare.

This wasn't going to end well, Tracy grimly predicted and wondered if she would be better off if she just handed Micah's case over to someone else in the firm.

But who? Everyone was superbusy.

Besides, she'd already taken steps to get the case rolling, already had her own take on things and, from what she could see, Micah seemed to trust her, something that was all-important in a case and not always all that easy to earn or negotiate.

She would just have to get a grip on herself. She just had to keep in mind that thinking of Micah in any other terms than as her client would compromise the case. She couldn't properly represent someone she was sleeping with.

The unbidden thought had her jaw dropping down to practically her desk.

Where the hell had that come from?

How had she gone from "cute guy" to making him her bed partner? Talk about getting carried away.

And, more than likely since he'd made no real moves on her other than as her client, he wasn't attracted to her. Micah had been nothing if not a complete gentleman and she was willing to bet that he would remain that way no matter how long they had to work on this case.

So, she concluded with feeling, if she didn't allow herself to get carried away by her own thoughts, everything was under control.

Squaring her shoulders, Tracy rose from her desk and collected her notes. Depositing them into her briefcase, she got ready to leave. She had a case waiting for her in court.

Weary at the end of a long day, Tracy was finally heading home. But first, she would make a quick stop at Micah's house.

Uneasy about the pit stop, she told herself that she was only doing this for the same reason she'd had Jewel stop by the office instead of discussing the case with her over the telephone. Since, as far as Donovan Defense was concerned, this case involved possible unlawful access to highly classified top secret information, talking about it on the telephone was asking for trouble.

Wire tapping was illegal—unless special waivers

were granted by the district attorney. But she'd be a fool to believe that Micah's phone wasn't being tapped. So she felt it safer to assume that someone might be listening in on her call to Micah. She didn't want to risk jeopardizing the case in any way.

For all she knew, someone was framing Micah for reasons all their own. It sounded far-fetched but not entirely impossible. Which was why she was here, on his doorstep again. The stop wasn't out of her way. And besides, the man deserved to get an update. His very freedom hung in the balance.

Tracy had barely touched the doorbell when the door swung open.

"Hi." Micah stood in front of her wearing jeans, a blue V-neck sweater that should have had a shirt beneath it but didn't, and he was barefoot. His dark hair was carelessly tousled and he looked more like his sons' older brother than their father.

He was also breathless.

She felt her gut tightening unexpectedly. "Am I interrupting something?" she asked him uncertainly. Maybe she should have at least called ahead.

"No, no, c'mon in. I was just playing a game with the boys," he told her, running a hand through his hair and trying to get it into some semblance of neatness. "Greg's feeling a lot better, so we thought we'd celebrate by playing a game Gary came up with," he explained. Stepping back, he allowed her more than enough space to walk in. He looked at her, mildly confused. "Remind me—did we have an appointment for tonight that I seem to have forgotten about?"

She should have definitely called, Tracy upbraided herself. *Too late now.*

"No, I just thought I'd stop by to give you an update," she explained, then added, "Talking on the phone about this case just didn't seem quite right somehow."

Micah smiled, nodding. He read between the lines and picked up what she wasn't saying. "The company does have a habit of making a person feel completely paranoid," he agreed.

She still felt bad about interrupting him when he was playing with his sons. She began to edge away. "Look, since you're busy, maybe I should just—" she began.

He stopped her before she could finish her statement. "Right now, I'm losing, so I'm not too busy."

Standing back on the threshold, she hesitated for a moment. Still, she was here now. She might as well stay.

"Well, if you don't mind—"

"I don't mind," he said, his eyes holding hers.

She felt as if he was talking directly to her, not to his lawyer or to the person gathering information on his case, but to *her.* To the part of her that wasn't an attorney but a woman.

"I won," Gary crowed, sailing into the room and unwittingly shattering the moment.

Picking up the boy, Micah swung his older son around as if he were a small jet plane. "Yes, you did, but I'll get you next time—unless Greg does," he added, grinning at his younger son.

She noticed that the boy beamed in response.

Well, Micah Muldare certainly has fatherhood down pat, she thought.

There was no way she would allow him to be separated from his sons, she silently vowed. No matter what she had to do, Micah Muldare would remain with these precious boys.

Chapter Eight

As Tracy walked into Micah's living room, she said, "I have one of my firm's private investigators looking into your case." She saw the sudden apprehensive expression in his eyes. He was afraid of information being leaked. This special top-secret program had to be hell to live with. "Don't worry, Jewel is very discreet."

"Jewel?" Micah echoed. What kind of a private investigator had a name that sounded as if it belonged to a model, or a Country-Western singer? He felt less than reassured.

Tracy could almost read the thoughts going through his mind. Was that a good or a bad thing?

And if she could, was he transparent to others, as well? That could definitely be a problem.

A moment later, she decided she could second-guess

what was going on in his mind because she was so tuned in to his case, so that made it all right.

She smiled reassuringly at him. “We can’t help the names our parents give us.”

They were in agreement on that, Micah thought as he considered the name his parents had given him.

“I guess not,” he replied. “I never much cared for my own name,” he admitted. “When I was a kid, I thought it sounded antiquated, like something that belonged to a prospector who was close to a hundred years old.”

She wondered if that was his assessment of it, or if some bully had taunted him. Rolling it over in her mind, she decided that, unless she was mistaken, Micah wasn’t the type who would put up with a bully.

“It’s not so bad,” she countered. “Right now, it’s rather unique.”

“Unique is good?” he asked, mildly amused.

“Unique is always good,” she replied. “Who wants to be like everyone else?” As if he could possibly be lumped in with everyone else. She had a feeling that Micah Muldare had stood out in a crowd right from the start.

Maybe he saw the picture a little more clearly because he had kids, Micah thought, but his attorney definitely didn’t remember his playground days.

“Oh, I don’t know. Maybe every kid under the age of twenty,” he suggested. “That’s why I had everyone calling me ‘Mike” when I was growing up.”

“Mike,” she repeated, toying with the name, rolling it around on her tongue. “No,” she decided, shaking her head. “‘Mike’ doesn’t cut it. I like Micah better.”

Why didn't that surprise him? The woman struck him as someone who definitely didn't march to the same drummer as everyone else.

"So I guess I'll keep it."

My God, he suddenly thought. Was he flirting with her? Until a second ago, he'd just assumed that all that—flirting, male-female dynamics—was behind him. That his life was now set in stone. He had his sons and his career, and that was all he needed or wanted.

But now his career was in serious jeopardy, dangling dangerously by a thread and if, through some twist of fate, he was found guilty, then he wouldn't have his sons, either. He'd have to leave the boys with his aunt while he was in prison. He couldn't believe that with all this going on, he was reacting to the woman that fate—and in an odd way, Donovan Defense—had brought into his life. Reacting to her on a very basic level.

He hadn't gone this route since he'd first dated Ella.

Almost self-conscious, Micah cleared his throat. "Can I offer you dinner? I made shepherd's pie. It's Greg's favorite."

The selection in her refrigerator hadn't improved any since yesterday. Grocery shopping wasn't exactly high on her list of priorities and she tended to forget to do it.

That was why there were phone numbers to at least half a dozen takeout restaurants anchored down by various magnets on the front of her refrigerator door. They offered her a wide variety of food to choose from. From what she'd sampled of Micah's cooking, he was head and shoulders above what the restaurants she ordered from could deliver.

"I can't impose on you like that again," she demurred, although with little verve. She was hoping he'd talk her into staying.

"Sure you can," Micah told her. He was already leading the way to the kitchen. He glanced toward his sons. "Can't she, boys?"

"Yeah," Gary piped up. "She can."

Rather than add his voice to his brother's, Greg quietly came over to her and took Tracy's hand in his, as if the four-year-old had every intention of escorting her to the kitchen.

Amused, moved, Tracy left her hand in the boy's small one—the part of it that he actually managed to hold—and allowed herself to be led off.

"I guess I can't fight all three of you," she said, surrendering.

Gary's small brow scrunched up as he looked up at her. "We're not fighting you," he pointed out, confused.

"Daddy doesn't like fighting," Greg informed her solemnly.

"It's an expression, boys," Micah explained. His back was to them as he carefully spooned out a portion of the shepherd's pie for his unexpected guest.

"What's a 'spression?" Gary asked, no more enlightened than he had been a minute ago. His brow was still furrowed.

"It's something that grown-ups say," Tracy told him, crouching down to Gary's level. "Like when they use metaphors."

Gary appeared to be completely willing to accept

her first sentence. It was the second one that had the furrows in his brow deepening into wavy lines. "Huh?"

Tracy glanced over her shoulder at Micah. "I went too far, didn't I?"

He laughed. "Don't let it bother you. I do the same thing all the time. But I found if you don't talk down to them, they get a better command of the language faster than if you use baby-sized words." He spared his older son a warm glance. "Which is why they're both smart as whips, right, Gary?"

There was a tinge of uncertainty in the boy's blue eyes, but he bobbed his head up and down with pronounced enthusiasm.

"Hear that, Greg? Daddy says we're whips." He made a noise like a whip cracking down on its target.

Greg echoed the sound and the two were off and running into the family room to play another new game they'd just made up.

"Hard to believe he was so sick yesterday," Micah marveled as he put the plate with her dinner on it into the microwave. He pressed the numbers for a minute and a half, confident that would be warm enough.

"Too bad adults can't bounce back so fast," she agreed, thinking how nice it would be to have all that energy.

"He didn't always," Micah remembered. "For a while there, I wasn't sure how long I would even have him in my life." He blew out a breath that sounded more like a deep-rooted sigh. And then, switching topics, he pushed the mood that threatened to engulf him aside. "That doctor you referred us to, Dr. Connor, Greg was crazy about her. People tend to think that kids don't really have feelings or react the same way as adults do, but I noticed that Greg really reacted to Dr. Connor's positive attitude. She treated him as if he were a little person. To be honest, I've been looking for someone like that ever since the boys' old pediatrician retired." His eyes held hers for a moment. "I really can't thank you enough."

She ignored the shiver that materialized out of nowhere and slid down her spine. Or tried to.

"Glad I could help," she told him. "Like I said, Dr. Connor is a friend of a friend, and as far as I know, no one has ever had a bad thing to say about her. She loves kids and she's extremely dedicated."

The microwave signaled that the minute and a half was up. Micah gingerly removed the plate from the turntable and placed it in front of his attorney.

"Careful," he warned as he handed her silverware. "The plate's hot."

The corner of her mouth curved. "I had a hunch," she deadpanned. "The steam kind of gave it away." She was about to sink her fork into it, then stopped. She looked at him, slightly confused. He was standing behind the stool next to hers. There was nothing in front of him. "You're not eating?"

"I had dinner with the boys," he explained.

"Oh." Tracy glanced down at her dinner. The aroma that wafted up from it was still tempting, but slightly less than a moment before. "That's okay," she told him. "I'm used to eating alone."

"Oh, God." Micah laughed, shaking his head. Moving over to the casserole pan, he spooned out half a serving onto a plate and then brought it back to the counter. He slid onto the stool beside hers. "I don't think I've ever heard anything quite so sad-sounding—at least not in a long while."

Was he mocking her, or just saying she sounded pathetic? The words had just slipped out. "I didn't mean to make you feel guilty—"

"You didn't. Compassionate, maybe, but not guilty." Micah slid a forkful of mashed potatoes into his mouth.

"Aren't you going to warm it up?" she asked. After all, he'd warmed up her plate, she just assumed that he'd want to eat his portion warm, too. Who ate their mashed potatoes cold?

"I like to eat it cold," he told her. "I developed a taste for cold food when I was in college—half the time the old stove in my studio apartment wouldn't work. I didn't have enough money to get it fixed and the super took weeks to show up—if at all. I got used to eating all my meals cold." She seemed unconvinced. "It was okay—unless I was eating frozen pizza," he laughed.

The shepherd's pie was comprised of beef, gravy, as well as lots of peas, all covered by a thick layer of mashed potatoes. Micah had sprinkled shredded sharp cheddar over it, then baked the casserole.

Tracy looked from the casserole to the serving on Micah's plate. "So you really don't mind eating cold mashed potatoes?"

He wondered if she realized that she was wrinkling her nose as she asked. It made her appear more like a teenager than an attorney.

"Nope. Actually, I've learned to like it better than hot mashed potatoes."

"Well, you're certainly easy to please," she commented. Less than a beat later, she realized how that might have sounded to him. "Um, I mean when it comes to food."

The smile on his lips absolved her of any blunder, real or imagined, on her part. He nodded. "I know what you meant."

She tried to steer the conversation in a slightly different direction. "This is really good."

"Thanks. I try not to serve anything bad more than once."

Again, she couldn't tell if he was being serious, or just pulling her leg. Not that she really minded the latter. After all the tension of dealing with high-powered clients all day long, this was almost like kicking back and relaxing.

"And, like I said, this is one of Greg's favorites. The good thing about it is that the boys don't realize that they're eating their vegetables, as well. Like most kids, they think if it's good for you, it has to taste awful."

"So this is just a sneaky way to get them to eat their peas?" she asked, amused.

He grinned. "You do what you have to do."

"Very clever," she said, applauding his technique. "Fatherhood looks good on you," she couldn't help commenting. He laughed softly in response. She hadn't expected that sort of reaction. "What? Did I say something funny?"

"No, it's just that your comment about fatherhood

started me thinking. Before Gary and Greg came along, I thought I'd be perfectly happy with things just the way they were—just Ella and me. I didn't need anything else. To be honest," he confided, "I didn't think I had it in me to be a good father. I figured I'd make a lousy one."

Well, that certainly wasn't the case. "Why would you think that?"

He shrugged. "I really didn't have much of a blueprint to go on."

He had no male role model, no real father figure to emulate. She'd forgotten about that. "Because your father was killed when you were so young?" she asked sympathetically.

"Well, there's that," he agreed, but that wasn't what he'd actually meant. "But even before then, my father wasn't exactly father-of-the-year material."

All this was so long ago, he rationalized that he wasn't really telling tales out of school. There were times that he barely remembered his father. And when he did remember, he felt that he was better off if he didn't.

"My father was kind of short-tempered," Micah explained. "He thought that I should be a small carbon copy of him and anticipate whatever he wanted me to do. Instead, I was more boy than man and that didn't exactly please him."

She thought back to what she'd read in the information she'd gathered about him. "You were twelve, right?"

"Right. I'd turned twelve the week before the car accident," he recalled. Whenever he did think about the accident, he never thought about how close he himself had come to dying, just that he had lost his parents. For the most part, though, he did his best to block the memory altogether.

Suddenly, she caught herself feeling sorry for the twelve-year-old who been expected to "man up." "Well, at twelve, you should have just been able to be allowed to be all boy."

Micah laughed shortly, remembering. "Not exactly the way he saw it."

What about his mother? Did she intervene? Mothers were supposed to protect their children—not that all did. "What did your mother say?" she asked.

"My mother agreed with everything my father ever said about anything," he told her. She detected a note of sorrow in his voice. Someone else would have felt slighted, or blamed their mother for not taking their side. That he didn't, that he seemed just to miss her, spoke volumes about him. "It was easier on her that way," he explained.

"Well, even though you didn't have an example to go on, you turned out to be a wonderful father," she observed. "Anyone can see that the boys utterly adore you."

Finished with her meal, Tracy pushed the plate over to the side. That was when she noticed the mug on the corner of the counter. The slogan World's Greatest Mom was embossed on it in multicolored flowers.

For a moment, all she could see was the mug. An unsettling feeling slipped over her. Was there a woman in the picture she hadn't met yet? And why would that matter to her?

But it did.

A lot.

"Who's that for?" she asked, trying to sound as nonchalant as possible, even though she caught herself feeling more than a little distressed about the mug's existence and its mysterious recipient.

At bottom, none of this made any difference to the case or how she was going to represent Micah, she argued silently. So why did she feel so disappointed?

Micah picked up the mug, a lopsided grin gracing his lips. "The boys gave that to me on Mother's Day," he was saying.

She did her best to suppress the laugh of relief that suddenly bubbled up within her. "They gave that to you, huh? Aren't your boys a wee bit confused?"

"That's what I thought at first," he said, appearing to agree with her. But then he continued. "But I *have* been both mother and father to them for the last two years, so I guess they thought I deserved it."

He turned the mug around in his hands. The smile on his lips was pure love. For just a second, pending charges notwithstanding, she envied him more than she thought possible.

"I just didn't have the heart to argue with them," he concluded.

"I understand."

And, oddly enough, she did. He was making perfect sense to her. Little feelings were at stake. Besides, his sons had unconsciously given him a wonderful compliment. That he had filled both roles for them and they were not just aware of it, but grateful. How often did *that* kind of thing happen?

"The boys love you very much," she told him. She took the mug from him and looked it over herself. "You're very lucky to have them."

"I know." If not for them, he wasn't sure if he could have made it through these past two years. And then he looked up at her, finding himself curious about her. Had she remained evasive so as to separate her private life from her professional one? "And you really don't have any kids?"

There was that knife again, twisting in her stomach. Allowing the emptiness to all but consume her.

"No," she finally said. It was more of a whisper than a normal response. "I don't." *I would have, had she lived. Lila would have been three by now. She could have made friends with your sons, played with them. Instead...instead Lila's playing with angels.*

She felt her throat tightening up until she had to concentrate on breathing to get through the feelings her stillborn daughter generated.

He'd struck a nerve, Micah thought. The topic was obviously a sore one for her. Was that because she'd had a child and then lost it? Or because she couldn't have any? Or was it just that she felt her time would never come?

"Sorry," he apologized with feeling, remembering that he'd already asked her about having children last night and she hadn't answered him. "I didn't mean to pry. I've got no business asking you questions like that."

She was being way too sensitive. It had happened and she'd moved on. Time to act like it. "You're entitled to know about your attorney," she replied, pulling herself together and away from the whirlpool that threatened to suck her into its depths. "Anything else you want to know?" she asked. "Go ahead, ask me anything that's on your mind. I'll do my best to give you as honest an answer as I can."

In his world, that was doublespeak for sharing only partial intelligence while keeping the rest a secret, usually for security reasons.

But she wasn't part of that world, he reminded himself.

Or was she?

She wasn't quite prepared for the bluntness of his first question. "Are you married?"

It took her a moment before she replied. "No."

"Good." She looked at him sharply. What had he meant by that? The next beat, he explained, "I wouldn't want to be dragging you away from your husband and dinner."

That made her laugh. "If I had a husband, I'd be bringing him here—on second thought, no, I wouldn't. He'd want to know why I couldn't cook as well as you. You know, I was only half kidding last night about you opening up your own restaurant. But tonight convinced me that last night wasn't just a fluke. I really think you could do very well opening up your own place."

The smile she saw on his face in response to her heartfelt compliment had the middle of her stomach tightening again while the rest of her grew very, very warm.

She wasn't sure just how much of that she could attribute to the hot meal, but she did her very best to pin the blame there—and not on the man who had prepared it.

Chapter Nine

It was almost a week later. Although there had been several phone calls between them, Tracy had deliberately not allowed herself to come over to his house on some pretext as she made her way home. She knew better than to think "out of sight, out of mind" actually worked, but something was going on with her. Something she didn't quite understand and it made her very nervous. Especially whenever she was around Micah.

In short, she was reacting to Micah. To his home life, to his family.

To him.

And that was decidedly bad, not just because of the conflict of interest it could possibly represent but it was bad for her, personally.

In the courtroom, there was no question about it,

she was a dynamo. But when it came to her own home court, well, that was an entirely different story. Her emotions had a habit of tripping her up, so she had learned, long ago, to just block them out. She'd gotten rather good at that, or so she'd believed up until now. She was not a person who made the same mistake twice and she'd discovered that leading with your heart, or any part other than your head, was asking for trouble with a capital T.

Been there, done that. And once was more than enough for her.

But Jewel had stopped by her office today with an update on what her I.T. guy, Neal, had uncovered on Micah's supposedly "scrubbed" laptop. The news was very hopeful—but only up to a point. Jewel had carefully explained all that to her and now she was standing before Micah, trying to find a way to couch her words so that he was apprised of the situation, but didn't instantly take it to mean he was now in the clear.

Because he wasn't. Not yet.

She began again, following him to the kitchen, which apparently seemed to be his favorite room in the house when he was trying to destress.

"My investigator's I.T. guy managed to dig up what was going on with your laptop that made your bosses so suspicious."

Taking a couple of beers out of the refrigerator, he turned to look at her just before he set the bottles on the counter. "Donovan gave him access?" he asked, more than a little surprised.

Right now, even *he* couldn't get access. Placed on

restricted duty, he was given a regular laptop that had none of the high-security-clearance software on it. And even then, he'd been subjected to a couple of unannounced spot checks where someone from the human resources department would come up to his desk and put their hands on his laptop, halting all activity. He would have to step aside and wait while the other person ran a check on it to make sure it hadn't been accessed again.

Each time, he'd cooperated, but it set his teeth on edge. Until this was resolved, he was a pariah.

"No." Sitting down on the stool, she picked up the bottle he offered her. "Donovan still has your original laptop locked away."

Frowning, Micah removed both bottle caps. What was she telling him? "Then how…?"

"Don't look at me, I haven't a clue. But he did resurrect all the erased files as well as pin down just when they were breached. Jewel says what he does is damn close to black magic, but apparently, if this Neal person can't access your computer, then it's somewhere at the bottom of the ocean." She paused to take a small sip. Beer was something she nursed rather than drank in regular, long sips. "Fortunately for you, yours isn't. Neal pieced things together and says as far as he can tell, your laptop was picked at random by this crew of cyber hackers to be part of a botnet."

Micah had command of a wide spectrum of information and knew his way around a great deal of physics, different disciplines of math and a wide variety of software needed to implement this knowledge. But what his attorney was talking about was a whole different, unknown world to him.

"A what?"

She found it rather comforting that someone of his caliber was as mystified as she was when Jewel had first tried to explain the existing situation to her. Tracy had absolutely no doubt that Micah was rather brilliant when it came to doing what he did for the company he worked for, which was why it was so nice to know he could be stumped, just like her.

She explained it to him the way Jewel had explained it to her. "The hackers formed a network of infected computers, which they control remotely—"

The frown on his handsome face deepened. "Doesn't *anyone* need to be in the same room as their equipment anymore?"

To him, the first requirement was always close proximity. Had this—as well as he—gone the way of the dinosaur?

Tracy shrugged as she absently ran the tip of her finger along the lip of the beer bottle. "Apparently not. Anyway, these hackers were using your laptop among others to troll still other computers, looking for credit card numbers, bank accounts, things that can enable them to steal identities, empty out bank accounts and God only knows what else. Jewel said that as far as Neal could see, the hackers didn't realize that there were top secret files and restricted information on your computer. Otherwise, if they had, that information would have been the first thing to go, auctioned off to the highest bidder. The hackers were just using your laptop, just like all the others, as a jumping-off point for their little million-dollar scheme."

Maybe his brain had slipped behind a cloud, Micah thought, but he wasn't following this. "And that means?" Micah pressed, frustrated.

Jewel and her update had in turn placed her on the receiving end of a great deal of information this afternoon. By the time Jewel left, Tracy felt as if she'd just attended a technical school and received a crash course in the dark side of having a computer.

"They were using your computer, as well as all the others they initially hacked into, to bounce around their I.P. address so that if anyone does realize what's going on, they can't be traced. Instead, you and the owners of those other computers bear the brunt of the blame." She looked at him pointedly. "In short, you were set up and framed."

"But if this Neal guy found out that this was what they were doing—that I was a victim like the others—then I'm in the clear." He blew out a long breath. "God, that's a relief."

"Well, relief's not quite here yet," she cautioned. She hated raining on Micah's parade, but she didn't want him breaking out the champagne bottle just yet. Not when he was still under suspicion.

About to tip back his bottle and take a long swig, he stopped and looked at Tracy. "What are you saying?" he asked.

"That your company and the customer they're working for—which I imagine has to be the government—" She held up her hand before he could begin to deny her assumption. "It's okay, I know you can't confirm that. I'm just giving you my hunch. Anyway, your company and the customer can claim that this is actually bigger than they first imagined and that you could very possibly be part of this network of hackers who had created the botnet to begin with."

He began to protest that that was absurd. That he had no idea how to do any of this, but he knew it was all futile. She might be on his side and believe he was innocent, but he knew that in the company's eyes, he was still guilty until proven otherwise.

The light that had completely lit up his face went out. "So, I'm back to square zero." It wasn't a question, but a painful assumption.

"No," Tracy quickly corrected. "It's not square zero."

"And why's that?" he challenged, wanting desperately to have *something* to hang on to.

"Because," Tracy patiently explained, "now we know that there's a ring out there and when there's this substantial a ring, there's got to be some kind of an investigation going on, either on the local police level, or the FBI level—or maybe even a joint task force, for all we know."

He supposed it was something. "And how do you go about finding out if this task force or investigation is going on? Is that what Jewel is going to be looking into?" he asked.

She smiled. "Even as we speak. But I also have a cousin on the police force I intend to put the squeeze on," she told him. "I'm going to have him ask around for me, see if he can pick up any useful intel about these hackers."

What she was saying all sounded well and good in theory. But he knew a little bit about how the real world worked. It wasn't anywhere near as neat and tidy as she was suggesting.

"Don't they frown on things like that?" he pointed out. "Answering questions for a civilian?"

Her smile widened. When it came to her work, her confidence was unshakable. He had nothing to worry about. "I can be very persuasive when I want to be," she told Micah.

He in turn watched her for a long moment. There was a determined expression on her face that utterly captivated him.

"I guess I'm lucky that you're in my corner," he finally said, and then he paused, his thoughts switching to something very basic. He didn't like loose ends. "You know, we haven't even talked about your fee yet."

"Sure we did," she reminded him. The beer, she noted suddenly, was hitting her funny. And then she remembered that, as was becoming more and more frequent, she'd had a protein bar for lunch, and breakfast had been a thought that had never been realized. "I told you I was taking the case pro bono."

He remembered that part. He also remembered what he'd said to it. "And I said no, you're not. That I pay my own way. I might have to make payments from now until you're collecting social security checks, but I always pay my bills. *Always,*" he emphasized.

She laughed and without thinking, she brushed the

palm of her hand along his check. "You are a very stubborn man."

Maybe it was because he'd felt like an emotional yo-yo, first down, then up and then leveled out only to find himself rising up again. That kind of thing made a man lose his bearings. Or maybe it was because he'd just been alone far too long. He loved his sons more than his life, but there was still this void in his life, a void he tried not to think about or acknowledge. But it was still there.

There were a dozen excuses to look to, but for whatever reason, the light touch of her fingers along his skin stirred him. It woke up things within him that were best left sleeping. Best left sleeping because once awakened, they didn't easily return to a hibernating state.

When he thought about it later, he wasn't altogether sure if that was the reason, or if there was some other explanation for what he did next. But while it was happening, he didn't want to conduct a self-examination. There was no point.

There was this need within him and it was demanding to be appeased, at least just a little.

The next moment, he took her hand, bringing her to her feet even as he was gaining his. He stood away from the counter where they'd both been sitting, his eyes never leaving hers.

And then, without saying a word, he slipped his hands into her hair, framed her face between them, lowered his mouth to hers and did what men had been doing since the very beginning of time: he kissed the person who held such an attraction for him.

His blood heated instantly.

He deepened the kiss, taking himself with it.

It was then, as his lips took possession of hers, that Tracy realized she'd been waiting for this. Holding her breath for this.

Craving this from the bottom of her very toes—and the soul she rarely even thought about.

Rather than pull away, protesting that they shouldn't be doing this, shouldn't be allowing their weakness to get the better of them, Tracy gave herself permission—just for a second—to sink as far down into the kiss as she possibly could.

With any luck, she might not surface for a while.

There was a rushing sound in her ears. Her heartbeat? Or something else?

She didn't know, didn't care.

Because this kiss was everything she'd imagined it would be—and more.

Better.

For that split second that she'd indulged herself, her head had gone spinning, and her pulse set a brand new world record for hammering wildly.

Her body leaned into his as she hooked her arms around his neck. She couldn't remember feeling this wonderful before, this exhilarated. The man certainly knew his way around women, was all she could think of—and be grateful for.

Strawberries.

She tasted of strawberries.

He had to be losing his mind, Micah thought. This

impetuous move wasn't him. It bore no resemblance to the man he had become. If anything, this was the first-year college student he had once been. Free to follow his sense of pleasure no matter where it led.

No, this was something more, he argued. Something with substance. He could feel it in his bones.

Didn't that make it worse? There was no place for this in his life. He'd had love, but that chapter of his life was supposed to be over.

Wasn't it?

Damn it, man, get a grip, he silently ordered himself.

The order went unheeded. He couldn't make himself pull back. She made him feel far more intoxicated than the beer he'd been drinking.

Suddenly, there was space between them. Their lips were no longer sealed to each other. For a second, he felt almost disoriented.

Flustered, the imprint of her lips blurred from the pressure of his, Tracy took in a ragged breath after forcing herself to break contact. She struggled, trying desperately to regain some semblance of control over herself.

What had come over her?

"We shouldn't be doing this," she told him. Near breathless, her voice lacked conviction.

He knew she was right, but he still challenged her. "Why?"

Her mind had been reduced to a single-cell amoeba. She struggled to think. "Because—because it's a conflict of interest."

Micah took her protest to mean something entirely different. "Are you with someone else?" he asked.

Stunned by the question, she could only stare at him. "What?" And then she replayed his words. "No," she declared with feeling.

"Then there's no interest to conflict," he maintained, reaching for her again.

Tracy took a shaky step back to keep herself from falling into his arms again.

"Yes, there is," she insisted. "I'm your lawyer." God, but she wanted to kiss him again. So badly that her teeth ached. "I can't be emotionally involved with you."

Her choice of words surprised him. But rather than retreat or take the way out she offered, Micah looked at her for a long moment before finally asking, "Are you emotionally involved with me?"

Too late she realized that she hadn't worded her protest correctly. "No," she insisted, her voice quivering. And then she said, "No, I'm not," more firmly.

He gazed into her eyes and had his answer. She was protesting far too much—undoubtedly to convince herself as well as him?

Micah inclined his head. She thought he was going to release her. Instead, he stunned her by saying, "Okay, then you're fired."

It took effort not to allow her jaw to drop open. "What?"

"I said you're fired," he repeated mildly. For good measure, he added, "Your services are no longer needed." And then he grinned. With a flourish of his hand, he declared, "Voilà, no more conflict of interest."

Fired? How he could fire her just like that? Was he out of his mind? He could still be in very real trouble here.

"But—"

Her protest died on her lips as, once again, he covered them with his own.

Struggling with herself, Tracy put her hands up against his chest, creating a wedge between them as she managed to push him back. "You can't fire me," she protested. "You need me."

"Lady," he murmured, kissing the side of her neck, melting her in her tracks. "You don't know the half of it."

Her heart raced wildly again, this time pounding so hard and so quickly, she had trouble catching her breath.

Okay, she'd allow herself one more kiss. Just one more kiss, she promised, and then she'd call a halt to this, tell him that he was being incredibly hasty and foolish and a whole host of other things, as well, ending it by saying that one of them had to be sensible. Obviously, that role had to belong to her.

In a second, in just another second, she'd tell him all that and more.

More.

The single word shimmered in her head, a silent entreaty to the man who was knocking out all the carefully laid foundations of her world. Very effectively reducing her to a pile of palpitating rubble.

She had one last card to play, however unenthusiastically.

"What about your sons?" she asked as, tapping the last of her strength, she created yet another chasm between their lips.

"Let them get their own women," he told her, kissing her again.

Melting her again.

Creating complete and utter chaos inside of her.

He didn't understand, she thought, desperately trying to pull her brain into some kind of functioning order so she could be relatively coherent when she finally did speak.

"No, I mean…"

Her voice trailed off as another assault on her throat rendered her incapable of completing even a single sentence, a single thought.

Everything seemed to be going up in flames.

"I know exactly what you mean," Micah told her, whispering the words into her ear.

As he did so, he wound up creating yet another tidal wave inside her as his warm breath caressed her cheek and throat, making every fiber of her being yearn for things it had no business wanting.

Oh, but she did.

She wanted them.

She wanted him.

The very next moment she went airborne. She would have let loose with a little shriek of surprise had his lips not been covering hers.

He'd swept her off her feet and up into his arms in a single movement. One more mind-numbing kiss and she was being carried. It was then that she realized her eyes were shut.

Opening them, she found he was carrying her up the stairs. To his room, she thought a beat later. Or maybe hoped.

"Am I really fired?" she asked him hoarsely.

His eyes were dark, unfathomable. Reaching his room, still holding her, he closed the door with his elbow. "Yes. I don't want you compromising your ethics."

"Okay," she whispered.

Tracy threaded her arms around his neck and stopped resisting what she wanted more than anything in the world at this very moment.

Him.

Chapter Ten

She felt as if she'd been transported to a timeless place where nothing else mattered. Nothing else existed but the man who enflamed her and everything was wrapped in a warm, hazy blanket.

Tracy was aware of every touch of his hand, every pass of his lips. Acutely aware of the effect he had on her, both body and soul.

There were no alarms in her head, no hesitation, no impeding thoughts that warned her that she would regret doing this, that she needed to retreat while she still could. Those were thoughts for a person who *could* think rationally, not a woman who passionately missed the feeling of being one with someone, so much so that she ached.

Not that, during her brief marriage, she'd actually

felt as one with her husband. Making love with him counted as some of the loneliest times in her life.

But what was happening now, *this* was what she'd missed about making love. He engaged not just her body, but her mind and every fiber of her being.

Seduced her.

Even the thought that he would actually go so far as to fire her didn't jar her. She wasn't altogether sure just how he had managed it, but Micah had taken away any need for her to feel guilty.

But even if she had felt guilty, or hesitant, or could actually enumerate reasons not to immerse herself in him, the spell that Micah's sensuous lips cast on her would have quickly made short work of any roadblock.

At this point, as he wove his magic around her, Tracy counted herself lucky if she could remember her full name.

She was tingling.

Anticipating.

Her whole body was on fire and there was only one way to deal with that situation. Only one way to put out the fire.

But if he was in any hurry to sate himself, Micah gave her no indication. Rather, he behaved as if time had completely stood still and become his ally. Either that, or he had all the time in the world to acquaint himself with every inch of her body, to explore it in depth, section by section. Inch by inch.

It got to the point that she was positive she was climaxing just from the mere *thought* of their ultimately coming together. Little eruptions fed into one another, growing larger and more powerful by the moment. In part that was because her clothes continued to disappear from her body. Micah removed each piece one by one. Methodically. With patience.

Every newly exposed area was touched, kissed and, just like that, very effectively set on fire.

She was twisting in his arms, moaning and breathing hard, all but driving him out of his mind.

It was a double-edged sword.

Micah wanted nothing more than to lose himself in this woman, to physically join with her and become, just for one wild, intoxicating moment, one.

But even as desire slammed into his body, making demands, begging for that final, breathtaking surge of euphoria, he held himself in check, going slow. Pleasuring her, and simultaneously making himself wild with anticipation of the final moment.

But it was far from easy.

Her body was sleek and toned, moving into his touch and then twisting away as enjoyment snaked its way through her.

The look of pure desire in her eyes made it incredibly difficult for him to go at this slow pace. And when Tracy tugged away his clothing from his body, he came very close to losing it. To just tossing his patience to the wind and taking her right then and there, on the king-sized bed where he had spent all those long, lonely nights.

He would have thought, just before the outset, that thoughts of his late wife would have stopped him, would have caused him to get a grip on himself. But just the opposite occurred.

It was almost as if Ella had stepped back and just before vanishing, had whispered her approval of this woman who had so effortlessly captured the hearts of his sons.

And if he secretly expected to be disappointed with this first foray into lovemaking after more than twenty-four months of voluntary celibacy, he was more than pleasantly surprised.

It didn't happen.

Instead, as he went on kissing her, caressing her, discovering all of her secret pulse points, the intensity of his reaction, his very anticipation, continued to grow. To grow to such a volume that it was becoming increasingly difficult to contain.

He wasn't sure just how much longer he could hold out.

Tracy was far from experienced. To her, lovemaking wasn't casual, or undertaken because too much alcohol was involved and caution was being tossed to the winds. She had never come to a man in that condition.

Her only real requirement was that affection had to exist on some level for any of this to happen. Preferably very strong affection.

The way it was now.

Granted, she'd had a beer with Micah, but that drink in no way impaired her judgment. As much as her head was spinning right at this point, her thinking had been completely clear at the outset.

She wanted this, had been denying to herself that she wanted this with every single atom within her body.

Tracy arched against the incredible magic of his lips and tongue as they branded her. She didn't know where she wanted him to anoint her next. It was as if every square inch of her wanted its turn at the same time.

Immediately.

Twisting into him, Tracy surprised him by suddenly pulling his face closer to hers, sealing her mouth to his while urgently pressing her throbbing body against his rock-solid one.

Anticipation scissored through her, making it oh so very difficult for her to contain herself.

Yet somehow, she managed.

Just as she was ready to straddle him, to take the lead and join their two bodies, Micah slid his body along hers again.

Electricity radiated all through her, chased along by another jolt of anticipation.

With the palms of his hands bracketing her face so that he could look directly into her eyes, Micah entered her with a forceful and yet, somehow, incredibly gentle thrust.

Tracy sucked in her breath, her heart hammering hard. The timeless dance began.

The tempo built and increased as his hips rocked against hers more and more urgently.

Without realizing it, Tracy dug her fingers into his shoulders, holding on as she instinctively matched move for move—until she and Micah finally hit the very highest peak.

Together.

It was sheer ecstasy.

Tracy bit down hard on her lower lip to keep the cry of pure, guttural enjoyment from escaping and exploding in the air. There was still the tiniest part of her anchored to the world and that part was mindful of not awakening his sons. This was a time for sheer pleasure, not for having to come up with necessary explanations to pint-sized, inquisitive people.

She felt Micah shiver beneath her hands. Felt his sigh of contentment echoing through his body before it actually emerged.

That excited her even more.

Even as the euphoria abated, they remained sealed, almost closer than they had been as the crescendo had been building.

It seemed almost like a mini-eternity later when he finally raised his head to look at her.

His head, she realized belatedly, had been resting on her shoulder. The simple action seemed so natural, so right, she felt as if it had been that way forever.

As if she'd been created to be the other half of his whole.

The smile on his lips when he looked at her went straight to her gut, turning lights on within her as it made its way all through her.

Ever so lightly, because he wanted an unobstructed view, Micah brushed aside the stray strands of hair that had fallen into her face.

His smile deepened.

As did her reaction to it.

"Hi," he murmured. The smile easily slid into his eyes. And into her soul.

"Hi," she echoed back.

Very gently, he shifted his weight from her, lying down at her side and tucking her against him. There was concern in his voice as he asked, "I didn't hurt you, did I?"

"I'm not sure," Tracy admitted. And then she saw the look of apprehension come into his eyes. She strove to lighten the mood. "That was my very first out-of-body experience, and I'm not altogether sure of anything right now."

The corners of his eyes crinkled as he grinned. "Out-of-body experience, huh?"

She nodded her head slowly, as if afraid that she would be dizzy again. "Uh-huh."

"I think I felt a little bit of that happening myself," Micah admitted.

Raising himself up on his elbow, he looked down at her. With lovemaking behind him, he'd expected to feel guilt beginning to encroach over him at this point. But he only felt a fresh wave of desire.

He was more surprised by that than he could possibly say.

Trailing his fingertips along her tempting, supple body slowly, Micah watched in fascination as he saw her abdomen quiver in response.

"If you feel up to it," he whispered against her ear, "I'd like to go back on that wild roller-coaster ride again."

His breath was warm, creating excitement within her all over again.

As to his suggestion, this was something new. Neither her husband, nor the less-than-handful of others before him, had ever voiced a desire to go back for seconds. And even if they had wanted to make love with her for a second time in one encounter, she was more than certain that they wouldn't have asked her if she felt up to it. They would have just gone ahead and done it.

A tenderness toward Micah began to take root within her.

"An encore?" Tracy asked, both incredulous and amused.

He hadn't thought of it in those terms. The word made him grin again. "If you like."

A laugh bubbled up within her in response to his words and to his grin. She nodded her head ever so slightly. "I'd like."

She could have sworn that half a heartbeat before Micah's lips came down on hers, she heard him whisper, "Perfect."

That did it for her. Tracy didn't need anything else to make her respond enthusiastically, to throw herself with gusto into a second round of lovemaking.

A second round that ultimately turned out to be even more teeth-jarringly satisfying than the first round.

It was close to two in the morning when Tracy opened her eyes. The realization that somehow she'd managed to fall asleep in his arms now roused her into a wakeful state.

The fog cleared from her brain. A beat later, she couldn't recall ever feeling so very contented in her life.

Lovemaking, cures what ails you, she thought, amused even though she knew she should have felt upset with herself at this glaring breach of behavior.

There was no excuse for what she'd done.

He was a man, men did these kinds of thing all the time. But it was different for her. This just wasn't like her.

God knew she certainly didn't take lovemaking casually.

And yet, they'd come together—wildly and passionately—three times before she'd drifted off, exhausted and happy.

Three times.

And she'd loved every second of it.

This was a completely new side of her, Tracy couldn't help thinking. *Learn something every day,* she mused. And then she looked over to her left.

Micah was breathing evenly. He was still asleep. She needed to make her retreat now, before he woke up and tempted her to stay.

If he wanted her to stay, she reminded herself. Just because they'd made love didn't mean that he was about to swear his undying love or his allegiance to her, or even his mild interest in her.

Last night was last night, and now was now. She had to remember that and not allow herself to get carried away. Men made love to women all the time and it meant less than nothing to them.

It meant far more than that to her, even if she didn't want it to.

Ever so slowly, almost in slow motion, Tracy moved her legs until they were clear of the bed and she could draw herself up into a sitting position. Clearing the bed was a process that was equally painstakingly slow.

She didn't want to take a chance on inadvertently waking him up.

Moonlight filtered into the room and she could see where most of her clothes were scattered on the floor. If she moved carefully, she could gather them together and slip out of the room without waking him. She could get dressed in the bathroom she'd noticed down the hall.

Separating herself from the bed, Tracy slowly rose and then quietly made her way over to her clothes.

So far, so good.

"Leaving?"

She'd almost screamed, but managed to clamp her lips shut at the last minute.

The question, posed in a voice that hadn't a trace of sleep in it, had her freezing in place, as if a layer of ice had been sprayed on her limbs.

Her breath trapped in her throat, Tracy turned around and looked at the man who had turned her world upside down, made her forsake her ethics, and had reduced her to the consistency of wonton soup.

Micah's eyes were open and he was watching her. For how long?

"You're awake," she finally heard herself say.

Humor curved the corners of his mouth. "Looks

that way." Micah sat up, the tangled sheet barely offering him the courtesy of strategic cover. "Can't stay the night?" he questioned.

"I thought it might be easier for you if you didn't have to explain to the boys in the morning what I was doing here. Or explain it to your aunt, for that matter."

"The boys wouldn't think anything of it," he told her easily. "Most likely, they'd be happy to see you here and want to play. As for my aunt, she wouldn't need an explanation. I'm pretty sure she'd know what you were doing here." The light was poor, but he was almost certain Tracy was blushing. He found that oddly stirring and appealing. "And, if I know her, after discovering you in my bed, Aunt Sheila would probably set off a whole box of fireworks to celebrate."

She looked at him uncertainly. That didn't make any sense to her. "Celebrate?"

He nodded. "She's been after me to get back into 'the game,' as she puts it, for a year now." His eyes met hers and he patted the space beside him. The space that still retained her warmth.

For a second, Tracy was fiercely tempted to drop the clothes she was holding and slip back into bed beside him. But she was well aware that if she gave in at this point, it would be harder on her in the long run.

She'd slipped and weakened, but it was better just to have this one instance than to consciously set up the groundwork for a brief, albeit absolutely delicious, interlude. She knew herself. Happy as she'd be, she would wind up holding her breath, waiting for it all to end.

And even though maybe Micah had forgotten—or

thought he could just plow his way through this—he still needed a lawyer and she'd do him more good in that capacity than as his part-time lover. At least there, as his lawyer, she knew what she was doing.

As his lover, she hadn't a clue.

"I'd still better go," she told him, hugging her clothes to her as if they could somehow shield her from her own feelings.

His eyes still held hers. Very slowly, he nodded. "I won't hold you against your will."

Tracy began to protest. "It's not that it's against my—"

Shut up, Tracy, she upbraided herself sharply. *Just take the easy way out.*

"It's okay," he told her, not wanting her to have to struggle with her conscience. "You need to do what you think is right. Oh, by the way," he called after her just as she reached for the doorknob.

Turning, Tracy looked over her shoulder at him, not trusting herself to go back. Was he calling her back? she wondered. "Yes?"

"You're not fired anymore."

It was hard to see with just the moonlight illuminating the room, especially since the upper part of his torso was in shadow, but she could have sworn he was grinning as he lay back down.

After a moment, she slipped out of the room. But she had to force herself to do it.

Chapter Eleven

In an attempt to distract herself and keep her mind from endlessly reliving every exquisite second of her one night with Micah, Tracy threw herself into her work with even more verve than usual.

Ordinarily, she was blessed with laserlike focus and the ability to shut out every extraneous distraction.

Ordinarily.

But her life had taken a turn that by no means could be described as "ordinary." There definitely had been nothing ordinary about making love with Micah Muldare.

Consequently, despite her very best efforts and intentions, Tracy's mind kept wandering and finding its way back to Micah and the magical experience that they had shared together. But even when she allowed herself a few moments to revel and relive, Tracy mocked herself for the direction that her thoughts and feelings were taking.

"You know damn well he couldn't possibly be reacting to what happened the same way you are," she muttered to herself as she deleted an entire paragraph she'd just written. It read as if it had been constructed by a five-year-old.

"Who are you talking to?"

Tracy's head jerked up. She struggled not to allow her embarrassment to color her cheeks a bright, telltale shade of pink.

She pressed her lips together and tried to sound calm as she asked Kate Manetti, "How long have you been standing there?"

Kate grinned. It was an amused grin, but a sympathetic one, as well. "Long enough to realize that someone has finally rung your chimes," she quipped. Crossing the threshold, Kate closed the door behind her before she approached her friend's desk. "Nice to know you're human like the rest of us."

Tracy shrugged carelessly. "I don't know what you're talking about."

The smile on Kate's lips was tolerant. And then she repeated, word for word, what she'd just heard as she was walking by her friend's office.

"'You know damn well he couldn't possibly be reacting to what happened the same way you are.'" She leaned over Tracy's desk, getting closer to her. "Ring any bells?"

"I was just going over this case." Tracy nodded at

the computer screen. "I guess I must have said what I was thinking out loud." Okay, so it was lame, Tracy freely admitted. But it was the best she could come up with, cornered like this.

"Uh-huh." She looked at Tracy knowingly. "Your nose might not be growing, but your cheeks are getting pinker and pinker, Pinocchio. I'd suggest coming clean before you turn into a bright, flaming shade of hot pink. It wouldn't look good on you."

"There's nothing to come clean about," Tracy insisted, banking down her desperation.

Kate shrugged, as if what her friend said made no difference one way or another.

"Suit yourself," she said, shoving her hands into her pockets. "Oh, I almost forgot, while you were in court this morning, 'nothing' called and was switched into my office by mistake. I took a message." She extracted a small pink piece of paper expressly used to write down phone messages. Before handing it to Tracy, Kate held it up as if comparing the color of the paper to the color that was gracing Tracy's cheek. "Almost there," she observed.

A few choice words hovered on the tip of Tracy's tongue, but she managed to swallow them without uttering a single one. She pulled the message from Kate's fingers and glanced at it.

"He's confirming tonight's meeting. Where's it going to be?" Kate teased, then went on to create the appropriate scenario. "At some intimate little restaurant, a table for two with steamy candlelight the only illumination in the place?"

Oh, damn. Tracy stared at the small pink square of paper. Their meeting. She'd forgotten all about it. She'd left time and place up to him, wanting to allow him to feel as if he had some control over the situation. And it had slipped her mind.

How was she going to face him? she asked herself, a wave of something close to almost panic washing over her.

Concerned now, Kate leaned over the desk again. "Hey, are you all right?"

"No," Tracy confessed. The very fact that she had just made that admission told her that she was in a weakened frame of mind. Maybe she should just skip the meeting, reschedule it and go home.

Kate sat down opposite her. "Want to talk about it?"

The reply came without hesitation, without even a second's debate. "No." She was accustomed to fending for herself.

"Well, I'm not going anywhere until you do," Kate informed the other woman without any bravado.

She must have seen the flash of impatience in Tracy's eyes. "I'm not being nosy," Kate told her quietly. "I'm being a friend. And concerned. This isn't like you," she said, referring to her behavior.

No, no it wasn't. Or maybe it actually was and that other persona, the focused one who won case after case by doggedly working on every scrap of information that was tossed her way, wasn't really her.

At this point, Tracy honestly didn't know which was real and which was not.

Taking a deep breath, she dragged her hand through

her hair, a sure sign that she felt, consciously or unconsciously, that she had her back against the wall and was outmatched and outgunned.

A burst of feeling passed through her. Looking up at Kate, she said, "I slept with him."

She said it so quietly. Perplexed, cocking her head so that her ear was closer to Tracy's mouth, Kate asked, "What?"

And then, as if it was all on some five-second-delay relay, the words registered in Kate's head. Her eyes widened.

"Slept with who?" Kate asked and then, that too seemed to answer itself. "Muldare?" Kate asked in a hushed whisper, her eyes never leaving Tracy's face.

Tracy's mouth had gone entirely dry so rather than speak, she just nodded her head.

"How was he?" Kate asked. "Never mind," she said, waving a dismissive hand at her own question. "I can see how he was."

Startled, Tracy looked at her. Was she that transparent? And if Kate could see, did that mean that Micah could, too? What had Micah seen when he looked at her? She sought to somehow tamp down her mounting dismay and quiet her nerves. "What do you mean?"

"Honey, you're making as much sense as a melted popsicle. He rocked your world, plain and simple. I can see that and all I can say is that it's about damn time!" Kate concluded, obviously happy for her friend.

"He didn't rock my world," Tracy protested, trying her best to sound dismissive of the very idea. She had a feeling that she wasn't being very successful.

"Oh, no?" Kate seemed to keep from laughing at the denial. "Then why do you look as if you'd have trouble remembering your own phone number if I asked you to recite it quickly?"

Tracy released a noise that sounded almost like a hiss as she looked off into oblivion—the same place that her mental faculties had run off to. But then, as if to show Kate that she was wrong, she recited the aforementioned phone number.

But Kate shook her head. "Honey, don't fight it so hard. Trust me. This is a good thing," she assured her friend.

"He's a client," Tracy lamented.

"Yes," Kate allowed, "he is that. But he's also a *man,*" she emphasized, then added, "and a hunk, from the one time I did see him. No shame in reacting to a good-looking man."

"But he's a *client.*" Tracy stressed the word as she repeated herself. There was more than a faint note of distress in her voice. Distress at her behavior and more than that, distress over the way she felt. The man made her want to run barefoot through a field of clovers, but at the same time, she knew she was asking for trouble. And setting herself up for a huge and exceedingly painful fall.

"Yes," Kate agreed, "he is. But he's not always going to be one." Her eyes were kind as she continued. "Look, I'm trying to give you the benefit of my experience because I care about you. If it's a choice between the man and the client, pick the man, give up the client. You won't regret it."

Tracy blew out a long, draining breath. "Easy for you to say."

"Actually, it's not," Kate contradicted. "But I don't regret what happened for a minute. And, as it happens—" her eyes crinkled, sharing the satisfied smile that was on her lips "—I got to have my cake and eat it, too."

Tracy rolled her eyes. "I'm not even going to ask what that means."

"I'm perfectly willing to share," Kate said.

Kate might have been willing to share, but right at this moment, she didn't know if she was up to being on the receiving end of that "sharing experience." She had things to work out in her head first, not the least of which was that maybe Micah would be better served with another attorney, one whose judgment couldn't be viewed as compromised.

Tracy rose. Grabbing her oversized purse out of the bottom drawer, she slung it over her shoulder.

"Can't spare the time right now," she told Kate, hiding behind her schedule. She glanced at the pink piece of paper on her desk. Any port in a storm. "I've got an appointment to keep."

Kate was on her feet, as well. "You go, girl," she said with an approving laugh.

For the third time in the last thirty minutes, Tracy told herself to stop chewing on her lower lip. It would get mangled by the time she got to her destination.

Her nerves were square-dancing over this first post-sleepover meeting with Micah. Then there was the fact that she hated being late and she was going to be. Not terribly, just enough to annoy her.

She should have gotten this message sooner, she thought as she turned right and finally drove into her development. That way, she would have felt more prepared.

An uneasiness ate away at her, an uneasiness that something was wrong, although she couldn't put her finger on it. But to start with, he asked her to come to his house. At this time in the afternoon, he shouldn't *be* in his house, he should be at work.

Why wasn't he at work? Was something else wrong? The man already had more than enough piled on his plate. Questions filled her head, colliding with those nerves in her stomach. The anticipation and uncertainty didn't help.

Okay, so she had elected to stay away, but that didn't mean he wasn't supposed to try to get in touch with her. But he hadn't. She hadn't heard from him in three days and didn't know if it was because he was busy with work, or busy regretting what had happened between them.

Most likely, this meeting was to tell her that he'd decided to engage another lawyer, one who could keep her priorities straight and her clothes on.

That still didn't explain what he was doing home at this hour.

She could feel her cheeks beginning to burn again and quickly talked herself into a calm state. Or at least calmer than she'd just been.

But her heart was still in her throat as she pulled up

at his curb. Getting out, she noticed that his aunt's car wasn't in the driveway or anywhere to be seen for that matter. His was the only vehicle in the driveway. Was that a good sign or a bad one?

What did it all mean? she silently demanded, driving herself positively crazy.

Reaching the front door, Tracy hesitated. For one second, she came very close to just turning around and going back to her car, making a beeline for her house. But that would have been hiding and cowardly, something that would have haunted her for a good long while.

So instead, she rang the doorbell before anything else stopped her. And then she waited. And did her best to brace herself for this first encounter after their night of passionate lovemaking.

It probably meant nothing to him, she reasoned, evaporating from his brain the moment it was over. For her, it was a whole other story.

She could hear the boys calling to their father, loudly announcing that there was someone at the door. She listened to them calling back and forth a couple of times and then she heard the rather loud click of the lock. The sound probably meant freedom to so many people. To her, it was the cell door closing.

The front door opened and she was face-to-face with Micah. The quandary she'd been dealing with, trying to decide what first words to utter, vanished. His complexion was pale, there was sweat on his forehead and his watery eyes looked as if he'd encountered a severe allergen.

"Are you all right?" she asked, then gave weight to her question. "You're as pale as a ghost."

He would have waved away her comment if it hadn't taken such strength to lift his arm. "Probably the lighting," he mumbled.

The hell it was, she thought. He was deliberately avoiding her eyes. Something was definitely wrong.

"Is the lighting making you perspire, too?" she challenged.

He shrugged, thinking to appease her with a partial surrender. "Okay, I'm feeling a little off today," he admitted.

"You didn't feel good yesterday, either," Gary piped up, reminding him. The little boy looked at Tracy. "He said he couldn't give us our piggyback ride to bed," Gary told her. "He said he was giving us a check in the rain," he added solemnly.

Not to be left out, Greg told her, "Daddy's tummy hurts."

This didn't sound good, Tracy thought. Turning to look at Micah, she frowned. The man was definitely sweating.

"Would you like to amend your original statement?" she suggested.

He looked from one son to the other. So much for filial support. "I live with stool pigeons."

Greg's eyes grew huge. "Where are they, Daddy?" he asked excitedly, his head sweeping from side to side as he scanned the area. "Where are the pigeons?"

"We don't have pigeons, dummy," Gary informed his brother with a haughty, older and wiser air.

Greg was not that easily dissuaded. "But Daddy said that—"

Tracy decided to come to the rescue before this devolved into an argument.

"Your dad was just making a joke, honey," Tracy told him. "A very weak joke," she added, looking pointedly at Micah. She tried again. "Now, want to tell me what's wrong?"

He had never been one who enjoyed being fussed over and he definitely didn't like admitting he was feeling as weak as a broken pipe cleaner.

"Nothing," he insisted, but it came out more like a murmur. "I probably ate something I shouldn't have. Or maybe it's the flu," he speculated, giving her a large spectrum to work with that would hopefully get her off his back.

She doubted it was either, but she played along for a moment. "Have you taken anything for it?"

"No. What'll you give me?" he asked, forcing a weak smile to his lips. It faded almost instantly.

Her eyes narrowed. This wasn't the time to play games. "A hard time if you don't tell me what's going on," she warned.

He closed his eyes for a moment. The room had tilted and he was definitely feeling sick. "Can I take a rain check?" he asked seriously. "I'm not up to matching wits with you right now."

That came as no surprise. "I'd say you weren't up to matching wits with an amoeba right now." She touched his forehead with her fingers to confirm her hunch. "You've got a fever."

Micah did his best to smile mischievously. "You have that effect on me."

She wasn't listening to his feeble attempts to distract her. Her concern was turning into worry. "What else are you feeling?"

Sick to his stomach and unsteady on his feet, but he didn't want to admit that, especially not when his sons were within earshot.

"Just tired."

He was a damn poor liar. "Anything hurt? Specifically, does your lower right quadrant have any pain?"

He would have laughed if he could. She'd zeroed in on the pain. "Want to play doctor?"

Instead of answering him, Tracy began to press her fingers slowly along the area in question. Each time she did, she saw him wince and heard him suck in his breath, struggling not to cry out.

Okay, that did it. She was convinced.

"What's your aunt's number?" she asked him out loud. They were going to need the woman.

Micah didn't understand. And the room was beginning to tilt. Again. "Why do you want to know?"

"Because I need her to come over to watch the boys." She flashed a quick, reassuring smile at his sons. The last thing she needed or wanted was to have them panicking. It was bad enough that she was worried.

"But I'm here," he protested.

"But you won't be for long," she countered. "I'm taking you to the E.R."

"No, you're not. I just need some rest. I'll be fine in the morning. I shouldn't have called you." He'd done it in a moment of weakness, thinking that perhaps if she was around, he'd be distracted enough not to feel this sick. In essence, he was using a distraction to distract him, he realized.

Micah saw the stubborn expression on her face and told her, "You're overreacting."

She knew, after their night together, that he had no scars. Which meant that he still had all his organs intact. And that in turn, along with his wincing, told her all she needed to know.

"And you're having an appendicitis attack."

Chapter Twelve

Micah stared at her as if she'd just suggested that he was coming down with Dutch Elm's disease. Both, to him, were equally unlikely since he was neither a teenager, nor a tree. Besides, he didn't get sick. Ever. Not even last year when those around him in the office were dropping like flies from the flu. The fact that he felt weak and nauseous, and this searing pain slashed through him, was irrelevant.

"No," he said firmly, "I'm not."

If he thought that was the end of it, he should have known better. He was beginning to learn that Tracy had the tenacity of a junkyard dog when she latched on to something.

She looked at him pointedly and asked, "Did you have it removed when you were a teenager?"

He wanted to say yes, because that would end her assault, but he didn't want to lie in front of Gary and Greg. "No."

His stubbornness was setting her teeth on edge, but to play fair, especially since his sons were listening intently, Tracy reviewed the facts.

"You're running a fever, you look pale and sweaty, you admitted that you feel sick and your lower right quadrant hurts to the touch. If I press a little harder—" all she had to do was stretch out her fingertips and he instantly moved back, out of range "—I'll probably find that it's swollen, as well." She looked at him, an attorney who had just delivered her summation. "You have appendicitis and it's not something you want to fool around with."

"Is he going to die?" Gary asked, clearly beginning to panic.

"Only if he doesn't go to the hospital," she told the boy in a reassuring voice.

"Go to the hospital, Daddy," Greg pleaded, wrapping his hands around his father's arm as if to give weight to his entreaty. "I can take you in my wagon if you can't walk."

"He can't fit in your wagon, stupid," Gary told his brother haughtily. Even so, there was real fear in the older boy's eyes as he watched his father. He was just as worried as Greg, but trying very hard not to show it. "You're not gonna die, right, Daddy?" His lower lip trembled slightly as he added in a hoarse whisper, "Not like Mommy, right?"

"Not if I have anything to say about it," Tracy said

firmly. The fact that she was able to assert herself this way without a hearty protest from Micah indicated how sick he really was. It was time to stop talking and start driving. "I need Sheila's phone number." This time it was an order, not a request.

"I know it!" Gary piped up, excited that he could help.

Tracy gave him a wide smile. "Good man." She pulled out her cell phone. "Tell me her number and I'll call her. The sooner I can get her here, the sooner I can take your dad to the emergency room."

The familiar term struck a responsive chord for Greg. He patted his father's arm, as if to set him at ease. "Just like you do with me, Daddy. Don't worry, they're real nice."

Meanwhile, Gary was reciting the numbers in his great-aunt's phone number very carefully. Tracy hit each on the keypad.

Less than five minutes later, it was all arranged. Sheila was coming right over. Fifteen minutes later, the woman was using the key Micah had given her and came in. One look at her face told Tracy that Micah's aunt was trying not to appear as concerned as she felt.

But her eyes gave her away.

The moment she was inside, the boys came running up to her, throwing their arms around her waist and seeking the warmth, comfort and reassurance that she had come to represent in their lives.

"Daddy's sick," Gary told her, wanting to be the first with the news.

"I know, honey," Sheila replied. "Tracy told me when she called."

Greg turned to her for the reassurance he still so desperately needed. He asked her the same question he'd asked his father. "He's not gonna die, is he?"

Sheila hugged both boys to her, then, bending, she kissed the top of each blond head. "He's going to be just fine. This is your dad we're talking about. He's always fine." But even as she said it, Sheila's eyes met Tracy's, silently seeking the reassurance from her that she was giving the boys.

The moment Sheila had arrived, Tracy immediately began to draw Micah up to his feet. She wedged her slim shoulder beneath his armpit in order to give him the support he needed. Her one goal was to get him to her car, parked at the curb.

"Yes, he is," Tracy answered in an almost alien, no-nonsense voice no one in the room had ever heard her use before.

It occurred to her at that moment that somehow, through some wild twist of fate, she had been designated to be the "strong one" and while she didn't much care for the role—she would have liked to have had someone to emotionally lean on herself—she accepted it without complaint. All that mattered was getting Micah to the hospital before he got any worse.

"Let's go, Mr. Invincible," she coaxed, taking small, measured steps so as not to throw him off. Passing Sheila, she promised, "I'll call you as soon as I know anything."

For the sake of her nephew's sons, the older woman forced a smile to her lips.

"I'd appreciate that," she told Tracy. She didn't need to add that she'd be waiting by the phone for her call. That went without saying.

Gary broke away from Sheila and hurried over to the front door. Yanking on it as hard as he could, he managed to open it for Tracy and his father.

"Thank you," she told the boy. It struck her that the little boy was acting more like a young man than a child his age. The maturity level of both boys astounded her at times. "I'll take good care of him," she told the little boy as she walked slowly past him, keeping Micah's arm draped across the back of her shoulders.

"Okay," he replied. She saw Greg's lower lip quiver a little. He was old enough to sense that there were some things that promises couldn't cover, no matter how well intentioned.

It felt like an eternity had gone by before she finally got Micah to the car and into the front passenger seat. The second he was in the car, she switched into high gear and quickly rounded the trunk, all but throwing herself into the driver's seat. Glancing to make sure he was buckled up, she gunned the engine.

Less than thirty seconds later, they were pealing away from the curb, and then out of the development.

He was too quiet, she thought, weaving her way onto the main drag that ultimately led to the freeway. That worried her a great deal.

And then he spoke and she found herself missing

the silence. She really didn't want to have to argue with Micah.

"You scared the boys," he told her, each word measured and struggling to emerge. His breathing was labored.

"No," she contradicted calmly, silently congratulating herself on her performance, "you did. With your sweaty body and your pale face."

Micah had his seat belt on, but he was sitting slightly hunched over rather than ramrod straight the way he usually did. Added to that, his right hand was pressed hard against the source of the radiating pain. Even so, he made a concentrated effort to lighten the mood.

"I didn't hear you complaining the other night," he told her.

She slanted a quick look at him. So, he wasn't pretending that it never happened. She took a grain of comfort from that. "Well, at least you still have your sense of humor. That's hopeful."

He glanced down at the speedometer. "You're going too fast."

She'd all but flown onto the freeway, tenser than she could ever remember being. She couldn't shake the feeling that she didn't have much time to get him to the hospital. "No, I'm not."

"Okay," he relented. "For an airplane, you're not, but for a car, you are." He sucked in air as a sharp pain sliced through him. Eyes closed, Micah struggled past it and did his best to go on talking as if nothing was wrong. "I thought the object was to get me there in one piece."

"It is. And the sooner the better."

Though she had no intentions of telling him, Tracy somehow attempted to outrace time. If she didn't get to the hospital as quickly as humanly possible, she would live to regret it.

And Micah wouldn't live at all.

He'd undoubtedly laugh at her "intuition," but that didn't change the fact that it was there and it felt extremely real to her. She couldn't ignore that.

In less than twenty minutes, feeling as if she'd run all the way instead of driven, Tracy was pulling up to the left side of the hospital and the E.R. entrance. Stopping at the valet station, Tracy turned off the ignition.

That was when Micah began to rouse himself. He'd dozed off to escape the pain. Awake, he was having an extremely difficult time focusing.

Turning toward Tracy, Micah asked, "Have we landed yet?"

Rather than take exception to his choice of words, she merely said yes as she jumped out of the car and once again rounded the vehicle to get to his side. By the time she'd started to help him to his feet, a hospital attendant was bringing over one of the hospital's wheelchairs from the E.R.

With Tracy on one side of him and the attendant on the other, they started to slowly lower Micah into the seat. He felt unmanned by the help. Grasping the armrests, he announced curtly, "I can do this on my own."

"By all means, go ahead," Tracy told him.

Hands raised as if to surrender all contact, she

stepped back. But she watched Micah like a hawk. He was growing progressively weaker, but she also knew that his pride was at stake and since she'd gotten him here where he could be taken care of, she could cut Micah a little slack when it came to the self-esteem department.

However, the moment he was seated, Tracy immediately took possession of the wheelchair and all but propelled him through the electronic doors that sprang open to admit them.

The instant she was inside, a nurse and an orderly approached them. And for the first time since she'd stood on Micah's doorstep earlier today, Tracy felt that everything *was* going to be all right.

"Hi," she greeted the duo. "He has appendicitis."

They took it from there.

Fidgeting, Tracy looked at her watch.

It was three minutes later than the last time she'd looked at it. Impatience and worry rifled through her, alternating in strength.

Micah had been in the operating room for one hour and twenty minutes.

The queasy feeling in her stomach threatened to devour her from the inside out. Why the hell was it taking so long?

The first hour she'd been fine. She was aware that appendectomies took approximately an hour to perform, so she felt that everything was going well and there was no need for concern. She'd already called

Sheila and the boys with an update, telling them that she'd diagnosed Micah correctly and he'd been taken off to surgery in very short order. There was every reason to believe that this man with an excellent constitution would be fine and good as new in a short amount of time.

But her self-assurance had begun waning as the minutes ticked away in slow motion, feeding into each other and eroding her confidence with every passing moment.

What if she'd brought him here too late?

If she'd stopped by last night instead of tonight, she could have brought him to the hospital a lot sooner and that might have made all the difference in the world. She sincerely doubted that he'd gotten this bad just overnight. She was willing to bet that this appendicitis had been days in the making.

Why had she played those games with herself? Why had she pretended to distance herself from him and what had happened between them? She knew it had, just as she knew that she was reacting to what had happened in a very real, very dangerous way.

She was falling in love with him.

What if she'd brought him here too late? her mind taunted.

Tracy stopped pacing for a moment and stared accusingly at the operating room's double doors across the way. She'd watched Micah being rolled into the room on a gurney, pumped full of morphine and feeling absolutely no pain.

She had been the one with the pain as she watched him disappear behind those doors almost two hours ago.

Why wasn't anyone coming out to apprise her of what was going on?

Dear God, what would she tell his sons if the unthinkable happened?

If…?

"Ms. Ryan?"

Startled, Tracy swung around to see a tall, gaunt man dressed in blue hospital livery—operating room livery—slipping off his surgical mask. A second later, it hung about his neck, looking as worn out as he did.

Fearful, praying she was just being paranoid, she hurried over to the man.

"Yes, I'm Tracy Ryan." It took everything she had not to grab his arm and grill him. She did her best to sound calm—or at least sane—as she asked, "How is he?"

The surgeon paused. Was he tired or trying for dramatic effect? She did her best to look patient.

Finally, he said, "You got him here just in time. Half an hour longer and we might be having an entirely different conversation," he told her honestly. "In a different part of the hospital."

The morgue was located in the basement. She didn't want to even go there. Instead, she tried to get the surgeon to give her some reassuring words. So she spoonfed them to him.

"So he's going to be all right?" She searched his face.

The surgeon, Dr. Firestone, nodded. "He's going to be fine. We got it all."

She wasn't sure she was following him. "All?"

The surgeon rotated his shoulders for a moment before answering. "His appendix burst just as we were making the first incision. It took a long time to mop up everything from the cavity, so to speak. We had to be sure he wasn't going to come down with peritonitis," he explained. "That was why the operation took twice as long as it normally does. This is ordinarily a very simple surgery," he assured her.

She'd heard all she needed to. Micah would be all right. Life could go back to being on track. "When can I see him?" she asked.

Firestone glanced at the overhead clock on the opposite wall out of habit rather than need. "He'll be in recovery for about an hour, then they'll take him up to his room. You can see him then."

Overcome for a moment, she pressed her lips together, suddenly struggling to get herself under control. When she did—and could finally speak—her voice was almost inaudible.

"Thank you, Doctor." She put out her hand to him.

His hands were large and hamlike. It was hard to envision them as the hands of a gifted surgeon, yet they were and he was. He enveloped her hand in his own.

"No, thank *you* for getting him here just in time. That man owes his life to you." Firestone smiled at her. "I wouldn't let him forget that too soon." Patting her hand, the surgeon rose again. "Now, if you'll excuse me, I've been dying for a roast beef sandwich for the last hour. It's time to reward myself," he added with a wink.

Tracy marveled that the man could actually eat after having his hands inside a man's abdomen. But that was why he was a doctor and she wasn't. Her mind jumped from one topic to another as huge waves of relief washed over her.

He would be all right. Micah was going to live. She felt like cheering.

Instead, taking in a long, shaky breath, she waited a couple of minutes before she called Sheila again. There was no reason to alarm the woman by sounding as if she'd just run all the way to the hospital, dragging Micah's body behind her. If she sounded breathless, Sheila would undoubtedly think the worst.

And there was no longer any reason to think that way.

Smiling to herself, Tracy began to dial.

His eyelids felt as if they were made of lead and each weighed a ton. It took him several attempts before he finally opened his eyes and *kept* them open.

Focusing them was another story. That was tricky.

Eventually, in what seemed like hours but in reality was no more than several minutes, Micah managed to see.

It still took a second before he realized he was looking at Tracy.

Was she real? Or was he just imagining her again?

She'd been in his dreams more than once since they'd made love. And each time, he'd only become aware of that after the fact. After the dream was over and he woke up.

That made it harder to hold on to.

Each dream about her had surprised him, as if he hadn't expected her to haunt his mind like that, not when he'd made such a conscious effort *not* to think about her during his waking hours.

But he had no control over the night.

It wasn't that he'd felt disloyal to Ella when he'd made love with Tracy. Ella had been a selfless woman and she would have wanted him to move on, to find someone new. To find someone to care for their sons. The problem was that he didn't want to experience ever again that gut-wrenching emptiness that had swallowed him whole when Ella had died. He was old enough to know that love seemed to go hand in hand with that awful specter, the specter of losing the one who meant the most to him.

He'd already put himself out there because he loved his sons and, of course, Sheila. He was determined not to put himself out there because of a woman. To love only to lose. Once was enough, thank you.

But his subconscious, which had wantonly pulled Tracy into his dreams, taunted him with the fact that he had no real control over that.

Love was a mysterious force that had many slaves, but no master. God knew that he certainly didn't have a say in it. He'd fallen hard for Ella and now he felt himself falling hard for Tracy, as well, God help him.

He could, of course, go on running from striking up relationships, but something told him that he was pretty much doomed. The yearning for Tracy had all but become a fact of life for him.

God knew, even in his weakened state, he was extremely glad she was there.

"Are you real?" he asked her hoarsely.

She'd been sitting here in his room for the past hour, waiting for him to open his eyes. Praying that the doctor hadn't made a mistake and that he *was* going to be all right.

Tracy rose from the vinyl chair and came over to his bed. Ever so gently, she cupped his cheek and smiled into his eyes. "Welcome back, stranger."

"Yeah, you're real," he murmured. And then, with a sigh, his eyes closed again. He was fast asleep.

Tracy's mouth curved as she shook her head. "Not much of a conversationalist, are you?"

He went on sleeping.

Tracy knew she should leave. She had a ton of case files to catch up on, not to mention that she wanted to stop by Micah's house and reassure the boys in person that their father would be all right.

She had some very good reasons why she should be on her way, but she was still recovering from her own ordeal. Waiting for word about his surgery while struggling not to think the worst had taken a great deal out of her. She felt too tired to drive.

It was really no contest. She decided to stay a little longer, just to recharge.

And to watch him sleep.

She smiled to herself. Seeing Micah's chest rise and fall was exceedingly comforting and reassuring. He was going to be all right. She'd gotten him to the hospital in time.

Happy beyond words, Tracy sat down again.

Chapter Thirteen

"See, I told you he was all right."

"But he's not moving."

"He's sleeping, stupid. See? His chest is going up and down. That means he's alive."

Unlike the first voice, the second two voices did not blend in with his dream.

Until this very second, as the voices filtered into his semiconsciousness, Micah hadn't even realized that he *was* dreaming. He'd vaguely thought that he was just experiencing disjointed bits and pieces of something he couldn't quite get hold of.

Since his wife had died, if he dreamed at all, it was to relive that awful day when she'd left him standing alone by her hospital bed, feeling incredibly helpless and lost. And so angry at the world he could barely contain it.

But just now—whatever "now" was—the woman in his dream hadn't been Ella. There'd been a different face, a different voice echoing off stage that he'd somehow *known* belonged to the woman. And there had been no despair, no sense of anger, just a strange, strong sensation of…hope.

That was it.

Hope.

And it was *her* voice he'd heard in his head, her voice he'd felt in his soul.

Tracy's voice.

But at the very end, it had been joined by smaller, childlike voices. His sons' voices. Which was when he'd opened his eyes.

Joy as well as a sense of well-being filled him as he looked at his sons being brought in by Tracy. His aunt was right next to her. The boys had wide, relieved smiles on their faces as they came running up to him, jockeying for the same space next to him right beside his bed.

"I want to be next to Daddy, I'm older," Gary cried, pulling rank.

"No, I want to be next to him," Greg cried. Unlike his brother's voice, which was filled with self-importance, his voice was trembling.

"Boys, your daddy has two sides," Tracy gently pointed out.

Taking Gary by the hand, she circumvented the foot of the hospital bed and led the boy to the left side of the bed. The boy had to share the space with an IV drip, but he was small enough not to need much room. To give the boys their moment, she moved a couple of steps back, assuming the place of an outsider, rather than the person who had been instrumental in arranging everything for the past three days. Ever since she'd brought Micah to the emergency room.

Each boy grabbed one of Micah's hands, grasping it between both of theirs and hanging on as if to keep him from suddenly leaving them. It was obvious, despite Gary's blustery bravado, that both boys had been very afraid that he'd be taken away from them just like their mother had been.

"We missed you, Daddy," Gary declared loudly.

"Yeah, missed you, Daddy," Greg echoed, not to be left out.

"And I missed you guys," Micah told them, squeezing each little hand that clutched at his. "All of you," he added, looking first at his aunt, then at the woman who had ushered his sons into the room. The woman who had infiltrated his sleep.

Much as he wanted to see the boys, Micah couldn't help wondering if she was breaking some sort of protocol bringing them in. He'd learned that she was the kind of woman who made things happen the way she wanted them to, not necessarily the way they were *supposed* to.

"Are you sure it's okay for them to be here?" he asked Tracy.

"Well, I had to smuggle them in inside my purse," Tracy deadpanned, "but I'm fairly certain it's okay." And then, unable to maintain her serious face, she grinned. "Don't worry, it's safe for them to be here. Last anyone checked, appendicitis wasn't catching."

He knew that, he just thought that Gary and Greg might be too young to be allowed on the floor. But, since he was in a single-care unit, there was no other patient in the room who could have been contagious.

Out of the corner of his eye, he saw Sheila nod authoritatively, backing up Tracy's cheerfully stated assurance.

Belatedly, he realized that his sons were talking to him.

"Did it hurt a lot, Daddy?" Gary asked him. "When they cut the bad thing out of you, did it hurt?" There was concern in the young blue eyes.

"I didn't feel a thing," Micah told the boy. He steered the conversation away from him and any fears they still harbored, hoping to dispel them. "So, what have you two been up to while I've been lying around here?" he asked.

The boys gleefully threw themselves into answering his question. The next fifteen minutes were spent with each boy trying to talk louder than his brother, relaying their exploits. Micah had expected to hear about video games, television shows and playtime spent with a few of their friends who lived nearby in the development. What he *wasn't* expecting was a report about "all the neat places Tracy took us to. She even made Aunt Sheila come with us," Gary informed him importantly.

He'd proceeded, with Greg's input, to tell his father about the amusement park Tracy had taken them to in

San Diego as well as the new animated movie that had opened in the local theater that weekend.

Greg came closer to him and confided in a whisper that nonetheless carried throughout the room, "Tracy's a lot of fun, Daddy."

His eyes momentarily meeting Tracy's, the corners of Micah's mouth curved in more of a grin than a smile as he told his younger son, "You don't know the half of it, Greg."

After a few more minutes of nonstop details, Sheila stepped forward and interrupted. "Boys, your dad looks a little tired." She looked from one boy to the other. "Why don't we let him rest?"

Looking disappointed, the two boys dutifully nodded. And then Greg piped up, "Can we come back and see him tomorrow?"

"I'm afraid not, boys," Tracy told them.

Gary's shoulders drooped. "Why not?" he asked.

"Because," Tracy said, then paused for half a beat before breaking her big surprise, "your dad's going to be coming home tomorrow."

The boys lit up like Christmas trees. For his part, Micah was stunned.

"Really, Daddy?" Greg asked excitedly.

"Tracy said so, so it's gotta be true," Gary maintained.

Greg was still a little uncertain and eyed his father questioningly. Micah responded by saying, "What she said," as he nodded at Tracy, although his uncertainty was clearly evident in his face. This was the first he'd heard about being discharged. Was she just trying to placate his sons?

"I talked to the doctor this morning," Tracy explained to her semiskeptical audience. "And he said that your daddy's healing really well so there's no reason not to let him come home. So he'll be there before you know it," Tracy promised.

"I'll take the boys outside," Sheila offered amid their cheering, then added, "Let the two of you have a few minutes alone."

Not waiting for a response, the older woman took each little boy by the hand and ushered her grandnephews out of the room.

"Thanks for bringing them," he said to Tracy when the boys' echoing goodbyes faded, and his sons had left the hospital room.

She shrugged carelessly, as if she couldn't take credit for a matter that had been really out of her hands. "It was either that, or risk having them hike out here on their own. They wanted to see that you were doing all right with their own eyes. I'm afraid that you seem to have raised a couple of skeptics," Tracy concluded with a soft laugh.

His sons weren't the only ones who were skeptical. He'd gotten very restless in the past few hours. "Am I really going home tomorrow?" he asked her, adding, "I haven't been able to see the doctor yet today."

It wasn't for lack of trying. He'd asked the nurse on duty several times if his doctor was coming in to make his hospital rounds and if not, could he get a call put through to the man's office. The nurse had told him that as far as she knew, the doctor was due in sometime before six. To Micah, that was code for "before the end of the world." So far, the man hadn't been by to see him.

"I cornered him early this morning, just as he was coming into his office," Tracy told him.

She had plenty of practice, ambushing witnesses who were reluctant to testify at one trial or another. Because of that, she'd learned how to be both resourceful and persuasive. The former often required being several steps ahead of her quarry.

Micah looked at his attorney with more than a little admiration in his eyes. The woman knew how to get things done. Rather than off-putting, he found her take-charge attitude both compelling and stirring. A few more pieces of his dream came back to him.

He smiled broadly. "Remind me to fire you when I get a little stronger."

She knew exactly what he was referring to. Trying to look serious, she still couldn't help smiling. "Don't bite off more than you can chew," she warned him.

"I wasn't planning on chewing," he told her, humor highlighted in his eyes. "Unless, of course, you want me to."

She laughed then and shook her head. *This is just temporary. Enjoy it but don't get used to it. He's just vulnerable right now. Like you are.*

"One step at a time, Micah," she advised. "Let's get you home and healed first."

He caught her hand. Lacing his fingers through hers, he looked at her. Didn't she realize that she was good for what ailed him?

"Haven't you heard?' he asked her. "Making love with a beautiful, intelligent woman is all part of the new healing plan."

"No, I haven't heard. Sounds intriguing," she admitted. "But right now, I have to get your tribe back home and then duck into my office for a few hours." She didn't even want to think about what had to be piling up on her desk. The past three days, because of the boys—and Micah—she'd been out more than she'd been in. "My contact at the police department said that they think they might be getting closer to breaking this identity theft case." She looked at him pointedly. "I don't have to tell you that once they do, once the whole story comes out, you'll be exonerated."

Other than his sons' welfare, clearing his name had become the most important thing in the world to him. But right now, while still very important, it wasn't in quite the same life-or-death category as it had been only a month ago. Things had happened. Things that placed his life in a different focus than it had been before.

He'd begun to feel again, feel in a way he had been so very certain he would never feel again. He'd been convinced that those particular emotions had been numbed, disconnected. Severed.

But he'd been proven wrong.

He thought of all that this woman he hadn't even known a short while ago had done for him. For his family. "Saying thank-you doesn't seem like nearly enough," he told her.

Tracy shook her head. "I'm superstitious about things like that," she admitted. "Don't thank me yet.

Save your thanks for when we put this whole thing to rest," she cautioned.

"All right." His eyes smiled into hers. "But I can practice saying thank-you."

The man was wonderfully incorrigible. With so little encouragement, she could become entirely used to this, to his family…

Stop. What the hell are you doing? You don't want to go there. You don't want to get hurt again. Good things don't last, remember?

Drawing in a breath, she took a moment to pull herself together. "*After* you've got your strength back," she told him. "Remember?"

"I remember," he echoed, then told her with a wicked, if a little weak, grin. "But I'm working on it."

Brushing her lips quickly against his—it was all she would allow herself and besides, he didn't need to be tempted in his condition—Tracy said, "Don't get too ambitious. Slow and steady is what usually gets a person there."

The last thing she wanted was for the man to jeopardize himself. After all, he'd just had an operation. His stitches were still fresh. Any undue acrobatics and he might break them before his incision was healed.

But there was another part of her, a part that needed to feel loved, if only fleetingly and superficially. Something was better than nothing, and that part urged her on, whispering, *You don't know how much longer this is going to go on, take advantage of the situation while you can.*

Tracy wasn't about to try to deceive herself by pretending this could continue indefinitely. There was a finite timetable out there with the name of this affair on it. She was a big girl now and she knew that. She accepted it because she knew that life was harsh with no happily ever after.

But there was happiness, if only for a very little while, and why shouldn't she allow herself to revel in it? As long as she accepted the fact that it would fade away like the morning fog, leaving no trace, she would be all right. She'd survive. Just like she always had.

"Thanks, again," Micah said to her as he let go of her hand.

She placed her index finger lightly against his lips. "Like I said, don't thank me yet." Her eyes held his for a moment. "Later," she said in a whisper that sounded more like a promise.

To both of them.

"You know, that young woman is just an absolute godsend," Sheila told her nephew the next afternoon as she fluffed up his pillow for him.

The doctor had signed him out of the hospital earlier that morning, just as Tracy had said. And she, bringing along his sons and his aunt, had arrived to pick him up and bring him back home. But once he was back in his familiar surroundings, Tracy had begged off his aunt's invitation to lunch, saying she would do Micah more good back at the office.

He didn't know about that, but he kept his protest to himself, afraid that perhaps, like his sons, he was becoming too attached to her.

Rather than retreat to the bed in his room, Micah had opted to camp out on the sofa in the family room. At least there he could be around his sons and also near the kitchen where his aunt could usually be found when she was at his house, puttering around.

"Lean forward," Sheila instructed as she tucked the pillow back in behind his head. "She came right in and took charge of everything. Never saw anything like it," his aunt marveled. "After she brought you to the hospital and waited around to make sure that you were all right, she didn't just call to tell me, she came by after she left you to reassure the boys in person. She stayed talking to them until they were all out of questions. Came back the next day and got them involved in things so that they wouldn't worry about you."

Taking a breath, Sheila debated going on, then decided that it was best to be honest.

"To tell you the truth, I thought I was going to resent her take-charge attitude—you know how I like to have the upper hand when it comes to you and the boys—but she did it in a way that made me feel relieved, not resentful." Sheila laughed softly, shaking her head in wonder. "I'd say that was a pretty unique quality to have. Looks to me like she's the whole package," she told her nephew.

"I mean, I knew Tracy was a very good lawyer. Maizie wouldn't have recommended her if she wasn't, but I didn't know she was going to be so capable and yet so nice." Sheila looked quite happy as she looked at him meaningfully. "She should be able to put that company of yours in their place."

Satisfaction echoed in every word Sheila uttered. She had been both horrified and angrily indignant when she'd first learned about the accusation leveled against her nephew. Micah was as honest and upstanding as anyone could be.

"The very idea, treating you like a criminal after all that time you put in with them, especially these last couple of years. You practically worked around the clock for those people."

That, he thought, was less about dedication on his part than it was about trying to bury himself in his work so that he wouldn't think about losing Ella and how devastated that had made him.

Defending Donovan Defense came automatically for him. You didn't become the top in this field by being lax and laid-back. He'd known all about that when he'd signed on to the black programs.

"They have to be careful, Aunt Sheila. Donovan Defense is responsible for a good part of the country's defense missiles."

That carried no weight with Sheila. She fisted her hands against her hips, her very stance a challenge. "And you're what, the enemy?"

"No, but my laptop was compromised and they're geared to think the worst and be suspicious until they're shown otherwise." There was no other way to proceed and he knew that. Unfortunately, this time around they were proceeding against him.

Sheila took his face in her hand the way she'd done countless times when he'd been a small boy. Since he was a man now, with a man's face, all she managed to be able to hold was his chin. She gave it a quick, affectionate squeeze before releasing it.

"Anyone can see that this is not a face that belongs to an enemy conspirator. This is the face of a good, decent, honest man who loves both his country and his family."

"Be that as it may," Micah allowed, "it's still something that they want to verify themselves."

Until just a little while ago, he'd been afraid of getting railroaded. But now that fear had abated. He wasn't sure if it was because he'd faced death and beaten it, or because he had such supreme faith in the woman who had been thrust into his life. But for whatever reason, he was now confident that it might take a while, but things would be sorted out. And in the end, he would be cleared.

The only questions that remained were how long it would take and what would he use for income until that happened. He had a thirty-day grace period, after which action against him would be taken or he might be let go pending further investigation. In either case he wouldn't have a salary or health coverage.

Some catch he was. How could he possibly entertain thoughts of getting serious with Tracy? What did he have to offer her? An instant family with accumulated bills? Not exactly appealing to a woman who had looks, brains and was most obviously going somewhere. He, in thirty days, had gone from being a man with a future to a man whose future had turned into a huge question mark.

He didn't want her remaining with him, even for a

little while, out of some sense of obligation or, worse yet, out of pity.

Yet what else could keep her with him, he silently challenged.

"You're awfully quiet," Sheila observed. "Has my talking tired you out?" she asked with an amused smile.

No, but realizing I have nothing to offer Tracy does make me tired.

"I think I am a little tired," he admitted. "If you don't mind, maybe I'll just take a nap before dinner."

"I don't mind," she assured him, then confided, "I'm just happy you're around to do *anything*. I know you well enough to know that if that woman hadn't forcibly taken you to the hospital—well, I don't want to think about that," she said, emotion welling up within her. "By all means, take a nap," she said, then promised, "I'll be very quiet."

He closed his eyes, pretending to take a nap. But rather than fall asleep, Micah couldn't help thinking about how lonely life would be once Tracy was no longer in it.

Chapter Fourteen

Micah discovered that as his strength slowly returned, so did, to a lesser degree, his confidence. Specifically, that his feelings for Tracy were not futile.

Rather than simply continuing to believe that he had nothing to offer this woman, he felt a surge of determination to prove himself.

Granted, he currently faced having no salary, no job and the possibility, if things went horribly wrong, of incarceration for quite a long time.

But all that could be turned around with a little bit of luck. Luck that hinged on what that joined task force comprised of the local police department and the FBI could uncover. While he hated having the outcome of his fate in the hands of complete strangers, he now felt that at least there was a chance that things might work out.

With growing impatience that he was nonetheless trying to keep under wraps, Micah glanced at his watch. It was almost six o'clock. Anticipation hummed through the veins of his healing body.

She'd be here soon.

Not that there was any actual arrangement to that effect, at least not in so many words. But in the past two weeks, ever since he'd come home from the hospital, Tracy had stopped by around this time every day after work. And on the weekend, she'd found one excuse after another to come over even earlier in the day.

He knew that technically they were working on and building up his case, but he'd like to think that even if they weren't, she'd still find a reason to stop over.

But even if his case was the *only* reason she came, he wouldn't allow that to bother him. The way he felt about Tracy, he would work with whatever he could get—and build the foundation of his relationship on that.

The doorbell rang.

Pushing himself up from the easy chair where he'd been sitting, Micah rose to his feet and began to make his way to the door. In the background he heard his sons scrambling, obviously with the same goal in mind. They were arguing about who could get to the front door first.

He barely made it there before they did. Opening the door, he smiled broadly at the person standing on the other side.

Tracy.

She wore a light aqua jacket with a matching pencil skirt. Four-inch tan heels turned the business suit into something impossibly sexy in his eyes. He could feel the very air around him brightened instantly.

"Hi," he said, stepping back to allow her in.

Crossing the threshold, Tracy frowned. "What are you doing out of bed?" she asked. Usually, it was Sheila who let her in. Micah had been camped out on the family room sofa. A quick glance around told her that Sheila wasn't around.

"Just what a man wants to hear from a beautiful woman," Micah said warmly, shutting the door again.

She gave him a full appraisal. If the case against Micah came down to an actual hearing, she needed him to be strong. That meant no setbacks due to the operation. "That man better get back into bed if he knows what's good for him."

His eyes washed over her. She found herself growing rather warm. He dropped his voice several levels as Gary and Greg all but tumbled into the room.

"I know exactly what's good for me."

Tracy stood perfectly still in order to keep the shiver from giving her away. It wasn't easy. If she wasn't careful, she would start believing him.

"At least lie down on the sofa," she said just before she turned and threw her arms open to his sons. The little boys all but plowed into her, small arms reaching as far as they could in an attempted embrace around her waist. Grinning at her fan club, Tracy hugged them close and asked, "How are my two favorite men?"

"We missed you, Tracy," Greg told her solemnly.

She'd been here for more than three hours yesterday, but she never grew tired of hearing the boys express their feelings for her. "And I missed you, but we each have things we have to do, right?"

The boys bobbed their heads up and down in vigorous agreement. She had a feeling that they would have easily agreed to anything. Too bad that quality would fade away by the time they reached manhood, she thought.

Straightening, Tracy's attention was drawn back to their father, the man who invaded her dreams lately. It was a bad sign and she knew it. She had become used to having him in her life. That would make it twice as hard on her when they went their separate ways, as they inevitably would.

What made it even worse was that she would miss his little boys like crazy.

"Oh, before I forget. Here." Digging into her purse, Tracy pulled out an envelope and held it out to him.

For a moment, he just stared at it, puzzled. The logo in the corner had a broad, bold embossed double *D,* one capitalized letter within the other. That was Donovan Defense's logo.

What was Tracy doing with an envelope from Donovan? he wondered.

"Trying out your X-ray vision?" she asked, mildly amused when he made no effort to take the envelope from her hand, but went on staring at it.

Micah blinked and looked at her. He knew she'd said something, but the words had gone right by him without registering.

"What?"

Tracy kept a straight face for at least part of her answer. "Well, you're staring at the envelope as if you were trying to see inside it. Most people open envelopes to accomplish that, so I was just wondering if you'd been blessed with X-ray vision recently and were trying it out just now."

"Very funny," he muttered.

Taking the envelope from her, he slid his finger into a small space and ripped it open. What was inside the envelope was definitely *not* funny.

It was a check.

A check equal to his semi-weekly net salary. Raising his eyes, he looked at her. There were times he forgot that she was, first and foremost—at least in her own eyes—his attorney.

"What's this?"

"It hasn't been that long, has it?" she asked, pretending to be surprised. "Most people would recognize it as a paycheck. Did they get the amount wrong?" she asked, moving so that she was able to peer around his shoulder at the check.

"No, but—" He didn't understand. It didn't make sense. Glancing one last time at the check, he looked at her again. "They told me that I was being put on suspended leave without pay as of two weeks ago. How did you get this?"

She shrugged casually, trying not to appear as pleased with herself as she secretly was. This hadn't been easy. Not because she wasn't right but because Donovan had dug in its heels at first and resisted.

"I could say I charmed it out of your supervisor, but the truth's a lot less colorful. You had an emergency appendectomy," she reminded him.

He realized that, but didn't see the connection. "Yeah, so?"

"So," she said slowly, "you had the surgery just before you were scheduled to be put on that leave without pay."

"Okay." He still wasn't seeing what the connection between that and the sizable check he was holding was. What was he missing?

"That puts you specifically on sick leave," she said, enunciating each word. This had taken some digging into policy terms on her part. "They cannot take action against you or deprive you of your salary while you're on sick leave. Even if you were supposed to be terminated and this happened one day before you were to be officially terminated, the company would have to provide you with both health coverage *and* your salary for at least the next six weeks." She smiled at him. "That's just the way the coverage is written. You'll be getting another check just like this one in another two weeks."

"And the operation?" he asked, trying to absorb this reversal. He'd gone from a man once more submerged in debt—this time with no salary coming in, as well—to a man who was solvent.

"It's all covered," she told him. "Hospital, surgeon, anesthesia—everything. Your company insurance will take care of all of it."

Micah released the breath he'd been unconsciously holding all this time. This was a huge load off his shoulders—and his mind. And he owed all to this tenacious woman.

"You are incredible," he told her with no small amount of admiration.

Tracy shrugged her slim shoulders. She was accustomed to clients' gratitude. But she didn't want him being grateful to her. She didn't want him to feel that he was in her debt. The idea made her uncomfortable.

She tried to make light of it by joking, "I've been told that once or twice."

"By mostly grateful women and gnarled old men, I hope," Micah said.

Maybe having him a little grateful *wasn't* such a bad thing, she decided.

"Gnarled," she repeated with a nod of her head. "Every last one of them."

He laughed and kissed her without thinking or stopping to censor himself around his sons. The gleeful burst of applause behind him reminded him that they were definitely not alone.

"We have an audience," she pointed out, gently separating herself from him and turning instead to the boys.

"Do you like Daddy?" Greg asked her. It was hard to miss the hopeful note in his voice.

Yes, I do. But saying that out loud would only get the boys' hopes up and she didn't want to be responsible for disappointing them in the long run. Greg and Gary's relationship with their father was important. So she would have to be the bad guy when Micah and she moved on.

She did the only thing she could. She was evasive. "He's very nice man."

It amazed her how sharp children could be, and how they wouldn't always docilely accept evasion when they wanted an answer.

"But do you *like* him?" Micah's younger son stressed again.

Her eyes briefly met Micah's. She couldn't play it safe. There was no point in being evasive. After what they had done and what she'd shared with him, even if she said nothing in response to the boy's question, Micah would know how she felt. Unless he was utterly stupid—and he wasn't. The man had to be aware that she cared about him.

Besides, she had a feeling that Greg and Gary would keep after her until she gave them a definitive answer.

"Yes," she finally said quietly. "I like your father."

She expected the boys to smile. The smile on Micah's face, however, was a revelation. It blossomed and spread until it was positively brilliant. Still, she was afraid to read too much into it. Better safe than sorry.

"Well, this calls for a celebration," he finally said, holding up the check. The check and being back on salary for the duration of his sick leave was a good cover for what he actually wanted to celebrate. What had him really hopeful and in a celebratory mood was what Tracy had just allowed to slip.

Whether she knew it or not, she'd admitted to having feelings for him. Which was fine with him because he more than had feelings for her. He was rather certain that he was falling in love with her.

"Wait," Tracy said, suddenly realizing just what he was proposing. She didn't want him getting carried away. "You're not going to cook, are you?"

"That was the plan, yes," he told her. He didn't understand why she seemed so apprehensive. "Why?"

"Because you'd have to be standing up, at least most of the time, that's why." Did she have to spell everything out for him? For an intelligent man, there were times she felt he had no common sense. At least not when it came to his own limitations.

"Well, I haven't mastered cooking from a reclining position," he teased. "So you've got me there."

As he made his way, albeit slowly, to the kitchen, Tracy moved in front of him, blocking his access. "You're still not 100 percent well," she pointed out. "You don't want to push it. Who knows, tiring yourself out like that might impede your recovery."

While he had to admit that he liked her fussing over him, he wasn't exactly a delicate piece of china. "They took out my appendix, Tracy. They didn't do a heart transplant."

"They plant hearts?" Gary asked, clearly confused.

"I'll explain later," Micah promised. "It's complicated."

"Cutting is cutting," Tracy was stubbornly insisting. Up until now, Sheila had been doing all the cooking since he'd returned from the hospital, but Tracy knew that the woman had been invited to see a movie with some of her girlfriends and Micah, being Micah, had most likely insisted that she go.

"So what do you suggest?" he asked. Right now, she

was quicker than he was and he had no doubt that she would continue jockeying for position and blocking his way. He didn't have enough strength to strong-arm her, although the idea of doing a little wrestling was not without its appeal. "Do *you* want to do the cooking?" He watched her face for a reaction to his suggestion.

Tracy sighed, knowing that a woman her age *should* know how to cook, but she'd always been so busy, between college, law school and then her career, that take-out had become a way of life for her.

"That all depends," she answered.

"On what?" He hated to admit it, but she was right about his standing up too long. Micah retreated to the family room and sat down on the sofa, waiting for her to answer.

She knew she could bluff her way through this, but for the most part, she liked to think of herself as an honest person, especially when it came to dealing with Micah and the boys. That meant not pretending she could master something she couldn't.

She plowed ahead and owned up to her shortcoming. "On whether or not you'd like to pay a return visit to the E.R., this time accompanied by your sons."

Amusement highlighted his face. He had a feeling that she wasn't being unduly modest. "That bad?"

"Well, it's not good," she said. "I've been known to burn water. Or more accurately, burn away water and scorch the pot it was boiling in."

He laughed, shaking his head. "That's not entirely hopeless."

Tracy looked at him, stunned. "And just what would you consider entirely hopeless?"

Micah kept a perfectly straight face and answered, "If you'd burned down the house, as well, *that* would have been hopeless."

She pretended to consider what he said. "No, I have to admit, I've never done that. Of course, I haven't done all that much cooking, either." She wasn't proud of it, but it was what it was. "The only appliance I have a nodding acquaintance with in the kitchen besides my refrigerator is my microwave. I can heat up leftovers with the best of them."

He liked that she had a sense of humor about what she considered was a shortcoming. A lot of women would have become defensive. But then, she wasn't a lot of women. Which was why he was so attracted to her.

For a moment, Micah considered ordering out, then dismissed it. Where was the challenge in that? Besides, cooking together brought people closer and she'd be doing the "heavy lifting," so to speak, so she couldn't complain that he was pushing himself. He was more than happy to take on the role of a mentor.

Her mentor.

He did like the sound of that. "Tell you what," he proposed. "How do you feel about getting a cooking lesson?"

Tracy stared at him. "You want to teach me how to cook something?" she asked, just to be certain she hadn't misunderstood him.

"That was implied in the word *lesson,*" he confirmed.

She remembered when her ex had tried to teach her how to play tennis. Ten minutes into it, he was screaming at her, telling her how hopeless she was. She didn't want that happening with Micah.

"I don't think that's such a good idea," she told him quietly.

"That's all right," Micah assured her. "Because I do."

She was far more skeptical than he was optimistic, she thought. The man had nothing to base his faith on, while she had witnessed herself in the kitchen. Talk about two left feet—or, in this case, two left hands—she was definitely in that hopeless category.

"You have fire insurance on the house?" she asked him.

"You're not going to be burning anything down," Micah told her. "So stop worrying."

"Wish I had your faith," she murmured under her breath.

He'd heard her and gave her hand an encouraging squeeze.

"Don't worry. I've got enough faith for both of us. We're going to start you off with something simple," he promised. "I'm going to teach you how to make beef stroganoff."

That didn't sound simple to her. Tracy groaned, anticipating the fiasco ahead. "It's your funeral," she predicted.

"First thing we're going to work on," he told her, leading the way to the kitchen, "is your attitude. Tell yourself that you're going to do it, you're going to make beef stroganoff."

"I could do that," she acknowledged. "But I'm not in the habit of lying to myself."

Unless it's about you, about us. Because when it came to that, she'd willingly fallen into a trap by stopping in every evening. By getting so involved with his sons. By getting so involved with him. Each part of that spelled disaster. Put it all together and it became a giant prediction.

"You won't be lying," he told her firmly. "Because you're going to make this meal and it's going to be very good."

Obviously the man had incredibly low standards. Out loud she mocked, "And if we all clap our hands, Tinker Bell will come alive."

"Tinker Bell *is* alive," Greg piped up and then just the slightest bit of uncertainty entered his eyes as he asked, "Isn't she?"

Great, now she was blowing up the little boy's fantasy. Nice going, Trace.

"Absolutely," Tracy told the boy with feeling.

Well, she had almost blown that one, she thought, feeling less than happy with herself.

"Are you ready?" Micah asked her.

The question is, are you? she wondered. "As I'll ever be," she said.

"Okay, we'll start by having you slice these mushrooms." He placed an eight-ounce box of whole mushrooms before the cutting board on the counter.

Tracy mentally rolled up her sleeves and started slicing.

Chapter Fifteen

Tracy had always believed that the Christmas season was the season for miracles. Which meant that if there were any miracles to be had, that was when they were supposed to occur, before and around the third week in December.

But at this point, she was beginning to think that perhaps July should be regarded as the season for miracles as well.

First and foremost, of course, was the fact that a little less than two hundred and fifty years ago, a struggling patchwork quilt of colonies banded together to call themselves a fledgling country, and, with a ragtag army of soldiers, fought for and actually won their independence from a country that at the time had the best-trained army in the world.

Of secondary and only slightly lesser magnitude was the miracle that had occurred here tonight. She had made an entire dinner and not only had no one died, but no one had even gotten sick.

Tracy was still somewhat in shock and marveling over that as she first collected and then proceeded to wash the dishes that had been pressed into service so that Micah, the boys and she could consume this landmark meal.

She looked over her shoulder at Micah. She had had to practically bully him into sitting at the kitchen table while she worked rather than having him stand beside her, helping her with the dishes.

As far as she could see, Micah appeared to be fine, as did Greg and Gary, but maybe they were trying to spare her feelings and hiding the truth.

"You're sure you're not feeling queasy or anything?" she asked Micah for the third time.

He laughed at her. "We're fine, aren't we, boys?" Two heads bobbed enthusiastically up and down in response to his question. "See? The meal was really very good. No one's turning even a light shade of green. Know what I think?"

She turned down the water from the faucet in order to hear him more clearly. "No, what?"

"I think you've been holding out on us so that you didn't have to take your turn at cooking." For the last two weeks, Sheila had been doing the cooking, but before his unscheduled trip to the hospital for his appendectomy, he had cooked for Tracy when she stopped by.

"I've a different theory about what just happened," she told him.

Micah cocked his head, curious to hear what she came up with. "Which is?"

Finished washing—she'd found washing the dishes oddly therapeutic—she picked up a dish towel and dried her hands. "I'm having a lovely dream and I'm about to wake up any minute to find that none of this really happened. That I'm still the person who burns water."

"There's a way to test that theory, you know," he told her.

His voice was whimsical and playful. Anticipation suddenly reared its head. "Oh? And what would that be?"

"I'll show you." Getting up, Micah crossed to her.

Since she didn't know what to expect, he caught her by surprise. Framing her face with his hands, he leaned over and kissed her.

Tracy was vaguely aware of childish giggles in the background, but those quickly faded as the depth of his kiss drew her into a shining, beautiful world. This in turn brought about the rushing of blood and the heating of her skin.

She melted against him before she realized that she shouldn't be doing this. He was still recovering from surgery. Besides, the boys were standing right there and they were far too young to be taught about a new level of chemistry achieved between a man and a woman.

Reluctantly, Tracy drew back, her heart beating a

lot harder than when, eons ago, she had participated in a 5 K marathon.

"Micah," she whispered huskily, "the boys are watching."

"Yes, I know." He laughed as he took a step back. "Well, it was either this, or letting the boys pinch you. They pinch hard," he confided in a stage whisper that had the boys giggling again.

She was confused and having only half of her brain functioning didn't help any. "What?"

"As in 'pinch me, I must be dreaming,'" he prompted, referring to the famous disclaimer about dreaming. "I thought this might be preferable to you."

She pressed her lips together, savoring the taste of him. Her pulse went up several notches. "Definitely preferable," she agreed.

But even as she said it, Tracy knew she had to leave. There was just too much longing, too much desire ricocheting through her body for her to successfully ignore it for any length of time. And she couldn't very well act on her feelings. The man wasn't finished healing.

"Maybe I'd better leave on a high note," she suggested.

"Don't go." He laced his hand through hers, but his eyes were what actually held her prisoner. "The boys will be going to bed in a little while."

"That's why I'm going," she told him. "You're still in the process of healing."

The smile on his lips was positively wicked. He wasn't about to give up so easily. "We could see how much progress I've actually made."

God, talk about tempting. Tracy drew in a long, fortifying breath. She had to be the strong one here today, even though she wanted nothing more than to be with him. Time was growing short for her. She had a strong hunch that the case would be resolved very soon and then he wouldn't need her anymore. She'd had no excuse to hide behind as to why she kept dropping by, no excuse to give herself as to why she kept giving in to her desire to see him. Words like love and commitment weren't needed here, not as long as she could hide behind working on his case.

Once that was gone, she would be, too.

The thought filled her with almost insurmountable sadness.

"Tempting though that sounds, I'm going to have to pass on that," she told him, sounding far more firm than she felt.

But he'd seen the flicker of desire in her eyes and that gave him all the encouragement he needed. "You could do all the work," he proposed, whispering into her ear so that neither one of the boys could overhear him. "I'll just lie there and you can have your way with me. I won't tell a soul."

If she felt any hotter, she would burst into flames. Just the feel of his breath along her skin sent her temperature soaring, never mind what he was saying.

"You are not making it easy to say no," she whispered back.

His eyes held hers as he replied, quite audibly, "I want to make it impossible to say no."

The phone rang then. Tracy was both disappointed

and relieved at the intrusion. But maybe it was for the best, she consoled herself.

"Telephone," she announced, backing up toward the wall.

"I know," Micah acknowledged, amused. "I recognize the sound."

Since she was now closer to the wall phone than he was, Tracy picked up the receiver and answered it. "Muldare residence."

Out of the corner of her eye, she saw Micah grinning at her. Most likely it was because of the greeting she'd just offered, but since he had an all-male household, the caller might think he or she had the wrong number if they heard a woman just saying, "Hello."

"Micah Muldare, please," a gruff male voice requested. There was something vaguely familiar about it, but she didn't waste time trying to pin a face to the voice. So far there was no reason for it.

Micah held out his hand for the receiver, but Tracy had one more thing she felt needed to be answered. "Who shall I say is calling?"

"Sid Greene."

Tracy's eyes widened. Greene was Micah's supervisor's supervisor. He was the one she'd dealt with when she got Micah his salary reinstalled for the duration of his recuperation.

Why was he calling? It made no sense for him to be calling Micah while the two sides were embroiled in this legal battle.

"Mr. Greene, this is Theresa Ryan, Mr. Muldare's attorney," she reminded him in case it had slipped his mind. He dealt with a great many people each day and she wasn't vain enough to think that she stood out. "Whatever you have to say to him, you can say to me."

She heard an impatient huff on the other end of the line. "I need to talk to him directly about a project that he wrote a white paper for."

A white paper, Tracy had come to learn, was a technical paper, usually the definitive explanation of the steps involved in the creation of a product or a procedure that was regarded as the go-to document. Which made the person who wrote the white paper the go-to person for that particular product or procedure.

In this case, she assumed it was Micah.

She had a gut feeling this was a good thing.

"Just a minute, please, Mr. Greene. I'll see if he's available." The next moment, Micah took the receiver. "He's available," she managed to say into the mouthpiece before Micah put the receiver to his ear.

Bracing himself—he had no idea what to expect—Micah said, "Hello, Mr. Greene? This is Micah Muldare."

It was obvious that the man on the other end was uncomfortable. It was also obvious that he considered this call to be of the utmost necessity.

Known to be a straightforward man, Greene got right down to business. "Questions have come up about the ground-to-air missile project. We've had to lay off a lot of people in the last couple of years."

The man wasn't saying anything that he didn't already know, Micah thought, but he continued to wait patiently for some kind of enlightenment.

"There's no one left who was part of the original team. The ones who are left know squat about this particular project and we don't have time to bring them up to speed even if we could." Greene paused, as if debating whether or not to make the next admission. When he spoke again, it was almost grudgingly. "We stand to lose the contract if the customer's questions aren't satisfactorily addressed. Now your bulldog of an attorney told me all about your surgery so I know it's too soon for you to come in, but if I send someone over with a company laptop, could you review the questions and answer them as soon as possible?"

Micah was stunned. It took him a second to find his tongue. "I thought I wasn't supposed to have any access to the company's database."

"Yeah, well, in a perfect world, things might be different," Greene allowed. "But in this world, time is money and the customer's satisfaction trumps everything else. Besides, your attorney informed me that there's a federal task force investigating this network of hackers who got into your computer. She even brought in several special agents who made the case that your laptop was randomly targeted, just like the others were. In which case, none of this was your fault and you're innocent of the charges against you. I've been informed that the agents have to dot all their Is and cross all their Ts, but it looks like they'll be pressing charges and clearing you in the very near future. So, can we just put this aside for the good of the company and have you get to work, Muldare?"

"Absolutely," Micah responded. A flood of emotions suddenly washed all over him. He was stunned, flabbergasted and exceedingly pleased and relieved.

"Good. I'll send MacAfee over tomorrow morning with the laptop. Good to have things back to normal," Greene confided, then, belatedly, he thought to ask, "How are you feeling, Muldare?" It was a personal question and Greene was uncomfortable with personal questions—asking or answering them—but the moment called for it.

Micah was still high on relief. "I'm getting better by the minute."

"Excellent. That's what I like to hear," he said with genuine feeling. And then his voice dropped several octaves. "Between the two of us," he said, "I never believed a word of the charges brought up against you, Muldare."

Micah knew the man was only paying lip service to the event, but as far as he was concerned, it didn't matter. He had his job back and more important, his good name.

And he knew who he had to thank for all of it, he thought, slanting a glance toward Tracy.

"Thank you, sir," he said to Greene for form's sake. The line went dead the next moment. That resolved, Greene had moved on to something else.

"What was that all about?" Tracy asked as Micah hung up the phone.

"It's over."

Tracy felt an icy wave wash over her. She didn't like the sound of that.

Don't anticipate, she ordered herself angrily.

"What's over?" she asked, struggling to keep her voice level, detached.

His grin went from one ear to the other. "I think the case against me just disappeared."

"Why?" she asked eagerly. She knew how much being cleared meant to him. It went beyond a paycheck, it was the principle of the thing. They had questioned his loyalty, his character. And now he was vindicated. "What happened?"

"Well," he said honestly, "mainly you." He was well aware that the verdict could have easily gone the opposite way if she hadn't started investigating, hadn't personally hounded the task force and hadn't taken it upon herself to corner Greene on his home turf. "It looks like Greene took your defense to heart. He said that the FBI is on the cusp of bringing in the hackers and that he believed you when you told him that my laptop just happened to be hacked at random. He wants to send over a company laptop tomorrow so that I can start answering some questions that came up on an old project I handled."

That would be the government, she thought, knowing that Micah wasn't able to specify who or confirm her suspicions when she guessed. But for all intents and purposes, the identity of the "customer" in this case was an open secret.

She gleaned the important thing out of what he was telling her. "So we won."

He nodded. If he grinned any harder, his face would split open. "We won."

The all important word caught the boys' attention,

drawing it away from the video game they had begun playing in the family room.

"Yay! We won," Greg and Gary both shouted excitedly. Then Gary looked from Tracy to his father. "What did we win?"

"Daddy gets to go back to work as soon as he gets better," Tracy told the boy. She would have added that Micah won back his good name, but the boys were too young to understand what that actually meant, or why a good reputation was so important. That was a lesson for another day.

Yes, a day you won't be here for, she reminded herself. She could feel sadness encroaching on her and did her best to block it. This was Micah's time and she had to be happy for him, not sad for herself.

"Did we win you, too?" Greg asked out of the blue.

She stared at the little boy, his question rendering her momentarily speechless. How had he come up with that? He was far too young to intuit the connection between her and charges against their father.

"I was just here to help your daddy with his case," she told him.

"But you're not going to go away just because he won, right?" Gary asked. When she didn't answer him immediately, he turned to his father. "Is she, Daddy?" he asked nervously.

"That's up to Tracy," Micah told his son. "We can't hold her here if she wants to go."

"Yes, we can," Greg insisted. To prove it, he latched onto her hand, holding it as tight as he could. And then he looked up at her and made his case by begging. "Stay with us. Please."

"Sweetheart, I can't stay." She caressed the small, serious face, missing him already. Missing all of them. She could feel her heart aching. "Your daddy doesn't need me anymore."

"I didn't say that," Micah countered quietly.

Her heart jumped as she turned to look at him. For a moment…

But she was just fooling herself, Tracy upbraided herself. Micah hadn't told her that her services weren't needed any longer in so many words, but there was no need to say anything. It was a given. He'd won the case. The charges would be dropped.

It was all over but the shouting. A few details to iron out—perhaps some compensation for pain and suffering over the baseless accusation might even be given—and then life would go back to normal for him. And to a solitary existence for her. She desperately tried to make her peace with that.

It wasn't easy.

She did her best to sound cheerful. "After I take care of a few loose ends, you won't need a lawyer anymore."

"No, I won't," Micah agreed. "But that doesn't mean that I won't need you." He saw the startled look on her face and told himself it was a good thing. "Hey, I taught you how to cook. I don't want anyone else reaping the fruits of my labor."

Her expression gave nothing away. "So you want me to hang around for my cooking?"

He took her hands in his. He didn't want to play

around anymore. He wanted her to know what was in his heart. A heart that would slip back into a comatose state if she left.

"Well, maybe I wouldn't go that far," he allowed. "About your cooking," he clarified, "not about you hanging around. I want you to 'hang around' for other reasons."

She could hardly breathe. "What other reasons?" she asked, her eyes never leaving his.

"Well, to begin with, I've gotten very used to seeing you every day. At my age, I'm not sure if I could stand any drastic changes and not having you around qualifies as an extremely drastic change."

"So you're asking me to stop by every day?" she deadpanned.

"No, I want more than that," he told her seriously. "A lot more." He regrouped, trying to work his way into a proposal. Admittedly, he was way out of practice. "In case you haven't noticed, the boys love you."

"The boys," Tracy repeated. She'd argued fearlessly before judges that made other, far more seasoned lawyers cower. Why then was she so nervous putting herself out there now?

Because what Micah said could crush her if it was the wrong thing. Still, she couldn't keep hiding indefinitely. This was it. She needed him to spell out exactly what he meant—and if it wasn't what she was hoping he meant, then she needed to find out sooner, not later. And go.

"What about you?" she finally asked him. If her

mouth were any dryer, it could have been named a national desert.

Micah didn't answer right away. Instead, he grinned at her. "I thought you knew."

"Knew what?" she asked, tension all but electrocuting her.

"That I'm one of the boys, too."

His eyes held hers for a long moment. He'd never thought he would ever be saying these words again, ever be feeling these emotions again. But Tracy had brought him back from the dead and however unintentionally, made him see that he could love again.

"I love you, Tracy. I love your independence, your feistiness, I love the way you dig in and don't give up and I love the way you effortlessly give of yourself without expecting anything back in return. Whether you know it or not, you saved me," he told her. And then he realized what she probably thought he meant and he was quick to set her straight. "Not my career, me. I didn't think I could ever fall in love again. It's nice to be proven wrong."

He drew her closer, wrapping his arms around her. "Marry me, Tracy." He felt one of the boys tugging on his shirt. Looking down, he saw Gary.

"Marry us," the boy whispered loudly, as if to remind him that he wasn't alone in this.

"Marry us," Micah amended. "We promise you'll never regret it."

At this point, Greg and Gary were all but jumping up and down. "Yeah, marry us, Tracy. Please?" Gary proposed as soulfully as he could manage.

"Pleas-eeze?" Greg added his voice to the plea.

Tracy blocked the laugh that bubbled up in her throat. She didn't want to hurt the boys' feelings by having them think she was laughing at them. "How can I say no?"

"Then don't," Micah coaxed. "Say yes."

Her eyes were smiling as she said, "Yes."

Greg and Gary instantly cheered. As for their father, he wasn't cheering. But there was a reason for that. He was too busy kissing their new mom-to-be, and the boys were more than just okay with that.

* * * * *

"Where are you staying?" Nate asked.

Michelle frowned. "What do you mean? This is my home. I'm staying here."

"I have a contract that says you're not."

"You can't throw me out of my own house." Dread tightened like a fist in her gut.

"This badge says I can."

"Before we continue this argument, can you go feed your cat? The distressed cries are driving me crazy."

"What are you talking about? I don't have a cat."

She blinked in surprise. "Don't you hear that? It's been crying for the last five minutes."

He cocked his head as he listened. The plaintive wail came again, weaker now.

"That's not a cat." He moved to the front door, flung it open, and charged coatless into the blizzard. "It's a—"

The wind grabbed his last word and garbled it, but it sounded as if he'd said *baby*.

Dear Reader,

Every little girl dreams of being a princess. Fairytales foster the fantasies of life—peril, humour, love and happily-ever-after. It's my joy to bring you three stories based loosely on three fairytales. This is Sleeping Beauty's story.

This book is dedicated to my nieces, and I'll share a story about Ashley. When she was in high school she and three of her friends decided to dress up as princesses for Halloween. She chose Cinderella, and her mother helped her find a pretty blue dress that was full and swished when she moved. She put her blonde hair up in a bun and wore long white gloves. She looked as if she'd walked from the pages of the fairytale.

Sadly, she arrived on Halloween to find not one of her friends dressed up as promised. It could have been a disaster. Instead Cinderella became the belle of the ball. Everyone made a big deal of her all day long. And that evening, when she went trick or treating with her younger sisters, people praised her and asked if they could take her picture. That day she was a true princess.

Do you have a princess moment? I hope so.

Happy reading!

Teresa Carpenter

THE SHERIFF'S DOORSTEP BABY

BY
TERESA CARPENTER

First published in Great Britain 2012
by Mills & Boon, an imprint of Harlequin (UK) Limited,
Eton House, 18-24 Paradise Road, Richmond, Surrey TW9 1SR

ISBN: 978 0 263 89453 0
ebook ISBN: 978 1 408 97127 7

23-0812

Harlequin (UK) policy is to use papers that are natural, renewable and recyclable products and made from wood grown in sustainable forests. The logging and manufacturing processes conform to the legal environmental regulations of the country of origin.

Printed and bound in Spain
by Blackprint CPI, Barcelona

Teresa Carpenter believes in the power of unconditional love, and that there's no better place to find it than between the pages of a romance novel. Reading is a passion for Teresa—a passion that led to a calling. She began writing more than twenty years ago, and marks the sale of her first book as one of her happiest memories. Teresa gives back to her craft by volunteering her time to Romance Writers of America on a local and national level.

A fifth-generation Californian, she lives in San Diego, within miles of her extensive family, and knows that with their help she can accomplish anything. She takes particular joy and pride in her nieces and nephews, who are all bright, fit, shining stars of the future. If she's not at a family event you'll usually find her at home—reading, writing, or playing with her adopted Chihuahua Jefe.

For my nieces Amanda, Ashley, Sammy, Erika, Michelle, Gabrielle and Rachel.

You are everything a heroine should be: beautiful, smart, talented and loving.

I'm proud of you all.

PROLOGUE

"DADDY! Daddy! You're here."

"Mama! Hi! Over here."

Arms flung wide, ten-year-old Michelle Ross twirled in a wide circle, her long blond curls and wide pink skirt flowing out around her. She determinedly ignored the excited calls of her friends as their parents arrived to visit.

For the first time ever she felt beautiful.

She loved Princess Camp, even if her dad didn't come to parents' day. He said he would, but he promised lots of things that didn't happen. Duty first.

She begged and begged Daddy to be able to come. And of course, he said no. And continued to say no until Aunt Yvonne finally stepped in to plead Michelle's case. She had to behave all of June and July—which had been torture—but come August she'd been off to camp. And all that boring good behavior paid off.

She shared a cabin with Elle and Amanda. They instantly became BFFs and did everything together. And Michelle loved it all, even the etiquette classes. A princess needed to know how to conduct herself!

"Michelle, these are my parents." Dragging a dark-haired man by his hand, Elle proudly presented her father. "Daddy, Mama, Michelle is in my cabin. She's Beauty. I'm Belle and Amanda is Rapunzel. We're going to do a dance for the talent show. Sleeping Beauty had the gift of song, so Michelle's going to sing."

"Hello, Michelle." Elle's father greeted her and shook her hand. "What a lovely young woman you are. I can see why you're Beauty."

She giggled and dropped into a shallow curtsy. "It's so nice to meet you."

"What lovely manners," Elle's mother said with a kind smile.

"The pleasure is all ours." Her dad tugged on Elle's dark red ponytail. "I can't wait to see you girls dance. And to hear you sing, Michelle."

"The talent show isn't until after dinner," Elle advised him. "Come on. I want to show you my cabin, and the pool, and the gazebo."

He laughed indulgently. "We're coming, Elle. But what about your friend?"

"Oh. Michelle's waiting for her dad. Right?"

"Yes—" Michelle nodded and put hope into her voice "—he should be along anytime."

Elle's mom looked down the empty drive and frowned. "I don't like leaving you alone out here."

"I have to stay in the courtyard," Michelle reassured her. "I'll be fine."

"Elle, I think we should ask your friend to keep us company until her dad comes along."

"Yeah." Elle grabbed Michelle's hand, swung it back

and forth. “Come with us. Your dad can find us when he gets here.”

“Maybe.” Michelle bit her lip. She should wait for Daddy. She was excited to show her dad around camp, to tell him what she’d learned, and how much she loved her time here. More than anything she wanted him to hear her sing and to impress on him that she should come back next year. But the truth was he probably wouldn’t even show. He meant his promises when he made them, yet the need to protect and serve took first place every time.

But Elle’s daddy thought Michelle was pretty and she wanted to go with them.

“I guess I can look around with you until he gets here.”

“Yippee!” Elle smiled and together they skipped ahead.

They showed Elle’s parents the cabin and the pool. And when they headed back to the main cabin, The Castle, Michelle looked around hopefully and glanced toward the parking lot, but saw no sign of her dad.

She got ready for the talent show with Elle and Amanda and pretended not to be nervous as she checked the audience repeatedly for her father.

“Come on, Michelle.” Amanda grabbed her hand and tugged her away from the wings. “It’s our turn.”

Michelle frantically searched the crowd one last time but there was no denying the inevitable. Another promise broken. Daddy wouldn’t see her sing. She sighed her disappointment and followed her friends onstage.

CHAPTER ONE

HANDS braced on his hips, Sheriff Nate Connor stood looking down at the strange beauty sleeping on his couch. Rolled up in his fleece throw, purple-and-pink-striped socks peeked out from one end and sunshine-yellow hair cascaded from the other.

With a muffled curse he holstered the nine millimeter he'd palmed when he found his front door unlocked. Not that he'd really expected to need it, but a soldier was always prepared. Even in River Run, where the population was less than five thousand.

Luck and skill had kept him from shooting himself when he tripped over the guitar case negligently left in the entry hall.

He considered reaching for his handcuffs, but the woman wasn't a complete stranger. He'd seen sufficient pictures here in this house and on his predecessor's desk to recognize the pretty flow of hair. He was enough of a lawman to figure out she was his new landlord.

And they'd met briefly at her father's funeral seven months ago.

Yeah, he knew who sleeping beauty was. The question was why?

Why was she here and why did she think she could make herself at home on his couch?

He'd had his own plans for that couch. Today was supposed to have been his first day off in over a month. The storm changed that. An overnight delivery truck had skidded on ice and ended up on its side in the pass, blocking traffic in both directions. By the time they got it cleared up, they were in the middle of a full-blown blizzard, and he'd given up any hope of regaining his day off.

A surge of wind knocking branches against the house punctuated the thought.

After a ten-hour day, he'd planned to come home, heat up a frozen dinner and watch the game he'd recorded earlier.

Plans delayed by his uninvited guest's possession of said couch.

A soft snore came from the fleece-wrapped bundle. Nate's dark brows slammed together in a scowl. Now that was irritating. Not because the sound annoyed him, but because it didn't. It had been cute.

He had no room in his life for soft and cute, no patience for trespassing blondes interrupting the last of his day off.

In the past seven months he'd heard nothing from Michelle Ross. Now she slept tucked up on his couch. She may own the place but he had a contract stating it was his for the next four months. He didn't know what brought her to town, but she wasn't staying here.

A matter he meant to take up with her right now.

"Ms. Ross."

No response.

"Ms. Ross." Advancing on the couch, he repeated the demand for her attention, and then again, louder each time. She stirred and then settled against the cushions, sighing as she pulled the throw tighter around herself.

Finally he leaned down and shook her shoulder. "Come on, beauty, wake up."

She stirred and mumbled something.

Instinctively, he leaned closer to hear what she said.

But suddenly she turned and her lips brushed his. That's when her eyes opened. Lovely eyes that brought the green of spring to a late-winter's storm. And that thought distracted him long enough for her to wrap her arms around his neck and draw him down for a deeper kiss.

Questions of who and why and what disappeared in a rush of sensation. She felt warm and soft, and tasted oh, so sweet. This was what home should feel like, what a welcome should taste like.

Nate threaded his hands in all that hair and sank into the moment. After the day he'd had, he let the heat of the kiss sweep him away.

Michelle dreamed of a man on a white horse riding through the forest. Tall and strong, he carried a sword and sought a beautiful princess, ready to save her from all her woes. Michelle was both the princess and not. She liked the safety the knight represented, but it never came free and she wanted to save herself.

Only fools and optimists believed in love. Which left her out. She was nobody's fool. And she'd given up on optimism early in life. She preferred to control her own destiny than hope for the best.

Now the knight was on top of her, holding her gently, his hands fisted in her hair, broad shoulders blocking out the world. He smelled like the fleece that held her in warmth and comfort, of the woods and man. But he was heat and power and his lips were on hers and she didn't care if there was a price. Safe had never felt so good.

She arched into the kiss, opening her lips at the demand of his, welcoming him in, savoring the spicy taste of the man who held her so securely.

His hand moved in a sweeping caress from her head to her waist, where skin met skin. The shock of his cold fingers reached beyond Michelle's lethargy.

Her eyes flew open and she realized this was no dream, no Prince Charming of childish imaginings, but a flesh-and-blood man with a bold kiss and cold hands.

She broke off the kiss, planted both palms flat against his chest and pushed. "Back up, buddy!"

For a moment, just a heartbeat, he held the embrace, and then he released her and surged to his feet.

"Hell. I must be more tired than I thought." He scrubbed both hands over a face a shade too ordinary to be considered handsome. Straight dark eyebrows topped fierce gray eyes. Cut military-short, his hair was a tawny blend of brown, blond and red. Temper, or maybe it was passion, brought a ruddy hue to his cheeks.

The khaki uniform so like her father's had her narrowing her eyes on him as she swung her feet to the floor and sat up. Pain throbbed in her ankle, but she ignored it.

"Who are you and what are you doing in my house?" she demanded. "Besides accosting me?"

"You mean my home?" His hands went to his hips, and he met her glare for glare. "And you kissed me."

She raised brows at him. "A neat trick for someone asleep. I inherited this house from my father."

"And I rented it from him."

That surprised her. "He didn't tell me anything about renting the house. When did that happen?"

"Ben rented me a room when I first moved to town and I continued to rent the place when he moved in with his lady friend almost a year ago."

"Dad had a girlfriend?" She'd been dreaming of princesses and white knights, but clearly she'd fallen down the rabbit hole. As far as she knew, Dad had never had a lady friend.

"I remember you now, from my father's funeral." Usually great with names, she reached for his and came up short. The funeral had been hard for her. She took a stab. "Gabe?"

"Nate." He corrected. "Nate Connor."

"Well, Nate, it seems you took over Dad's job, and you took over his house."

His expression frosted over. "What are you implying?"

"Nothing nefarious." She waved off his paranoia. "I'm just saying this is my house."

She'd only come back to River Run to sell the house so she could move to Los Angeles and pursue her songwriting career.

She'd escaped this town when she graduated from

high school—couldn't leave the little burg fast enough—and nothing had changed since. With her dad's passing the small town had even less going for it now than it had when she was a kid.

So no, she hadn't crept through Dead Man's Pass praying to a deity she hadn't spoken to in way too long to be kicked out of her own home.

"It's your house, but it's rented to me. I have a contract if you'd like to see it." Nate crossed his arms over his chest, causing his biceps to pop. "You didn't talk to your dad much, did you?"

The truth she'd come to acknowledge since her dad's passing hit her hard. Hearing the censure from the current sheriff didn't help.

"You don't know anything about my relationship with my father." Anger had her pushing to her feet. The ankle she'd injured walking up the snow-covered path from the car to the front door protested at the sudden motion, at the sudden weight, and gave out on her.

He caught her before she could fall, putting those impressive biceps to work, his grip under her elbows easily holding her weight off the sore foot.

"Are you okay?" Exasperation sat alongside concern in the question.

"Fine." She attempted to shrug off his touch, but he held firm until she was seated once again. "I tripped on something on the way up the walk."

He frowned. "I'll check it out tomorrow. Do you need ice for your ankle?"

It irked to hear him playing host in her house. She

shook her head. "I'm fine. How long did you know my dad?"

"Three years," he said as he shrugged out of his jacket and hung it on the newel post.

She waited, hearing the cry of a kitten in the lull, but that was all he shared. Great. Her father had been the same all her life, bound by duty, determined to steal all the joy from her life. Now it seemed there'd been more to him than she remembered, but the bearer of the news was no more talkative than her father had been.

"Not very long," she challenged.

"Not compared to twenty-five years, no. But I talked to him, worked with him, spent time with him. You let a complete stranger make funeral arrangements."

Shame burned in her. That had been the lowest time in her life. A bad week capped off by the loss of her father. Yeah, she should have come home and taken care of the details of Dad's funeral, but she'd been trying to save her job, trying to hold together the fraying edges of her life.

In the end she'd only been delaying the inevitable.

"I thanked you for your help." She tried to find a smile and a little of her patented charm to ease the way with him. She'd learned early in life that a pretty girl had power, and she wielded the tool of her looks like any other talent.

But she was too weary, too annoyed with him and the crying of his cat, to bother. Or maybe she was too unsettled by the taste of him still in her mouth to summon a smile.

And what had that been about anyway? She was supposed to have kissed him in her sleep? Right.

So okay, she'd been kissing the knight in her dream. Coincidence. By no means did that translate into smooching a stranger in her sleep.

"Huh." He dismissed her claim of gratitude. "Where are you staying?"

She frowned. "What do you mean? This is my home, I'm staying here."

"I have a contract that says you're not."

"You can't throw me out of my own house." Dread tightened like a fist in her gut. She couldn't afford to pay for alternative accommodations.

"This badge says I can."

"Please." She gestured to her swollen foot. "I couldn't leave if I wanted. I can't drive."

He drew a set of keys from his pants pocket. "I can take you wherever you need to go."

Sleet blew against the window as the wind roared, a timely reminder of the harsh weather.

"I'm not leaving." Defiant, she crossed her arms over her chest and made a show of settling back into the couch. The tension from the long trip was back as she faced being expelled from her own home, the stress aggravated by the cries of distress from the kitten deep in the house.

"Oh, you are."

She shook her head, holding up a staying hand. "Before we continue this argument, can you go feed your cat? The distressful cries are driving me crazy."

"What are you talking about? I don't have a cat."

She blinked in surprise. "Well, then one is trying to get in. Don't you hear that? It's been crying for the last five minutes."

This should be interesting. Would the big bad sheriff help the stray or leave it to fend for itself in the storm he was so ready to toss her out into?

He cocked his head as he listened. The roaring wind covered the sound for a moment and then the plaintive wail came again, weaker now. Poor kitty.

"That's not a cat." Suddenly his expression changed, became harder—something she couldn't have imagined—and determined. Urgent now he moved to the front door, flung it open, and charged coatless into the blizzard. "It's a—"

The wind grabbed his last word and garbled it, but it sounded like he'd said *baby.* Unbelieving, she hobbled over to the door, righted her suitcase, which had fallen, and set it and her guitar case against the wall.

Using the door for support, she peered into the darkness and screamed when Nate loomed up in front of her. He carried a baby seat. The howling she'd mistaken for a cat's yowls had turned to faint whimpers.

"My God. Hurry," she urged him. "A baby! What if I hadn't heard him crying?" She slowly followed Nate to the couch, where he set the carrier down. "Poor thing, he's shivering. And look how red his skin is."

"Hypothermia. Get him out of the seat and his clothes," Nate ordered. "Put him inside your shirt and wrap up in the fleece. Don't rub his skin. I'll get the fire going."

Michelle sat down and pulled a damp blue blanket

away to get at the straps holding the baby in the seat. Quiet now, eyes closed, the infant shook so hard the seat moved. A dingy white cap covered the child's head, but he wore no socks and his thin outfit offered little protection against the elements, including his own blanket.

Next she unbuttoned her pink-and-purple plaid flannel shirt and pulled her T-shirt from her jeans. Her heart broke as she lifted the tiny body, quickly stripped him down to his diaper and then cuddled him to her chest under her shirt. Teeth chattering at the chill he brought with him, she wrapped them both in the warm fleece blanket.

"His hands and feet are freezing cold," she reported, happy to see the fire going. Already the room felt warmer. "How could anyone leave a baby out in a storm like that? It's inhumane."

"Yes, it is." Ice dripped from the words as Nate came to stand over her. "It's neglect and child endangerment. I hope you have a good lawyer."

CHAPTER TWO

"THAT's not funny." Glaring up into the sheriff's cold gray eyes, Michelle carefully shifted the baby so his nose wasn't pressed into her.

"It's not meant to be." He tapped his badge. "I don't joke about the law."

"And I don't abandon defenseless babies."

"No, you just break into houses."

"It's my house," she reminded him through gritted teeth. "So there's no reason I wouldn't have brought the baby inside."

"You knew it was a boy," he said, arms braced across his broad chest.

"A guess from the blue blanket. And it hasn't been substantiated yet. You called him a boy, too."

"He arrived at the same time you did."

"You don't know what time I got here." She narrowed her eyes at him. "Seems to me he arrived at the same time you did."

How dare he accuse her of such an atrocious act? She fully admitted she looked out for number one. You had to put yourself first when no one else did. But she had a soft spot for kids, got along with them better than a lot of adults.

She narrowed her eyes at him. "And as you're so quick to claim, it's your doorstep." She made a point of pulling open the neck of her shirt and looking from the baby to the man. "I think he has your eyes."

His frown turned ferocious. "That's not my kid."

"Are you sure?" she persisted just to aggravate him. "He looks about three or four months old. Think back about a year, something will come to you."

"There is no possibility the child is mine."

"How can you be so sure? A lot of men have vague memories when it comes to things like this."

"I know."

"Oh, right." She rolled her eyes at his arrogance. *"You know."*

"I haven't been with a woman since I moved to River Run." Acknowledgment of what he'd revealed came sharp on the heels of his outburst. "Ah, hell."

"Why?" The word burst from her. Shocked, she ran her gaze over him. "You're not bad-looking and your body is smoking hot."

"I have my reasons, which are none of your business." The grimness of his tone warned her the topic was closed.

"Okay." She valued her own privacy too much to disrespect other people's rights to the same. "We've established he's not mine and not yours, so who is he? Was the seat all that was with him? Was there a diaper bag? Maybe there's a note."

"I'll check." Happy for action, he headed for the door.

While he was gone she went through the seat. She found a pacifier and a soggy piece of paper. She was trying to shake it open when Nate returned with a diaper bag.

"What's that?" he demanded.

"It was in the seat." She handed the paper to him. "I think it's the note we're looking for."

Sitting beside her, he carefully unfolded the paper and spread the note. He took up a good portion of the couch and Michelle would have moved away from the large bulk of him, but she wanted to see the note.

Plus he was warm. And he smelled good.

So instead of sensibly moving away, she scooted closer and peered over his large arm. Pretending not to notice his big hands and the thick width of his wrist, she read the note.

Nate,

This is your cosin Jack. I never wanted a kid. Im too old and I cant take care of him and work. I gotta work to stay outta the joint. Jack talked good about you. He was good to me so Im giving his kid to you. If you don't want him giv him to some body to giv him a good home.

"Well, I'm off the hook. Too bad for you," Michelle muttered. The letter offended her. She knew desperation, knew self-absorption, and she could never abandon a child. She suddenly had new respect for her father, who'd at least accepted the responsibility of raising her.

"Joint?" she sneered.

"She means jail."

"I know what joint means. She's barely literate, but that's no excuse for abandoning her baby. How could she give her son away? What about your cousin Jack? Where is he?"

"Dead."

Oh, man. "I'm sorry. What happened?"

"He was killed in a bar fight five months ago."

"Oh."

"Don't say it like that." The eyes he turned on her were grieving. "Like he was a lowlife drunk. Jack was a nice guy, but he was troubled. He should never have followed me into the service. Some men aren't meant to be killers. A stint on the front line messed him up good, and then they sent him home. But the damage was done. He began drinking, had a hard time keeping a job."

Nate rubbed a hand over the back of his neck. "He was excited about the baby. Becoming a father was the first thing he cared about in a long time. And then he was gone. He didn't even get to see his son."

"I'm sorry," she said again, with more feeling this time. It was a sad story. She looked down at the lump of the baby under her shirt and thought he had a hard time ahead of him. She didn't remember her mother, she'd died when Michelle was two, but she had been loved, coddled during those first formative years. Little Jack didn't even have that.

When she looked up, she found the sheriff watching her.

"You need to call Child Services."

"Why?"

Her eyebrows lifted, giving away her surprise. "So they can come get Jack, of course."

He shook his head. "They'd only try to locate his next of kin, and that's me, so there's no need to call them."

"But you aren't equipped to take care of him."

"No," he said grimly, "but it looks like I have little choice."

"So what does that mean? What are you going to do?"

He shrugged. "Raise him."

She blinked at him. "Just like that?"

"Yeah."

"Wow." What did it say about him that he hadn't even hesitated? That he was honorable? Responsible? Both fit with him being a sheriff. "You're not even going to think about it?"

"My uncle took me in, taught me what it meant to be a man. Jack was like a brother to me. Of course I'm going to take care of his kid."

"That's huge. There aren't many men I know who would just take a baby in like that."

"Then they aren't men."

That was a pretty tough stance. But after a moment's thought, Michelle nodded. He was right. One thing she could say about her dad, he'd never tried to give her away.

"Do you have to start tonight? Couldn't you call Child Services to take him until you move into your new place and get all the gear you'll need?" How could she work on the house with a baby around? They required care and feeding, and quiet.

His hands went to his hips and he shook his head, his expression forbidding.

"Ms. Ross, if anyone is leaving tonight, it's you. As it is, you'll be leaving first thing in the morning. Because this is my place for the next four months."

"But I need to sell the house. And I need to make improvements."

"Not my problem."

"But it's my house."

"And I have a lease. We've been over this."

"But—"

He held up a hand. "There are rental laws. Read them. Then we'll talk."

Michelle wanted to bite the offending hand. Arrogant jerk. It wasn't her fault her father rented the place without letting her know. She had the right to move on with her life and selling this house was a big part of that.

But she was smart enough to know pressing the issue wouldn't gain her any points, so she retreated.

She nodded at the note. "What about the mother? She didn't sign the note. Do you know her?"

"I met her. Wasn't impressed." The very flatness of his tone spoke volumes. "She has a criminal record so she won't get another chance to hurt Jack."

"Understand I have no sympathy for the woman, but it's possible she knocked. We were arguing and the storm is loud."

"Then she should have knocked harder—" there was no give in his response "—waited for me to open the door and talked to me."

"You might have said no."

"That's no excuse."

"No, but it's a possibility she wasn't willing to risk. Wait..." Michelle suddenly noticed something was different. "He's stopped shivering. I heard that's bad."

"Maybe not." His calm response took the edge off her panic. "If he were still in the cold, yes. But he's been warming up. The need to shiver is gone. Is he still breathing?"

She froze, worried for a moment he'd stopped, but she felt the soft heat of his breath against her chest.

"Yeah." She glanced down at her misshaped T-shirt. "I'd feel better if I could see him."

Nate stepped over, grabbed the neck of her undershirt in both hands and effortlessly tore an eight-inch rip down the front. Michelle gasped, shocked by his outrageous action.

"Hey!" she protested, glowering at him.

"You said you wanted to see the baby. Now you can."

Yeah, and the swell of her breasts and the pink lace of her bra. She pulled her flannel shirt closed over herself and the baby.

"I thought the point was to keep the baby warm."

"Right. And skin-to-skin is the best way. Warm fluids would be good, too."

She nodded toward the diaper bag. "There's probably stuff to make a bottle in there. Do you think you can handle it or should we trade places?"

"If I'm going to raise him, I may as well learn how to feed him now." He grabbed a bottle and a tin of formula from the diaper bag and headed for the kitchen.

Michelle frowned after him. Most people would

probably find that admirable. She just found it annoying. It was just as much a fault to have to do everything yourself as to want everyone else to do it for you.

Then again she may just be reacting to her disappointment in not getting to see the baby pressed to Nate's bare chest.

She imagined it would be a pretty impressive sight.

Thinking about it, she decided, no, her annoyance had nothing to do with being denied an erotic peek and everything to do with Sheriff Nate Connor being an arrogant pain in the butt.

In the kitchen Nate leaned against the counter and curled his shaking hands into fists.

How righteous he sounded when he told her he'd be raising Jack. Little did she know the internal fight he went through.

What did he know about raising a kid? Nothing. Sure his uncle had taken him in, but he'd been a stupid teenager and Uncle Stan already had a kid, so taking on Nate had been nothing new. And the Lord knew Nate was already messed up so there was little Uncle Stan could do to damage him.

Not so with Jack. He was an infant with his whole life spread out before him. The damage Nate could do encompassed everything from the baby's health to his spiritual upraising. Nate groaned. Hell, he couldn't remember the last time he went to church, the last time he'd done more than take the Lord's name in vain.

New rule—no cursing.

Because he was a father now, no matter how freaked

the notion made him. Because he was no coward and no quitter. He owed Uncle Stan and Jack, so Nate reached for the can of formula and began to read.

He would learn and he would adjust. And he and baby Jack would be just fine.

The baby stirred against Michelle and she looked down into frowning gray eyes. Jack was awake.

"Hey, little guy, how are you doing?" She smiled in relief and to assure him she was a friend. His color had improved and she cuddled him close and rubbed a finger over the downy softness of wispy wheat-colored hair. "Are you feeling better?"

He blinked at her, which she took as a yes.

"Bad news, buddy, your mom, the lowlife witch—" Michelle's sweet tone never changed as she dealt the insult "—dropped you on Cousin Nate's doorstep in the middle of the biggest storm of the season."

He stared at her with sober eyes, taking in every word she spoke.

"Hopefully, your daddy was smarter than your mommy." She nodded at the alertness in his gaze. "The good news is your cousin Nate says he's going to raise you." Chewing the inside of her cheek, she sighed. "Actually, I'm not going to lie to you. It's a good news-bad news thing. He'll be a rock for you, but he'll have impossible expectations. At least that's how it was with my dad."

His little face crumpled and he began to whimper.

"Oh, shoot." Michelle gently bounced Jack, trying to

calm him. "No, baby, don't cry. Shh. Maybe I'm wrong. Maybe Nate is different."

"Different from what?" a deep voice demanded.

Flinching internally, she carefully controlled her expression when she met Nate's challenging gaze.

"I was warning him how difficult it can be to live with a sheriff."

He lifted one dark brow, silent reproach in the gesture. "Thanks for undermining me before I've even met the kid."

"The truth is the truth."

"Being sheriff is what I do." He handed her the full bottle. "It's not who I am."

"I was raised by a lawman." The warm bottle felt good in her hand. She checked the temperature of the formula on her wrist. Perfect, of course. She fed it to Jack, who latched onto the nipple and sucked, his little hands coming up to rest on the bottle. "I know what wearing that uniform means. Long hours, community service, duty first. Family a far and distant second."

"You don't know anything about me. I won't be judged by the actions of another."

"Fine. Prove me wrong."

"I would." Nate settled into the corner of the couch. "But you won't be around to see. You just want to sell this house and head back to the city."

He was right. And she wouldn't apologize for wanting to move forward with her life. "I'm not going back to San Francisco. I'm moving to Los Angeles."

"Really?" He lifted one dark brow. "Following some guy south?"

She snorted. As if she'd move across town for some guy. "My agent thinks it'll be better for my songwriting career. And now who's judging?"

"I'm just calling it as I see it."

"There's nothing in this town for me anymore."

"You've never believed there was anything here for you," he said.

Michelle glanced up from the sweet baby to study the stoic sheriff. How did he know her so well when they'd only met briefly at the funeral before today? She didn't think Dad had been the type to talk about his absent daughter. Maybe she'd been wrong about that.

"You were wrong then and you're wrong now."

"Wrong?" Could he read minds now?

"About what the town has to offer."

"I don't have anything in common with the people here. I want more."

"More what?"

The same question her dad had always had for her. She didn't know! She just knew this town lacked what she needed.

"More everything. More music, more options, more money, more entertainment, more men, more people who want more."

And Dad had never understood, never accepted how important music was to her, that songwriting wasn't just a dream but what drove her.

"Shallow. I guess you're right after all. River Run has character, people with heart and integrity who care about their neighbors, where life is more important than entertainment and meeting strangers in the street."

No surprise, Sheriff Nate Connor didn't understand, either. Why that hurt she couldn't say.

She ran the back of her finger over baby Jack's powder-soft cheek, wishing him a better life in River Run than she'd had. "He's asleep again."

"Good. Hypothermia is hard on the system."

"Is the storm going to get better or worse tomorrow?"

"Why? You have somewhere you gotta be?" he mocked her.

"Just answer the question."

"Worse. This was only supposed to be a light snow flurry, but a massive cold front pushed down from Alaska causing blizzard conditions. It's supposed to get worse before it gets better. We've battened down the town and advised people to stay inside except for emergencies."

Nodding, she tucked the fleece-wrapped baby in the crook of the couch and set his bottle on the oak coffee table.

"Then I should get at least one of my other suitcases tonight." She reached for her shoes.

Nate didn't move. "You're not going out in the storm. Didn't you hear me say I advised the townspeople to stay inside?"

"This is an emergency."

"You're safe and sound inside a warm house. There's food and water, and a flushing toilet. How is this an emergency?"

His long-suffering expression made her grit her teeth. "I need clothes. I have a change of underwear in my overnight case, but not clothes." She tugged at her ripped T-shirt. "And the ones I have on came into contact with a Neanderthal."

"You can borrow something of mine." He shrugged off her sarcasm. "Nobody is going back out into the storm."

Shooting daggers at him, because she'd hoped he'd offer to get the cases for her, she made her way around the table to the middle of the room. Her ankle throbbed but held her weight.

"Ten minutes ago you were ready to send me on my way."

"That was before I'd been back outside. The storm has worsened."

"All the more reason to go now. I'm going to get my suitcase and you can't stop me."

He laughed. And pushed to his feet with a lithe grace that spoke of muscle and discipline and the easy strength to make her do anything he wanted her to.

Aggravating man.

"You don't scare me." Still she couldn't prevent taking an instinctive step back. And immediately felt her ankle turn. Pain streaked through her foot and she started to fall.

She screamed.

The baby cried.

And the lights went out.

CHAPTER THREE

"I'VE got you." Nate caught a bundle of soft female curves in his arms. She smelled of something fruity, clean and tart…and good enough to eat.

Too bad she was prickly as a porcupine. Because it looked as if he was stuck with her for a couple of days.

"I'm fine." She twisted against him, seeking release. "You've made your point. I'm not going outside."

"Stay still." He shifted his hold from her arms to her waist, practically spanning the narrow width with his hands. She was tinier than he'd thought. "You're going to hurt yourself worse than you already have."

"The baby is crying."

"We'll get to Jack in a minute." For some reason Nate couldn't let Michelle go. She'd untucked her shirt when she stuck the baby under the hem and the thumb of his right hand rested on the silky warmth of her skin. It wasn't personal, he assured himself. It wasn't Michelle he wanted.

It just felt so good to hold a woman in his arms.

But he had enough common sense to know the landlord who wanted to sell his house out from under him was not the place to kick-start his libido.

He had no choice but to let her stay for a couple of days, but after that she'd be gone. Either to a place in town or preferably back to the city to stay until his lease ended and she could return to do her thing without his bumping into her.

She stopped struggling, going totally still. The lights were out but the fire gave off enough light for him to realize the dark shook her.

He could handle a woman's tears. When your mother cried at the drop of a hat, you learned to cope or became an emotional wreck yourself. Still the long day—days—and the baby must have him off his game, because he really didn't want to see the tears sparkling in Michelle's emerald-bright eyes fall. Already he knew enough about her to know she'd hate putting on a tearful display for him.

"What's wrong, Michelle? Are you afraid of the dark?"

Anger instantly sparked, wiping the distress from her face, replacing it with haughty distain.

"Of course not." Her chin lifted and instead of pulling away from him she stepped forward until her pink flannel shirt brushed against the khaki of his uniform. "I'm at my best in the dark."

His body reacted with a rush. Holy sh— Moly.

Ding! Ding! Ding! Round one to Michelle.

A warrior knew the advantages of a timely retreat. He quickly released her and took two steps back, narrowly missing the coffee table and a fall of his own.

She flipped her hair and flashed him a glance of triumph as she moved to pick up the baby and coo at him.

Not a tear in sight, and she seemed to have forgotten her missing suitcases.

Mission accomplished. So it hadn't been a total defeat.

"Good. Then keep an eye on Jack. I'm going to go get some flashlights and candles. Plus I have to make some calls. I may be a few minutes."

"Okay." But she couldn't prevent a flinch of uncertainty.

"Don't let the fire go out."

"Don't worry."

"I'll be as fast as I can and we'll get some light in here."

"Thanks. I think the dark upsets Jack."

Nate stared down at Jack held snuggly in her arms and an unexpected rush of emotion swelled up in him. The baby had Nate's uncle's eyes, the resemblance especially strong with Jack scowling like he was doing now.

How Nate had loved that old man.

Funny, he'd always thought of Uncle Stan as old, but hell, at forty-two his uncle had only been ten years older than Nate was now when he took in a wild fourteen-year-old.

He'd been in a bad place but Uncle Stan took no guff from him. There'd been no bluff in the man, but he'd cared. He'd been as free with his affections as he'd been with his disciplines. Nate had needed both.

He'd learned how a real man acted.

How proud Uncle Stan would be of baby Jack. Though it hurt Nate to admit it, he was glad his uncle hadn't seen Jack Sr.'s spiral into drunken obscureness.

He wouldn't have blamed Nate—Stan believed a man was responsible for his own choices—but it would have killed him to see Jack's pain, and the weakness that took him over.

The baby, the continuance of the Connor family, would have thrilled Uncle Stan. Michelle was surprised by Nate's willingness to take the baby on, but Nate owed Uncle Stan and Jack too much, loved them too much, to shame them by turning away baby Jack.

Which meant for the time being he needed Michelle. At least for tonight; beyond that, he'd see.

"Right." He mocked her claim that Jack was the one afraid of the dark.

She hit him with a scorching glare, but all she said, was "Food would be good, too."

Her bravado and the underlying vulnerability got to him. He called himself a chump but once he'd gathered the flashlights, candles and a battery lantern he returned to the living room.

He lit candles and placed them on the mantel, handed her a flashlight and set the blazing lantern on the coffee table. But it was her smile that lit up the room.

"Double chump," he muttered as he escaped to the kitchen. The phones were out, too, so he used his cell to call the county supervisor's office to get the status of the utilities. He learned the storm had taken out several major hubs. And then the line went dead as his phone beeped and informed him he was out of service.

"Great."

The need to fix the problems pressed at him, but there was literally nothing he could do except prepare for the cold night ahead. The loss of electricity meant they'd have no working heater.

He grabbed a box from the utility room and piled in his stash from the refrigerator and cupboard, tossed in utensils and topped it with plates, mugs, a pan and napkins. Next he used the flashlight he'd kept to find two sleeping bags in the attached garage.

Why he bothered to go to so much trouble for a woman so self-absorbed she rarely contacted the father who obviously adored her, Nate didn't know. And sure she was watching the baby, but she hadn't even offered to help. No doubt she expected to be waited on hand and foot. Well, that wouldn't wash here. He expected people to pull their own weight and since her temporary stay was on his dime, she'd just have to meet his expectations.

He frowned, remembering what he'd overheard her telling Jack. That kids of sheriffs had to live with high expectations and little freedom. It made him recall the early days with his uncle Stan. That's exactly how he'd felt. The restrictions had chafed badly, but it had also felt good to know someone cared about where he was and what he was doing. To have someone who checked up on him and made sure he had something to eat.

It took two trips to get everything to the living room and Michelle was sitting on the hearth pawing through the food box when he came back with the sleeping bags.

"Big boy, you are my hero." The sultry look of anticipation on her face made him wish she were gazing at him instead of the stew she was transferring from plastic container to cast-iron pot. "I'm starved, and this smells really good."

When she put her finger in her mouth to clean off a smudge of gravy, he had to disguise a groan with a cough.

That brought her attention up from the food.

"You're not catching a cold, are you?"

Was that real concern in her voice?

"Because you're a parent now, you have to take better care of yourself."

Nate rolled his eyes. He should have known better.

"Thanks for your concern." The sarcasm slid off his tongue before he could rein it in. Damn, now he'd have to put up with the sulks for an hour while she pouted around. He moderated his tone. "But I'm fine."

Unoffended, she flashed him a dimpled grin. "I'm just saying. No more wandering around in the cold without a jacket."

Surprised by her easy response, Nate felt some of the tension in his shoulders lessen. Maybe the woman had a few redeeming qualities.

"Yes, Mother."

"Oh." Her green eyes widened and then narrowed dangerously. "You didn't go there."

He had. And her huff made him add, "You want a cap and slippers to go with that advice?"

"You're going to pay for that, buster." She promised retribution. "Now you get to play chef."

She pushed the heavy pot into the flames of the fire. And to punctuate her point she stood, dusted off her curvy butt and hobbled back to the couch, where she claimed her seat in the corner. Arms crossed over her chest plumped up her breasts, pushing pink lace and considerable cleavage into view.

"I like it steaming hot," she said with a slow lick of her lips.

Oh, devious, devious woman. The wanton knew exactly how to make a man pay. And it had nothing to do with cooking supper.

Determined to keep his composure, he put his back to the tempting sight of the contrary female.

"You're fickle, Ms. Ross. First I'm your hero, then I'm a sorry fellow tasked with heating your stew."

He glanced over his shoulder, taking in the cozy scene backlit by the encompassing darkness. Baby sleeping, a tiny blanket-wrapped bundle; smug woman, pretty in pink flannel. As she caught his gaze, she flipped her hair in a gesture no doubt learned in the cradle. The long tresses looked like flowing gold in the firelight.

"Cooked steaming hot," he emphasized.

She lifted a brow. "I wasn't talking about the stew."

Michelle bit back a laugh. She swore the man almost swallowed his tongue.

Served him right. Calling her *mother.* The nerve.

Stew was good, though. As if on cue, her stomach growled. Not loud enough to be heard, thank goodness, but a definite reminder it had been close to nine hours since she last ate.

"But it'll do for now," she purred, taking satisfaction in seeing his shoulders brace as if ready for a fight. Better prepare, big boy, she was here to fight for her inheritance, and she wouldn't let a massive he-man stand in her way.

Flirting came as natural to her as breathing. And if a little harmless seduction threw him off his stride, good. It might get her what she wanted and no way would she fall for River Run's newest lawman.

"You'll mind your manners if you want a serving," he calmly responded.

Ah. A challenge.

"You'd really deny an injured woman a simple meal?" she chastised in a wounded voice, soft and just a little accusatory.

He just shook his head without turning and dished up two bowls of the savory stew. Then he opened a foil-wrapped loaf of bread and cut two big slices, putting one in each of the bowls. Walking over, he handed one of the bowls to her.

"Thank you." She reached eagerly for the meal, too hungry to pretend otherwise. The first bite tasted divine and she moaned in pleasure. "Excellent. Did you make this?"

"No," he said from the brown corduroy recliner next to her. "A friend cooked it for me." He eyed her over his steaming bowl. "You're going to be trouble."

It wasn't a question, but she nodded. She didn't usually reveal her weaknesses, especially to strong competitors, but weariness and desperation drove her to the point of honesty.

"I need to stay here," she said bravely.

"And if I say no?"

She chewed carefully, the yummy stew suddenly sitting heavy in her stomach. "You can't."

"We both know I should."

"I don't know that," she denied. "I think we can help each other out here."

That stopped him midbite. He lifted one dark eyebrow. "How's that?"

"I need a place to stay." She choked out the words, then cleared her throat and put determination in the rest. "And you need help with little Jack."

"Hmm. Seems I could hire someone who won't cause trouble to do that."

"But you don't have to pay me." Hmm. "Much."

He laughed. A hearty, rusty-sounding bark that came from deep inside him and startled the baby awake.

Michelle immediately reached for the baby, her first instinct to soothe and settle him, and then her healthy sense of self-preservation kicked in. So instead she cooed to little Jack on her way to handing him to Nate.

Let him see what he'd be dealing with without in-house assistance.

"Here you go." She held the crying child out to Nate.

"Humph." He set his bowl on the coffee table and took the squalling baby into his arms.

The trick worked because the baby continued to cry no matter what Nate did to soothe him. Then she felt bad because Jack refused to be mollified. Nate patted him, talked to him, put him over his shoulder and held him in his lap. Actually he was very good with the baby, holding him well and confidently.

But nothing made Jack happy.

Once she finished eating she set her dishes aside and took him so Nate could finish his meal.

She thought she'd be able calm the child, even hummed a little song for him, which seemed to be working and then it wasn't. Instead he worked himself into a full screaming fit. So much for her plan. And her ego.

"I changed his diaper," she said even as she checked him again to make sure he was still dry. "And he just had a bottle. I don't know why he's so upset."

"Maybe he's still hungry," Nate offered. "Do you think he'd like some stew?"

"He's too small to eat that. Or any solids. How old did you say he was?"

"Four months."

Did that mean Jack could have food? She wasn't sure. "I don't know. I had a coworker with a new baby. I think she started feeding her little girl about this age. But if so, it was only soft cereal or pureed fruits and vegetables."

"Yeah, well, we don't have any of that. I'm going to give him a little of the broth."

Michelle hesitated, still unsure, but the frantic crying wore at her nerves. At this point she was willing to give it a try. She gratefully released the baby into Nate's care.

"Be careful," she urged him. "Make sure you don't get any chunks of food. And don't give him too much. It's rich and his system won't be used to it."

"Let's see if he even likes it." Nate dipped the tip of his spoon in the thick broth and brought it to the shrieking baby's mouth, touching the tiny tongue with a small taste. For a moment there was no change, but Nate tried it again. This time the crying stuttered as Jack worked his tongue against his lips, but his little body still shuddered with the force of his sobs.

"That's promising." Nate fed him another small sip.

"Not too fast," she cautioned as blessed silence surrounded them.

"He likes it."

"I'm sure he does. It's got more flavor than anything else he's ever eaten."

"It shut him up." Nate sent her a superior look as he continued to feed the baby. "You can't argue with the results."

"I can if he gets sick later," she shot back. "I think that's enough."

"Okay. One more." He talked to the baby, explained this was the last bite, but he could have another bottle later. And Nate continued to talk to Jack after he lifted him to his shoulder, telling him about the storm and how Jack had to do his part to help them all have a good night under the trying circumstances.

He talked until Jack fell asleep.

"Good job." She applauded. "Hopefully he's out for a while."

"I guess it's too much to hope he's out for the night?"

"Afraid so. Speaking of which, who gets him for the night? Are you ready to agree to my terms?"

He sighed, the baby lifting and falling with the movement of his broad chest. "Trouble with a capital *T*."

She grinned at the resignation in his voice. "Just saying. Life will be so much easier with me around."

"Huk."

What kind of noise was that?

"You okay?" She couldn't tell if he was choking or trying not to laugh. Maybe a little of both?

He reprimanded her with the flash of diamond-sharp eyes as he fought to get himself under control.

"Witch. Lucky for me I don't need to make a decision tonight." He nodded at a couple of sleeping bags she hadn't noticed before. "We'll be sleeping together down here next to the fire."

CHAPTER FOUR

MICHELLE'S spine snapped straight. "What do you mean sleep together? Why do we have to sleep down here?"

"The heater is electric," Nate stated calmly. "That means there's no heat upstairs."

"Surely we'd be warm enough under our blankets? I don't remember sleeping down here as a kid."

"Your dad told me he changed from gas to electric some years ago. Probably felt it was safer." He stood and set the baby in the seat. "But if you want to try finding enough blankets to huddle under, be my guest. Jack and I are sleeping down here next to the fire."

As if he cared less what she chose to do, he gathered the dirty dishes and pot of stew and carried it all into the kitchen.

Obviously no help would be coming from that direction. Michelle bit her lip and eyed the distance to the stairs. The twelve feet seemed daunting enough considering her foot had given out when she'd barely passed the coffee table before the lights went out. Add in the stairs and the walk down the hall while carrying her overnight bag and gathering extra blankets along the way, and she saw the impossibility of the challenge.

"I'll sleep on the couch," she announced when Nate returned to the room.

"Suit yourself." He offered no argument. But he stood and surveyed her with his hands braced on his hips. "It'll be a little lumpy once I remove the mattress from the Hide-A-Bed, but you can keep the cushions."

Though it seemed an obvious question, she didn't ask why he didn't just pull out the Hide-A-Bed and use it as is. He'd already stated his intent to be close to the fire.

Plus she didn't want to share a bed with Nate Connor. He was too big, too gruff, too dominating to share such a small space with. There'd be no getting away from him.

She could still feel the imprint of his body on hers, remember the taste of him on her tongue. The memories made sharing a bed with him too tempting and way too dangerous.

Nope, not going there. The couch made total sense. She wouldn't have to walk up the stairs. She'd be near the fire. And she'd have the necessary distance from the sexy but aggravating sheriff.

Her game plan set, she glanced up to see Nate zipping the two sleeping bags together.

"Hey, I need one of those over here."

"Nope," he said without looking up. "I'm too big to share one sleeping bag with the baby."

Measuring the width of his shoulders, she really couldn't argue with the statement. "Then he can sleep with me."

"Nope." He finished with the bags and draped them over the back of the chair. Next he picked up the heavy coffee table and easily moved it across the room, opening up the space in front of the fire. Then he turned toward the couch. "I'm going to need you to move."

"Why not?" She held out a hand, silently asking for assistance in rising.

"Because you're going to get cold and end up down on the mattress with us." He grasped her hand and pulled her to her feet.

She practically flew off the couch, ending up way too close to him. She looked into his eyes, pretended to be unaffected by the show of strength. The man was solid as a rock and warm as sun-baked stone.

"That seems easy to predict since you won't give me a sleeping bag." Making no attempt to move out of his way, she lazily twirled a strand of hair around her finger. "I'm disappointed in you, Nate. Trying to maneuver me into sleeping with you on our first date."

A ferocious scowl crashed over his brow, making him look like an angry lion.

"Woman, are you crazy? We're snowed in. We are not, nor will we ever be, dating."

"Really?" she challenged in a totally reasonable tone. "I cooked for you. You revealed your sexual history. And we necked on the couch. Sounds like a date to me."

His glower intensified through her recitation. "You *are* insane."

"Maybe." She shrugged, pleased at riling him. "But I'm not easy. You're going to have to work harder than that to get me between the sleeping bags."

He cringed.

Not a great reaction for her ego, but she didn't let it

show. And it had been a bad pun. "Can you at least find me some blankets?"

He wanted to say no, his reluctance was written all over him. But he picked up a flashlight and turned for the stairs. The noise announcing his annoyance would have been a huff coming from a woman, but it was too low and rough to be considered anything other than a growl.

Rather than take the chance that his temper would have him tossing the cushions beyond her reach, she removed them and set them beside the couch. She tried to pull out the bed but couldn't get good purchase with her bad foot.

Jack stirred so she lifted him, sat and hummed softly until he settled into sleep again.

Nate returned with a large navy blue comforter and a couple of pillows. He dropped everything on the far side of the room and came to stand over her.

"How's he doing?" For all their differences, Jack represented neutral ground.

"He's restless," she said quietly, hoping not to disturb the sleeping baby. "I'm sure he misses his mom."

"He's going to have to get over that." Nate's tone was grim.

"So you don't think she'll be back? She may not be much of a mother, but she's all he's ever known."

"If she has any smarts at all, she better not show up here. If I see her again, I'll press charges for child endangerment. Which reminds me, I need you to write out a statement."

Michelle shrank from the idea. It spoke of an involvement she preferred to stay away from. But Jack's welfare demanded she do the right thing.

"Can it wait until the morning? I'm wiped."

He gave one short nod. "I guess. Let's get these beds put together."

He made short work of it, easily pulling out the Hide-A-Bed and stripping off the mattress then folding it back up and putting the cushions back in place.

Considering his grouchiness she watched in wonder as he brought over the comforter, draped it in half over the couch and tossed a pillow on the end away from the fire. Next he placed the mattress vertically in front of the fire and spread out the doubled-up sleeping bags.

When the beds were done, he came for Jack.

"I'm sure you remember where the bathroom is," he mentioned as he rose from placing the baby between the sleeping bags.

She nodded but lost track of the comment when he stripped off his shirt, giving her the view she'd missed earlier. She'd been right—he was ripped. *Impressive* was too mild a word for how fine he looked.

She was so distracted she failed to notice his hands move toward his belt buckle.

"Weren't you headed to the bathroom?" he demanded.

"What?" She took in his stance and grinned. "Don't mind me. I'm not shy," she assured him. "But since you appear to be, I'll respect your sensibilities."

Picking up her suitcase, she limped toward the hall. A sigh sounded behind her, and then a large hand took the case from her and Nate disappeared down the hall, his broad shoulders shadowed against the light he carried. He turned through a door and the light dimmed.

Her hero yet again. How could she have forgotten a light?

The man had such a protective streak she was no longer surprised he'd taken on Jack so easily. He returned so quickly she had no time to step out of his way. Suddenly she found herself pressed up against all that gorgeous skin.

Oh, my. Warm and hard, he felt so good she wanted to melt into all that masculine heat. He must have taken time somewhere along the line to wash up because he smelled yummy. She recognized the smell of his soap from the throw she'd been wrapped up in earlier. It was even better on his heated skin.

"Mmm. You do smell good." She restrained the urge to lick the hard pecs in front of her. Instead she lifted her gaze to his. "Almost good enough to make me forget my vow to never get involved with a man in law enforcement."

"You tempt me, Ms. Ross." Long-fingered hands wrapped around her waist and lifted her into the air. He turned so they traded places, and then he let her feet touch the ground. But rather than release her, he bent over her, his lips just an inch away from hers. His minty breath was an enticing invitation that whispered over her skin. She was about to meet him halfway, when he shifted his head to speak in her ear. "But it's best if we don't complicate this relationship more than necessary."

"Complicated doesn't scare me," she bluffed.

Okay, that felt a little too real. Maybe she needed to dial it back a bit.

Why encourage him when she agreed with his decree? Starting something with anyone in River Run smacked of stupidity. Starting something with the sheriff would be a mistake of major proportions.

He lifted a dark brow as he straightened. "That's because you don't stick around for the complications."

"Ouch!" She flinched, exaggerating her hurt to hide the pain. "That's just mean."

"Sometimes the truth hurts."

"Indeed. But I have to wonder. Is your fear of complications responsible for your long dry spell? Are you a simple man, Sheriff?"

"Give the lady a prize." He mocked her. "I spend my days solving problems and keeping order. When I get home, I want peace and quiet, not to juggle the needs and demands of three different women and their well-meaning friends and relatives."

"Ah." She nodded sagely but made no effort to hide the glee in her eyes. "Now I understand. A virile, strong-bodied man like you comes to town unattached. The matchmakers probably swarmed all over you."

She tapped her finger against her lips as she contemplated him. "Which means one of two things happened. Either you accepted their cleverly casual offers for a home-cooked meal and found yourself set up with a number of lovely companions eager to follow up with a date. And you made the mistake of trying to juggle the women while you figured out who you really wanted to date. Or you saw the minefield ahead of you and decided not to risk precious body parts by alienating matchees. Or matchmakers."

"You can laugh, but I'm rather fond of all my body parts."

She grinned. "I imagine you are. My guess is it was the former. There are a lot of nice ladies with single relatives in town."

"So there are." He chucked her under the chin. "No need to blow your vow now. Use all the soap you want."

With that he closed the door in her face.

She blinked at the wooden barrier. Oh, he wasn't getting away with that. She wasn't through playing with him yet. She yanked the door open and stepped into the hall. Nate was at the end and before she could challenge him he turned. Light flowed over his broad back, highlighting a vivid scar running from his left collarbone across his shoulder blade and under his arm.

It was a shocking blight on the perfect canvas of his muscular body. Between one thundering heartbeat and another she knew he would hate for her to mention it. Wouldn't want to talk about it.

Here was his reason for keeping to himself.

She remembered her dad telling her his new deputy sheriff had been in the army, that he'd been a Ranger or something. Everything she knew about special forces told her his body was a weapon. Which probably told her why he was a sheriff in Podunk River Run instead of still fighting the good fight.

As a woman who knew the value of beauty, she understood his inclination to hide the imperfection. And she respected his right to privacy.

She retreated into the bathroom and closed the door.

Wrapped in Nate's throw, Michelle cuddled under the comforter, clenching her teeth to keep them from chattering. It galled her big-time, but Nate had been right. The couch sat under the window. And the distance from the fire was too great to offset the icy glass over her.

Giving in, she gathered her covers and her pillow and used the dim light of the fire to make her way to the middle of the room and the cozy bed where Jack and Nate slept.

Just being closer to the fire helped and she eyed the makeshift bed, wondering if there was a way she could join them without waking Nate. Hearing him gloat was the last thing she wanted at two in the morning.

He slept on his back and easily took up half the space on the mattress. Jack slept about a foot to the left of Nate, which left about eighteen inches for Michelle to squeeze into.

No way she could climb into the sleeping bag without waking both males so she wouldn't even try. She set the pillow down next to Jack, drew the comforter around herself and, trying for stealth, lay down on the edge of the mattress.

She sighed, but before her head even hit the pillow, Nate erupted into action.

He leaped over Jack, caught her around the middle and rolled with her. Comforter and pillow went flying. Instinctively Michelle threw her arms up in self-defense.

Nate blocked the move, caught her right arm, twisted and flipped her. She screamed, in pain and fright.

The baby began to cry.

"Nate." She spit out carpet fibers and called his name. "Nate, it's me—Michelle."

"Michelle?"

The weight he used to contain her shifted, tensing then relaxing, and suddenly the fight went out of him and he sprawled full-length over her body. He went into a rant of creative and foul curses.

"Hell, woman, are you insane? I'm a soldier. You can't sneak up on me when I'm sleeping. I could have broken your neck."

"My neck is fine. But you may break something else if you don't move," she wheezed out, no longer nervous. "Can I have my arm back? Please."

"Good Lord." Two hands appeared on either side of her and his weight disappeared. A moment later, he flipped her again, gently this time, and his hands ran lightly over her, checking for injuries. "I'm sorry. Are you hurt? Where?"

"Nate. Stop." She grabbed his hands and held them still. She couldn't get her breath back with his hands on her. "I'm fine. You were right. I got cold and moved to the mattress. I didn't mean to startle you."

"Right." He scrubbed his face. Glanced at Jack, who'd been jostled awake by Nate's abrupt departure from the bed, and then back at her. "Look, some habits die hard. Do me a favor, next time announce you're joining me in bed."

"Next time?" She swallowed hard. "You are feeling lucky."

His eyebrows drew together as he processed her comment while clearly still shaken. He shook his head. "Smart-ass."

"What can I say? You bring out the best in me."

"Jack's crying and I'm freezing my butt off. Let's go to bed."

Currently her body was overheated from proximity to him. Maybe she should rethink the whole sleeping-together thing?

No, then he'd know she was running scared.

She allowed him to help her to her feet. She grabbed the crying baby, singing softly to soothe him, while Nate straightened the bedding.

Wrapping the throw around the baby, she watched with interest as Nate unzipped the sleeping bags.

"Why are you unlinking them?"

"With the extra body heat and the comforter we don't need the additional warmth."

"And with the three of us it would be a tad cozy?"

He lifted one bare shoulder, let it drop. "Yeah, there's that."

"Good plan."

"I thought so." He nodded toward Jack. "He's probably hungry. Christy was still taking a bottle at night at that age."

"Christy? You have a daughter?"

His head whipped around and there was no sign of sleep in the gaze that cut through her. "Christy is my friend's daughter. He died in combat."

"And you came to River Run to check up on her?" The guy really did have an overactive protective gene.

"Something like that." He was defensive.

Telling herself it was none of her business, Michelle expressed sorrow over the loss of his friend and asked if he'd get the bottle for Jack.

While he went to the kitchen to clean the bottle, she and Jack got settled on the mattress. The baby continued to fuss until Nate finished making the bottle with the water he had warming by the fire.

She concentrated on Jack, paying no attention as Nate joined them in the bed. Right, as if she could ignore a six-foot-three-inch mass of muscle and testosterone. But she was determined to pretend nonchalance.

He settled against his pillow with a sigh.

Jack put his tiny hand on Nate's biceps, and Michelle could swear he sighed, too.

She turned on her side, facing the baby, and plumped up her pillow. Her eyes blinked as she slid her feet over the cool nylon of the sleeping bag. She focused on the bottle, saw it was almost gone. Her feet encountered a firm, warm surface. She sighed and slid into sleep.

Nate sat up to burp Jack and felt Michelle's toes dig into his calf as she moved with him. Sound asleep, she had an innocence about her that belied her tough exterior. And drew him far more than he could afford.

The truth was he found too much about her way too tempting. He dismissed her bravado; saw it for the shield it was. Some might see her aggression as manipulation and her flippancy as fake, but he heard the self-honesty driving it and appreciated the bluntness.

Her patience and connection with Jack awed Nate. He would have been lost without her tonight.

She was beautiful and knew it. Used it. This woman knew games he'd never even heard of. And wanted no part of. High maintenance thy name was Michelle Ross.

She'd been right. He was a simple man, and he wanted a simple life. He'd deal with taking in Jack because he had to, because he was family.

Nate had originally moved here to support his best friend's widow, to watch over his infant daughter. Nate and Kim had been friends for three years. He knew he could count on her help with Jack.

As soon as the storm ended, he'd call Kim; make a date to talk to her about what he needed for Jack.

Now was definitely not the time to let his irrational attraction for Sleeping Beauty sway him from his set path. But as he set the snoozing baby between them and sank back onto his pillow he made no effort to move away from her seeking toes. The human connection felt too good to lose.

His last thought before fading into sleep was a prayer that the storm ended soon. Spending time housebound with a woman he had no business desiring was his idea of torture.

CHAPTER FIVE

THE next two days were absolute torture. Being cooped up with a bear of a man and a traumatized infant did not make for lots of fun.

Luckily Michelle's foot healed up pretty fast and got her off the couch and puttering around between bouts of watching Jack.

Child care was not in her plans when she headed home to sell her dad's house, but poor Jack was miserable. Obviously he missed his mother, plus his experience from the day before had left him with a cold. Bottom line he was unhappy when he was awake and his cold kept him from sleeping more than a few minutes at a time.

She and Nate settled into a grudging truce as they shared baby duty. She thought his patience would run out, but reluctantly acknowledged he held up his end. He'd prop Jack against his shoulder and go about his business. And he was always busy. He kept the fire going, cooked, cleaned, did dishes, handled the trash.

On the first day, she watched him make tuna sandwiches, mostly one-handed, for lunch and later he did paperwork at his desk. She took the baby, and by the second day he'd devised a sling that helped to leave his hands free.

Because she liked to cook, she helped with the meals and left the rest to him. She spent the remainder of her time wandering through the house taking stock.

She was surprised to find her room remained the same as she'd left it, complete with purple curtains, butterflies, musical notes and pop-star posters.

The house was in good shape, better than she would have thought, but then her dad had always demanded she help out with some new project. From gardening and fixing a broken step to repairing a toilet and building her tree house he'd always had something he needed her help with. She had to admit the fix-it knowledge had come in handy over the years.

And she'd loved her tree house. He'd made her a castle. They'd built it together the first year she went to Princess Camp. And she'd used it clear through her senior year in high school.

Late the second day she followed Nate up to the attic to see if there was any baby furniture they could use. There wasn't. Her mother might have kept that kind of thing. Her dad got rid of anything they weren't currently using.

What they did find was a very dusty wooden rocking chair. At her insistence Nate carried it down to the garage.

"This is filthy. And one of the arms is warped." He dusted off his hands after setting it down. "The only thing it's good for is firewood."

"We'll see." She bounced Jack on her hip. "Yes, it's

dirty but it's sturdy. A little sanding and a good cleaning is all it needs."

He lifted a skeptical brow. "You're on your own there. Speaking of firewood, I have to replenish our supply."

"Okay, let me put my jacket on and I'll help."

"You have Jack." He reached for a hooded coat he kept in the garage. "I can handle it."

"Stubborn man," she muttered as he headed out the back door. She carried Jack into the living room, placed him in the middle of the mattress and piled up a barricade of pillows between him and the hearth. As he'd barely mastered turning over, she figured he couldn't get far in the few minutes it took her to help Nate.

Dragging on her jacket, she arrived back in the garage in time to hold the door open so Nate didn't have to struggle to get it while carrying the large load of wood. A gesture he accepted with a less than gracious grunt.

Rolling her eyes at his back, she stepped out the back door to walk the short distance to the wood shed but a hard hand wrapped around her elbow and pulled her to a stop.

"Stay inside," he insisted. "It's too slick out there for your weak ankle. You'll only end up on your pretty ass."

"Ohh, so you think I have a pretty tush?" She wiggled her butt enticingly. "I think yours is nice, too."

"Nut." He shook his head, but the corner of his mouth quirked up just a little. "Now go back inside. I can do this. What I can't do is take care of Jack and you, too."

"Fine." She flounced around on her heel and promptly felt her foot slide on a frozen patch, going out from under her. Luckily, his hand on her arm kept her from falling.

"Careful." He pulled her close, clamping her to his sturdy frame.

Humor fled as she clung to him. The last thing she needed was to hurt herself worse than she already had, especially when her ankle was still on the mend.

Breathless from the near fall, she gazed up at him. "Thank you."

He picked her up and set her inside the garage door. "Does everything always have to be about sex with you?"

Indignant, her hands went to her hips. "How is 'thank you' about sex?"

"I don't know." He threw his gloved hands up, revealing his frustration. "It's the way you talk, everything sounds sexy."

Well, yeah. Using her sexuality usually got her what she wanted. And okay, she'd admit to an attraction to all that raw masculinity. But he was being far too sensitive. Sometimes "thank you" just meant "thank you." Defensive, she tossed his argument back at him.

"Or maybe it's the way you hear it. I just came out to help. You're the one who started talking about my ass."

His eyes narrowed in a scowl and he opened his mouth. Then he obviously thought better of it because he closed his mouth with a click of his teeth.

After a deep breath, he said, "Just hold the door. This will only take a few more minutes."

"Yes, sir." She gave him a pert salute.

Looking at the dark clouds and heavy snowfall, she rubbed her hands together for warmth and wished for the storm to end soon.

The attack began with a close-range sniper shot. Nate heard the whining echo as he caught his best friend in his arms. He went down under Quentin's dead weight. Gunfire broke out. Shouts and then screams rent the air. Return mortar fire boomed and the foundation shook.

Nate dragged Quentin inside. Shafts of light were thick with dust and sand. Paper-thin walls offered little protection but Nate bent over Quentin, calling his name, demanding an answer. His heart in his throat, he checked for a pulse and his hand came back bloody.

The building suddenly exploded. Nate threw his body over Quentin. A lancing pain tore through Nate's shoulder. And then everything went black.

Nate sat straight up in bed. The sound of mortar fire rang in his ears. Sweat beaded his brow and he pushed out of the sleeping bag to pace the chilly room. He grabbed a T-shirt to wipe his face, wishing it was that easy to wipe out his memories.

No, that was wrong. Quentin deserved better from Nate.

He'd told Command they needed to change up the routine. A smart soldier knew predictable was deadly. But nothing about the damn war was logical. So the simple changing of the guard had turned bloody. Worse, he'd changed shifts with Quentin. Their positions should have been reversed.

Nate should be dead and Quentin should be with his wife and daughter.

His blood was on Nate's hands. The first shot had killed him and Nate's efforts to shield him from the blast had been worthless and had nearly cost him his arm.

Nate walked to the kitchen, opened the refrigerator and stared at the contents unseeingly.

Quentin had had so little time with his beautiful daughter, Christy, but he'd loved her so much. He never talked about her, as if he wanted to protect her from the vileness of the war and their everyday life. But he showed Nate pictures, would just hand over a stack without a word. And Nate savored every candid shot of the plump little girl with his buddy's nose and hair and her mother's eyes.

Those pictures of home, of an innocent child filled with the joy of life and discovery, were what kept Nate going. When the sand and the heat and the hatred got to be too much, he'd remember Christy's smile and remind himself he was here to make the world a better, safer place for her.

And sometimes he actually believed it.

He closed the refrigerator door and began to pace, the terrazzo tile icy under his bare feet. Wait… He swung back to the refrigerator and pulled the door open. The light was on. Good, the electricity was back. That meant the storm must be abating.

Thank God.

He used to relive the nightmare of that day in his dreams every night. They'd become less frequent over the past year. He knew exactly what brought it on now: his decision to raise Jack.

They'd saved Nate's arm, but his career was over.

He hadn't hesitated when he returned stateside—he'd moved to River Run. He owed it to his friend to look after his family. And that's what he'd done for the past three years.

"Are you okay?" Michelle's soft voice came out of the darkness.

He gave a harsh laugh. "Yeah, I'm just fine."

"Couldn't sleep?" She leaned a hip against the counter and crossed one pink polka-dot-socked foot over the other.

"Touch of heartburn from the chili tonight." He pounded his chest for emphasis. It wasn't a total lie; it just wasn't what woke him.

She opened a cupboard and tossed him a bottle of antacids. "Sorry. I like spicy. Next time I'll go lighter on the jalapeños."

"No," he said, sorry he'd picked on her food. "Don't." He popped the chalky tablets. "It's worth the burn."

Her smile lit up the dark room. Some of the tension eased in his chest. He told himself it was the fast-acting antacids.

"I'm sorry I woke you."

"It wasn't you. Jack was restless." Her eyes went misty soft. "I saw your scar. My father told me you almost lost your arm in the war. Is that what disturbed your sleep? Bad dreams?"

He froze. "I don't talk about that."

"Maybe you should. Maybe it would help you sleep."

"It's over. My arm is fine. No good comes from rehashing old business."

"No good comes from bottling up old wounds. Talking can help."

"I've heard that psychobabble before." He crossed his arms over his chest. "What possible good can come from splitting my veins open and bleeding emotions?"

"Maybe you'd find some peace."

"What do you want to hear? That I cost my best friend his life? Or that I'd give my arm to have him back? What's the cost of a limb compared to the life of a husband and father?"

She blanched but didn't back down. "Life isn't that simple. You were in a war."

"We traded duty. He was shot as I was relieving him. If our positions had been reversed, I'd be the one sent home in a pine box."

"And if you hadn't changed assignments, the shooter might have shot to the right or the left and your friend would still be gone. You can play the if game all night long, but it doesn't change anything," she said softly. "Death happens."

"Quentin's death is on my hands. It's not something I can be philosophical about."

"I guess not. Try remembering you didn't kill him."

"Right." He mocked her. "I'll remember that."

She tried to shrug off his rudeness, but he saw the cringe she couldn't hide. Why didn't she just go back to bed?

"So Christy is Quentin's daughter. She and her mother are what brought you to River Run?"

"How—" Her knowledge stunned Nate until he remembered he'd mentioned Christy their first night together. "They don't concern you."

"Oh." The animation went out of her face. "Good night then."

He was such a moron. This was his problem. And no business of hers. But he figured she'd only been trying to help. He needed to cut her some slack.

"So Jack was restless?" he said quickly before she could leave and go back to bed.

"Yes." She rubbed her hands over her arms, seeking warmth. "He doesn't like the powdered milk bottles as well as his formula bottles. I think it upsets his stomach a little."

"Speaking of which…" He walked past her, inhaled the sweet scent of lotion that made her skin so silky soft and pulled open the refrigerator, showing her the light.

"We have electricity." She clapped her hands. "That means the storm is over, right?"

"It means the hub is up and working."

"Oh, come on, give me some hope here." She closed the refrigerator door and leaned back against it, putting her way too close. "I'm stir-crazy. I need to see something besides the inside of this house. Even the slim pickings in River Run will do."

"For once we're in agreement." He stepped back and bumped into the counter. She smelled too good, looked too soft, and he found it too easy to remember how sweet she tasted. Being alone with her like this was not good. Not for him. "I appreciate your cooking, but I can really go for some of Luigi's Pizza."

"Oh, my God, Luigi's Pizza! How could I forget

Luigi's Pizza? Their pepperoni is to die for. I swear I ate there three times a week my senior year in high school." She sighed over the memory, her breasts rising and falling under the soft fabric of his T-shirt. He forced his eyes back to her face. "You are so on. As soon as the snowplows clear the roads we have a date."

She flounced back to bed, and he scrubbed his hands over his face. That really hadn't gone according to plan.

"Freedom." Michelle flung her arms out wide, embracing the beautiful outdoors. Crisp and clear, the air still held the icy bite of winter but a single ray of sunshine promised the storm truly had ended. "My kingdom for freedom."

And the roads were plowed, including their driveway—one of the perks of living with the sheriff. Nate had taken off at first light promising to be back by early afternoon to take her grocery shopping.

He missed that deadline by several hours. No surprise.

She'd brooded for a while at being under the thumb of another lawman, the pacing and waiting taking her back to too many memories from the past.

Like the time she walked to school through huge drifts of snow one year after a storm knocked out power for three days. The snow had stopped and Dad was gone so she got dressed and trudged to the school four blocks away, only to find out Dad had forgotten to tell her school was canceled for the rest of the week. She was out the next week because of a bad case of bronchitis and missed the field trip to the capitol building in Sacramento.

After a while she shook off the negativity of being out of control. Instead she and Jack went out to the garage and started sanding the rocker. Okay, she sanded and Jack slept in a blanket-draped drawer, the point being they kept busy until Nate showed up.

Now they were off to town for some much-needed supplies.

And much-needed company.

If she had to spend another minute alone with hunky sheriff Nate, she might spontaneously combust. Something about the man kept her body on a low-level buzz.

"Wouldn't that be queendom?" Nate came out of the house carrying Jack in his car seat.

He wasn't immune to her, either. Sometimes she caught him looking at her with such heat she wanted to eliminate the space between them and forget they could barely tolerate being in the same room together.

Oh, yeah, she needed civilization bad.

"Queendom. I like that. But right now I'll settle for River Run."

"I bet that's something you never thought you'd say."

"You got that right." She strapped her seat belt on. "Luigi's, driver, and make it quick."

Nate gave her an askance glance before he put his big SUV in gear and rolled forward.

"You're a little tipsy on your freedom there, aren't you?"

"Yes." She sighed, making no effort to deny it. "It was getting so I couldn't breathe. It didn't seem to bother you. But then you left at the crack of dawn. You've been free all day."

"I've been working. And I hadn't had a break in close to a month. I was glad to be able to get some things done that I'd been putting off."

"I got some song writing done, too. But I'm still happy to be free." She breathed deeply, let it out slowly. "Did you put an arrest warrant out for Jack's mom?"

"No." His hands fisted on the wheel. "But I listed her as a person of interest, which means information on her will be forwarded to me if she shows up on the grid anywhere we share info."

"What will you do when you find her?"

"I don't know," he admitted, surprising her. "I hate how she abandoned Jack. It's hard for me to get past that. He's probably better off without her."

"Probably?"

"Some women aren't meant to be mothers."

Now that was interesting. Did he speak from personal experience or just from what he'd seen?

"And you feel confident in making that decision for him?"

The look he gave her sliced her to the bone. Which made her wonder why. Why was she pushing? Obviously her question pricked a sore spot for him. But it was none of her business. And sure, Jack was a cute kid, but the last thing she needed was to get emotionally involved in this mess.

"Never mind," she said as if his look hadn't cut her off at the knees. "I'm sure you'll work it all out." Seeing they were still in the driveway, she waved her fingers at him. "Luigi's! Forthwith."

"Freak." He sighed and pulled into the street.

"You have no sense of fun," she informed him.

"I know how to have fun," he stated evenly.

"Jack is the one I feel sorry for. You really should put a little effort in for his sake."

"Don't tell me how to raise Jack."

"I'm just saying the kid deserves a chance."

"Cut it out." He sent her a sideways glare. "I know how to have a good time as much as the next guy."

"Doing what?" she demanded, not believing him for a minute. She'd never met a man that was more work-oriented, except for her father and that wasn't saying much. "What do you do for fun? Play football with the guys? Go fishing? My dad liked to fish. Or are you a secret gamer? Confess, you get your thrills on *Grand Theft Auto*, don't you?"

"What's *Grand Theft Auto*?"

She shook her head in exaggerated disappointment. "Now that's just sad."

"I'm a law enforcement officer. Why would I play something called *Grand Theft Auto*?"

"Oh, I don't know, for the vicarious thrill? Or maybe because *it's fun*?"

Now it was a killer glare. "I don't have to explain myself to you."

"No, you don't." Satisfied she'd riled him, she wiggled more comfortably into her seat. "If you put on the siren so we get to Luigi's extra fast, I'll let you play *Grand Theft Auto* when we get home."

"That's not going to happen."

"It would in my queendom."

He shook his head, but she saw the corner of his mouth quirk up. A smile. They rode in silence for several blocks.

"I work out. And I like to bowl," he finally muttered.

Pleased with herself, she drew an exclamation point in the condensation on the window.

CHAPTER SIX

LUIGI'S was packed. Seemed everyone had a case of cabin fever and decided to eat out tonight. Nate bounced Jack and scanned the room looking for Kim and Christy.

The kid weighed next to nothing. Nate could hold him in one hand. Not that he would. He still worried he might break the little guy.

It was hard to remember Christy was ever this small. He'd thought he was being a help to Kim in those early days. And he probably was, but he knew now she'd needed so much more than he'd given her.

He'd gone ahead with his plan to call her and asked her to meet him here tonight. With Michelle along it wasn't quite what he'd had in mind, but it was a start. And with Kim there nobody was likely to get the wrong idea about him and Michelle. Especially Michelle.

He spotted Kim talking to her neighbor David, an average-size man with dark hair and a trim mustache. She laughed at something he said, and then she caught sight of Nate and waved. The man picked up Christy and the small group started making its way through the restaurant toward him.

"Looks like your friend has company," Michelle observed. "Maybe we should look for a bigger booth."

He turned and found her tucking a high chair in at the end of a booth. "That won't be necessary. David won't be joining us."

"I'm betting he will," she contradicted him, her gaze on the group about to join them. "I hope you don't have any feelings in that direction."

"What do you mean?" he demanded. "Why do you say that?"

"Because it looks to me like the widow is smitten with David."

"You're wrong." He dismissed her claim. Kim still loved Quentin. Nate would know if that had changed. Quentin may be gone but his spirit was irreplaceable.

"Hi, Nate." Kim greeted him with a big hug. "This was a great idea. You know David, right? It's such a crush in here. You don't mind if he joins us, do you?"

Michelle jumped in. "Of course not. Hi, I'm Michelle Ross."

"Sheriff Ross's daughter." Kim patted Michelle's shoulder in unspoken sympathy. "I'm Kim and this is my daughter, Christy. She's three, and she'll talk your ear off if you let her."

"Michelle." David greeted Michelle with a fond smile. "It's good to see you. May I say how sorry I am about your father's passing? The whole town misses him. I would have been at the services, but I covered the office so my father could go."

"Thank you." Michelle graciously offered her hand and Dave swallowed it up in his large mitts. She didn't seem to notice as she continued. "Those two did like to cast a line together. I was always happy when your dad was free on Saturday mornings. It meant I got some extra beauty sleep."

Nate scowled at the chitchat. He didn't care for the way David hung on to Michelle's hand. The man needed to move on. Didn't he see they were blocking traffic standing around the table?

He made a point of scanning the area. "Sorry, buddy," he told David, "but it doesn't look like any of the bigger booths are available."

"Don't be ridiculous, Nate." Kim waved him off. "We can squeeze in here." She slid onto the bench seat and pulled David in beside her. "Here, there's room in the window for the baby seat." She lowered the handle and shoved the seat on the window ledge.

Unhappy with the way things were shaking out, Nate glanced at Michelle. She winked and scooted in to sit across from Kim. He narrowed his eyes at her, but she just smiled and released Jack from his seat.

"I see you finally got that peach-fuzz mustache to grow in properly," she teased David.

"Brat." He grinned and swiped fingers over the hair framing his upper lip.

"He had such a baby face when he first joined his dad's dental practice, the older ladies gave him a bad time. So he decided to grow a mustache to look older."

"It worked, too." He shook a finger at Michelle. "And it was never as bad as you make out."

"Of course not." She looked at Kim and mouthed, "Peach fuzz."

Kim laughed. She inspected David. “I like it.”

Nate shifted in his seat, feeling like an outsider. Thankfully, the waitress arrived to take their order. After a brief consult he ordered one vegetarian and one meat-lover’s pizza.

“Mommy, can I have my juice?” Christy asked.

Kim pulled a sippy cup from her purse and David passed it to the little girl.

Once she had her drink, Christy patted Nate’s hand and pointed at Jack. “Baby.”

“That’s right.” He bopped her nose with a finger. “That’s Jack.”

“He sure is a cutie,” Kim told Michelle. “How old is he?”

“Around four months.”

“I didn’t know you had a son,” David said. “I’m surprised your dad wasn’t crowing about his grandson every chance he got.”

“Oh, no.” Michelle shook her head, her gold hair brushing over her shoulders. She cocked her thumb in his direction. “He’s Nate’s.”

Clearly shocked, Kim’s gaze ricocheted around as if she didn’t know where to look. She finally took refuge in snagging David’s gaze.

Nate realized he should have taken charge of the introductions. Found a time to make an explanation to Kim when they didn’t have an audience. He wanted her help, but he didn’t want to put his life on display for strangers.

“Ah, Nate,” Michelle whispered.

Used to hiding his emotions, he flicked an expressionless glare at David, wishing him away. He'd prefer Michelle wasn't there, either, and not just because she kept digging her elbow into his ribs.

"Kim, I can explain," he began.

"Nate, you don't have to—"

"I want to. We've been friends for years—"

"Nate—" Michelle suddenly shoved at him "—I really need to talk to you."

He turned his head and looked down at her. "Not now." He focused on Kim. "Jack was a surprise."

"Please, you two, don't argue," Kim implored. "This is a special time for you."

"Kim, it's not what you think," Michelle countered.

Again Kim's gaze went to David, and Nate thought she was wishing for some privacy. He echoed that sentiment. He knew he was handling this badly. He should have planned out what he was going to say, but he'd been distracted by Michelle. And Jack, of course.

"Kim, I was really hoping—"

Michelle stopped him by turning his head toward her, and grinding her mouth on his.

For a moment his mind went blank. And his body took over, responding to the sweet softness of her lips under his. He opened his mouth, tasting her, devouring, her before his brain reengaged.

Furious, he grabbed her hand and pulled her from the booth.

Michelle let Nate drag her away from the table, stopping only long enough to hand Jack over to Kim with a grateful smile.

He kept hold of her hand until they reached the video games at the back of the room near the restrooms.

"Are you insane?" he demanded. "I'm trying to explain the situation to Kim. I have a personal interest in making sure she fully understands what's going on."

"I know." She tugged at the hem of her waist-length sweater. "You're welcome."

"That settles it. You are nuts."

"No, I'm saving you from yourself. I get it, okay. I know your grand plan was to get together with the widow and raise your kids together." She was pretty good at reading people—as a songwriter she observed life—and interpersonal relationships. Plus, the man was as transparent as cellophane.

"You couldn't be more wrong. Her husband was my best friend. She's like a sister to me." His affront couldn't be more obvious, and she realized she'd misread the situation. His ire showed in his stance. "You have no right interfering in my personal affairs. Or giving Kim the impression that something is going on between us."

"Me? The way you bumbled that explanation, the woman thinks I had your baby!"

"No."

"Yes. Look, I know you think you need to play hero because you feel responsible for Kim being a widow—"

"You don't know anything about me, or my intentions. The last thing I am is a hero."

"Whatever. This is what I see, you're fixated on the past and she's ready to move on."

"What? Who with—David?" He scoffed. "Now you're being ridiculous. Kim still loves Quentin."

She sighed. Men could be so dense. "She'll always love Quentin but she's also a young vital woman with a full life ahead of her. She's found a new love. She and David are a couple. You're going to have to deal."

"You don't know what you're talking about." He dismissed her claim. "How could you? You haven't spoken to anyone in town for seven months."

"How can you be a law enforcement officer and not see what's in front of your eyes?"

"Maybe because there's nothing to see."

Aggravated by his failure to listen to her, she grabbed his broad shoulders and tried to turn him toward the table they'd just left.

He didn't budge.

With a sigh she walked around him, forcing him to turn to keep track of her or stand facing the back wall.

When he faced her, she waved her hand, inviting him to take in the couple cooing at the baby. As they watched, Kim lifted her face to David's for a kiss. Ouch.

Michelle rolled her gaze up to Nate. He stood, hands on hips, his eyes locked on the wife of his best friend embracing another man. His expression never changed as the seconds ticked by and she wondered what he was thinking.

Deciding she'd give him a moment alone, she patted his arm and headed back to the booth. She went two steps before his arm wrapped around her waist and he swept her into his arms.

"Hey..." She pushed against his chest.

"Just saying thanks." He bent his head to hers and claimed her mouth. Slanting his head, he deepened the kiss with a sweep of his tongue. No hesitation, no holding back, no distractions, this kiss was unlike any others they'd shared. He held her with care, with urgency. He tasted good and felt better.

The pizza parlor disappeared as she melted against him, and his heat surrounded her. The buzz she constantly fought to ignore ignited into full-blown tingles. Desire flowed hot through her blood as she opened to his sensual demand.

Needing to get closer she went onto her tiptoes and circled his neck with her arms. And suddenly she felt like she floated on air, Nate her only anchor in a swirling mist of sensation.

Someone jostled her from behind.

"Excuse me," a young voice said, followed by teenaged giggles.

"Sheriff Nate has a girl."

The shrill announcement echoed through Michelle's head, disrupting her passionate haze.

"That kiss was hot," a girlish voice replied in awe.

Michelle's eyes popped open and she stared into Nate's heated gaze. A breath shuddered through his wide chest, her body moving along with his. That's when she realized the floating sensation came from the fact he held her aloft.

"You…" She cleared her throat. "You should put me down."

He leaned over and her feet gently settled on the

ground. For a moment his hands lingered on her waist and then he released her.

She brushed the back of her fingers down his cheek. "Well done."

"What?" She took satisfaction in hearing the rasp of desire in the word.

"You used me. And I don't even care."

"You started it."

She held up a hand. "Don't push it. Your pride needed a booster shot and I was handy. I get it. Don't do it again."

Facing the room, she tugged at the hem of her purple sweater and willed her overheated body to settle down.

"You know you have to correct the impression Jack is our child."

"Nobody would believe that."

She shook her head at his obtuseness. "You'll see."

"Come on." A hand in the small of her back ushered her forward.

The man really had no clue. They'd gone half a dozen steps when a couple stopped them to congratulate them on their little bundle of joy. Michelle flicked him a telling glance, smiled at the couple and moved on to their booth.

She scooted in, slid a piece of meat-lover's pizza onto her plate and took a big bite. Jack slept against Kim's shoulder. Michelle eyed the hands clasped together on the table and felt a smidgen of sympathy for Nate.

A moment later he slid in beside her and reached for his own slice. In a disconnected part of her brain she noticed that both of them had taken the meat pie while Kim and David had both chosen the veggie.

"Please tell them the truth," she prompted him.

He shrugged. "It's my business."

"And my reputation," she countered.

"You're leaving town, what do you care?"

"I care." She faced the couple avidly drinking in their debate. "Kim, Jack isn't my child. He's Nate's cousin's boy."

"Oh." Kim looked confused. "I thought Jack passed away a few months ago."

"Yes, and his girlfriend was pregnant. She left the baby on Nate's porch the first night of the storm."

"Oh, my God," Kim exclaimed. She softly rubbed the sleeping baby's back. "His mother left him in the storm? He could have died."

"Luckily, I heard him crying."

Kim glanced back and forth between Michelle and Nate, her expression a curious combination of understanding and skepticism.

"Why didn't you just say so?" Kim asked Nate.

His cheeks turned ruddy. "This didn't seem the place to go into it. I'm not used to discussing my business in such an open forum."

Kim's gaze shifted to Michelle, pinning her to her seat. "And where do you fit into the picture?"

"I was at the house when Nate found the baby. We've been stuck together for three days."

"Because she broke into my house."

"My house," she corrected through clenched teeth. "And that's what you choose to share?"

Smug, he lifted one shoulder, let it drop.

Aggrieved all over again. Michelle turned to David. "Who is this gal Dad was shacked up with? I didn't know he'd moved out of the house."

"Ah." David blinked in surprise at suddenly being in the hot seat of the volatile conversation. "You know, he and Dolly had been friends for years. That mild heart attack he had just before his birthday last year scared him. Shortly after your visit he moved in with her."

Silence followed the explanation. Dad and Dolly… lovers? Michelle would never have guessed. Then again, she tended to shy away from any notion of Dad and a lover in the same thought.

"More pizza, please." Christy's small voice piped into the stillness. Kim reached for a veggie slice, but the little girl spoke up. "No, Mommy, I want pepperoni."

"Here you go, sweet thing." Nate placed a small slice on her plate.

"Thank you, Uncle Nate." She smiled, grabbed a round bite of pepperoni and popped it in her mouth.

Kim reached over and patted Nate's hand. "Jack couldn't be in better hands."

"Yet, I'm already making mistakes."

Annoyed as she was at his closemouthed attitude, Michelle felt a little sorry for him. Tonight was definitely not going as he'd planned. Time for a change of mood.

"You'll fix it," she stated confidently. "You better—" she smiled at him, showing a lot of teeth "—or I'll sue you for child support."

Next to her Nate went very still, and then he threw

back his head and laughed out loud. He pushed a fall of hair behind her ear.

"You'd probably get it, too."

"Oh, believe it. Judge Austin is my godfather."

Still chuckling, he groaned. "Of course he is."

"You know, Nate, I have Christy's baby furniture stored in the garage. You're welcome to use it for Jack. There's a crib, and a changing table. Plus I think I still have her baby swing."

"Kim, that would be great. I don't know what to say."

"Thank you?"

"Of course. Thank you. I'll pick it up tomorrow."

"I have a truck," David said. "You must be really busy with the aftermath of the storm. Why don't I pack it up and bring it over? Then, if you're not available, I can help set it up."

Nate nodded and expressed his thanks. He managed to sound sincere even though Michelle knew deep down he was totally frustrated.

His phone beeped. He pulled it from his pocket and checked the screen. "I have to take this," he said and slid from the booth to step into the lobby.

"Mommy, can I ride the pony?" Christy pointed at a shiny brown pony with a red saddle.

"I'll take her," David volunteered and lifted the girl into his arms. They wandered off toward the pony.

"Here." Michelle reached for Jack's carrier. "Let's put him in his seat. Your poor arm is probably ready to fall off." She stood, gently took the baby and tucked him into place.

"You're good for him," Kim observed.

"Jack? He's a sweetheart."

"I meant Nate."

"Ha." Michelle made no effort to hide her derision. "We're lucky we didn't kill each other during the storm."

"Hmm. Like that killer kiss?"

"Please. He was punishing me because I was right."

Kim lifted one fine eyebrow. "And it hurt so good?"

Michelle grinned and fanned herself. "I didn't say I didn't like it."

"I've never seen him laugh like that. We're usually lucky to get a few chuckles out of him."

Michelle set Jack's carrier on the bench seat and sat down next to him, her attention wandering to Nate, who stood staring intently out the front window while he dealt with his call.

"Yeah, well, he's not a lighthearted guy."

"No, he's not," Kim agreed with a sigh. "And that's what I love about David."

"Nate seemed a little surprised by David." Michelle liked Kim; she was smart, perceptive and not threatened by Michelle, which sometimes women were. "I think he's put you on a pedestal."

"Which is why I haven't mentioned David." She met Michelle square in the eye. "I think you saved us both from an embarrassing moment."

Michelle simply stared back. Kim sighed.

"I love Nate like a brother. He was a lifesaver after Quentin died. But I'm not a stone statue. I deserve true love. I had it once and I won't settle for less this time. Nate is one of the best men I know. But he doesn't understand because a strong relationship is not something he's ever known. I want it for him. He deserves to be loved. He deserves someone who can make him laugh out loud."

CHAPTER SEVEN

STILL half-asleep Michelle pushed open the bathroom door and stepped inside. She promptly bumped into a steam-slicked body.

Instantly alert she stepped back and ogled Nate in nothing but a towel. His shoulders looked impossibly wide over a broad chest and a rippling six-pack.

The man was fine. And better than a cup of Joe first thing in the morning.

"Mmm. Good morning."

She got a growl in response.

Too bad he was a bad-tempered Neanderthal.

She reached for her toothbrush and took a peek at her own reflection. Her hair was a wild explosion of curls and her face devoid of makeup, but she wore her midnight-blue shorty pajamas. Not too bad a showing first thing in the morning.

"The room is taken," he said around his own toothbrush.

"I don't mind sharing," she assured him.

"I do," he barked.

She ignored him, enjoying instead the play of muscles in his arm and abdomen as he cleaned his teeth.

"Why aren't you using the master suite?" she asked him. "You could have a bathroom all to yourself there."

"I was already settled in my room when your dad decided to move out. I had the house to myself so I saw no reason to move. You take it."

"I'm good in my old room. I won't be here long enough to need the bigger room."

"Thank God."

"Hey, I'm helping you out here," she reminded him. "Have you thought what you're going to do now your girlfriend has found someone new?"

"Not funny. I need to talk to Kim," he declared as he rinsed his brush and returned it to the medicine cabinet, which was meticulously in order. "This thing with David may not be serious."

She rolled her eyes, amazed at his ability for self-deception. "She was kissing him in public."

"We were kissing in public. There's nothing serious between us."

He had her there. And if his easy dismissal of their embrace stung a little, she pretended not to notice.

"It looked serious to me."

"That's not what I need to talk to her about. I want to discuss Jack's care. She'll be able to help me explore my options."

She relaxed and nodded. "Closure is a good thing."

"Ouch!" He pulled his razor away from a bleeding nick. "There's no need for anything girly like closure." He glared at her reflection in the mirror. "Can I have some privacy, please?"

Sighing, she tugged at the hem of her pajama top and

for a moment it molded to the naked breasts beneath the thin cloth. His gaze lowered and his jaw clenched.

Satisfied, she turned on her heel.

"Seems to me you're the one acting like a girl," she ventured. "Next time lock the door if you're so modest."

A curse sounded from the other side of the closed door.

She smirked, suddenly looking forward to the day.

Twenty minutes later she shuffled down the stairs, Jack in her arms, to find Nate walking out the front door.

"Hey." She stopped him. "We need to make plans for shopping. The cupboards are bare and Jack has needs."

He turned to face her, a scowl drawing his dark brows together. He rubbed his temple as his gaze glazed over and his thoughts focused inward.

They'd planned to do some grocery shopping after dinner last night, but it turned out he needed to go back to the office. Instead they swung by the market and he ran in to pick up some formula and diapers. She'd almost kissed him again when she also found coffee and milk in the bag.

But kissing the man was getting to be a habit she needed to break. Seriously, did she have no sense of self-preservation?

He came toward her almost as if he'd read her mind and meant to test her resolve. It took everything in her to hold her ground. He stopped next to her and bent to kiss Jack on the top of his head.

"We're not going to get everything we need here in

River Run. We need to drive down to Sacramento to hit one of the big warehouse stores and a Wal-Mart."

Her heart sung at that decree. "Excellent idea."

"I'll work it out so I leave early. Can you be ready at three?"

"You bet. Jack and I'll be here with our shopping shoes on."

"Uncle Nate is going to be late," Michelle informed Jack after getting off the phone with Nate. He was a cop. Of course he was going to be late. "Get used to it."

She used the extra time to wander out into the backyard. She already had a list of supplies for work on the rocking chair, and changes she'd decided on for updating the kitchen, master suite and downstairs bathroom.

She intended to do the inside work herself; the outside work, not so much. Gardening had been her dad's thing, not hers. The yard work she'd hire out. But she spied the tree house and her heart melted.

That was something her dad had really done right.

Some of her happiest memories were the two years she went to Princess Camp and the hours spent in her castle tree house. The castle started out painted lavender, but in her teen years she toned the color down to a soft gray. By the weathered look of it her dad hadn't done anything with it since she moved away. She mentally added lavender paint to her list.

And a note to call Elle and Amanda. Thoughts of Princess Camp reminded her she hadn't spoken to her longtime friends since before she arrived in River Run.

Her cell rang and she fished her phone from her jeans pocket. Speak of the princesses.

"Elle, I was just thinking about you and Amanda."

"Really? Am I supposed to be telepathic to communicate now? What's wrong with the phone? See I picked up my cell, punched a number and there you were on the other end."

"Witch. Don't pick on me. I'm stuck in the middle of nowhere and until yesterday a storm had knocked out electricity and phone services. It's downright primitive."

"A storm knocked out services for three days?"

"Technically two days, but spring is a day away and we have snow on the ground. You live in San Diego. You wouldn't understand."

"Hmm. You have me there. So how long are you planning to stay in the back of beyond? I'm anxious to see you."

"Bad news. It's going to be longer than I thought. Turns out my dad rented his house to the new sheriff. His lease isn't up for a few months."

"So you can't work on the house?" Elle demanded, eagerness adding a lilt to the question. "Come stay with me, we can scope out L.A. on weekends and find you a place while you're waiting for the tenant to vacate the house."

Everything in Michelle leaped at the suggestion, but she'd given her word to help Nate with Jack. And with Jack's light weight resting trustingly against her shoulder, she couldn't discount her promise.

"I can't."

"What? Why not? If you're thinking of the rent, don't. I have it covered."

"You are the greatest. But you have to stop tempting me, because I have to stay. I made a commitment."

"You hate that place."

"I know. It's complicated."

"Ah." A knowing quality entered Elle's voice. "There's a man involved."

A vision of Nate half-naked in the bathroom this morning streamed through her mind. She sighed and kissed Jack's downy-soft hair.

"Two actually."

"Hmm." Elle hummed knowingly. "That would be complicated. Promise me it's not going to keep you from moving south."

"Not a chance."

"Good. Listen, I have a meeting. Keep in touch, and I don't mean telepathically."

"Very funny. Can you tell what I'm thinking now?"

She laughed. "There's the Michelle I know and love. Tootles."

Michelle disconnected, a grin lifting her mood. She missed her friends.

The time on the phone caught her attention. Nate should be here soon. She moved inside to finish getting ready. In case he arrived on time she wanted to be waiting when he got there.

Too late. Apparently he was early, which was almost as bad as being late.

He came skipping down the stairs as she entered the

front hall. He must have been faster than he'd thought because he'd obviously showered and changed.

He wore black slacks and a long-sleeved, light blue shirt with a navy pin-striped tie and carried a black blazer.

She whistled her appreciation. "Don't you look pretty? Do you always dress so formal to go shopping?"

"I have an appointment with an attorney about assuming custody of Jack," Nate said, hooking his jacket over the end of the banister. "I had to put the mayor off and hurry home because the attorney couldn't adjust the appointment without moving it back two weeks. Child Protective Services needs a copy of the petition. So I'm going to have to drop you at the warehouse store and catch up with you after the meeting."

"Of course you have to make the appointment." She indicated her sweater and jeans. "It'll just take me a minute to change."

"There's no need. And we're already running late."

"I can't go like this. I'll be quick." She thrust Jack into Nate's arms and waved to the baby's gear. "I'll be there before you get Jack loaded up and strapped in." She dashed up the stairs.

Knowing she'd never live it down if she didn't meet her promised speed limit, she kicked her shoes off on the way to the closet, pulled out black pumps and a short black skirt. It took two minutes to shimmy out of her jeans and into the skirt. She looked into the mirror and nodded—the light pink sweater was fine. She clicked a wide black belt around her waist and ran out the door.

At the bottom of the stairs she slipped into the

pumps, grabbed her purse and the jacket she noticed Nate had left hanging over the banister and strolled out to the SUV.

Nate was just closing the garage door as she walked up. The once-over he gave her was gratifying. The obvious male approval stroked her ego. But when he opened his mouth she knew it wouldn't be to compliment her shoes.

"You forgot your jacket," she said and thrust the black garment into his hands. And then she made a point of reaching her seat before he slid into his.

While strapping in she glanced behind her to make sure Jack was properly situated and noticed he sat in a new seat. He was scoring big today. Along with the furniture they dropped off earlier Kim had brought a bag of clothes Christy had outgrown. Gender neutral, of course.

He wore a pair of brown jeans with a pale yellow shirt with a bee buzzing along the front. Under it he wore a white onesie and on top should be a bib that read Got Formula.

"What happened to Jack's bib?" she asked Nate as they hit the road.

"I threw it away."

"What? Why?"

"It was purple."

"It was white."

"With purple writing. He's a boy, he's not going to wear purple."

"He can't read, doesn't know the difference between

purple and polka dots and—pay attention here because this is really important—he's only four months old."

"Which only means I have to protect his manhood until he can do it himself."

"And purple lettering is over the line?"

"Yes."

She shook her head at his unrelenting masculine stance. No wonder men and women didn't understand each other. They were taught from birth to be contrary.

"What time is your appointment?" she asked, changing the subject.

"Four-thirty."

She glanced at her watch—three-twenty. Sacramento was a good hour and a half from River Run.

"Will he wait if you're late?"

"He said he'd wait as long as he could."

"You'd better go straight there." She stated the obvious. "Jack's future is more important than a few supplies. How did you choose this lawyer?"

"Dolly recommended him."

Dolly, retired attorney and Dad's girlfriend. Michelle knew she'd have to go see the woman, but she dreaded the thought. She really didn't want to talk about her dad's relationship or their mutual loss.

He turned right onto the on ramp to Highway 80 and then glanced her way. "You're sure you don't mind waiting?"

"Not when it's best for Jack."

"Best? I'm a sheriff," he said, facing forward again. "I heard you warning him against the perils of living with a lawman."

"There's that, but you've been very good with him, patient and caring. And at least you're trying, which is more than can be said for the woman who dropped him off."

"I thought you were giving her the benefit of the doubt."

"I never said that. I said she may have knocked and we didn't hear her. That didn't mean it was acceptable for her to leave him in the freezing cold."

"I'm glad to hear it." He loosened the tie around his neck.

Michelle meant what she said. And she meant to leave it at that but she couldn't.

"I know she doesn't deserve a second chance. That there's no excuse for leaving her baby in a dangerous situation. I get that, I really do. But there's this tiny part of me that keeps saying I'd have done anything to know my mom."

Silence met her revelation, leaving her feeling exposed. She glanced at Nate's hard profile, found no hint of his thoughts and turned her gaze to the tree-rich scene out her window.

"I guess it's not something you can understand if you grew up with your mom."

There was a sigh beside her. "My mom should never have had a child. She had the maturity of a fifteen-year-old. Which is a personal assessment, not a professional one. Everything was always about her. And if it was too hard, or took too long, she didn't want to be bothered."

"Sounds rough." She'd longed for some freedom, a

little less supervision, but it seemed you could have too much of a good thing.

"It wasn't bad when my dad was alive. He loved taking care of her. He was proud of his home and his family. He took care of everything. She cooked. She had a weekly menu that she repeated week after week."

Okay, that part didn't sound so bad. The Lord knew her dad hadn't been very imaginative in the kitchen.

"And then Dad died."

She flinched. That was bad. "How old were you?"

"Six."

"That's pretty young."

"She could barely function after my dad died. Everything fell to me. I had to get us up for work and school. I had to remind her to shop for food and to pay the bills. I kept expecting her to become the mom, but she never did. She loved me but my needs were always second to hers. I don't want that for Jack."

Of course he wouldn't. His mother had robbed him of a childhood. Michelle understood where he was coming from, but that little voice continued to call to her.

"But you loved her, too."

His shoulders tensed and for a moment she didn't think he'd respond.

"Yeah." It was grudgingly offered.

"Do you think your life would have been better without her?" she wondered aloud.

"It's hard to say," he answered, unsure. "Foster care is no picnic. But there are good people in the system, as well."

"So you're sure this is what you want to do? You want full custody?"

"I owe it to Jack, to my Uncle Stan."

And that wasn't a hard choice to contemplate. The silence grew between them until finally she had to ask.

"Have you heard anything on his mother's whereabouts?"

He slid Michelle a sideways glance. "You're like a dog with a bone, aren't you?"

"That must mean yes." She grinned. "What have you learned?"

"Not much. She and Jack lived in Carson City. Searching across states complicates things, but I'll find her."

"And then?"

He lifted one shoulder, let it drop. "I don't know. The letter made it clear she was done with Jack. She wanted me to assume custody. Or give him to a good home. She couldn't be any clearer in her intentions. Finding her probably won't change anything."

"But you don't know that."

"I know Jack's future is too important to base it on maybes and what-ifs. And the attorney made it clear on the phone if I wait to assume custody, Child Services may step in."

Traffic was light so Nate pulled up to the attorney's office only ten minutes late. It helped that Michelle had agreed to wait.

She surprised him sometimes. She wore her siren facade so well that when she showed signs of depth it caught him off guard. Heaven help him, but he'd told her more about himself than anyone else, ever.

Why was that? What was there about her that made him open up?

She wondered why he had so little sympathy for Jack's mom; he could tell her he knew how it felt to be left in a storm.

He'd been a latchkey kid. They'd lived only a block from the school so he walked, and one day when he was in the first grade he'd run home through the rain only to huddle wet and cold on the doorstep for over an hour waiting for her to get home.

As he'd told Michelle, he firmly believed some women weren't meant to be mothers.

He stepped out of the vehicle and grabbed his jacket. When he saw no movement from her, he bent down to ask, "Aren't you going to come in and wait in the lobby?"

She shook her head, causing her hair to shimmer like gold in the dying sunshine. "Jack is asleep. We'll wait here. Take as long as you need."

He nodded and turned to enter the modern glass building. The entrance faced the small parking lot and Ted Watkins was waiting at the door.

They shook hands and he gestured to the SUV where he could clearly see Michelle.

"Would your friend like to come in? We have a nice waiting room."

"Thank you. But the baby is asleep."

"You have Jack with you?" Ted's gaze went back to the SUV. "Good. I'd like to meet him."

"Why?" Nate's protective hackles rose.

"Because it makes it more personal when I see and talk to the people involved in a case. Child custody cases are extremely personal so I want that connection. I'd also like to document his condition, take some pictures for the file."

"For what reason?" This really wasn't going how Nate had expected. "The trauma he experienced from being left in the storm has passed."

He spread his hands. "It may not ever come into play, but I prefer to be prepared. And as an officer of the court I can add my evaluation along with the custody documentation."

Watkins cocked his head and met Nate stare for stare.

"Is there a reason you don't want me to meet the boy?" the attorney asked point-blank.

"No." Nate relaxed a little. He got the impression Ted Watkins wouldn't relent until he determined for himself that Jack was okay. Nate knew his size and air of command intimidated most people. The fact that Watkins didn't let that deter him told Nate everything he needed to know. The man was tough, not afraid of a fight.

He was in the right hands.

"Good, then shall we ask your friend and Jack to join us?"

CHAPTER EIGHT

"I SAW the baby furniture in the room across the hall. I guess David delivered everything."

"He did." Keeping her attention on the array of stains and paint on the shelf, Michelle smiled at Nate's terse tone. "Between the three of us we got it all upstairs and put together. I like Kim. And David. They seem really happy together."

"You already made your point there," he said grimly. "We're not going to talk about their relationship."

"Okay, fine. What did the attorney say?" After being introduced to the lawyer, she and Jack had waited in the reception area while Nate finished his business.

"Can't we talk about the weather?"

Concerned, she stopped and faced him. "It was that bad?"

"No." His expression softened and he cupped the side of her face in his large hand. Briefly, gently, he swept his thumb along her cheek before dropping his hand.

"I liked him. He doesn't anticipate any problem with the court granting me full custody."

"Good." She forced a smile, pretending she didn't already miss his touch. He was an uptight lawman, in a go-nowhere town, and he stood between her and what she needed to do to get out of said nowhere town. Yet a single caress melted her insides.

That was just wrong.

Intent on self-preservation, she turned back to the shelves. They'd already been to the warehouse store to pick up food and baby supplies. They were now at Wal-Mart and had half the baby section loaded into two carts. Jack sat propped up between her oversize purse and a Spider-Man fleece blanket Nate insisted he needed.

Her last chore was to gather the items on her home improvement list. Best to stay on task.

"Whoa." Nate's hand closed around the tin of lavender paint Michelle moved toward her cart. "I said no purple."

"It's not purple. It's lavender."

"Which is just froufrou for purple." He put it back on the shelf. "It's not going in Jack's room."

Michelle tried to reach around him to retrieve the can of paint, but he blocked the shelves with his big body. Hands crossed over his chest, he sidestepped every time she did.

"It's not for Jack's room," she assured him, feinting one way then quickly back the other hoping to catch him off guard. He simply wrapped one long arm around her waist and reeled her in.

"I don't want it anywhere in the house," he declared.

Suddenly breathless and way too close to his taut, muscular body she went still, ending their crazy dance for power.

"Enough." She planted both hands on her hips. "It's not for the house, either. It's for outside."

"You want to paint my house purple? Oh, hell no."

That got her back up. "My house," she corrected. "I'll paint it any color I choose."

"Not while I'm living there," he responded. "New rule, I get veto power over all improvement projects."

"I don't think so. You haven't put a single bit of yourself in the house. And for the baby's room your idea of decorating is a stuffed bear, a dump truck and a Spider-Man blanket."

"It's a really cool truck."

She threw up her hands. "He's four months old!"

"He's a boy. And he's not going to live in a purple house."

"I give up." She sighed. "The paint is for my castle."

He blinked at her. "What?"

"My castle in the backyard." He still looked blank so she laid it out for him. "Castle. In the tree. In the backyard."

"The tree house?" Comprehension dawned. "That eyesore? I've been waiting for a free day to tear that thing down. It would already be gone by now except for the storm."

Anxiety ripped through her. She was lucky she'd made it home in time to save her beloved haven.

"Is the structure even sound? It's probably ready to fall to the ground."

"It's sound. I had to add a couple of nails here and there but it felt sturdy when I climbed up there yesterday."

"Good Lord." Clearly appalled, he demanded, "Tell me you didn't take Jack up there."

"Oh, yeah, we're a team. I had him in the sling while I was swinging the hammer." Sarcasm screamed through her chipper tone.

"Well, who knows about someone who'd paint any type of house purple?" But he stepped aside and let her retrieve the lavender paint.

An overwhelming sense of sadness hit her as she set the can in the cart. It had nothing to do with the stupid argument—the silly dance had almost been fun. But hearing how close she'd come to losing the tree house made her realize she'd soon be walking away from all of it—the house, the yard, the town. Reality brought on a melancholy she couldn't hide as tears burned her eyes.

"Hey," Nate said softly. He stepped closer, patted her shoulder. "Are you okay? Come on, this can't be about the color of the house."

She shook her head. "It's not that."

"Then what is it?"

His hand fell to the small of her back, a comforting touch. Without thought she leaned into him about to confess her unexpected wave of nostalgia.

Good God. She stopped, straightened away from him, then carefully put the length of the cart between them.

What was she thinking? She knew better than to reveal her weaknesses. Especially to a lawman trained to spot and exploit the weaknesses of his adversaries.

And despite their close circumstances, they were adversaries.

"It's nothing." She dismissed his concern with a dab at the corner of her eye. "I got a speck of dust in my eye."

"Dust?" He lifted one dark brow.

"Yes." That was it. No more letting her affection for Jack soften her toward his uncle. Surely that's all it was, a little residual connection. "I'm starved. Didn't you promise me dinner? Italian sounds good."

It simply wasn't possible she was falling for the sheriff.

Jack's cries reached Michelle in stereo through the barely open door and the baby monitor on her nightstand. She peeled one eye open, sighed and then forced the other open and her body into motion.

The first move had her moaning as muscles rarely used screamed in discomfort. With the near loss of her beloved tree house fresh in her mind, she went right to work on the remaining repairs and repainting. Nate may consider it a waste of time, stating the new owners could simply tear it down, but it was important to Michelle to bring it to its original glory. It represented the best part of her childhood, a visual reminder her dad had cared for her.

With the help of an electric sander she spent the day getting it ready for its pretty dressing of lavender paint. But tonight her arms and shoulders were feeling the pain of her gain.

No time to stretch with Jack demanding attention from across the hall, but she'd peek in Nate's medicine cabinet for some muscle rub before she went back to bed.

She frowned when the cries suddenly stopped. Not a good sign. A good baby, Jack rarely cried except for his 2:00 a.m. feeding. He'd already figured out if he didn't make himself heard there would be no bottle, and so he announced himself—loudly—until he saw the whites of her eyes.

At least that had been their schedule for the past four nights.

She pushed the door all the way open and found the reason for the change in routine. Nate stood with the baby cradled against his bare chest, Jack's head resting on Nate's shoulder as he rocked him slowly back and forth.

The sight of man and baby together took Michelle's breath away. Her heart wrenched and she wondered what it was about a tough man holding a baby that made a woman's knees go weak? A psychologist would probably explain it as something primal, dealing with procreation and survival of the species.

Whatever. She felt primal all right, lust at its purest level.

Dressed only in lightweight knit pajama bottoms, he personified masculine perfection—broad shoulders, trim torso, taut butt. Muscles flexed and flowed with the controlled back-and-forth motion.

Just yum.

He was gorgeous. Not even the scar detracted from the sheer beauty of his form.

"Hey," he said, sleep giving him a sexy rumble.

She shifted restlessly, and the satin of her nightie brushed over her sensitive nipples. She shivered even as heat raced through her blood.

"Hey." She crossed her arms over her chest, because her body had ideas she had more sense than to give in to. "Nothing wrong with this boy's lungs."

He laughed. "No. What are you doing up?"

"We agreed I'd watch the kid."

"Sure. During the day. I figured we'd split night duty. You had last night. Tonight is my turn."

"Seriously?"

"Yeah." Jack whimpered and began to wiggle, showing his displeasure with the chitchat delaying his feeding. "But since you're up, can you take him while I get his bottle?"

She took Jack and sung to him softly while Nate disappeared. A few minutes later she heard a ding too close to be from the kitchen downstairs. Curious, she stepped into the hall and encountered Nate coming back from the fourth bedroom, which he'd converted into his office.

He was shaking a bottle he'd obviously just made.

"Are you cheating?" she demanded.

He grinned. "Did I forget to tell you I have a minifridge and microwave in my office?"

"You didn't." She would have noticed when she prowled through the house.

"Okay, I bought them off one of my deputies, who was moving in with his girlfriend. It seemed like a good idea."

"Hmm." She accepted the bottle, fed it to Jack and

moved back into the baby's room and the office chair Nate had brought into the room.

He continued to surprise her with his dedication to the whole father thing. "Is it really so easy for you to assume this role?"

He shrugged, a sensual roll of bone and muscle. "Hell no. But it was my choice, no point in moaning about it."

"No, but it's got to be an adjustment."

"You have no idea." He ran both hands through his hair, sending the sleep-tousled mass into further disarray. "Everything has changed. I have to factor him in to every decision I make. Even at work I'm aware there's someone counting on me at home."

"I know," she empathized. "He's young enough and good enough I can put him in the portable crib while I'm working, but I'm constantly aware of him. And not only do I have to think about feeding and changing him, I worry about the logistics of keeping him in view but safe from paint fumes or dust particles."

"I saw the paint you got. It's kid-safe."

"Yes, but I still don't want him breathing in a lot of it. We're becoming a great team. He's a real guy's guy. He was kicking it to the sound of the power tools today."

Nate barked out a laugh and then his gaze turned intense.

"I know I've given you grief, but you've been a lifesaver. I really couldn't have done this without you."

"Thanks. I guess we're a team, too." She shifted her gaze away from the half-naked glory of him to the baby in her arms. Nice guy Nate combined with the fabulous body made him way too appealing.

"Have you thought about what you're going to do when I'm gone?" She pushed the reminder of her looming departure at him along with an internal lecture to take note.

Her goal was to spiff up the house, sell it and move to Los Angeles to get on with her life. She needed to stick to the plan.

Jack chose that moment to smile at her around the nipple in his mouth and he reached out and petted her cheek.

Her insides melted at the trust looking at her from that tiny face. She closed her eyes and pictured L.A.

"I've thought about it." Nate huffed out a frustrated breath in answer to her question about his future plans. "And I talked to Kim. She's given me a list of names to contact for nanny service. She says he's too young for most day-care centers and that they won't take a baby until they're potty-trained."

"A nanny is probably better with your hours anyway."

"True." He propped himself against the doorjamb, his broad frame nearly filling the opening. "It doesn't happen often but there are nights when I'm called out." He gave her a lazy smile. "Fair warning, you might have to cover for me some night."

"Familiar territory," she assured him.

"Right. You would understand. Anyway, it's pretty clear I'm going to need someone to live in."

"I was right, wasn't I? You were thinking you and Kim could team up to raise the kids. That a wife might be a better bet than a nanny?"

"It crossed my mind." He grimaced. "It wasn't my finest moment."

"No," she agreed. "You both deserve better."

He hung his head, shook it in despair. "I vowed I'd always take care of Kim and Christy. It's the least I can do."

"And I'd say you've met that vow." She carefully removed the bottle. Jack made a few sucking motions and then settled into sleep.

"I'll burp him." Nate came over and gently took Jack. She handed him a receiving blanket to use as a burp cloth and then crossed her legs and unabashedly watched man and baby.

She couldn't help herself. It was like constantly playing with a sore tooth—it wasn't good for you but you couldn't stop doing it.

"Maybe it wouldn't be such a bad solution," she conceded, thinking about his reaction to David. Maybe it was more than protecting his friend's place in her heart. Could Nate be jealous?

"Do you love her?" Something had driven her to ask the question. She shouldn't care. Didn't, she assured herself. It was only for Jack's sake that she pushed. It wouldn't be fair to him if Nate jumped into a relationship for the wrong reasons.

He went still. The question obviously caught him off guard. And she could see him thinking it through. So what did that mean?

"Yes," he finally declared.

She nodded, not surprised by his response. She knew Kim meant a lot to him, first because of what she'd meant to Quentin, but also from what Kim told her, the two of them had been through a lot together these last few years.

Now the pinch of resentment Michelle felt, *that* surprised her.

She cocked her head, and met him stare for stare. "Do you want her?"

"Ah, hell." No hesitation now, no need to think it through.

She had him. He cared for Kim, but it was clear his feelings for the other woman were no more romantic than hers were for him. And that wasn't going to change.

"So not a solution."

"It was only a passing thought."

"Why did you trade duty with him?"

"What?" Nate alternated rubbing Jack's back and patting him gently. She found it enthralling to watch his big hands tenderly handle the boy.

"With Quentin," she clarified. "Why did you guys switch duty?"

He sighed. "It was his anniversary and he had a chance to do a video chat with Kim, but it had to be early, so I took his shift."

"So you would have chosen to take that from him?"

He scowled. "Of course not. I knew how much he missed her. How he longed to see his kid."

"If you wouldn't change what led to the two of you being where you were when Quentin got shot, you can't continue to blame yourself."

"Wait." He rubbed a fist over his forehead, as if trying to push the information through. "No. If we hadn't traded—"

"Then Kim wouldn't have those last fond memories of him."

His eyes flashed. "But he'd be alive."

"You don't know that," she said softly. "If you're going to change one element, then other factors could change, as well. The sniper may have chosen the other target and Quentin could still be dead."

"No. You're mixing things up."

"I'm saying the only way to change what happened is to have denied Quentin time with his wife and daughter. And even then there's no guarantee he wouldn't still be gone."

Jack burped, the sound loud in the sudden silence. Nate spent the next few minutes putting Jack back in his bed.

She realized she wasn't going to get an answer. That she'd pressed Nate as far as she could. She pushed to her feet and walked to the door, satin sliding sensually over her body. Halfway through the door she stopped and glanced at him over her shoulder.

"You're a good guy, Nate. You should give yourself a break."

CHAPTER NINE

On Michelle's first day off, she gratefully left Jack in Nate's care, strapped on the tool belt her dad had given her when she was eight and strolled out the front door. The belt felt familiar on her hips and she ran her finger along the notches her dad added to fit her growing figure through the years.

She was supposed to have yesterday off. But it got postponed when the mayor demanded Nate participate in a meeting with the local school district.

Putting aside her annoyance at having her schedule disrespected—she'd expected it, hadn't she—she skipped down the porch steps and strode across the yard.

She'd noticed a couple of fence boards were loose after the storm so she walked the perimeter of the property making repairs where she could and taking notes on boards that needed replacing.

For the front she decided a new coat of paint would do a lot to perk up the curb appeal. Luckily the yard was in good repair because she didn't mind wielding a hammer, but gardening had never been her thing.

Not that Dad hadn't recruited her help there, too. She eyed the early-blooming irises, remembering how helping Dad plant the flower bed around the stone bird-bath had earned her freedom from being grounded to go to the Spring Fling Ball with Timothy Smart in junior high. She deemed the dirt under her fingernails a worthwhile payment when Timmy gave her her first kiss at the dance.

Oh, yeah, she had a fondness for irises. She grinned. How Dad would have freaked if he knew. Then she shook her head—who was she kidding? Of course he'd known. He may not have made it to her graduation from junior high to high school, but he always knew what was happening with her. He'd had spies everywhere. It was one of the reasons she'd been so hot to skip town.

With a sigh she walked down the side of the house, along the cement walk her father had put in when she was all of four or five. Even then he had her helping him. She remembered holding the hose over the wheelbarrow while he mixed the concrete.

At the end of the walk she stopped and stared down at her tiny handprints imbedded in the cement, her father's large prints were there, too, on either side of hers. She remembered how he'd tickled her neck with his whiskers making her laugh, as he leaned over her to press his hands in the wet cement.

Now he was gone. There'd be no more projects. Tears stung her eyes and she ran her finger along the notches again. The tool belt would be a reminder of her dad for the rest of her life.

Ten minutes after his shift ended Nate got a text message from Michelle advising him he'd invited Kim and

David for dinner to thank them for their help last week and he should get home as soon as possible.

He'd invited them? No.

Guilt tightened the muscles across his shoulders as he acknowledged he should have. Worse, he would have but the whole David thing continued to annoy him. Kim should have told him she was seeing someone.

Obviously Michelle had picked up his slack and made the arrangements. Not that it was any of her business.

And he told her so thirty minutes later when he confronted her in his kitchen.

"Well, if you would have handled it, I wouldn't have had to," she informed him. "And you're late."

"It's not a nine-to-five job. I was wrapping up a meeting with a neighborhood watch group when I got your text."

"You could have let me know you'd be late." She gave him a chiding glare along with a set of pot holders. "I'm trying to put on a party here. Can you drain the noodles?"

"I didn't ask for a party. Kim is my friend. She knows I'm grateful for the furniture. I already told her so." He dumped the noodles into the colander, turning his face away from the rising steam.

He noticed she'd hung new curtains. Gone were the dull white ruffles and in their place a soft yellow wafted in the light breeze. They looked fresh and clean against the crisp white of the newly painted trim.

"Oh? So you've talked to her since they delivered the furniture?"

"Well, no." He set the pan back on the stove. "Come on. Friends don't have to keep repeating themselves."

"Not usually, but this was a big favor and it involved more than Kim. You barely know David and he put in a big effort."

Replacing Nate at the stove, she pulled another pan forward and lifted the lid. The scents of garlic and bacon filled the air.

"Him." He used his hip to push her aside and lifted the heavy pan to pour the contents over the noodles. "This looks great. What is it?"

"Yes, David. Kim cares for him." She edged in next to him and began to fold the creamy mixture into the noodles. "If you care for Kim like you say you do, you'll make an effort with David. It's spaghetti carbonara."

He licked a finger. "Tasty."

"Glad you like it. You can set the table."

"I'll tell you what I don't like." He opened the cupboard with the plates. "David."

"You don't know him. This dinner will help remedy that."

Catching her looking at him from the corner of her emerald eyes Nate braced himself for what was coming. He'd already revealed way too much to her the other night. Sitting there in a pink little bit of nothing that clung to her curves as faithfully as a lover, she'd raked him over the coals both emotionally and physically.

"She told me you're like a brother to her."

"Yeah," he admitted with no small sense of relief, "which doesn't make it any easier to see her with David."

"She deserves to be loved, Nate. After all she's suffered, she deserves to be happy. You want that for her, don't you? And for her to be taken care of? Isn't that what Quentin would want for her?"

God, she had his number. Knew just what keys to tap. And she was right about all of it. He wanted Kim and Christy to have everything they needed and wanted. Whether it was him to give it to them or not.

"David makes her happy," Michelle said in a whisper as if the softness would make it easier to accept. And then she turned brisk. "Never mind the table. I've got the rest of this. You should go change if you plan to. They'll be here in fifteen minutes. Oh, and I invited Dolly, too."

"Of course," he muttered as he left the room. "The more the merrier."

Actually Dolly was a great addition to the party. It gave him someone to talk to other than David.

Michelle picked up the plates and followed Nate from the room, watching as he jogged up the stairs. He moved with a lithe grace that was a pure joy to see.

But he was totally off-limits. She'd lectured herself severely on staying detached. This whole dinner party was just an excuse to talk to Dolly.

This morning it had finally clicked with Michelle, duh, that if Nate was renting the house, he must be paying rent. When she asked where he was sending the payments to, he told her Dolly because that was where he had been sending it and he'd never been notified to send it anywhere else.

Dolly was a retired attorney. It stood to reason she'd know where the money was. Michelle should have thought about her dad's affairs before now. She knew he didn't own much beyond the house and a truck older than she was, but there may be something she should take care of.

Michelle liked Dolly. She and Dad had been friends forever. But Michelle didn't know what to think about her dad and Dolly hooking up. It was just such a foreign concept for Michelle to think of him in that way. Anyway, she preferred this meeting with the woman be informal.

So far so good. The carbonara was a hit. Nate actually appeared to be giving David a fair shake, helped along by Dolly's easy chatter. Christy was enthralled with Jack and wanted to treat him like a doll, but otherwise so far so good.

The chill brought on by the storm a week ago was gone, replaced by the warm days of spring. With both the front and back doors open a breeze blew through the house making it easy for them to linger at the table.

Now came the hard part. They'd all carried their plates into the kitchen and the others were headed for the living room. It was Michelle's chance to get the older woman alone.

"Dolly, would you like to see the work I've done refurbishing my dad's old rocking chair?"

"Sure." The petite, white-haired woman turned at Michelle's invitation. "I don't remember him having a rocker."

"We found it in the attic when we went looking for baby furniture. None of my baby stuff was there. I'm kind of surprised the rocker was. Dad believed in use it or lose it."

"That's exactly how he was." Dolly laughed. "I swear if I didn't eat fast enough, half my meal ended up in the trash."

"He was always after me to eat, so he didn't do that to me. But I did have to explain to a teacher once that he'd thrown my homework away."

"Oh, goodness." Dolly's brown eyes danced with mirth. "That ranks right up there with the dog eating it."

"Exactly." Feeling justified even after all these years, Michelle led the way into the garage. "The teacher wouldn't let me make it up until I had my dad call him and admit he'd trashed it."

Laughing together, she met Dolly's gaze and suddenly her throat swelled up and tears filled her eyes. She swallowed and blinked, seeking control. Instead the tears overflowed and rained down her cheeks.

She missed her dad.

While she was in San Francisco it hadn't been so bad, probably because she was used to being alone there. She'd had her friends, especially Amanda, but her dad had little to do with her life in the city. He'd visit a couple of times a year, always made a point to come to her gigs. And she'd always been so proud when he sat in the audience.

Coming home and not finding Dad here felt wrong. The situation with Nate and Jack kept her busy and distracted, but the truth was she kept expecting to see her dad, to run into him when she entered a room.

Of course she didn't. Not physically, but there was evidence of him everywhere.

She tried to pretend she was fine, because if she pretended hard enough eventually she really would be fine. It was hard, though,

"Oh, my dear." Dolly's arms wrapped her in sympathy, in comfort. "I miss him, too. Every day."

They stood, tears flowing, locked together in love and sorrow for a man gone but not forgotten, who'd been important to each of them in different ways.

After a few minutes, Michelle pulled away, walked to the workbench and brought back a box of tissues. She offered a couple to Dolly.

"Thank you." The older woman mopped her eyes and dabbed at her nose. She looked dewy but none the worse for wear.

Michelle knew her eyes were red-rimmed and her nose rivaled Rudolph's, but she pushed the notion aside.

"I've been so mad at him," she confessed.

"Oh, my dear. Why?"

"For not telling me he was sick." She plucked at the damp tissue. "I could have spent more time with him if I'd known. Made him take better care of himself."

"After his scare, he did change his diet and begin exercising more. He was trying."

More tears leaked out. "I never thought of us as being that close. He was always rushing off to take care of business. And the distance just got worse when I moved to the city."

"Oh, sweetheart. I loved your father, but when it came to expressing his emotions, he was a complete cotton head. You don't want to know how long it took him to kiss me the first time."

Michelle threw up a staying hand.

"No, I really don't." She confirmed with a half-hysterical laugh. "That's not a picture I want in my head."

"Of course," Dolly said with a bit of a twinkle. "What I'm trying to say is he may not have said so often, but he loved you very much."

Michelle shook her head and tossed the used tissues in a bin at the end of the workbench. Not often?

Try rare as fairy dust.

She'd only ever heard him say those three little words once a year on her birthday, and then only when he thought she was asleep. She heard it for the first time when she was eight. Every birthday after that, she'd pretended to be asleep early, just to hear the words.

"With Mom gone, it was just the two of us. We should have been tight. But—"

"He put you second." Dolly nodded, her well-defined brows puckered in a frown. "I saw it as you were growing up. It's one of the few things we argued about. It was his self-defense mechanism after your mom died. He needed work and the sense of duty to help him cope, to give him focus. He genuinely couldn't see what it was doing to you."

Choked up, Michelle stared at her feet, focusing on the black sneakers with the bright pink trim. She frowned at a white smudge of paint on the toe.

"He was the job."

"Yes, beyond anything else, he was the job. But I also know it hurt him to know he failed you."

"He didn't fail me," she insisted. "I learned to cope,

too. And I knew if I truly needed him, he'd be there for me."

"I'm glad you realize that." Dolly's smile was sad. "He had his way, you know, of showing his love. Taking out the trash without being asked. Handling little fix-its around the house before they became big fix-its. Drawing me into projects so we spent time together."

Michelle thought of the reminders of her dad she'd found while updating the house to sell, how she kept coming across projects he insisted they work on together. She thought of her tool belt and swallowed hard.

Yes, that was exactly his way.

"I want him back."

"Me, too." Dolly kissed Michelle's cheek. "We'll just have to keep him close in our hearts. Now, where is that rocking chair?"

"Rocking chair?" Michelle blanked for a minute, and then remembered her gambit to get Dolly alone. She still needed to talk to the woman about her father's affairs. She hadn't meant to get so emotional.

"It's over here." She hit the button to lift the garage door and let in the light, then led Dolly to where the mission-style rocker sat on a tarp on the far side of the garage.

"I've stripped it, sanded the treads until they were even and used wood glue to tighten the dowels. Now it's ready to be stained."

"Oh, my dear. You've done a wonderful job. This is a beautiful piece." She sighed. "And I know why your dad kept it."

"Really?" Surprised, Michelle demanded, "Why? How?"

"Your father had a picture of this chair in his things. It's of you and your mother. She's holding you against her shoulder and you're both asleep. It's very Madonna-like."

"Oh." The vision left Michelle speechless.

"It's beautiful. And was obviously a prized possession of your father's."

"Can I have the picture?"

"Of course." Dolly squeezed her hands. "I have all his things for you. And we can go over his estate whenever you're ready."

"His estate? I didn't think he had anything besides the house. I was just going to ask after the rent for this place."

"There's that, yes. But your father lived simply and saved. He had a college fund for you that you never used. And of course there was his life insurance, which has been placed in an account for you at his bank."

"I had no idea." Stunned, Michelle's mind whirled. She'd pulled into town with the last of her savings in her pocket and a desperate plan to turn it into a nest egg to finance a new life in Los Angeles.

It never occurred to her Dad had any assets beyond the house. The windfall was bittersweet, she could use the money, but it came at such a high price.

"I'm sorry." Dolly's voice trembled a little. "I should have made a better attempt to talk to you at the funeral, but it was such a difficult time for me."

"Stop." Michelle hugged the woman. "I understand. Tell me the rest."

"I tried to reach you afterward, but the contact information I found was no longer good."

Michelle grimaced, remembering the loss of yet another job, of having to mooch off Amanda while she tried to find something new in an ever shrinking job market.

"It was a difficult time for me, too."

"I'd like to hear about it," Dolly said with sincerity. "Why don't you come over some day this week? We can talk and I can give you your dad's things."

Michelle had been so reluctant going into this meeting but at the end she felt closer to both her father and Dolly.

She nodded. "I'd like that."

"So you're serious about this David guy?" Nate followed Kim to a small SUV parked at the curb. She'd brought another box of baby things and he'd volunteered to carry them inside.

Michelle's instincts appeared to be on target where Kim and David were concerned, but he wanted to hear it from Kim.

"Come on, Nate. He's not that 'David guy.' You two have met a couple of times. He's a well-respected member of the community." She popped her trunk and then stood back so he could reach the box.

"Huh." In no hurry, he leaned a hip against the dark green vehicle and crossed his arms over his chest.

"We've bumped into each other at a few events. But I don't know the man."

"Considering your occupation, that's a good thing." Both her tone and posture challenged.

He had to concede her point. And her defense of David indicated her emotions were engaged.

Seemed emotions were on the playbill today. From where he stood he saw Michelle and Dolly wrapped together with the waterworks flowing. A frown drew his brows together. It wasn't like Michelle to get all weepy.

"Nate." Kim called his name and he shifted his gaze to her.

"Yeah."

"I want you to give David a chance," she implored him. "He's important to me."

"I see." Well, there was his confirmation. He flicked a glance toward the garage. Michelle had been right. She appeared more composed and he nodded.

"I'm glad you understand." Kim wrapped him in a hug. "You're important to me, too. In a different way."

He patted her on the back. "I'll always be here if you need me."

"I know you don't have to be." She stepped back and gave him a watery smile. "But you will be. You were a good friend to Quentin."

"I'm your friend, too."

"Yes. But you came here and helped me and Christy because of him. I'm not too proud to say we needed you. That I was glad for your help even though you owed us nothing."

He shoved his hands in his pockets and looked away. Michelle and Dolly were inspecting the rocker.

"I wouldn't say nothing."

"I would," Kim insisted. "Quentin was a soldier to the bone, he knew the drill, accepted the risks. We both did. He wouldn't have wanted you to take a bullet because of his choices."

"It's not fair. He had a wife and child. Nobody would have missed me."

"Oh, my God, Nate." Kim pushed the strawberry-blond hair away from her face with both hands. "That is so not true. I hope you don't believe that."

"It's true enough," he argued gruffly. "Nobody depended on me like you depended on Quentin."

"Your cousin Jack needed you. He would have been lost without you."

"Not even Jack could help Jack."

"But you did. He tried because of you."

"I didn't do him any favors. He joined the service because of me. And the war killed him, in a slow and painful process."

"Stop it this instant. You are not responsible for the decisions other people make. War is hell. It breaks the strong and the weak. Jack loved you. He respected you. And he deserves your respect in return." Impassioned she pointed toward the house. "And if you want to talk about someone needing you, let's talk about Jack's son."

"Okay." He pulled her in for a fierce hug. "Settle down."

"Let me go." She pushed away, fire flashing in her blue eyes. "I won't listen to you bad-mouth yourself.

You're one of the best men I know and no one gets to trash talk my friend, not even you."

"All right. You win." Unable to meet her gaze he stared at the toes of his boots. "I'm wonderful."

"Darn right," she snapped, clearly unappeased. "Now say it with a little more conviction. You talk some sense into him. I'm done trying."

Nate looked up to see whose mercy Kim had tossed him to and saw Michelle stood on the curb a few feet away. Why would Kim think Michelle had any sway over him?

He wondered how much she'd heard. Not that it mattered. She pretty much poked her little nose wherever she wanted.

Kim reached into the back of the SUV and lifted the box out. He held out his hands but she walked right by him.

"Hey, I thought I was carrying that."

"That was before I was mad at you. Now I can get it myself." She jutted her chin and narrowed her eyes at him. "And make friends with David, you big lug. You'll like each other if you give it half a chance."

She stormed up the walk and David came out when she reached the porch and took the box. Great.

With a sigh Nate closed the rear door of the SUV. Michelle came over and leaned against it next to him.

"I'll never understand women."

"That's because you're a man and you have to complicate things."

"Me? She's mad because I said Quentin should be here instead of me."

"She's mad because you devalued yourself. And if your life means nothing, does that mean the last three years spent helping her mean nothing?"

"Of course not."

"You blame yourself for both Quentin's and Jack's deaths, but have you ever thought that by taking responsibility you're robbing them of their dignity?"

Appalled, he shook his head. "I'd never do that."

"Life is a series of decisions, actions and consequences. They put us in a certain place at a certain time and life happens. Sometimes you meet that special someone. Or make the deal of a lifetime. Or you could die. Jack struggled in the end, but the same man that raised you raised him. I have to believe at one point he was a strong, capable man. As was Quentin. By honoring their choices you honor their memories."

"Kim said something like that." He rubbed a hand around the back of his neck. He felt like he'd been put through the spin cycle. First Kim and then Michelle questioned his motives when he was just trying to do his best.

Funny how when Kim talked to him, his defenses crackled, but Michelle had a way of offering him options that empowered him.

"Smart woman. You should listen to her." She punched him in the arm and headed inside. After a few steps, she stopped and waved him along. "Come on. We're having ice-cream floats for dessert."

He followed her retreat with brooding eyes.

He had all the respect in the world for Jack and Quentin. But how was he supposed to shrug off their deaths when they seemed so pointless? And when they'd had so much to live for?

Still he needed to think about what Michelle and Kim were saying because he'd rather cut off his right arm than do anything to dishonor Quentin or Jack.

His cell buzzed in his pocket. He fished the phone out and flipped it open. A couple of minutes later, he went inside to make his excuses. He'd have to miss out on the ice-cream floats. There'd been an incident at Pete's Hardware and Nate had to go.

Luckily he escaped before he had to admit the women were right.

CHAPTER TEN

A WEEK later Michelle slowly rocked Jack as he took his bottle at 2:00 a.m. Tonight was Nate's turn, but he'd been called out to an accident on the main highway.

Her muscles ached with each motion of the chair. She'd finished painting the castle today. It looked great—soft lavender with white trim, a true castle in the sky.

She was a little surprised she was still here. As they'd planned, she'd met up with Dolly for lunch earlier in the week. Her dad had provided well for her in his death. She should have known he would, because he'd provided well for her in life, physically if not emotionally.

Excited, her immediate reaction was to take the money and run, waving to River Run via her rearview mirror.

And then she left the meeting and had her first hesitation when she strapped Jack into his car seat. How could she think of leaving him? He'd already lost his father and his mother. Yes, he loved Nate, the two of them were as close as a dog and his bone, but losing someone else would no doubt affect his little psyche.

Not to mention Nate had yet to find a sitter or nanny to take her place.

He'd allowed her to stay and start on the house in exchange for helping with Jack. Nate had needed the help, but so had she and he'd come through for her.

And truthfully living with him wasn't so bad. Sure his schedule could be erratic, but she'd also arrived home from running errands or visiting Kim to find Nate had started dinner or folded the laundry. They'd fallen into a rhythm and it worked.

Sure her circumstances had changed but she still needed to deal with selling the house. If she left now, she'd just have to come back to finish what she'd started. Once she got to Los Angeles she wanted to concentrate on the future, not be drawn back to the past.

Better to stay and see it through now.

Jack whimpered. Poor guy was in a bit of a mood tonight. She began to hum and when he opened his eyes to look at her she sang softly.

My American man opens his arms, opens his home
To a fatherless child, lost and alone.
He heats up the bottle, rocks him to and fro.
My American man is an everyday hero.

Jack smiled and her heart lurched. Yeah, here was the true reason she was staying. And oh, she had it bad.

She sang a while longer playing with the words to a song she'd been working on and he slid into sleep. She kissed him softly and put him in his crib, and then lingered for a moment, tucking the blanket around him, making sure he was sleeping soundly.

With a sigh, she turned to leave and found Nate standing in the doorway watching her. She stopped, caught by something in his expression. He looked tired, but more than that he looked tormented. And she knew it must have been bad tonight.

That he was in need tonight.

Again her heart lurched. Oh, man. She knew better than to let him close, to allow him in. That wasn't why she was staying.

But the pain in his eyes cut through all that.

"Hey," she said softly.

Without a word he walked to her, cupped her face in his hands and took her mouth with his. She tasted his desperation, his need, and gave him everything he craved, going on her toes to get closer to him.

He groaned and wrapped his arms around her, hugging her near and deepening the kiss. For long moments he ravaged her mouth, stealing her breath and her senses.

She thrilled to his touch, to the heat building between them. Inching closer she pressed her body to his, aligning thigh to thigh, hip to hip, breast to chest. Oh, yeah.

He lifted his head, pressed his forehead to hers. Breath ragged, he demanded, "My bed or yours?"

"I have a twin." She imagined the two of them squeezed onto the small bed and thought it wouldn't be such a bad thing. But bigger would be better.

"Mine then." He took her hand and turned for the door.

"The master has a king."

A smoldering glance pinned her over his shoulder. "Too much space."

Yeah, plus she really needed to make changes in there before she'd be comfortable thinking of it as anything other than Dad's room.

To prove she liked how Nate thought she pushed him through his door and followed him inside. Closing it behind her, she leaned back against wood. A quick glance confirmed Nate's baby monitor was active on his nightstand. Good.

Biting her lower lip in a sexy moue, she beckoned to him. His eyes blazed with desire, and he prowled back to her. Placing both hands on the wooden barrier either side of her head, he lowered his head and claimed her mouth with his. He ran his tongue along the seam of her mouth and softly nipped her bottom lip, punishing her for taunting him.

Or rewarding her.

"Ouch." She sighed. And then returned the favor, using her teeth on him, and rejoiced in his groan of need. Circling his neck with her arms, she allowed him to carry her to his bed, to lower her to her feet. "More." She threaded her fingers in his hair and pulled him to her for another heated kiss.

"This is probably a bad idea," she said when they came up for air. And then, her eyes on his, she slipped the straps of her cotton camisole off her shoulders. Anticipation flaring in his gaze, he hooked his thumbs in the sides and pushed the garment down her body, catching the waist of her pajama shorts along the way.

"Oh, I'm sure we'll regret it," he agreed, nibbling on her ear. "But I don't want to stop. Do you?"

"You could try to stop." Shivering under his intent stare, she reached for the buttons of his uniform. "But I'd hate to have to hurt you so early in our relationship."

He laughed. But he shook his head and stopped her. Instead he swept the covers back, letting them fall off the end, and then he pushed her gently down.

"No danger of that." He assured her, making quick work of stripping off his clothes. And lowering himself next to her.

He went to kiss her but she placed a finger against his lips to halt him. He nipped her finger then lifted a dark brow in question.

"Are you sure you wouldn't rather talk?"

"You're kidding me, right?"

"You're obviously upset from the accident."

"It was a fatality. Two dead, a child and his mother. I really don't want to talk about watching a man lose his family. I want to forget." He dipped his head and did something with his mouth that made lightning sing through her body.

"Make me forget," he said against her skin.

"Forget what?" She gasped, already lost under the skill of his hands and lips, arching as he played her like a delicate instrument.

She wrapped herself around him, giving, taking, wondering. From one moment to the next caress became demand, became the need for more, for harder, deeper, higher until she bowed under the exquisite flow of sensation. With a cry she clung to him, her ballast in the storm, and soared with him through the night.

Jack's soft whimpering woke Nate the next morning. Instantly alert, he opened his eyes to see it was before seven. No need for the woman in his arms to be up yet. God, she felt good against him, soft and warm and female. How could something that felt so right, be so wrong?

He kissed the bare curve of her shoulder and eased away from the temptation of her. Pulling on his jeans he crossed the hall to tend Jack.

"Hi, buddy." He greeted the baby. At the sound of his voice Jack stopped whimpering and smiled. "Sorry I missed your feeding last night. It couldn't be avoided."

He'd been feeling raw when he'd gotten home last night. Death was never easy. And the Lord knew Nate had seen more than his fair share of it. But it's not something a guy became accustomed to. At least he hoped he never got that callous.

He'd asked Michelle to help him forget. And she had helped. He hadn't truly forgotten, the victims deserved better than that, but she'd given him the distance he needed to cope with the memories.

Finding her standing over Jack dressed in a skimpy T-shirt and shorts, singing softly to the baby about everyday heroes, instantly relieved his distress. Her sensual beauty and sweet voice soothed him, the perfect foil for the devastation he'd come from.

Every day he fought the need to taste her again, to feel her in his arms. He understood she didn't fit in his life, that when she got the money from the house she'd be gone in a blink.

Last night, he hadn't cared.

Need overrode common sense and in the wee hours of a difficult night, he'd been drawn across the room, compelled to inhale her scent, to surround himself in her warmth. And her eager response eased his troubled soul.

He lifted Jack from his bed, made quick work of changing his diaper and carried him downstairs to prep his bottle. While the formula heated in the microwave, Nate got the coffee going.

He amazed himself with how adept he'd become with the routine. He should thank Michelle for that, too. She was so impressed with his decision to take in Jack, Nate hated the thought of looking like a freaked-out pansy handling the baby—which was how he'd really felt—so he'd faked it.

Reading instructions on the formula can, total pansy, making note of how the snaps and tapes and buckles went as he undid them so he could put them back. Watching Michelle, seeing how she did things. He'd been a total cheat. But it had worked. Now he only occasionally freaked out.

Jack squeaked and shifted to look at the microwave, a clue to Nate he'd missed hearing the bell.

He grinned at Jack. "I'll tell you this—" he lifted the boy so they met eye to eye "—my head may be all over the place, but I feel great."

"I'm feeling pretty good myself," Michelle drawled from the doorway.

He tucked Jack against his shoulder and met her gaze across the width of the room. "Hey."

"Good morning." She strolled over, circled his neck with one arm and kissed him softly. With a sigh she pulled away and walked to the coffeemaker to pour herself a cup of the strong brew.

"What's wrong with your head?" she asked after her first sip.

Jack began to protest the delay of his breakfast, so Nate pulled the baby's bottle from the microwave and fed it to him before responding.

She smelled of soap and a hint of mint and looked beautiful without a speck of makeup. His body tightened as images of her in his arms woke up his libido.

Forget Wheaties, the breakfast of champions stood in front of him, her sweet butter hair, cherry lips and peaches-and-cream skin made her look good enough to eat.

Oh, yeah, he wanted him some for breakfast.

Too bad all that sweetness was bad for him.

And he still had night mouth.

"I was messed up last night." Definitely not thinking straight. And her kiss just sent his morning ricocheting off course. What did it mean? "You helped. Thanks."

Was it a morning-after kiss? Or was it a she-thought-they'd-started-something kiss?

"A fatality must be difficult to deal with. Especially a child," she sympathized.

"You know, hold that thought." He pushed Jack into her arms. "And Jack. I'll be right back."

Either way she meant the kiss, he didn't want the final

marker of last night to be a mere peck on the mouth. Not when it was going to have to last him a lifetime.

He shot upstairs, hit the bathroom for a quick spit and shine, grabbed a shirt and headed back downstairs.

In the kitchen he rewrote history. Jack played with a rattle in the portable crib under the window and Michelle whisked something at the counter.

Grabbing her hand he whirled her into his arms and captured her mouth with his in a lover's kiss, swift and needy, a dance of tongues in a heated embrace. He drowned himself in her, sipping from the minty freshness of her lips.

He lifted his head once, but it was too soon. So he shifted to a new angle and sank into her again. And she was right there with him. She climbed onto his feet, lifted onto her toes and took him prisoner by circling him in her arms, surrendering to the passion consuming them.

The need to breathe broke them apart. Forehead to forehead he sawed for air as if he'd run a four-minute mile. She sighed and swayed into him. He had to set his knees to hold them up. He buried his nose in her hair, breathed deep of sunshine and hibiscus.

She turned her head and bit him on the arm.

"Ow!" He set her at arm's length. "What the hell?"

"My thought exactly." She threw back her head and propped her hands on her hips. "I know goodbye when it smacks me in the mouth. I shouldn't be surprised. You said you'd have regrets."

"But I don't," he denied.

"Looks like boo-hoo from where I'm standing."

The woman donned attitudes like other women wore accessories. Different occasions requiring different 'tudes. He saw just enough hurt in her defiant eyes to recognize her attack as a defensive move.

Fine. She wanted a fight?

He got right up in her grill. "No regrets." He made it clear. "Not a single one. You were the best time I've ever had."

"You bet your derriere I am."

She didn't blink. Didn't back down an inch, which was seriously hot. And an unwanted distraction.

He bit back a smile, knowing any show of amusement would only antagonize her more.

"I'm not a gambling man."

Her vibrant green eyes narrowed suspiciously.

"But?"

"No buts."

"Seriously?"

"There were no promises made. None inferred." This close to her, with the air sizzling between them, he almost regretted that. "We're both adults who know the score."

"Yet it won't happen again." It was a statement, which told him she'd come to the same conclusion.

"It's for the best."

Each breath brought her scent into him until he longed to eliminate the space between them. Instead he carefully stepped back.

"Don't you agree?"

"Yes." An odd twitch of her head accompanied the

agreement and then she swung around and picked up the whisk. "It's for the best."

She beat furiously at the poor concoction in the bowl.

He ached to go to her, to pull her stiff body into his and re-create the magic they'd made last night. But good as it had been there was no future in it.

And he knew in that moment why none of the women he'd interviewed for Jack's nanny were working out. None of them were Michelle.

Until he worked that out, he needed her help with Jack. It wouldn't be smart to get involved with her in any other capacity. Not for such a short amount of time.

Not when he was already half in love with her.

CHAPTER ELEVEN

It was her own fault, Michelle bemoaned as she bounced Jack on her hip and watched three little girls play ring-around-the-rosie with the coffee table. She allowed Kim and Dolly to gang up on her.

It took all her energy and ingenuity to take care of one little boy. What made them—or her—think she could take on four kids at one time?

The thing was Dolly and Kim were friends with two of Michelle's old classmates who had opened an internet cupcake pop business. It was a good news-bad news scenario. Good news for her classmates' business, bad news for Michelle, who was called on to babysit while everyone baked, dipped and shipped.

"Girls, let's head outside. I have apples and oranges for everyone."

As the girls shrieked their excitement, she ushered them outside.

No doubt about it, she'd gotten the rough end of the arrangement. She'd been looking forward to four o'clock, when the moms were supposed to pick up their young. That was before the phone call saying they needed another hour. Or two!

Nate was going to freak when he got home.

"Castle." Awe colored Christy's voice and lit up her big blue eyes as she took in the refurbished tree house. "I wanna go in the castle."

"Castle, castle." The other girls began to chant. They were all under four.

"Oh, no. No. No. No." Michelle tried to stop the stampede of three-year-olds, but it was no contest. They almost knocked her off her feet. She hugged Jack to her and prayed for a miracle.

"Girls, I can't take the baby up there and you can't go alone. Girls!" She glanced helplessly at the table and then back at the heads bobbing around the base of the tree. "There's fruit."

Giving up, she crossed the lawn at a trot, catching Christy around the waist and lifting her off the ladder leading up.

"Sorry, kids, but you're too small."

Too small and too many for her to handle on her own while also taking care of Jack.

The wailing started.

The girls scattered like cats after pigeons, each trying to get to the ladder when she chased another away. Delighted with the game, Jack giggled. Not so thrilled, Michelle growled under her breath.

"Stop. I said stop." Her stern tone had no impact on the tiny tots. Their merry shrieks were loud enough to pierce the eardrum.

"What's going on out here?" a male voice demanded.

Of course Nate was early. You could never count on a lawman's schedule. Late when you wanted them home, early when you needed extra time. But today she didn't care.

She swung around and found the sight of Nate standing on the back patio such a sight for frazzled nerves her standoffish attitude of the last two weeks vanished in an instant.

Rushing to his side, she thrust Jack into his arms.

"I'm never having kids," she announced. And turned back to corral the girls. She shook her head as she saw Christy was halfway up the ladder again. Definitely the instigator in this crowd.

Nate quickly passed Michelle, moving Jack into one arm and snagging Christy safely with his other. He blocked the ladder so the other little girls couldn't get up and turned to face Michelle, the two children perched smugly in his embrace, obviously unfazed by his stern demeanor.

"I asked what was going on."

Happy for a moment's respite, Michelle plopped down in a patio chair, grabbed an apple slice and bit off the end. Flavor exploded in her mouth, the sweetness and crunch as satisfying as the joy of handing over authority. Even if it only lasted for a brief moment.

"Where's Mama?" Christy asked.

"Good question," Nate told her. His gaze pinned Michelle. "Spill."

With a sigh she filled him in on the whole babysitting gig.

"How long ago did Kim call?"

She glanced at her watch. "An hour and a half."

The corner of his mouth lifted in a grim half smile and he pulled his cell out of his pocket.

"Hey," he said into the phone. "Your daughter is asking for you." Pause. "No, I'm not early. How's it going over there?" He listened for a few minutes, throwing in an occasional grunt. "How much longer do you think that's going to take? Another hour and a half?"

Michelle's heart sank. She threw up both hands in a staying motion and frantically shook her head. After five hours, she was more than ready to throw in the towel. In fact, give her a towel—a bubble bath sounded really good right about now.

Listening to him agree to additional time, she thought she better get some cupcake pops out of this or someone would pay.

"I can't believe you caved," she groused when he hung up. "Chump."

He laughed and set Christy down to play with her friends. "You started it."

"Last time I make that mistake," she assured him. It was good to hear him laugh again. The last couple of weeks had been very stiff between them. She'd missed him. "I thought I was such hot stuff because I've been taking care of Jack. But he's sweet and happy, and quiet. I'm telling you these girls are from a whole other planet."

"Michelle." He was totally patronizing.

"And they don't talk on their planet. They scream."

"You're tired."

"Completely wiped."

"Uncle Nate." Christy tugged on his pant leg. "We want to go in the castle."

"Yeah." The other two girls cheered. "We want to go in the castle!"

"That's their latest thing, but they can't go up alone and I couldn't help them and hold Jack, too." She waved to the fruit on the table. "I made them a snack. But I brought them out here and now all they're interested in is the castle."

"Well, they are little girls."

"Yeah."

"And you did spiff it up so it looks pretty enchanting."

"Yeah, it's pretty dope." He was trying to butter her up, and darned if it wasn't working.

"Well, we have the girls for another hour or more." Without shifting his attention from her, he carefully removed his badge from Jack's grasp and tucked it in his pants pocket. "Why don't we add some sandwiches and have a picnic in the *c-a-s-t-l-e*."

She perked up in an instant. She loved the idea. A tea party in the castle, how perfect. It had been way too long since she played princess.

"Excellent." She popped up, threw her arms around him, kissed him on the cheek and Jack on the mouth. "Tiaras! We're going to need tiaras."

"Hold it," Nate called after her as she skipped into the house. "We are not playing dress-up."

She simply wiggled her fingers at him over her shoulder. Of course they were playing dress-up. Why hadn't she thought of it sooner?

In her room she found everything she needed.

For all his quickness to toss clutter, her dad had left her room pretty much alone. After her conversations with Dolly, Michelle began to see signs of his affection all over the house. Here was another. And her heart warmed as she headed for the closet.

Since she'd always been a princess in her heart she had plenty of fluff and frills from the past. In her zest to clean things out she'd bagged most of it for Goodwill, so she knew right where to go.

She dumped the bag on the bed, plucked out the items they couldn't use and a couple of things with sharp edges and put the rest back in the bag. Draping a pink boa around her neck, she grabbed the bag and hurried downstairs.

In the kitchen Jack was in the portable crib, the girls sat like perfect angels at the table—yeah, she believed that—and Nate stood in front of the open refrigerator. She grabbed the grape jelly from the door and handed it to him.

"Three peanut-butter-and-jelly sandwiches cut into four triangles each," she instructed him. "And then can you find a box or a basket we can use to carry all the food?"

"Sure."

Ten minutes later they packed his sandwiches along with the ham-and-cheese she'd made, the sliced fruit, cookies, water, soda and juice packs into a huge basket.

"Ready," she announced and handed the food to Nate to carry.

"Yeah!" The girls clapped and jumped from their seats to follow him outside.

Michelle picked up Jack and then decided to detour by the living room for the throw and some pillows.

"Am I going to fit up there?" Nate demanded when she caught up with them at the ladder of the tree house.

She eyed his broad shoulders and had a moment's doubt. But she looked up and saw the opening and figured it might be tight, but he'd make it.

"My dad did, so you should," she assured him.

She went first and laid out the blanket and pillows, and then Nate handed her Jack and she tucked him between two of the pillows. Next the girls climbed up one at a time. And finally Nate joined them.

Instantly the spacious six-by-nine-foot room shrank to dollhouse proportions. Man, he was huge. And totally out of place at a princess tea party.

Yet here he was. And after they'd spent the last two weeks avoiding each other. He sat with his back to the wall, legs drawn up in front of him. The man was all male, all the time. The Lord knew she'd had a heck of a time pretending he didn't exist.

And yet he let Christy and her friends dress him up for the tea party. They wrapped a gauzy scarf around his neck, beads around his thick wrist and put stickers on his boots.

The pained expression on his face spoke volumes. And still he accepted a tiny sandwich triangle on a pink napkin as if Michelle offered him a gourmet treat.

"Thanks." He devoured the triangle in one bite. "I

have to say I'm impressed with the job you did on this tree house. I was ready to tear it down."

She threw him a chiding glare as she wrapped a sparkling pink necklace around a headband. "It was weathered but it's built well. A few nails and a fresh coat of paint was all it needed."

"You're making it sound easier than it was. You're such a girly girl, how do you even know how to do all the home repair stuff?"

"My dad." She put the makeshift tiara on Christy's head and pulled her fine brown hair free of the headband. "He was always dragging me into helping on some project or another. Building, plumbing, gardening—we did all kinds of stuff. Everything but electrical. I only got to watch him do electrical."

"That's actually smart. Electrical can be dangerous."

Christy preened and posed for the other two girls and they crowded closer, wanting tiaras of their own. Michelle reached for the shimmering blue beads and a plastic purple headband.

"Yeah, it didn't hurt my feelings not to mess with electricity."

"I suppose not."

"Dolly said drawing me into working with him was Dad's way of showing his love. Working on the house, seeing all the different projects we worked on together, it's like I've found him again."

"Then it's a good thing you came back."

Tears burned at the back of her eyes. She blinked them away, determined to keep them happy memories.

"Yes." She met his gaze. "I'm glad I came."

Red crystals woven through a soft cream scarf and wrapped around blond pigtails made up the last tiara. The girls giggled and practiced bowing to each other.

Michelle laughed and pulled out the plate she'd tucked into the bottom of the basket. Loading it with sandwiches, fruit and cookies, she handed it to Nate with both hands.

His eyes lit up and he eagerly reached for it. She held on to to the edge until he looked up with a question on his face.

"Thank you," she told him. "This is special for them. For me. We couldn't have done it without you."

He winked. "Just call me Prince Charming."

"Today has been so great," Amanda told Michelle as they settled at an outdoor table in a café on the wharf. "I'm going to miss you heaps when you move to Los Angeles. Promise you'll visit often."

"Now that I have some funds, you can bet I will. Los Angeles doesn't even seem real to me yet. It's going to be tough. And lonely."

"Elle is just down the road in San Diego. She's excited about your move. And this song is a winner, Mich. If you sent it to the record companies instead of the artists, they'd snap you up in a heartbeat."

"I'm a behind-the-scenes girl. Have been ever since that first year at Princess Camp."

Amanda rolled her eyes. "Most people get over stage fright."

Michelle just shook her head and ignored the years-long disagreement. The waiter came and went with their coffee order.

"You really think it will sell?" She bit her lip. "Everyday Hero" was so close to her heart, she had no objectivity on this one.

"I do." Amanda squeezed her hand in encouragement. "He sounds pretty special. Tell me about him."

Michelle hesitated; she was usually the one in control of her relationships. She never had trouble walking away. This time it didn't feel so easy. With a sigh she spilled her guts, telling Amanda all about Nate and Jack, and of finding peace with her father's memory.

"Girl, you are in trouble," Amanda declared after a sip of latte.

"I know. It feels like I'm a different person now than when I moved to River Run two months ago. I still want to succeed with my music, but the overwhelming desire to get to Los Angeles has eased up."

"Do you love him?"

"Jack? Yeah. He's such a sweetheart I defy anyone not to love him."

"You're so full of it. You know who I mean. If you care about this guy, maybe you should give it a chance."

"He's a cop, he lives in River Run, and he has enough baggage to fill a jumbo jet. Three strikes and he's out."

"Don't do that," her friend implored her. "Don't dismiss your feelings just because they're inconvenient. Love is worth fighting for."

"It's not love," Michelle denied emphatically. "I have more self-respect than to put myself second to a man's job again."

"Michelle, most relationships require compromise of some type. It's okay if you don't love him, but don't let childhood grievances keep you from finding true happiness."

"He's testing out a prospective nanny today." Michelle forced cheer into her voice. "Soon he won't need me and I'll be in Los Angeles glad that a fun time didn't keep me from pursuing my dreams."

"Or you could show a little backbone, fight for what you want and start a family with your sweetheart. And his little boy."

"Oh, you think you're funny." Michelle shook her finger at Amanda. "You are so not funny."

"I'm a little funny." Amanda grinned as she reached for her purse. "Coffee is my treat."

Michelle argued for the bill, but inside she thought Amanda wasn't funny, and the picture she painted held way too much appeal.

"How did you know it was Nate's birthday?" Kim demanded. "I've tried to pry the information from him for three years."

"He left his wallet on the sink, so I checked out his driver's license."

"You looked in his wallet?" Kim sounded awestruck over the phone line.

"Of course. There's a lot to learn about a man in his wallet. Just like a woman's purse. For instance, he's an organ donor, but no surprise there."

"Still it's pretty bold snooping behind his back."

"Oh, he was in the room."

Kim laughed. "That's bolder still."

"So I've reserved the event room at the bowling alley for Friday night. It has the four lanes right in the room. I need you to handle the invitations."

"Sure, I can do that. This is a great idea. A lot of people will be excited to attend."

Michelle believed it. People responded to Nate's strength of character and decency. But who knew she'd find those characteristics so appealing?

"Remember, it's a surprise."

"Got it. How are you going to get him there?"

"It's covered. Hank is going to call and report a fight about a half hour before Nate's shift ends. He's going to specifically ask for Nate to come out."

"That should work. This is a fine thing you're doing, Michelle. You've been good for him."

Michelle had no response to that. They'd certainly been good together, but a lack of any future scared him off. Actually the thought of a future would probably freak him out just as much. The good Lord knew it terrified her.

"He'll probably hate it. He's not one for drawing attention to himself. But he needs a little fuss made over him. I don't think he's had much of that in his life."

"Like I said, you're good for him."

CHAPTER TWELVE

NATE heard from his attorney around two on Friday afternoon. The courts had granted him full custody of Jack.

Raw emotion gripped Nate. He straight-up loved the boy. The depth of it shocked him.

When Jack first arrived Nate hadn't hesitated to accept responsibility for the child. Duty was as familiar to him as brushing his teeth, starting when he was six years old, and it fell to him to care for his mother.

Hell, he'd made a career of it.

With Jack it had become so much more than obligation.

Which was what made him reach into his bottom drawer and pull out the file on Alicia Carlton, Jack's mother. Nate had received notice of her whereabouts shortly after his first meeting with the attorney. Michelle's fervent wish for a mother's love and guidance was the only reason he hadn't pursued legal action against the woman.

She lived in Carson City, Nevada, not much more than an hour away, but clearly out of his jurisdiction.

Thirty-five and divorced, she had a lengthy file.

Mostly petty stuff, drug-related, but she spent a year in a secured facility five years ago for being in possession of stolen property.

No doubt about it Jack was better off without her in his life. Yet even with that thought ringing in his head, he closed the file and headed for the door.

He stopped at the dispatcher's desk. "I'm taking a couple of hours of personal time. I'll have my cell on. Hit me if you need me."

She nodded and Nate gave his second in command the same message on his way to his vehicle. An hour and twenty minutes later he pulled into the parking lot of a national restaurant chain and walked inside. He grabbed a seat at the counter and ordered a coffee while he assessed the situation.

One thing he couldn't get out of his head was the timing. Today was his birthday and his cousin Jack had always made a point of talking to him on his birthday. How odd the decision regarding Jack Jr. should be on today of all days. It was almost like Jack Sr. was giving a nod of approval. Nate didn't put a lot of stock in woo-woo stuff. But this felt right.

It took him a few minutes to spot Alicia.

He hardly recognized her. When he last saw her, she'd been four months pregnant, strung out, with sallow skin and her black hair a shaggy, matted mess. She'd barely acknowledged him as he spoke to Jack. His cousin had insisted she was clean, that it was the pregnancy that made her tired. Seemed she suffered from morning sickness.

She looked good today. Her hair was clean and pulled

back in a ponytail. Her skin had a healthy sheen and she smiled as she worked.

For the first time Nate saw what had attracted Jack to the woman. She sure didn't appear to be missing her son.

She must have felt the weight of his stare because she glanced up and spotted him. And there it all was for him to see. Fear first, followed by despair, and then hope, and finally resignation.

A lot of emotion in a flash of time, but she didn't try to bolt. She waved him over to a booth by the window before telling her boss she was taking a break.

"How is he?" she demanded as soon as she sat across from him.

Okay, she got points for going there first.

"You left him on the porch in the middle of a snow storm. I could be here to tell you he's dead."

She went white, all the healthy color leaving her face in a rush. "No." She shook her head in denial. "I'd know if he were gone. Somehow, I'd know."

"How could you know? You didn't even wait for me to open the door."

"No, but I saw you. I watched you go in. I couldn't stay, couldn't face you. I was at the lowest point in my life, but I knocked. And I left him in a better place."

"He could have died."

"Could have." She grabbed on to that. "So he's okay?"

"He's fine. Healthy. My attorney just notified me the courts have granted me full custody." He gave it to her straight, no sugar coating.

She went totally still, and then she nodded and her

whole body relaxed as she dropped her head into her hands on the table. No sound reached him, but by the way her shoulders shook, it appeared she was sobbing her heart out.

Her boss started toward the table. Nate flashed his badge and shook his head. The man backed off, but only as far as the cash register, where he kept an eye on the booth.

"Ms. Carlton," Nate said after a moment, and when she didn't respond he said, "Alicia."

One hand broke loose to grab a napkin, there were motions of mopping up, and then she slowly lifted her head.

"I'm okay," she told him and straightened her shoulders. She met his gaze with water-drenched brown eyes. "It was the right thing to do."

"You haven't changed your mind?" he asked her point-blank. If she was having doubts, he wanted to know now.

"No." Her body shuddered with a heavy sigh. "I said I reached my lowest point before I dropped him off at your place. I was wrong. Losing him was my lowest point. I went on a real bender after that. I was free, right? No baby to hold me back or to force me to work to take care of him."

She dabbed her eyes with the damp napkin. "But no matter what I did, or what I took or drank, I'd see his sweet face in my head. And I'd look at where I was or who I was with and I knew I'd done the right thing in giving him to you. I knew you'd keep him fed and warm and safe. Jack had such faith in you, I knew I could trust you, too."

"You look clean," he stated bluntly. Drugs were not something to tiptoe around.

"I am," she said with her chin up. "For over a month now. I'm doing the best I ever have before. Because of Jack. I was hoping if I stayed clean for a year, you might let me come see him."

He stared at her, searching for a break in her sincerity. He found none.

"But you don't want him back."

Her lips pressed together until they disappeared as if she had to force the words back, but she firmly shook her head. Tears welled again, but she pushed them back.

"I want what's best for him. And that ain't me. A month clean seems like forever. And I got to work at it every day. Real hard. It's best if you keep him." She nodded emphatically and dabbed at the corner of her eye, smiling sadly. "I thought he was a drag on me, but truth is I would be the drag on him. If you want to adopt him, I'll sign whatever you need."

"I'll have my attorney put the papers together." Nate climbed to his feet and put a twenty down for his coffee. "I'll be watching you," he told her, keeping his tone stern. She needed to know he meant what he said. "If you're clean for a year, we'll talk, see if you feel the same way. If you aren't clean, you won't get anywhere near him."

She swallowed hard, then nodded.

He turned away, took a couple of steps and then stopped. He reached into his pocket and pulled out his wallet again. This time he placed a picture Michelle had taken of Jack on the table.

The twenty still sat there and she reached right over it to snap up the picture. Tears flowed down her cheeks. "Thank you."

"Get ready," Kim squealed in excitement. "Hank just called to say a sheriff's car pulled into the lot."

Excited murmurs went around the room as people jockeyed for a good position to view Nate's surprise.

Michelle stared down at the text on her phone and knew it wasn't Nate driving up. He was going to be late. He'd been to Carson City and was still twenty minutes away. He had something to tell her, but he'd just gotten tagged for a call. He hoped it would be cleared before he got to town. He wanted her to put on something pretty and get Jack ready; they were going out to celebrate tonight.

Her first gut-wrenching reaction was disappointment. The same angry letdown she always experienced when her dad failed to show as expected for some special event.

Well, she knew just how to speed Nate along. Knowing he'd been called to a fight at Hank's Bowl, she texted back: Take your time, Jack and I are at a birthday party at the bowling alley. See you soon.

Her phone immediately rang. Before answering, she walked up next to the bowling lanes where the noise was the loudest. "Hey. I got your text."

"Michelle, are you okay?"

"What?"

"Are you and Jack okay? There was report of a fight."

"You're fighting traffic? Don't worry. We're fine here. Oh, my goodness. What a ruckus."

"Michelle! Go home."

"What? Home? I can barely hear you. Listen, we won't be much longer. We'll see you at the house. Say bye-bye to Daddy, Jack."

Jack cooed on cue, making Michelle grin.

"Wait," Nate demanded.

"Bye." She clicked shut the phone just as Nate's deputy entered the room and a loud boo went up.

Kim rushed up to the man to find out what was up, but Michelle wandered out to watch the parking lot.

Guilt racked her. But she was tired of the men in her life making her wait. Yes, she knew it was part of the job, but she hadn't chosen the job.

Sometimes family should come first.

It didn't help at all that Nate wasn't family. That she had no claim on him or Jack. Or that Nate knew nothing about the party. It didn't even matter that he was much better at keeping her informed of his whereabouts and schedule than her father ever was.

She'd wanted to give him something special and it was ruined because he was late. Glancing around at the crowd waiting to cheer his arrival, she almost regretted putting the surprise together. Almost.

But no. She reined in her emotions. Nate was not her father and she was no longer twelve years old waiting for him to show up at Princess Camp.

The truth was Nate deserved this moment of joy and

recognition. She had the feeling he'd had very few happy birthdays. Very few happy moments really.

She bit her lip. Well, it sounded like he'd gotten some good news today; hopefully it would be enough to put him in the mood for the party.

Okay, maybe it was a little mean to let Nate think they were in danger. But she made sure he knew they were both fine. And now he felt compelled to reach the bowling alley as quickly as possible, which was the point.

Ten minutes later Nate's SUV whipped into the lot. He looked grim as he made his way to the building.

Michelle bit her lip and backed into the event room. She hoped she hadn't spoiled his birthday by putting him in a bad mood with her call.

"He's here," she announced to the room.

"Are you sure?" Kim asked after the false alarm earlier.

"Yeah. I saw him."

The blonde clapped her hands. "Goody." She wrapped her arm around David's and dragged him over to crowd close to Michelle near the entrance. "My mother-in-law will probably only stay a short while. She's going to keep Christy overnight and she said she'd be happy to take Jack, too, so you and Nate can enjoy yourselves."

"That would be great." Michelle rubbed Jack's back, disconcerted at the thought of an evening without him. He'd become such a part of her life. "We'll see what Nate says."

A moment later he came charging into the room.

"Surprise!" voices shouted out from all around them.

Nate stopped as if he'd run into a brick wall. He surveyed all the people surrounding him, clearly surprised. Finally he grinned and reached out to shake hands. His gray gazed snagged hers with a promise of retribution before he disappeared in the crush of people.

She sighed and kissed Jack's cheek. "It's going to be all right."

Good. Let him wallow in the attention of his community for a while. He cared for these people whether he knew them as individuals or not. It was time he saw they recognized his dedication.

Yep, let them mellow him out a bit before he hunted her down.

Just as she relaxed with that notion, he appeared in front of her. His eyes flared with heated intent.

"You'll pay for this," he promised as he took Jack, holding the alert baby against his solid shoulder.

She thought that might be it for now. But no, he snaked a hard arm around her waist and jerked her close.

"And never scare me like that again." His head lowered and he kissed her, a slow deep claiming of her mouth by his. Not so much a caress as another promise.

Oh, yeah, if this was her punishment, give her more. She angled her head and challenged him to do his worst. Best? Hmm. Whatever.

A slap in the face, literally, brought her out of the sensual interlude.

She and Nate both pulled back to find Jack giggling and bouncing. Every day he gained better use of his limbs and he reached out and clocked her again.

"Whoa, kid." Nate caught Jack's arm. "We don't hit women in this family."

"He's just trying to show his love." Michelle grabbed the baby's fist and pretended to take a bite.

"Well, he's going to have to find a different way," Nate stated, pleasant but firm. "Because starting now, no hitting girls."

"You're right," she agreed, rubbing at the smudge of lipstick on his lower lip rather than look into his eyes. He was going to make such a good father and every day her departure loomed closer. "Good job, Daddy."

"Eeek." Jack squealed and waved his arms.

"Are you jealous?" Michelle demanded. "That's it, isn't it?" she teased the baby. "You want all my kisses for yourself."

Jack proved her right by leaning forward to give her a sloppy kiss on the mouth.

"Um." She laughed as she blotted her lips with the back of her hand. "I guess that says it all."

"Now I'm the jealous one," Nate complained.

"Don't worry." She leaned close to whisper. "I'm sure you'll get better with practice."

He caught her chin to hold her near for a lingering kiss where their only connection was mouth to mouth. Slowly, softly, he showed her he knew exactly how to excite her senses. When he lifted his head, she sighed.

"We'll practice more later."

Oh, my. Promises, promises. She didn't know whether to be thrilled or scared. She did know she should discourage him, but she couldn't quite bring herself to do so.

"Nate," a voice called out from the bowling lanes. "We need a man to complete our team."

"Go bowl," she ordered him. "There'll be dancing and karaoke later. It's your party. Have a good time."

"I intend to." He winked and turned to join the bowlers.

While he bowled she kept busy checking on the food and the music. With everything flowing nicely, she slipped out to the car to retrieve the jeans and black polo shirt she'd brought for Nate to change into.

While she was outside, she called the sheriff's office and asked the dispatcher to invite everyone to stop by when they had a chance. The woman was excited to hear from Michelle and assured her everyone would be contacted, both on and off duty because everyone would want to attend or at least stop by.

Tears welled in Michelle's eyes at the show of enthusiasm from Nate's coworkers. He thought he was so alone. But the truth was he collected people and didn't even know it.

Blinking back emotion, she told herself he hadn't worked his magic on her. She may not be running away from River Run anymore. Finding explanations for her father's behavior and seeing his actions through the eyes of an adult had helped her put the ghosts of her childhood behind her. But she was still determined to get to Los Angeles. That's where her future lay.

Back inside she handed off Nate's change of clothes and made a swing around the room, checking that all was well. She got caught up in the noise and gaiety of the party revelers, grabbed a beer, and strolled over to watch Nate bowl and let her momentary melancholy melt away.

CHAPTER THIRTEEN

NATE reluctantly let Jack go home with Kim's mother-in-law. Nate's plan earlier had been to spend the night with Jack and Michelle and it was hard to give that up. But the party was in full swing and she'd gone to a lot of trouble to give him this surprise. So he did his best to get out and mingle.

This was so not his thing. If not for Michelle, he would have been lost. As it was, he kept her in sight. Watching her having fun allowed him to relax and enjoy himself, too.

He killed it at bowling, beating both David and his dad. Okay, so maybe David wasn't so bad. And now Kim belted out a decent rendition of "Redneck Woman." Michelle rocked to the chorus, her hips swaying in sexy rhythm to the beat.

She wore a red minidress, the luxurious material shimmering when she moved. It was a turtleneck halter dress, blousy on the top and snug around her hips. Sheer vixen from head to toe.

He stepped up behind her and wrapped his arms around her waist, pulling her close and swaying along with her. She shimmied against him and then turned in the circle of his arms to face him.

"There's the birthday boy." She linked her arms around his neck. "Having fun?"

"I am."

She laughed. "No need to sound so surprised."

"I'm not a social guy," he said with a shrug.

"That was before you took on the community," she corrected him. "Now they've adopted you."

"Because of you." He had no illusions about that.

"Oh, no." The emphatic shake of her head echoed her denial. "It's all you. I just gave them a venue." She ran her hands over his shoulders, straightened his collar. "What did you want to tell me?"

He made a quick scan of the crowd filling the space. This wasn't the time or the place he'd planned, but good news was good news wherever they were.

"I heard from my attorney today. Jack is officially mine."

Her eyes lit up and she threw her body against him, hugging him tightly. "That is good news. He's so lucky to have you."

Her encouragement eased some of Nate's anxiety. "I'm glad you think so."

"I know so. I've watched the two of you together for the past six weeks. He loves you."

"This is different. The last six weeks felt temporary. This is the rest of our lives. And it is different, stronger. It's as if a link binds us now."

"That makes sense. It's official now."

"Yeah." The tightness in his gut eased even more.

"That sounds right. My feelings are the same. I love Jack either way, but now I know no one can take him from me." He told her about his trip over to Carson City and his talk with Jack's mother. "She offered to let me adopt him."

"Really? She said she wanted you to keep him?"

"Yes."

Michelle nodded. "See, even she sees it."

"You were right, that she needs to be a part of his life. If she stays clean, I think they'll be good for each other. If not, then I'll protect him any way I can."

"I have no doubt."

"Okay, everyone," Kim announced from the stage. "We're going to take a break from the karaoke entertainment so someone can give Nate a very special birthday present. Everyone, Michelle Ross."

Applause broke out. And Michelle wiggled out of his grasp.

"That's me." She stepped away, her gaze locked on his. "I hope you like it."

Nate followed her, stopping short of the stage. He crossed his arms over his chest and watched as she picked up a guitar and moved to the stool Kim had set in the middle of the raised dais.

Michelle adjusted the microphone, strummed an introductory riff and began to sing.

My American man wears a uniform,
Does his duty with honor and pride
He suffers every loss both friend and foe
My American man is an everyday hero.

She had the voice of an angel, low and rich, it grabbed him by the heart and squeezed.

My American man wears a badge and a gun.
Protects every man, woman, daughter and son.
His life he'd give and never say no.
My American man is an everyday hero.

My American man opens his arms, opens his home
To a fatherless child, lost and alone.
He heats up the bottle, rocks him to and fro.
My American man is an everyday hero.

My American man takes care of me just right.
He loves me passionately all through the night.
His kisses so sweet, his touch, oh, oh!
My American man is my everyday hero.

The words ended and the music faded away. Silence reigned for a beat of time, and then another before applause broke out, thundering through the room.

Without a word, Nate stepped up to the stage, took Michelle's hand and assisted her down.

"Did you like it?" Her eyes held both excitement and anxiety as she joined him.

Too choked up for words, he kissed her hand and drew her with him across the room.

As he got close to the door, he cleared his throat and called out a deputy's name. When he answered, Nate tossed the man the keys to his SUV. "Drop my vehicle off at my place on your way home."

Nate received a nod. Satisfied, he told Michelle, "Get your purse."

She shook her head. "I locked it in my car."

"Good. Give me the keys." He took them, and laced his fingers through hers. He waved to the crowd and then gave her hand a tug. "Let's go."

He talked little on the trip home, because he didn't know what to say.

She finally broke under the silence. "Are you really mad about the party?"

"No."

"Good." More silence followed. "Then why are you so quiet?"

"Nobody's ever gone to so much trouble for my birthday. Hell, nobody's ever gone to any trouble at all. Mom only remembered events where she got gifts. I got a token present or two at Christmas, but most of the gifts were from her to her. I had to remind her of my birthday." After he turned eight he gave up.

"Did it get any better when you moved in with your uncle?"

"Uncle Stan was simple—birthday, holiday, whatever—he'd pack Jack and me into the car and take us out to dinner. It marked the occasion and that was enough for him."

"My dad and your uncle Stan would have got along real well. That's what he always wanted to do. No surprise I always wanted a party."

"My money is on you."

"And you'd win."

Tonight he couldn't quite grasp it was all for him. Not until Michelle's birthday present. From the moment she stepped onstage, he'd wanted to be alone with her. She looked so pretty in the spotlight. Her silky blond hair flowing like liquid gold around bare white shoulders, lips as red as the dress inching up her long legs. Making him sound like a hero in a voice meant for the bedroom.

It was a gift he'd never forget.

Come to think of it, he'd received a few cards tonight, but thank God nobody else brought gifts. How uncomfortable would that be?

Only when he heard his voice fade did he realize he'd spoken his thought aloud.

"We put it on the invitation not to bring a gift," Michelle explained. "If someone wanted to give something they were encouraged to donate to the River Run Community Improvement Fund."

"I'm not sure you can do that."

"Sure we could. Nobody had to donate. But plenty did. Last I heard you raised twelve hundred dollars for the fund."

"Seriously?" He flashed a glance her way, watched her smother a yawn.

"Yeah." She grinned, her white teeth showing in the spill of a streetlight. "Pretty smart, huh? I knew you wouldn't want people giving you anything, but they're preprogrammed to give for birthdays, so I came up with the donation. The Community Improvement Fund seemed like a good choice, because everyone benefits."

"Brilliant. Are you going to spend the night with me?"

"Is that what you want?"

"More than anything."

"Even if it's not for the best?"

He pulled into the drive, put the car in Park and flipped off the ignition. He turned to her, reached out and cupped the back of her neck, the move instinctive, primal.

"You're leaving. I get that. I want the time we have left to be special."

"It's not the smart thing to do," she reminded him softly.

He drew her close until they were forehead to forehead. "I don't care." He angled his head, placed his lips on hers and gently, oh, so gently, kissed her.

She hesitated, but his care paid off. With a sigh she sank into the caress. Yes, this was what he needed, her in his arms. The taste of her, the warmth of her, his for the taking.

Minutes later he had her upstairs, slowly undressing her like the gift she was. He savored her, with his lips, with every stroke of his hands, with his whole body. And she responded beautifully. Embraced him wholeheartedly, even his scars, her acceptance giving him peace even as his body burned for her.

So receptive, so giving, her pleasure brought him pleasure. And he rocked them ever higher, sensation building on sensation, until anticipation splintered into indescribable satisfaction.

Heaven—he rolled them so he wouldn't crush her—must be something like this.

"Thank you," he said around a throat choked with emotion, "for everything."

Her hand trailed over his chest. "So you liked your song?"

"It's beautiful." He cleared his throat. "More than I deserve."

"Don't say that." She lifted onto her elbow next to him. "You are one of the best men I've ever met."

"There's nothing special about me," he denied.

She laid a finger over his lips, shushing him.

"Everything in that song is true. If you see the value of it, you have to see the value in yourself."

He frowned, wanting to argue with her logic but unable to do so.

Seeing she'd stumped him, she smiled and cuddled next to him again. "My agent loved it. She's sending it to an up-and-coming star in Nashville."

"Good luck." He sighed, feeling something deep inside settle. Life had never been better.

Jack was his now, safe and sound. As contentment led him into sleep, Nate tightened his arms around the beauty sleeping bonelessly beside him. Michelle was his, too. For as long as she stayed.

Michelle put the finishing touch to the chair rail in the master bedroom. She stepped back and admired the freshness of the room. As with all the renovations she'd done to the house, her improvements in here were mostly cosmetic, bringing the interior design from mid-eighties to the new millennium.

The chair rail circled the room in a soft cream; above it a mellow green paint three shades lighter than the sage green below the rail gave the room a serene feel. Cream curtains held back with sage ties dressed the window. A luxurious light green comforter with dark green vines flowing over it and mounds of pillows propped at the head made the bed an inviting bower. An artful rug in reverse colors and pattern from the comforter brought life to the serviceable beige carpet.

Pleased with the room she did a little happy dance. It hit the perfect balance, pretty without being too feminine. The dark wood of the furniture added the right masculine touch.

Satisfied, she headed in to check on the progress of the electrician in the master bath. She'd bought new light fixtures for the whole house. The electrician started the day inspecting the wiring throughout, and Michelle was happy to hear everything was in good shape. Now he was wrapping up the installation of the new fixtures.

Her cell rang before she reached the bathroom. She saw her agent's name and anticipation tingled up her spine.

"Hi, Denise. Tell me quick so I can breathe, do you have news about the song?"

"Girl, would I mess with you? Would I chatter on about nothing while you waited breathlessly for me to give you exciting news? It's not like you haven't been waiting for this news forever—"

"Denise, tell me now or I swear to you I will come through this line and scuff up your Jimmy Choos."

A husky laugh sounded. "Is that any way to talk to the woman who is going to make all your dreams come true?"

"Oh, my God." Michelle's heart stuttered. "She wants to buy the song?"

"She wants to buy the song."

Michelle screamed. Too excited to contain it she danced for real and when the electrician came running to see what happened, she grabbed him and danced some more.

"Ah, congratulations." Balding and in his fifties, the man gave her a twirl and a hug and then wiggled free and escaped back to the bathroom.

Michelle laughed and finally heard Denise calling her name. She put the cell back to her ear. "Sorry about that, I got a little carried away."

"You're entitled." Denise sounded almost as excited as Michelle felt. "It's a great song. I heard a man's voice, the inspiration for your song perhaps?"

"Electrician. Poor man now knows how it feels to be groped."

"It's his lucky day. And yours, too. I hope you're done with that house, because it's time to move to L.A."

"She's really, seriously interested in the song? Don't mess with me about this, Denise."

"Michelle, this is serious business. I would never mess with you over the sale of your song."

"I need to sit down." Michelle sank right down to the green rug.

"She loved the song. Wants to make it a lead on her next album."

"Shut up." This was so surreal. "Are you going to tell me who she is?"

"Rikki West, she won *Idol* a couple of years ago. Has been riding a wave to the top ever since."

"I can't believe it." Michelle couldn't be more thrilled. She loved Rikki West's voice. "I thought of her when I was writing it. This is perfect."

"It gets better." Denise practically purred. "She wants to meet you, to see what else you have."

"When? Where?" Okay, this had to be a dream. Michelle pinched herself because it was just too good to be true. The sting on her left arm did little to convince her she wasn't in some alternate reality.

"She's going to be in L.A. for an awards show next week. You need to get yourself down here now."

"Right." Michelle frowned, there was no reason the request should throw her. She'd always known the time would come for her to leave.

The first time Denise mentioned it Michelle had been too swept up in the moment to make the connection that going to L.A. meant leaving River Run. And Jack.

It meant the end of what she had with Nate.

Denise gave Michelle a few more details and signed off with another nudge to finish her business in River Run and get her butt to Los Angeles.

Her stomach churned and she flopped back on the carpet to stare up at the ceiling and try and make sense of what she was feeling.

Oh, God. She didn't want to go.

The biggest break of her career and her heart broke at the idea of leaving River Run and the family she'd found here.

No, she just felt attached because she was missing her dad, that's all. She'd reassigned her affections to keep from being so lonely. And sure she'd miss Nate and the baby for a few days. But her new life would soon distract her.

And she'd see them again. She still had to come back and sell the house. So no more moping. Today was going to be all about celebrating.

Needing her buzz back, she called Amanda in San Francisco and linked in Elle in San Diego. Both screamed when they heard her news.

"I knew it would happen." Elle calmed first. "You're so talented it was only a matter of time."

"And it's a great song," Amanda added. "I heard it when she came to town to record it. Patriotic is always in and it ends kind of like a love song, which is a nice touch. Makes me wonder if there's anything you want to tell us?"

No, not a thing. Michelle wasn't going down that road again.

"I can tell you Denise wants me in Los Angeles yesterday."

"Let me know when you make your reservations," Elle told her. "I'll drive up and help you find a place to live. We can celebrate."

"Count me in," Amanda demanded. "I'll take the weekend off from the museum and fly down, too. Heck, I'll bring the champagne."

CHAPTER FOURTEEN

"HEY, I got your message and yes, I'll be home at the regular time. See you tonight."

After leaving Michelle the voice mail, Nate flipped his cell closed and returned it to his pocket. She wanted to tell him something at dinner. He had a bad feeling he knew what it was.

She was leaving.

And he wasn't ready to hear it.

A glance at his watch told him he had two hours before end of shift. He bent his head down and put his attention into completing the budget report for the mayor. But Nate's mind soon wandered.

The two weeks since his birthday had shown him what it meant to be part of a loving family. Waking up to Michelle each morning, watching Jack learn something new every day, knowing she had his back at home—Nate never expected to know such joy.

After half an hour, he acknowledged the report was a no-go. He couldn't concentrate, couldn't stand to sit still. Pushing to his feet, he left his office. He needed to be busy. Stay busy.

He stopped at dispatch. "What do we have going on?"

"It's quiet," she told him. "But I just got a call from Frank over at the Sleepy Bear Motel. He says someone broke into all his units and stole the complimentary toiletries. I was going to send Nelson."

"I'll take it." A nuisance call was a perfect time-suck. And it would keep him distracted for the rest of his shift. "Have Nelson come in if it looks like Peters needs help."

Michelle sounded excited on the phone. He knew she'd scheduled the electrician to come today. She'd come to refurbish and sell the house. The electrician marked the end of that project. There was nothing more to hold her in town until his lease ended in two months.

The thought of her leaving tore him apart.

He could deny it no longer. He loved her.

He didn't know what he was going to do when she left town. He'd finally found the peace he sought in the arms of a siren. Michelle was not the shallow woman he'd first thought. Beautiful and strong, clever and funny, she was a survivor, like him. And he'd fallen in love.

Ten minutes later he arrived at the Sleepy Bear Motel to find the owner—Frank—nose to nose with Beverly, the owner of the local B and B. Uh-oh. Everyone knew of the ongoing feud between the gangly, gray-haired Frank and the plump, grandmotherly redhead.

This might take a little longer than he thought.

"Okay, let's break it up here." Nate quickly put himself between the two of them before the heated argument got out of control.

"Frank accused my grandson of stealing the toiletries." Beverly tried to get around Nate. "No one is going to call my grandson a thief."

It took him a few minutes to calm them down and separate them so he could conduct interviews. And then he had to find a spot to speak to one while keeping an eye on the other.

Just when he was wrapping up the statements, pleased to be only ten minutes past his end of shift, Frank's granddaughter showed up. She went ballistic when she heard Frank had accused the grandson.

"Grandpa, I told you he's smart. He doesn't have to steal. I love him."

Nate smothered a groan. He was tempted to order the lot of them down to the station, but that would only drag this out and he was already late. He reached for his phone to call Michelle and the grandson stormed in and, like his grandmother, immediately went nose to nose with Frank.

Nate pushed his phone into his pocket and went to break it up.

Tears blurring her vision, Michelle blew out the candles on the dining room table. In the kitchen she ditched the chicken medallions in artichoke sauce, pan and all, into the trash. Followed by the bread, the salad and the baked potatoes.

Ruined. Everything was ruined.

The food, the dinner, the joy in sharing her news with Nate, all of it ruined because of his tardiness, because he couldn't be bothered to call and tell her he was going to be late.

Bad enough to be late, but at least call, then she knew better than to expect him at any minute, knew to do something with the food before it grew cold, dry and wilted. Then she knew that her excitement had no foundation, that she was second to the job, again.

She scrubbed the tears from her face, furious at their appearance. She would not cry today.

It was the best day of her life.

She'd be damned if she'd cry.

She'd be damned if she'd stay in this hick town one more night.

She was right to leave River Run when she was younger, right that there was nothing here for her. Tonight proved that.

Her phone rang. She looked at the caller ID. Nate. Looked at the time, over an hour late. She rejected the call.

Chin up, shoulders back, she raced upstairs. In her room she threw her suitcases on the bed and began piling in clothes. She tried for order but folding was beyond her.

She shook with anger, with disappointment.

The betrayal was her own. He wasn't supposed to matter. Men were for fun and a means to an end. She knew that, had learned early to rely only on herself.

Because it hurt when she trusted someone with her heart and they let her down. And they always let her down. Second to the job again. It was the one thing she promised herself in a relationship. She must come first.

The disillusionment was all her fault. He was a lawman, so of course giving her priority was the one thing he couldn't promise her. And yeah, she'd been lying to herself every time she pretended she could walk away without looking back.

All the more reason to be gone when he got home. No need to put her pain on display. He didn't deserve her tears, didn't deserve her love.

Suddenly weak, she sank down on the side of the bed. Oh, God. She loved him.

Oh, yeah, she was a monster liar. How could she let this happen? She knew better than to leave her heart vulnerable. But he'd stolen past her guard with his broken soul and ready acceptance of Jack.

Jack. Oh, Lord.

Her throat tightened and she surged to her feet, seeking action to offset the need to think, to stop the emotions bombarding her from all sides.

The closet and drawers were empty so her gaze went to the walls, the bed. She hadn't touched this room mostly because she didn't want the mess in here where she slept but also because the nostalgia of it, in the face of her father's loss, made her feel safe, loved.

Another illusion.

Armed with anger and righteousness she stripped the walls of posters and pictures, of butterflies and musical notes. Books and trinkets got tossed into a box as she removed all evidence of herself from the room.

That done she carried her bags downstairs.

And there her emotion-driven adrenaline rush gave out on her. She looked at the door and couldn't bring herself to walk through it.

Her phone rang again. Nate again. She rejected it again.

As much as she hurt, the truth was Nate and Jack had her heart. She couldn't just leave. Instead she turned and headed out back, going where she always went as a child when she didn't know what to do and she needed to think.

She escaped to her castle.

By the time Nate got everything sorted out—all signs pointed to the new maid, who had missed her shift and was nowhere to be found—and got on the road home, he was nearly two hours late.

He tried Michelle's cell again. He'd finally managed a try twenty minutes ago but it went to voice mail. And it was the same now.

Aggravated, he tossed the phone into the passenger seat. Her refusal to answer was not good. Told him just how much trouble he faced.

He wasn't eager to hear her departure was imminent, yet he didn't want to hurt her, either. And this whole episode smacked of her father's neglect. Nate usually managed to connect with her to let her know he'd be late, but today's situation had been too volatile. Petty, yes, but emotions had been running hot.

He nearly tripped over her bags when he walked through the door. It reminded him of the day she arrived, of finding her asleep on his couch. Of the kiss that brought him to life. From that moment on, he hadn't been able to get her out of his head.

"Michelle," he called out and dread weighed heavy on him when silence answered him.

The very notion of losing her tore his soul in half. Yes, he had to let her go, but not like this, not on bad terms.

His nose led him to the kitchen. The savory scent of dinner lingered in the air and he found the remains of it in the trash. He rescued the pan, considered it another bad sign and continued his search for her.

Her room broke his heart. Seeing her childhood memories torn from the walls and stuffed in the trash shredded something deep inside him. It also told him he may be wrong about what she wanted to tell him. This was not careful packing. This was rage fueled by hurt.

More than ever he regretted taking the nuisance call. Not that he could know it would turn into such a fiasco, except a cop always knew a call could turn into something more.

He needed to find her. Needed to make this better. He backed into the hall and stared into Jack's empty room. It struck him, where was the baby?

He flipped open his phone, called Kim.

"Yeah, I have Jack. Michelle asked me to take him for the night. Are you sure she's not there? She was headed home to make dinner when she left here."

"The dinner is here." What was left of it. "She's not."

"She was excited about something but said she'd tell me about it tomorrow. She wanted to tell you first."

"I was a little late."

"Uh-oh."

"Yeah. Hey, thanks for watching Jack."

"Good luck."

He went back, checked every room looking for Michelle. She was nowhere yet everywhere. She'd taken a house stuck in the eighties and turned it into a modern, comfortable home. With paint and molding, new rugs and fixtures and a lot of hard work she'd changed it from sorry and dated to fresh and inviting.

He'd thought about buying the house from her, but no. He couldn't live here without her.

The quiet ate at him. He used to live in silence. There had been times when lack of noise meant the difference between survival or death. But that wasn't who he was anymore.

He was a dad now. Noise came with the territory.

He hadn't made a big deal of it when Michelle, talking to Jack, had first referred to him as Daddy, but the name felt good. He probably wouldn't have claimed the title without her, would just have gone on as Uncle Nate. But he wanted to be a dad, wanted the bond and responsibility implied by the title. Wanted to give Jack the love and connection he deserved.

And still it wouldn't be enough for Nate. Michelle completed their little family. These last couple of weeks of playing make-believe family showed him just what he'd be missing.

Sure he could hire someone to do the things she did but it wouldn't be the same. She challenged him, encouraged him, made him laugh. She sang like an angel and made love like a vixen. She wanted to be catered to yet worked like a dog when it mattered to her. He'd miss how she enjoyed cooking but got lazy over the laundry.

Most of all he'd miss her smile and the look in her eyes when she said his name.

The look in her eyes. The look that said she thought the world revolved around him. How could she look at him like that and not love him?

Ha. He laughed out loud. She loved him.

Hope energized him. If she loved him, he had a chance. Spurred to new action he moved from the hall to the kitchen.

He puzzled over whether the wreck in her bedroom happened before the trashing of the dinner when a light in the tree house caught his attention. Of course.

"Michelle," he called as he stepped outside. No response. Not surprised he powered his way up the ladder and shouldered through the child-size door.

Wrapped in a soft pink throw she slept with her head on a purple pillow shaped like a crown. The light behind her made her hair glow like ribbons of flowing gold. Again he remembered the day she first arrived.

Unhesitating he claimed his sleeping beauty with a kiss. He ran his tongue along the seam of her mouth and nibbled lightly on her bottom lip. Soon she blossomed under his attention, her passion awakening with her senses.

Michelle came awake to a warm embrace and the familiar taste of Nate. His kiss took her from slumberous to aroused from one racing heartbeat to the next. She longed to wrap her arms around his neck and hold on tight.

Instead she sighed and pushed against his chest. "I'm mad at you."

"Yeah, I got that from the pan in the trash."

"I worked hard on that dinner."

"I'm sorry I missed it. Sorry I upset you."

She narrowed her eyes at him. "You can do better than that."

"You're right." He swept a curl back from her face, his gaze following the gesture. And then his glance met hers and the intensity in his gray eyes made her breath catch. "I love you."

"Oh, no." Her heart rejoiced even as she denied his words. "Don't say that." Unable to hold his gaze she looked away. "Don't make this harder."

"I am going to make it hard." He kissed her cheek, the line of her jaw. "I'm going to fight for you."

"We're totally wrong for each other," she reminded him. "You love this town and I've been waiting to leave since the moment I got here."

"We belong together." He nudged her nose with his, then dipped down to kiss the corner of her mouth. She turned into the caress, instinctively seeking more, but he'd already moved on. "And you made your peace with River Run when you made peace with your father's memory."

"You're a cop." Let him argue that one after leaving her sitting for nearly two hours tonight. "I vowed never to be with a cop."

"Too late." He lowered his head to the curve of her neck. "We've been lovers for a month. These last two weeks waking up next to you have been magical."

"No."

"Ah, ah. Your honesty is one of the things I love most

about you." The heat of his tongue tasted her skin. "And we're more than lovers, we're a family."

"No." She shook her head. "No fair bringing Jack into this."

"All's fair in love and war." He breathed against her ear, making the cliché a carnal threat. "I'm a warrior in love. I'm going to fight to win."

"Nate."

"He loves you. We love you."

"Unfair, unfair." He was destroying her with his relentless pursuit combined with a delicious physical attack. How did she fight him when she couldn't think straight?

"I'm leaving."

"Stay. Marry me. Be Jack's mom."

"I sold my song," she whispered desperately as he nibbled on her earlobe. She needed a reminder of where her future was. "The one I wrote about you."

That stopped him. He lifted onto his elbow, ending his sensual assault to stare down at her. His expression revealed nothing but she could practically see his mind at work.

She held her breath. It was her song, but his, too, and he was a very private man.

Finally he nodded and she breathed. And then his face lit up with pride and joy for her. "Congratulations."

And that was the moment he won her over. His approval and excitement for her warmed her heart. She'd been waiting for this minute since she got the call. But everything she'd always wanted was suddenly at odds with what she'd never wanted but had found where she least expected.

"I need to be in Los Angeles next week."

She loved Nate, loved Jack, but how did she give up her dream?

"Michelle…" He cradled her face in his hands, demanded she look him in the eyes. "I was late tonight because a call went long. I hurt you and I'm sorry. I'm not going to lie to you. There are times you'll have to be second to my job, but I'm willing to be second to yours occasionally, too. We'll decide on a nanny so you can write and fly when you need to. As long as I'm first in your heart like you are in mine, we can make it work. Go to L.A. but come home to me."

"I can go to Los Angeles? And Nashville?" First in his heart. She liked the sound of that. Was it possible she could have it all? Love, a family and her career?

"Tell me you love me and I'll drive you to the airport. But you have to promise to marry me first."

She threw her arms around his neck and dragged him down to her, kissing him with everything in her. He wrapped her close and delivered on his erotic onslaught.

"Yes," she accepted, feeling lucky as the princess she used to dream of being. "I love you. Yes, I'll marry you. Yes, I'll be Jack's mom. But be warned. You proposed in a castle. I'll settle for nothing less than happily ever after."

He grinned. "No problem. I have my very own sleeping beauty." To prove it, he kissed her again.

* * * * *

A sneaky peek at next month...

Special Offers

Every month we put together collections and longer reads written by your favourite authors.

Here are some of next month's highlights— and don't miss our fabulous discount online!

On sale 17th August

On sale 7th September

On sale 7th September

Find out more at
www.millsandboon.co.uk/specialreleases

Visit us Online

0912/ST/MB384

Mills & Boon® Online

Discover more romance at
www.millsandboon.co.uk

- **FREE** online reads
- **Books** up to one month before shops
- **Browse our books** before you buy

...and much more!

For exclusive competitions and instant updates:

Like us on **facebook.com/romancehq**

Follow us on **twitter.com/millsandboonuk**

Join us on **community.millsandboon.co.uk**

Sign up for our FREE eNewsletter at
www.millsandboon.co.uk

WEB/M&B/RTL

By the same author:

Something More
Adventures in Prayer
My Personal Prayer Diary
Meeting God at Every Turn
Julie
The Helper
A Closer Walk
Light in My Darkest Night